The Haunting
of
Gallagher Hotel

K.T. Rose

COPYRIGHT

The Haunting of Gallagher Hotel

Copyright © 2020 by K.T. Rose

All rights reserved.

Written by: K.T. Rose
Cover Design: Pixel Labs

ABOUT THE AUTHOR

K.T. Rose is a horror, thriller, and dark fiction writer from Detroit, Michigan. She posts suspense and horror flash fiction on her blog at kyrobooks.com and is the author of a suspenseful short story series titled *Trinity of Horror*, an erotic thriller novel titled *When We Swing*, and *A Dark Web Horror Series*. She also writes paranormal horror novels and short stories.

MORE FROM K.T. ROSE

Trinity of Horror- Macabre Tales Volume 1
When suspicion meets desperation, the inner demons of desperate souls ignite.
https://mybook.to/3hs5FUT

Netted: A Serial Killer Thriller and Fast-Paced Suspense Series Box Set Books 1-3
https://mybook.to/1D0ntJP

**Netted: A Serial Killer Thiller and Fast-Paced Suspense
Book 1
The Beginning**
Can Dale and Jessica escape Father Paul, the dark web's most sadistic cult leader?
https://mybook.to/asJQ6Yo

**Netted: A Serial Killer Thiller and Fast-Paced Suspense
Book 2
Inside Out**
Is it possible to escape a cult that feeds on fear?
https://mybook.to/bKRr_

**Netted: A Serial Killer Thiller and Fast-Paced Suspense
Book 3
The Crash**
When time runs out, bodies will fall.
https://mybook.to/aeMfHJ

Trinity of Horror- Macabre Tales Volume 2
A normal summer day…drenched in blood.
https://mybook.to/Fqsg

The Haunting of Gallagher Hotel- A Chilling Haunted House Horror Novel
Pride and greed infect the soul, trapping the dead in Gallagher Hotel.

https://mybook.to/FbYFj

Stay connected with K.T. Rose by visiting:
https://www.kyrobooks.com/subscribe

ABOUT THE HAUNTING OF GALLAGHER HOTEL

Some hotels check you in. This one never lets you check out. In the Gallagher Hotel, every room holds a nightmare, and every guest becomes prey.

When Riley accepts a serving position at an exclusive party in the infamous Gallagher Hotel, she sees it as a chance to move past her son's tragic death. Instead, she steps into a supernatural nightmare. Together with Chris, a mysterious thief haunted by his own tortured history, she discovers the hotel's current owner isn't who she claims to be - but rather the vengeful spirit of an executed criminal. As malevolent forces trap them inside, Riley and Chris witness horrifying manifestations and uncover dark secrets hidden within the hotel's Victorian walls. The spiritual and material realms blur, and the body count rises. A sinister hotel manager reveals his true demonic nature, and ancient evils awaken. Can they expose the hotel's macabre history and survive the night, or will they join the ranks of the hotel's permanent ghostly residents?

The Haunting of Gallagher Hotel stands as the latest bone-chilling addition to K.T. Rose's horror collection. If you crave atmospheric hauntings, supernatural suspense, and relentless terror, then you'll be mesmerized by this blood-curdling tale.

Table of Contents

Chapter 1

She'd never forget the day she died.

Torches lit up the town square, illuminating scowling and shouting faces. The townspeople launched stones and spit, pegging Trudy's arms and face as she trudged through the abhorrent mob. She cringed when a pebble struck her cheek. Pain erupted, shooting through her face like lightning striking the earth.

Deputy Hill yanked her arm, leading her through the narrow path the townspeople created. Fists balled, Trudy groaned as the rope around her wrists dug into her skin. Her bare feet picked up glass shards and debris from the cobblestone path as she shuffled along.

She glared around at the angry faces and recognized the men, women, and children of Holloway. She'd done more for them than any God before her. Many of those people owned the very businesses that lined the stone slab she marched across that night. Building and financing the rows of wooden businesses lining the town's square accounted for half the things she'd done for Holloway. She fed the hungry, made clothes for cold children, and taught women's independence. The ever-growing list of the townspeople's wants was endless. At one point, she didn't mind the busy work. Fulfilling dreams of the once poor town kept her boisterous and distracted from her bitter reality. Trudy was Holloway's personal shepherd, making the people her needy sheep.

Hands snagged at her lavender tea gown, adding dirty prints to the blood drops and grime from the beatings in that putrid cell. She glared at the bare-faced man towering over her. The brim of his deputy hat cast a thick shadow, hiding his dark eyes and pale face.

The deputy would miss her. She was sure of it. He got off on the assaults that bruised her face. His heavy fists pounded her bones and scraped her skin until she confessed. And even after her confession, he continued with his evening visits, slamming her body into cinder block walls and passing off open-handed blows to her nose, cheeks, and eyes.

Trudy sighed. A bath with lavender and Epsom salt sounded good for the swelling. She didn't realize how bloated and purple her once beautiful, fairly smooth skin had become until she passed by the picture window in front of the town's jail just before they began her walk of shame. Her dark hair was matted to her forehead, washed by sweat and blood. Her plump lips were chapped and bloated with bruises.

Even then, her face pulsed with intense hurt. Pain shot through it whenever she winced.

The sea of convictions roared, growing louder as she drew closer to the opposite end of the square.

"Adulterer!" yelled a woman.

"Traitor!" screeched a boy.

"Murderer!" said a pot-bellied man.

Their accusations sent a sickening jolt through her bones. She watched the path underneath her slowing feet, fighting back the tears.

How could they turn on me like this?

"Why'd you do it?" Trudy glared over her shoulder to find the small voice. Off to the right, a pale, round-faced girl sobbed. Arms across her belly, she grasped the sides of her smock dress: one of Trudy's latest designs. She released it to Mary and Belle's Boutique not even a month prior. "I looked up to you," the girl shouted.

Trudy froze. The child would never understand. Holding the girl's crying eyes in her own, Trudy thought, *I did this for you.*

She caught the faces of women shouting and screeching, advocating her death.

I did it for all *of you.*

"Eyes front!" the deputy said, his authoritative baritone striking Trudy in the gut. She frowned and did what she was told: eyes forward, just like the man demanded. She watched her last stop approach in that ungrateful, dying town. *After all the work I've done, this is how it ends.* She swallowed the ball in her throat, bowed her head, and pressed on.

With every step, she drew closer to the burnt building just beyond the angry mob. Charred and blackened, there it sat, blending with the night beyond the crowd's orange flames. It moved her to tears to see her building reduced to rubble. The roof caved in, falling through the attic and second floor. The blasts left the double-paned windows bare, with nothing to see inside but burnt walls and a black staircase. A crooked beam leaned over the arched door frame where the door held onto the bottom hinges as the top had burned away.

She scoffed. The people got creative, tying the noose to the end of the lone beam. Underneath it, a wooden crate.

"You people are about to make a *serious* mistake," Trudy hissed.

"You should save your breath for your last words," the deputy said. He led her to the crate. "Step up."

Legs shaking, she placed a bare foot on the crate and hauled herself up. The ground seemed miles below. Her head lightened, and the jitters threatened to knock her onto the charred floor that used to be the honey-waxed porch outside the front door.

"Turn around," Deputy Hill said.

Trudy turned and faced the prosecuting crowd. She grunted when a stone slammed into her forehead, pushing her off balance. She caught her footing and fought to stand straight as dizziness whipped around her head.

A cluster of women, including her sisters Belle and Mary, stood amongst the mob. Their faces, glossed in tears, glimmered in the flickering lights. They held her glance for what felt like hours, their eyes begging for an answer.

Trudy had an answer for what she did, but didn't see the need to tell them. It was already too late.

Slowly, they turned and pushed their way through the excited crowd, sauntering off in their fine silk lampshade tunics. Trudy remembered the day she'd bought those for them. She purchased the boutique and the bakery for those girls; now, her heart raced as she cried. The backlash from the town was expected, but never from Mary and Belle. As she watched her sisters leave her behind, Trudy went dead inside for the fourth and final time in her life.

The deputy pulled the loop over her head and tightened the knot, fastening it. Her throat shrank, and butterflies circled her belly. Through heavy gasps, she said, "You know this town wouldn't have grown without me."

Deputy Hill stepped back and faced the crowd. He pulled a note from his trouser pocket and opened it. Then, he reached into the breast pocket of his tan deputy button-up and pulled out his reading glasses. He placed them on his face and looked over the note.

"You—you people wanted to bring money into this town," Trudy yelled. "I caught the train over to Detroit and made connections that brought the money here! I paid the price to make Holloway the train-stop town that it is today! *I* made this place into *Saloon Alley*! While you people collected money from tourists and travelers, I was out there making deals that made us rich!"

"Quiet, whore!" a man shouted.

"Hang the killer!" a woman yelled.

The deputy cleared his throat and raised a hand. The crowd fell silent.

"Trudy Mona Lisa Gallagher, on this day, June 19, 1921, you are hereby charged with the following crimes against the town of Holloway, Michigan: destruction of property, conspiracy to commit murder, murder, and arson. You have been formally convicted by the people of Holloway and me, Sheriff Deputy Davidson Lee Hill. You were not allowed a trial, as Judge Benjamin Rowles, District Attorney Allen Clyde Albright, and Sheriff Jay Kyle Louis have all perished on this very spot, along with Governor Brighton James Fisher, Mayor Richard Tucker, Mrs. Louise Fisher, Mrs. Patricia Tucker, Mrs. Madeleine Albright, and Mrs. Freda Albany Louis."

The mob gasped and fell into hushed chatter.

"Also amongst the dead are nineteen souls, including the hotel's waitstaff, maids, pianist, and bartender. I am sad to say that this will haunt Holloway forever.

"Our investigation concluded that you planted homemade explosives and barred those poor souls inside. You are sentenced to death by hanging on the grounds where your explosions claimed innocent lives. All that stand witness, aside from the townspeople of Holloway, are your two sisters, Mary Karen Welch and Belle Leanora Roth. Your husband, Ulysses Gallagher, God rest his soul, must flip and twist in his grave. He died in the muds of our enemy's territory for *all* of us. How you can defy him with your heinous behavior is beyond me." He moved his eyes from his note and onto the mob. "Trudy Gallagher has lain with politicians and bootleggers alike to push her own sinister agenda. She poisoned the streets of Holloway with hooch, prostitutes, thieves, and brawlers. She is an illness to this town and needs to be extinguished before she harms anyone else."

He turned to Trudy. "You are a disgrace, and in my opinion, hanging isn't enough of a punishment. I wanted the firing squad to take you down." He huffed. "However, after days of deliberation by the people of Holloway, this is the conclusion to your life of manipulation, greed, and murder.

"Reverend Pillars wanted to say a prayer for you, but the people would rather not waste any more time. However, they will grant you your last words, an attempt at getting an explanation, perhaps. What say you?"

Tears fell down her face as she perceived the risks associated with her lifestyle. Inhaling deep and pushing a weak breath through her shaking lips, she felt her chest swell due to the taunting accusations made against her. Keeping up with deals and tracking lies day in and day out was enough to drive anyone mad. But the rewards and freedom that came along with those risks changed her for the better. Trudy became the most powerful woman in Holloway. The prize was well deserved, and in the name of Ulysses, she'd claim the crown even after death.

"Did you hear me?" the deputy asked.

She smirked.

The people groaned and gasped.

6

Deputy Hill cleared his throat. "Murder is funny to you?"

She sighed and shook her head. "No." She looked him in the eye. "But I've never begged for anything before, and I won't start now. Those people deserved what they got, and if I had another chance, I'd do it again. No one stands in my way. Not you, not these people, and not the bastards who blew up." She scoffed. "In fact, if I had the chance, I'd do the same to all you ungrateful imbeciles." She glared at the faces of her persecutors. Faces that used to trust her before. Faces that she strived to keep happy. Faces that could burn in hell alongside the others. "I *always* win, and when you all go to sleep tonight, I want my words to sit deep in your conscience. I don't beg." She narrowed her eyes. "I *take*," she growled.

Deputy Hill nodded, disdain across his face. It tickled Trudy's heart to see him disappointed. He might take her life, but he'd never hear her apologize. He didn't deserve it, and neither did they.

"Burn in hell," he said.

Cheers filled the square as the deputy kicked the crate, sweeping it from underneath her.

Her body dropped, and the sound of snapping bones erupted in her ears.

PART I

Chapter 2

A warm breeze fluttered through the passenger window, blowing strands of Riley's hair across her face. She brushed it away and went back to poking at her phone, scrolling through Instagraph. She liked a vegan pudding recipe, and Debbie's new eggplant dress looked good on her thin ivory frame. Riley chuckled when she scrolled past Pastor Miller's golf pose. His broad smile stood out from the rolling green field in the background, and his visor and sunglasses hid his oily, reddening face. He leaned on his golf club's handle, which barely reached his wide hips. Riley grinned and then tapped the home button before dropping the phone in her tote—or "house on straps," as AJ liked to call it.

"I hope you're not too tired tomorrow when you get off," AJ said as he rolled the driver side window up a little. The sun kissed his tanned skin, casting a glow on his face. "Mom and Debbie are looking forward to s'mores and beers tomorrow night." He dropped his head and tapped on his knees with his index fingers, then gave a quick shrug. "But if you're too tired, I'd understand." He looked at her, citrine eyes full of disappointment.

Riley smiled. "It's nothing a coffee can't handle." She reached over the center console and rubbed the back of his neck. She knew something sat heavy on his mind. The entire hour ride was mostly silent.

"It's not too late to go back home, is it? Can't you call off? That way, you can finally get some rest."

Riley shook her head. "This job is easy money, AJ."

He scoffed. "Yeah, I know." He sighed. "I just wish you could take off." Disappointment loomed in his deep voice as his square, taut chin crumbled. "You promised

9

you'd spend more time relaxing, that's all. I worry when you overwork yourself. It isn't healthy, you know."

She grabbed his hand and squeezed. She couldn't deny her deep feelings for AJ. He was sweet and supportive, understanding the boundaries she set in place over the two years they hung out as "just friends" and the taller walls she put up once she started dating him. Yes, she made more time for him by calling him every day, telling him things only her estranged family knew about her, and spending evenings with him if she wasn't busy working or planning out her financials, noting how close she crept toward her goal. Sadly, her virtues didn't include a relationship or remarrying. It involved a journey she planned to take alone.

AJ knew that, but it never stopped him from trying to pull her closer, which worried her sometimes.

Avoiding his eyes, she peered up the street at the still intersection. Three teen girls stepped off the high curb in front of the Store and Go and jaywalked across the narrow street as they shouted exciting chatter at one another. Their tank tops fluttered carelessly in the summer breeze before they disappeared into Ray's Ice Cream Parlor. A brick Victorian mansion sat next to it. AJ parallel parked in front of the mansion, Riley's job for the night. The teal awning over the porch flapped against the soft breeze. Across it, in gigantic bold white letters, read: *Gallagher Hotel. Michigan's Most Haunted Building. Est. 1919.*

Riley scoffed. The brick walls, cement steps, and tall windows added an old-timey flair to the place. It looked and felt traditional. It reminded her of an apartment she lived in six years back, a mansion they converted into an apartment building. Her heart fluttered. The memory of that place clung tight, forcing her to revisit it often, unwillingly every time.

A young family pushed through the thick, glossy, arched wooden door of the mansion. Two small boys, barely big enough to walk, came out first, easing their way down the tall cement steps. Their parents watched with anxious glares as if they were ready to swoop the boys up if they tumbled down the steps or over the thin railing and into the rose bushes.

The headlights of the minivan parked behind AJ's sedan illuminated, and it started up, ready to take off whenever the family hopped inside.

AJ cocked his head. "That'll be us one day."

Riley's heart sank. She hated it when AJ talked like that. She felt the argument coming up. It had become a debate they'd never resolve, forcing her to saunter away from time to time. From the beginning, when they met at the church, they'd been good friends. The first time he told her he loved her knocked her out of sorts, making her break his heart for the first time of many. She'd made it clear to him repeatedly that she wasn't interested in starting a family again. She didn't want marriage and a kid. Well, she wanted a kid, but on her own. Constantly, she reminded him of her choice and how it defined her as a new woman. But when AJ was in a foul mood, it inevitably came up like vomit after drinking spoiled milk.

As badly as she needed to walk away from the idea and wished he'd understand that one solid rule about her, she liked his attention, his mind, and his thoughtfulness. AJ was the reason she got out of bed most days when she didn't have to work. Because of this, she vowed to never leave on an unpleasant note with him. He didn't deserve it, and she wouldn't dream of it. *Damage control. Fast and now,* she thought. She reached for a distraction. "AJ," she started, "I wish I didn't have to go in. *Trust me.* But Bruce said they needed someone to fill in as server and—"

11

"An overnight server," he reiterated. "I mean, what kind of gig is this? Why are you overworking yourself, Riley? You've been at it for months, working a hundred hours a week. You need to relax." The demand in his voice shook her. He meant business this time.

"AJ, I'm fine." She smiled. "See? I got a lot of sleep and…and I'm good. Don't worry about me." She nudged him in the arm. "Come on. You know you don't want to stay irritated, *AJ*."

He eased her nerves when he smiled and licked his full lips. "Okay." He raised his hands in defeat.

"Okay?"

"Alright. Only because your mind is made up. You're stubborn as shit; you know that, right?"

She leaned in and met his lips with hers. His warm softness pressed gently against her, soothing her worries. AJ knew better than to leave off with an argument. No matter how bad they'd fuss, they'd never leave or go to sleep angry. She'd closed too many chapters in her life on a sour note, only to revisit them in nightmares and cold sweats. AJ didn't need to join the list.

AJ sat back into the driver's seat and peered at the mansion. "You gotta admit, it's still a little weird."

She chuckled. "*Tell* me about it. I mean, look, apparently this place isn't a hotel anymore. It's a family restaurant."

"Did Bruce tell you that before he made you work again this week?"

"No. When I googled the name and directions, it was there. Aside from being Michigan's most haunted building, it's a place where people like to eat dinner."

AJ snickered. "I'll take my chicken breast with a side of trapped souls, please."

He laughed. Riley didn't. She only smiled and swallowed the lump forming in her throat. The tears wanted to rush forward, but she ate them just as she had for six years. Instead, she dropped her eyes to her forearm and gazed at her heart, forever etched in black ink. On her olive skin, multi pastel-colored butterflies fluttered about the weeping angel as its arm hung sheepishly over a tombstone that read: *Nicholas Charles Campbell. October 15, 2008-April 6, 2014.* Memories of his laughter and babble about butterflies and Moth Man softened her heart. A calm washed down her, bringing her back to her center.

AJ stopped his hysterics abruptly when he looked at her. His eyes widened. "I'm so sorry, baby." He reached in and pulled her close for one of his famous embraces.

"Oh God, AJ, come on," she said, laying her head on his shoulder. "I'm not *that* sensitive." She shrugged. "I—I mean, it was a funny joke."

"No, it wasn't," he said. "It was uncalled for and...I'm so sorry."

"Sorry for what? It wasn't your fault."

He pulled back and scowled. "Riley, please don't say that."

She sniffed and swatted the lone tear from her cheek. "You're right." She pulled down the visor. A small trail drew a faint line through her foundation. She opened her tote. "Who wants to be depressed at work, right?" She brushed her face with an olive foundation, covering the stray line.

He shook his head. "It was stupid of me to say—"

"It's alright. Just let it go," she said.

"Okay. Alright." He peered over at the hotel. "That's stupid," he mumbled under his breath.

"What?" Riley said.

"It's just, you're either a hotel or you're not. No reason to decide at the last minute to hire people to tend to their—what I'm guessing to be—*privileged* guests."

Patience for the discussion wore on her nerves. Riley pushed the visor closed and sucked in a deep breath. "I don't know anything about the guest list. I just know Bruce needs me to fill in tonight."

"Can I at least stay with you? They are giving you a room, right?"

She nodded. "Well, yeah, they're giving me a room. I doubt they'll let you stay. I'll probably be too busy to relax or even talk to you. It's a private party for honorary guests, and the pay is nice: one thousand for the night. I doubt they'll even *give* me time to relax."

"A thousand dollars is worth more than resting and taking a break?"

"AJ, I—"

"It's alright. You don't have to keep repeating it. It's just bullshit that I can't stay. Is it too late to ask?"

Riley looked at the ceiling. Sometimes, his clinginess was cute. But lately, it verged on overprotective. "Hun, there's no need for both of us to waste a beautiful night here. It might be crappy. It's probably some old locals doing local things at a local attraction. It'll probably be like bingo night at New Bethel."

He smirked. "Yeah."

14

She smiled big. He was finally sold. "Yeah. Who wants to put up with that? I mean, I need at least one of us to be in a good mood for service tomorrow afternoon."

Damn, she thought. *Left one hole just to dig a deeper one.*

"We agreed only to do morning services with Father Miller. You know how I feel about that hypocritical Father Doris. He makes afternoon service feel like a drag." He huffed and pulled a hand down his tanned face. "But if you have to work yourself to death *today*, then I guess we don't have a choice but to go into church late tomorrow."

Riley rolled her eyes. "AJ, you know I need the money."

"No, you don't. I'll take care of you," AJ said. The seriousness in his eyes filled her with guilt.

"AJ, I—"

He pulled his eyes away and threw himself back into the driver's seat again. That dreadful topic was coming, and it was the last thing she wanted to argue about.

"What about the adoption proceedings? I need—"

"Once we're married, we can have our *own* baby," he interrupted. He tilted his head and averted his eyes to the ceiling. He was as tired of this conversation as she was. So why did he keep bringing it up? Why did he expect her to change her mind about it? She'd made it clear before they fell in love that her decision stood stern: no marriage and no kids together. Why couldn't he understand that? Things were perfect the way they were. Why change them?

Riley hesitated to respond. It hurt to remind a man that devoted years of his life to a relationship with her that marrying him wasn't even on her "to do" list. The first go-around with Steve was enough. AJ knew that. *So why won't he let this go?* She *hated* that discussion. It was more uncomfortable than trying to reach out to her parents. The more they talked about it, the more she considered walking away.

Her heart dropped at the thought.

"I can't believe that after all this time, you still don't want to marry me."

Riley sighed. "It's— I don't know."

"What don't you know?" he snipped. "You love me, right?"

She caught his glare. His eyes, once cozy and sweet, brimmed with insecurity and hurt. "Yeah. You know I do." She flailed his square jaw between her fingers. "I just don't want to repeat the past. I don't want a future that reminds me of what happened to my family, not even a little. It hurts too much." It killed her to tell him that for the fiftieth time. For all the good he'd been in her life, he didn't deserve to wait around for a miracle to change her mind.

"I've known you for six years, and I can't..." He huffed. "I love you, Riley. I'd do anything for you. That's all."

Riley smiled, leaned in, and kissed his nose. "I know."

He moved his saddened glare to the hotel. "I know you gotta go in there and get to work. I'm not going to hold you up—"

"Don't do that," she said, narrowing her eyes at him. Once again, AJ didn't hold back on making her feel guilty about her virtues.

"What?"

She scoffed. "Whatever." She went to open the passenger door but stopped before pulling the lever. Ending on a decent note with AJ was a fair game. There was no telling how rough the night would be, especially if she was catering the event alone. She needed to see his smile in the morning. Not his saddened glare. "I have another minute," she said.

"Okay. What do you want to talk about?"

"Alright." She put an index finger to her lips. "Hmmm." She tapped. "What do I—"

"Do you think that place is haunted?" AJ asked, snatching her next thought.

She shook her head. "No way. It's a gimmick."

He shrugged. "I mean, it might be."

Riley dropped her brow. "What? You don't believe in that stuff, do you?"

He raised his shoulders to his ears. "Who knows? You might see a ghost."

Her eyes left him and laid on the dashboard. The thought of ghosts being real at all sent her heart thudding. Nick and Steve's ghostly figures would kill her on sight. She gulped. "I hope not," she said.

AJ frowned and rubbed her shoulder.

"It's okay," she said, pulling down the sun visor. She cleared her throat and ran her hands over her glossy dark hair, collecting strands that fell loose from her low ponytail. She puckered her lips, sure to spread her cherry lip gloss evenly, and dabbed her eyelids with her knuckle, careful not to smear her eyeliner. She hoped she could hold the waterworks for the second time.

Flipping the visor closed, she said, "I know you didn't mean anything by it. And no, I'm not interested in seeing any ghosts." She checked her white button-up and black slacks. All were pressed and crisp, just as she expected. "I gotta get going. Thanks for dropping me off. My car's out of the shop in—"

"It's my pleasure. As I said, I'm always here. Have a good evening, sweetheart," AJ said.

She inhaled deep and turned to AJ, who met her gaze with his winning smile.

She hummed and swayed her head slightly. "Please save me a massage for later. I'm going to need it."

He leaned over the center console and kissed her on the cheek. "I'll be waiting. How do you feel about a breakfast date?"

"As long as your French toast makes an appearance."

"With strawberries and whipped cream? Anything you want." He rubbed the back of her hand before pulling her toward him. She let out a playful yelp and giggled.

She closed her eyes, savoring his moist, warm goodness.

"I love you," she said once he pulled away.

"I love you more." He smiled at her, wiping all insecurities clean. "Now, what time do you get off again?"

"Cute," she said. "Seven, as you already know." She leaned in and kissed his cheek. "Bye," she whispered.

He waved. "Bye."

Getting out of the Malibu, she clutched her tote. The early evening sun kept the sky clear. Holly Avenue sat quietly before her as she rounded the car and stepped up the curb.

She looked over her shoulder to find AJ watching her. She smiled and waved at him. But even from where she stood, she could feel the disappointment in his eyes. She hated saying bye to AJ when he was worried about her. But duty called.

As she strolled up the cobblestone walkway, she gawked at the wooden door just up the steps. It was one of those fancy, glossy doors you'd find on a castle in a kid's storybook. She smiled. Nick used to beg her to read those stories to him every night after she tucked him in. His favorite was the one about the Moth King and the Butterfly Princess.

"I want to meet my princess one day," he'd say.

Riley promised he would.

The sweet memory made her smile as she scanned the banner across the awning again. Weariness threatened to knock her over right there. She shook her head, getting rid of the dizziness.

Shouldn't've drank that Ghoul so fast, she thought. That damn energy drink was enough to wake the dead. But once she got inside and got to work, it would wear off like it always had.

Riley had never been to Gallagher Hotel. Hell, she'd never been to *Holloway*. She was from Westland and rarely drove north of Hall Road where her favorite outdoor mall was. Because of the distance, a little over an hour, she had planned on turning the gig down. Eighty degrees on a Saturday, who wouldn't? And with graduation parties and weddings hungry for catering and waitstaff everywhere, she'd worked an average of fifty hours a week over the past few months. But Gallagher Hotel was different. They had requested her personally. She didn't bother telling AJ because he'd start in on his millions of questions and concerns. There was no need to worry him any more than he already was.

But how and why did they want her? Bruce didn't explain. She and Bruce had their hang-ups, with him lacking managing skills and being short-fused, there was no other way. Delighted and surprised, she wondered how they got her name and why they chose her instead of Bruce himself. She shook the thought. She was there now, ready to work, add one thousand dollars to her account, and prepared to look for a child to raise.

She smiled. Another child meant another chance to be a great mother. Better yet, this kid wouldn't have the burden of pumping her cursed blood through his or her veins. She'd get to be a mom again, and this time, she planned on doing things right.

Riley gazed up at the third floor of the hotel. The brick building seemed newer than the awning advertised. The double-pane windows looked like they belonged to a modern house, not a building put up in the early 20th century. No doubt, whoever owned the place had done some renovating.

"The most haunted building in Michigan," she mumbled to herself. "A gimmick, if you ask me."

She hoped that was the case. The mere idea of souls being trapped on earth was heinous. Everyone moved on to the other side. She believed it wholeheartedly. She trembled as Nick's round face and big brown eyes crossed her mind.

I hope you're not stuck where... Stop it, Riley! Now is not the time to beat yourself up.

20

She shook that eerie sensation. It had gotten easier to shake that daunting thought from her mind over time. But for some reason, for the first time in a long time, it clung like a leech.

Nick. Her only child. A true *love* child. Gone. Just like his father.

Nick's playful giggles sounded off deep in her ears. A cold tremor rolled down her back. His spirited laugh had never been so present since…

She blinked and peered over her shoulder. No one in sight other than AJ watching her. Her face warmed, and her chest swelled.

She struggled to flash AJ a faint smile. He waved again and started the engine.

"Get a grip, Riley," she griped through clenched teeth.

She took a sharp breath and proceeded for the door.

Chapter 3

"Chris!" Morgan's high-pitched voice tore him from sleep.

Chris winced at the swift nudge against his knee. Morgan's bastard strength shoved him out of a restless sleep, welcoming him to a crooked neck and sore back. He reached, stretching his arms out until he felt his shoulders crack, and then folded his arms. He huffed and rested his head against the back seat's leather headrest.

"We're almost there," Morgan added as she watched him with low, red eyes. Her short dark hair was a mess, and her deep brown face smiled hard at him.

Uncle Jay looked over his shoulder from the driver's seat. The bags around his dark eyes had blown up even more since they'd made their way out of Detroit. He said nothing, just as he hadn't said much over the last few weeks. He looked back at the highway.

Chris couldn't give two shits about Uncle Jay's mood. He gave the man fifty bucks for the one-hour trip. Uncle Jay could've said no if he was going to pout the entire time. Chris wasn't surprised by his uncle's new demeanor. No one was.

"Did you hear me?" Morgan asked.

"What?" Chris quipped. The woman was annoying, and to this day, he didn't understand why Uncle Jay kept her around.

"I said, we're almost there," Morgan contorted with a frustrated glance. She put the blunt to her lips and sucked down smoke, then blew it in his face.

Chris winced and glanced at the radio. 7:50. He frowned. "I said wake me when we get there," he snarled. He cleared the grogginess from his throat and waved the skunky smoke from his breathing space. He pressed the button on the door, freeing the smoke from the car through the opening window.

She shrugged a shoulder. "Oh well, you're up now," she shouted over the beating wind. Morgan smiled and handed the blunt to him.

He waved her off and rolled the window back up, opting for the air conditioner instead of fresh humid air.

"So, what? You don't smoke anymore?"

He cocked his head. "You know I don't smoke before work."

Morgan rolled her eyes. "You weren't always that way," she retorted.

A migraine rushed forward from the depths of his mind. "It's none of your business if I smoke or not," he said.

"Calm down. I'm just saying that people are acting brand new, that's all," she said. "Especially lately with all the changes going on."

Ignoring her, Chris let out a wide-mouthed yawn. No way she was about to drag him into a chat about those *changes*. She could piss Uncle Jay off by herself.

"Ugh, why couldn't you drive your car? You didn't tell us it'd take *forever* to get out here," she complained.

Uncle Jay scolded her. "You know he's not allowed, Morgan."

She smacked her lips. "Right." She smiled at Chris. "How could I forget?"

Chris scoffed. "How far out are we?"

"Like..." Morgan blew smoke out into the night air as the Impala charged past a semi-truck in the left lane. She picked her phone up from her lap. "The map says fifteen minutes."

Chris's blood boiled. "So you figured out a way to get maps working on airplane mode? Because I know for a fucking fact that I said airplane mode on all phones during this trip."

"Whatever. Calm down. We got lost because these directions you printed are shit."

"You can't read now?"

"Yes, I can read. I just don't understand garbage instructions on paper when my phone can tell me where to go."

"Uncle Jay, that's how you like them? Illiterate?"

"Ugh! Shut up. It's not the end of the world," she shouted, glaring him down as if she were sizing him up. "Why is it such a big deal anyway? It's not like you're going to be doing anything."

"You want them to track your shit? It'll show you were here, or around here, on the night shit went missing!" He grunted and flexed his jaw. *If Morgan wasn't a girl...* He turned his attention to the road outside. The darkening sky welcomed them into the early evening. Slim traffic left the highway open for them to pick up speed.

Uncle Jay must've noticed that too, because he was doing eighty-three miles per hour in the fast lane.

"Are you gonna tell us why you chose this place? You don't usually work out here. Well, at least when Brian was around you didn't."

Chris's stomach crawled at the sound of his roommate's name. "You don't know shit about what Brian and I used to do."

"You don't know shit about what Brain and I used to do," she mocked. "You miss your butt buddy, huh?"

"Uncle Jay, put this bitch in line before I do."

"Like you did with Carla?"

"Hey, children," Uncle Jay said. "Calm down. I'll have you two separated shortly."

"Whatever." Morgan rolled her eyes at Uncle Jay before turning her attention back to Chris. "How'd you find out about the place?"

"I got an invitation in the mail," Chris said.

She giggled. "Who gets invitations in the mail anymore, and to a party they didn't know existed? Can I see it?"

He pulled the invitation from the front pocket of his genuine leather backpack. The golden envelope shimmered in the setting sun as he passed it to her.

She opened it and pulled the invitation free.

She read, "'Christopher A. Styles, you have been cordially invited to join us for our annual feast and overnight stay at Gallagher Hotel, Michigan's most haunted building.' Ohhh, how *fancy*." She went on. "'Come join some of Michigan's elite as they wine and dine with the Midwest's finest.' Jay, this is all the way from Holloway, Michigan. A place we didn't know existed until today. But if Chris says it's worth his time, we have to stop everything for him, just like everyone else does, because he's *special*."

Her sarcastic undertone drove Chris up a wall. "Give me my shit back," he said. He reached for it.

She turned her body, rolled the window down, and hung the invitation out the window. It fluttered violently.

"Morgan, I swear to…"

"Ah ah ah," she said between bursts of laughter. "Don't say something you don't mean," she teased.

"Give me my shit!" he shouted over the thumping winds.

"Morgan!" Uncle Jay said.

"What? I'm not done reading," she growled. "Let me finish, and I swear I'll give it back."

Chris sat back and pursed his lips tight, holding back the urge to snap her neck and shove her from the moving car. The thought of her body rolling and skidding down the road made him smile a little.

"Alright," she said as she rolled the window up. "Where was I?" She cleared her throat. "'We will have a full waitstaff ready to serve you throughout the night, whether you're thirsty for our selection of fine wine or something from our imported whiskey collection or hungry for our fine cut steaks and delectable appetizers. Tour the Victorian mansion and meet one of our real-life ghosts.' Huh. Says they're friendly," she said. "Alright, here, take this shit."

She handed it over, and he snatched it.

"What's the real reason that you're coming out here?" she asked.

"You read the invitation."

"Chris, you ain't shit. There's nothing elite or fine about you."

He drew his head back, surprised. "I ain't what? Do you see these shoes? Limited edition Retro Jays. These jeans and hoodie cost more than your rent. My bag is worth more than your life. And my hair cut? More than your cheap weave. Bitch, get out of here. I *am* the elite. The finest wouldn't be fine if I weren't there as the centerpiece."

She sucked the smoke in and pushed it out. "Boy, my weave is worth more than you, everything you own, and your pathetic life. What does it say about the elite when you're just going in there to rob them like an underling parasite?"

"Oh, I see you learned a new word. Spell underling for us, will you?"

"Right after you spell 'jealous bitch boy.'"

Chris cocked his head. His face warmed over.

"Ain't got shit to say? *Of course* you don't, because the minute it's not about you and your shit, you throw a bitch fit. That's why Carla left your bitch-ass."

Vision glazed red, he smirked and sat quietly. Morgan liked, no, *loved* pushing his buttons. *If it weren't for Uncle Jay...*he thought. *She'd have gone the way of old TJ.*

He smirked. TJ. Chris hadn't thought of that name in a while. Since TJ was banned from the Gang almost five years ago, he kind of faded in everyone's memory. That's why it was best to stay off Uncle Jay's bad side, because he was a master at cleaning up messes, even if that meant wiping the culprit from the face of the earth.

They pulled up to the hotel, right in front. The curb was bare from the ice cream parlor to the Store and Go on the opposite corner. No people. No noise. Holloway could've been a ghost town.

"Damn, are you the only one staying here?" Morgan asked.

"What does it matter?" Chris asked. Her voice egged his migraine on, making him clench his teeth.

"This place looks so fancy. Look at it, Jay. It looks like a gothic mansion from one of those scary movies we watched. Don't look shit like no hotel." She turned to Chris. "How come we can't stay? I could use a vacation," she said.

"Because it's invitation-only, and you're a nobody."

"Fuck you."

"Watch it, bitch."

"Hey, man," Uncle Jay said. He pulled his hand down his face and peered at Chris in the rearview mirror. Frustration loomed in his tired eyes.

"You better get her before I do," Chris said.

"Is that a threat?" Morgan asked. "I hope you don't think—"

"Shut up, Morgan. I don't need this shit," Uncle Jay snapped. He hated it when they went at it. Chris knew it. But Morgan needed to be put in her place every now and again. The woman's mouth slashed nerves without a knife.

"Well, tell your shithead of a nephew to watch who the fuck he's talking to."

Chris's eye twitched, and he grinned. "Get your bitch, Uncle Jay."

She flicked the blunt at him. The cherry pecked his belly, leaving an ashy black mark on his new white t-shirt.

Face scorching, Chris reached over the passenger seat and grabbed a fist full of hair. He tightened his grip and pulled hard as he bit down on his bottom lip.

Morgan flailed her fists, hitting his jaw and right cheek one, two, three times. Each hit landed with an ear-piercing smack that shoved bright flashes before his eyes. But he gripped her hair tighter, yanking and pulling her up from the passenger seat.

"Hey, cut that shit out!" Uncle Jay grabbed Chris's arm, forcing him to loosen his grip, letting the hair fall loose from his fingers. Then Uncle Jay used his other hand to grab one of her flying hands and pinned it against her thigh. He sat her ass flat in the seat where she huffed, puffing her cheeks out. Chris sat back, cheek panging with hurt. He knew she left a bruise, feeling the pain evolve with every second that went by.

"Touch my girl again, and it's you and me. Disrespect him again, and I'm after your ass," Uncle Jay snarled.

Morgan smacked her lips. "Whatever." Her chest puffed with exasperated breaths.

Chris ran a hand down his face and threw the door open. He stepped out into the dead street. A humid breeze pushed through the sleepy downtown area, forcing its way into his face and around his thin frame.

Morgan rolled down her window. "Hey, Chris. Have a good time." She smiled and drove a straightened index finger across her throat.

Chris grunted at her and cocked his head, stretching his neck out.

He threw his backpack strap over his shoulder and slammed the door shut. He tapped on the roof of the car, and Uncle Jay rolled his window down.

"Seven, right?" he asked.

"Yep. Thanks again," Chris said.

"It's nothing," Uncle Jay said before pulling from the curb and getting back onto the street. He drove up to the red light just before the Store and Go storage containers.

Chris watched the car with a side-eye as he threw his head back and groaned at the darkening sky. His first night out in a week, and he'd already gotten into a fight. Morgan couldn't leave fast enough. She was knocking him off his game. Before he'd gotten in the car, he was proud; he'd found a new place to score before taking off for his new life. Gallagher Hotel was a blessing in disguise, as Mom would put it. The damned place had called him out, and he answered, finding it an excellent opportunity to begin his escape.

Once Uncle Jay made a right turn a block up the street, Chris dragged ass across the pavement. Every ache surged through him, from his face down to his toes. Aside from the fight, his sore back and legs reminded him of the night before. Working the grill at a popular midnight diner was tough, especially when the other cook sat on his ass and ate the entire shift. But Fat Pat was the owner's son; he could get away with that. However, Chris? Not so lucky.

The thought of the ten burners frying eggs and browning pancakes made him cringe. He hated it there almost as much as he hated breakfast food. But he needed it. Not only did it grant him short-term freedom from Uncle

Jay's basement over the last few weeks, but it was also a plausible front. It's not like he could put his actual job down on a loan application when it was time to buy a new car or that lakefront house he'd dreamed about for so many years. What could he do? He imagined himself walking into the bank wearing his best suit and dress shoes, dark hair slicked back and nails clean. He'd shake the loan officer's hand and go, "Hello, sir. Can you give me money? I'm a burglar." He'd aim his pistol at the man's head, open his leather sack, and say, "Now put the fucking money in the bag."

Even now, the daydream made him chuckle and his heart race.

He glared at the awning flapping in the soft winds. *The Most Haunted Building in Michigan*, it said.

He snickered. "The most *haunted* building in the state? Yeah. Okay." Chris slouched. "There better be something in there worth taking." It was reason number two for the trip, and a very crucial step in his plan.

He rounded the building, heading for the parking lot out back. As he strode, he looked up the length of the house. There were no cameras. He passed storm doors, and next to those, a set of double-paned glass doors. He stepped up to the storm doors first and pulled the rusted handles up; the door opened with ease. He tried with the back doors, but they didn't let up. He peered through the glass and smirked; there were chains around the knobs.

"Well that's interesting," he said.

He searched the parking lot to find nothing but a few cars parked back there: a candy red Lamborghini and a yellow Jeep Wrangler. Then there was a pearly white Charger fully suited with dark tints and smoky gray rims. He smiled at his car. He'd put so much into it and looked forward to the road trip that night.

31

Uncle Jay and the Gang didn't know Chris spent the first half of his shift the night before moving his car from his old house up to the hotel. His heart raised at the job well-done; he'd be out of town in no time, leaving them and the *changes* behind. He'd be on his way shortly, but first, he had to collect on whatever the hotel had to offer before he could escape the Gang's pending wrath.

He approached his Charger and popped the trunk. He pawed around the stuffed duffel bags, pulled out his pistol, and shoved it into the leather backpack. Then he patted his pockets down.

Chris leaned against the bumper and watched the building. It seemed quiet, not like a party was going on inside at all. *Good*, he thought, *no one to get in my way while I work*.

Chris turned and grabbed his hoodie, a red backpack full of toiletries, and his work clothes. A small chill went up his back. Choosing Gallagher Hotel was risky and far off from the rules set forth by Uncle Jay:

Rule #1: Make sure it's worth it.

Rule #2: Survey and survey again.

Rule #3: The exit is more important than the entrance.

Rule #4: Move fast and quiet.

Rule #5: Never leave empty-handed.

Rule #6: Do not get caught.

But the time to survey never came, and Gallagher Hotel was the best place for Chris to hide his car, collect some valuables, and then make his escape before Uncle Jay showed up in the morning. As planned, Chris would be halfway to Missouri, escaping his ruling and severe sentencing from the Gang.

He slammed the trunk and pulled his backpack over his shoulders.

Gallagher Hotel was historical, which meant artifacts. All he could think of was relics. His palms itched with anticipation as he walked toward the building. He couldn't wait to see those paintings, vases, crystal silverware, and jewelry. He gazed at the Lamborghini as he passed it. He wouldn't mind getting his hands on the keys to that thing either. Optimism took him. He had a good plan.

Brian would've probably gotten off on this. Too bad he wasn't around to confirm that. Carla would've loved this as well. Chris's chest sweltered over his thumping heart. Even the thought of her name burned his cheeks, making his gut turn.

Catering to her changed him. Made him…vulnerable.

Never again, he thought. *Never again will a chick…* He shook his head. *Not now. Not before work.*

As he approached the front of the mansion, the feeling from that day weeks ago washed him down, striking his nerves. Wishes crept through his mind. Questions and foreign doubts dragged his feet as they approached the cement steps.

Why didn't you whisk Brian away back then? Why'd you let him fool you?

"Chris." Carla's voice and olive, round, worried face sat behind Chris's eyes.

Chris shook his head and took deep breaths before stepping up the stairs.

"You alright?" Brian asked.

"Yeah. Yeah. I'm just—" Chris started. Then he froze and dropped his brow. He whipped around, searching the street. How was he hearing Brian's voice? For a second, he felt the heat of someone standing alongside him. But there was no one. Only him on the lonely street standing before the entrance.

"I have to tell you something." Carla's voice was so loud and present that he peered over his shoulder again. Nothing but cicadas starting up their night song.

"Focus up, fucker." Brian's voice broke the clashing shrills stirring in Chris's head. Chris whipped around.

Nothing.

No one.

He raced up the steps and stopped. He grunted and shook his head. Then he chuckled. "Alright. Alright, calm this whack shit down. You're alright." Morgan must've hit him in the head harder than he thought.

He pushed the door open, and the smell of grilled steak pushed past the threshold.

"Time to work. Focus and take what you put your hands on," Brian's voice.

Chris cocked his head. He must've caught a contact high from Morgan's trashy weed. *That's it.* Morgan poisoned his mind with voices and regrets, then she hit him in the face, shoving delusions between his ears. *That'll do it.*

His mind was fucking with him. *Morgan* fucked with him.

But he didn't have to worry about her anymore, and after tonight, Michigan would be a part of the distant past.

He stepped into the dim foyer, taken by the well-kept restaurant just past the threshold. The archway was gold, and old portraits of a man wearing three-piece suits sat on either side of the door. One was black and white; the other was full of soft colors. A copper vase sat below the black and white one.

Chris nodded, pleased as a smile crept across his face. He slowly pushed the door closed behind him and peered around. Still, no cameras.

"Oh, honey, close the door before you let the moths in and the cold air out," a woman said. Her burgundy dress hugged her tight, exposing her glossy ivory legs, outing the many hours she spent working out. At least she looked like she had been. She ran a hand through her silver hair, pushing it back. A gold chain dangled low, just below her perky breasts, and her golden bracelets slid down her slim arms. "Oh, sweetie. Where are my manners? I'm Brenda Scott, the Master of Ceremonies. You must be Christopher?"

"Just Chris is fine," he said.

"Oh, well, come on, let me show you to your room. We must hurry. All the guests are on their way to the parlor for drinks."

Chapter 4

Long scarlet curtains blocked the sun from the inside, keeping the ballroom dim. The smell of fresh steak loomed as a cool wind whisked through the ballroom, making Riley shudder a bit. Eerie classical music hummed below the chatty staff. Dark oak tables sat up against the walls with red, thin pillar candles flickering in the center of each one. The wallpaper looked old and gothic, the same color as the curtains but covered with a white gold stylized lily pattern.

She stepped slowly across the red and black marbled floor as if she'd stepped into a museum of the fancy. Each chair had a velvet burgundy cushion. Off to her right sat a long oak bar with a crystalline red triangle engraved in front of it. The row of stools separated at that point. She counted five on either side.

Riley peered around, clueless and nervous. She'd never worked an event on her own before. Without Matthew, Bruce, Kara, and Donna, she doubted she could take the place on by herself.

Luckily, the place was dead, with only a few patrons left behind enjoying their dinner at two tables against the walls. The waitstaff shuffled about, bursting in and out of the flopping kitchen doors straight ahead against the back wall. Some sat at tables counting down tips, and others were busy setting a long table in the center of the room. They carefully placed napkins, utensils, and glassware, starting her job for her.

"Hm," she mumbled to herself. They *have* a waitstaff, and there was no way these people were paid one thousand dollars a shift. Not with that minimal foot traffic, at least. So why was she requested? Maybe they didn't have a big enough staff to cover the event? She nodded. *Well, it makes sense, I guess.*

She walked past the threshold and stopped at the oak hostess station.

The host, a dusty-faced old man, looked up at her. His glare screamed self-importance, and his frown barked "ugh." *Allen* was stenciled into his cotton v-neck blouse like chalk to a chalkboard. His smile was as dull as his dark eyes. "Sorry, but we are closed for a special event," he said, speaking low and sluggish, almost droning.

"Yes, I'm here with KNR Catering. I was hired to help with the event tonight."

"Oh," he grumbled. He looked her up and down, then grimaced. "Bruce, you look a lot prettier than you did the last time we met."

Riley snickered. "Oh no, I'm not— He's my boss. He said I was requested personally?"

Allen glowered and sighed. "Oh well, fine, I suppose. I don't know why she—never mind. I guess we can work with you. Follow me."

He led her off to the right toward a set of steps.

Just before the steps hung a portrait of a pale man leaning on a pogo stick, sporting an evergreen kilt and a brown sack coat. His dark eyes were soft, and his smile was faint. The golden tag beneath him read *Ulysses Gallagher. An American Hero.*

"Hurry now," Allen beckoned. "We don't have all night." He stepped up the stairs, and she followed close behind.

"This is a really nice place," she said.

Allen said nothing as he led the way.

For the hell of it, Riley asked, "Hey, is this place *actually* haunted?"

"Have you ever been here before?" he asked.

"Uh, no. This is the first time I've heard of this place. It's the first time I've ever heard of Holloway, honestly."

"Well...welcome to my humble stomping grounds."

"It's a really beautiful hotel. I'm happy to be here."

"Hm," he said. "Good. And to answer your question, yes. The hauntings are real. You may see a ghost or two tonight."

Riley flashed a quick smile without responding.

On the platform, a portrait of the same man hung on the wall. In this one, he wore a top hat and a black suit. It was beautiful. His dark gaze was warning and curious as he smiled. Below his picture, it read *Mr. U. Gallagher. An American Hero*.

Is this one of the ghosts? Riley cocked her head, searching for another angle, hoping to catch enough light in the dim space.

Could that be the owner?

"Ah, I see you're taken by Mr. Gallagher."

"Is he one of them?" she asked.

"Sure," he said facetiously. "And if you see random bottles of whiskey floating around at any point throughout the night, it might be him."

"Pfft," she replied.

Allen winced. "Riley, do you believe in ghosts?"

"Oh no. I—have you seen him?"

He grinned. "Oh, *sweet* Riley. I've seen them all, talked to them, even. They are a lively bunch."

"Oh, well, I didn't mean to—"

"Shall we continue up the steps?" he interrupted. "I have to show you where you and our guests will stay before dinner and drinks begin. Most of them are already here."

"Yeah. Sure. After you."

He continued up the second flight of steps, and she followed.

The top of the staircase led to a hallway with matching carpet. They passed through the threshold and faced a wooden door with a golden number 1 on it. She peered around. The wallpaper was the same as the ballroom, and dim wall lights sat between each room door. The hallway ended with another staircase that led up to the next floor. To her left, there was a window covered in thick copper curtains.

Allen proceeded down the hall, facing the upcoming staircase. "There are seven rooms for guests. Even-numbered rooms on this side." Allen pointed to the right side of the hallway. "Odd on that side." He pointed to his left. "There are fresh linens in the closet here." He pointed to the thin door next to the staircase they'd just climbed. "That's all you need to know about this floor."

"What's upstairs?"

Allen narrowed his eyes at her. The darkness inside them was almost unhuman. It made her flinch. He spread a mischievous smile. "Well, aren't you curious?" he hissed.

She separated her lips to speak, but his gawking and defensive stance made her reconsider. She almost expected him to sprout horns and fangs.

"No, just…" She let out a nervous chuckle. "Never mind."

He lifted his brow. "Those stairs lead to the attic. It's off-limits to *everyone*. Do you understand?"

She gave a stiff nod.

"Good. I—"

Room 3's door opened, splashing yellow light on the dark carpet. A short black woman emerged, wearing a knee-length cocktail dress. She crossed her bare arms over her chest. Her hair was pulled back into a French bun. Glitzy diamonds glimmered across her neck, fingers, and wrists. Her hazel eyes scowled, displeased. "Excuse me. I wanted silk sheets! Do you people actually believe I'm going to lay my head on that cotton bullshit?! I know I told you that when I sent my invitation back."

Allen faced her; his sneaky smirk faded into a serviceman's smile. "Oh, of course, Ms. Paul. We'll be right with you."

Ms. Paul eyed Riley with disgust etched across her face.

"Uh. Hi, I'm Riley." Riley approached the woman and extended a hand while wearing her best service smile.

Ms. Paul *tsk*ed and looked past Riley to Allen. "Get my sheets," she barked.

Riley withdrew her hand. "I'm sorry. We'll get those right away."

"Thank you. And make it quick. I don't want to be late for drinks."

"Of course," Riley said as she watched the woman disappear into her room and slam the door behind her.

Allen let out a low cackle. "That's Ms. Natalie Paul. She's a part of the *needy* variety, someone who needs constant catering."

"She's dressed very elegantly. Is she famous or...?"

"Oh, she's famous, alright. If you're in the business of chopping people into pieces and dumping them into the Detroit River."

"Wh—what? Are you saying—"

"At least that's what the rumor is. But no one dares to turn her over to the police. Well, from my understanding, she owns them too. It's hard being a woman in her line of work, having to hit the hardest and do the most unimaginable things."

"Seriously?" Her chest heaved in surprise. Riley couldn't imagine that small woman doing such heinous things. She peered over her shoulder at the closed door. The number 3 glowed golden in the dim light.

"Room 5 isn't occupied right now," Allen went on. "Randy Moore got in early and made his way to the parlor. I imagine he's talking Room 1, the good Dr. Myles, to death. Or it could be the other way around. Either way, they are—"

"Everyone in the parlor already?" a muscular redhead said, sticking his head between the cracked door next to the linen closet. He set up shop in Room 2. The man was built like the Terminator and towered over Riley and Allen by about a foot. He watched them with his tight mug and unwelcoming glare.

"Why, yes, Lieutenant Marsh, most of them are."

"Call me Dan," he said in his thunderous baritone.

"Alright, *Dan*. We are waiting for one more person to show up while I'm getting our staff up to speed."

"Hi, I'm Riley." She waved at the man.

He stared at her and scrunched his face. "Nice to meet you."

"Dan here is a celebrated war hero from Keego Harbor. He's gotten many purple hearts from his tours in Iraq and—"

"Iran. It's my duty to protect and serve," he said matter-of-factly. "I've toured Saudi Arabia and Jordan. My men are amongst the best combatants in the world."

"Well, Dan, feel free to go meet the others downstairs. We are going to be starting shortly."

Dan nodded and stepped out into the hallway. He made his way to the stairs.

Allen searched the closet shelves lined with sheets on the top, towels and face rags in the middle, and plain white blankets on the bottom. He grabbed a pair of white silk sheets and handed them to Riley. "Go drop these off to Ms. Natalie Paul. I need to head downstairs. Meet me in the ballroom when you're done."

Riley headed for Room 3 and knocked.

The door opened, sending the sweet smell of lilacs into the hallway. Natalie stared back, impatience in her eyes.

"Here are your—"

Natalie snatched the sheets from Riley's grip and slammed the door in her face.

Riley flared her nostrils and let out a heavy sigh. "You're welcome," she said.

Chapter 5

The parlor was as dim as the ballroom. But instead of candles, on the side tables between four sets of copper recliners were golden lanterns, blemished with age.

The golden loveseats and couches looked like something out of a 1920s celebrity home. They circled the coffee table where Dan had situated his cocktail before sitting in the corner of one loveseat, resting an ankle on his opposite knee.

The walls were lined with shelves, all stacked high with red wine, white wine, or brown liquor. Just to the right of the brick fireplace, Riley picked up the bottle of Kentucky bourbon that had been waiting for her on an oak counter with a brown and white marbled surface. Next to the bottle sat a cluster of empty medium-sized crystal glasses. She filled each glass halfway before placing seven of them on a silver platter.

Riley steadied the platter of cocktails on her right palm and peered around the party. She averted eye contact with Allen, who stood with an older woman just behind Dan next to the fireplace. Allen's chuckling bellowed out over the soft chatter amongst Natalie and a clean-faced, olive-toned man. They'd already helped themselves to a glass china cabinet by the door leading to the kitchen. Natalie filled her glass with whiskey and sat the bottle on the oak table next to the china.

"I guess we have to serve ourselves," Natalie said before taking a sip.

Riley stepped past Dan, making her way for Natalie, whose drink was already half-empty. Embarrassed, she wanted to be sure to stay close by Natalie. *She's going to be the problem guest. I can feel it*, Riley thought. *Lord, give me strength.* She'd have to try a little harder to throw Riley though. Sticking close by was the best plan of action.

"Oh, yes, Brenda, tell me about it!" Allen said to the older woman, whose silver hair flapped lazily as she threw her head back with laughter. Her blood-red dress hugged her body, making her appear to be a fit thirty-year-old below the neck with a sixty-year-old face.

He caught Riley's eye and watched her with a sly grin. He waved her over. "Riley, I want to introduce you to someone."

The hairs on the back of Riley's neck stood straight. She painted on her most convincing smile and walked over as they watched a little too hard for Riley's comfort. Both wore conniving grins.

"Brenda," Allen started, "have you met the girl Bruce sent? She claims she was requested. Must be *special*."

Brenda's dark eyes widened. Without taking her eyes off Riley, she said, "Oh please, Allen. She's fine." She leaned in. "Thank you *so* much for coming at such short notice, darling."

"Hm," Allen said. He glared, laying an overbearing heat on her. "Perhaps you're right. She seems like a hard worker that likes to cater to people. You should've seen how she handled our guests earlier. She might work out just fine."

"I know she will." Brenda placed a hand on Riley's shoulder. The touch sent an electrifying shock through her. The woman reminded her a lot of the people she grew up around. There was a fake warmth about her.

"Excuse me," Riley said. "I have to—"

"We're only waiting on one more guest," Allen interrupted.

"Christopher, right?" Brenda asked. "He's here. I just showed him up to his room. He should be down in an instant. He said something about needing to change his shirt, and the poor boy had a fresh bruise on his cheek. He's probably attending to that." She sucked air between her teeth. "He looked like he'd just gotten into a scuffle." Brenda turned her attention to Riley. "How long have you been serving? Do you like it?"

"On and off for about ten years. It pays the bills."

"On and off? Well, what else have you done besides that?"

Riley paused, picking her next words carefully. She hated reliving the past. Sometimes, it was easier to pretend it never happened, and not talking about it was the best way to do so. Still, she couldn't blow Brenda off. So, she did the next best thing. She picked fragments of her botched young adulthood to discuss. "I took some classes here and there."

"You spent some time in school? Majoring in what?"

"Biology."

Brenda let out a smug chuckle. "What did you plan on doing with *that*?"

"Medical school, but I had to drop—"

"You know, Riley, that's where most people mess up. They think a higher education separates them from the masses of poor and underprivileged, when, in fact, you only stumble into the American Dream: debt up to your ears. You'll find yourself kissing some man's ass to keep a job that pays you half as much as your lazy and undereducated

46

male counterparts. If anything, it keeps you from being truly free," Brenda said. Her eyes went sullen.

Riley's palms began sweating. She readjusted the platter.

"Do you agree?" Brenda asked as she raised her thin eyebrow.

"Uh, I guess."

"You guess? Please don't be ashamed to agree with me, Riley. Men are the ones running this horrid world, after all. They get to run countries and swing their dicks around by starting wars and not giving a shit about the people that put them in a position of power."

"Oh please," a deep familiar voice said.

Riley and Brenda turned to find Dan sipping from his glass. He hadn't bothered to return the glance.

"I should get going," Riley said. Confrontation wasn't her thing. She turned until she felt a stern grasp on her shoulder.

"Oh, nonsense," Brenda said. "I'm interested in hearing what our prized war veteran has to say about the matter, and you should be too." She glared at the back of Dan's head. "Please, continue."

Riley peered at Dan and froze. She didn't realize a man was sitting next to him before. He ran his pale fingers over his pencil mustache as he watched the fireplace. He was the only guest wearing a black and white three-piece suit. She watched him sit still, gazing as if he was deaf to the people arguing around him.

"I'm only saying that things aren't as bad as women make them seem. Many women hold places of power. You're overreacting to nothing, getting all emotional."

Brenda winced at Dan. "Did you have any women in your platoon, Lieutenant?"

"You can call me Dan."

"*Lieutenant*, can you answer the question?"

Dan turned his head slightly, watching them with a side glare. "No. We spent nights stalking terrorists. We hid in the dunes, eyes in binoculars, waiting for the targets to leave their watchtower or their underground bunker. We laid low for days, soaking in the ninety-degree sun, and freezing our balls off in the forty-degree evenings, all just for that one shot because there was always only one chance. We stuck our dicks in bottles and pissed in them. We munched on MREs and drank dirty water. Women aren't built for such a job." He snickered. "Women can't be snipers because their bodies won't allow it."

"What do you mean?" Brenda growled.

The anxiety was getting to Riley's wrist, threatening to send the platter toppling over to the floor. She readjusted the platter and peered back at Dan. The man sitting next to him had gone. She frowned and looked around. He was nowhere in sight. Worry chewed on her nerves. "I should really get going," she said, convinced her eyes were playing dirty tricks on her. Maybe AJ was right. She needed a full night's rest.

"No, Riley, stay. Don't you want to hear what the man has to say?"

"Oh. Not really. He's entitled to his own theories." *Lord, please*, she thought.

"Excuse me," Natalie blurted. "Are there any appetizers here?" She looked over at the man she had been talking to. "Randy, are you hungry? Because I am."

He smirked and nodded.

"Excuse me. Can we get some service over here?" Natalie said.

"Watch what you say, army man," Brenda snarled. "You're in the presence of like-minded individuals."

Dan scoffed. "Who? Her?" He gave a quick point to Natalie.

"What about me?" Natalie asked.

"Nothing that concerns you. Go on and keep bleeding the china dry. I'm sure Little Miss here will bring your hors d'oeuvres shortly."

Natalie swaggered over. "You got some shit you wanna say to me?"

"Look, I don't want any trouble," Dan said. "I was just saying to this lady—"

"Brenda Scott. *Ms. Scott* to you," Brenda said.

"Excuse me. I was answering *Ms. Scott's* question about why I didn't have women in my platoon, and I explained that their monthly cycle was why they couldn't take part. They wouldn't've been able to lie in the sand for 49 hours at a time while waiting and watching. That's all."

"That sounds like a shit fucking excuse," Natalie snapped.

Dan's nostrils flared, and his face went deep red. "I don't make up excuses. I tell the truth!"

"No. No. It's bullshit. Let me tell you a story, soldier man…"

"My name is—"

"I'm going to call you whatever the *fuck* I want. Now shut up and listen. You've had your moment to throw your hissy fit and share how you feel about women. My oldest son thought he was going to pull that shit on me. He thought he'd tuck me away and take over my…conglomerate. But he was sorely mistaken. I sat outside his house in the bushes, waiting for him—fifty-two hours, to be exact. I could've sent my soldiers out to get him. Hell, I could've had him taken out on the spot. But I made him. Biologically, socially, physically, and financially. So it was only right that I handled him on my own. No help. These fifty-two-year-old bones were strong enough to pull it off without so much as a sliver of suspicion. Now you tell me what women can't do with the tools and training you got from our glorious government."

Dan stood from the couch and strode toward Natalie. "Is that a threat?"

Unmoved, Natalie peered up and met his eyes. "It could be if it were true." Her face softened under her smile as she took a sip from her glass. She winked and turned her back on him, heading to her spot next to Randy, whose eyes glowed with anticipation.

"Hey now," Allen said. "We're here to have a good time." He moved for the doorway to meet an olive-toned man, much younger than the others, and a chubby black man with a broad smile, enjoying the show.

Allen shook the young man's hand. "Welcome, Christopher. We've been waiting for you."

"It's Chris, and thank you," Chris said.

"Right." Allen turned on his toes. "Riley, go ahead and pop across the hall. There are a few trays of hors d'oeuvres on the counter. But first, make sure the guests have drinks."

"Of course," Riley said.

She headed for Natalie and Randy, who'd been joined by the black man.

"Rand, that motherfucker was close to getting his ass sliced. I don't give a fuck about a war hero. Everyone looks the same when they're drenched in blood," Natalie said under her breath.

Randy chuckled.

"Do you know what you should do? Get you a yacht and take it on Lake Michigan. It's the best way to relax," the man said.

"Uh huh," Natalie said as she finished her drink.

"Would you like a bourbon?" Riley asked the man.

He looked her up and down, then grinned. "Hi. I don't believe we've met. I'm Dr. Myles."

"Riley."

"Nice to meet you. You're such a gorgeous woman. You deserve a ride on my yacht." He snickered.

"Ugh," Natalie said. Randy chuckled.

"Excuse me?" Riley asked.

"Look, Riley, I have four cardiology practices, seven properties up north, and a dealership out in Detroit. All I'm saying is, if you want a better life, you can come work for me." He studied her with his greedy eyes again. This time, she fought the urge to vomit on his snakeskin shoes and white button-up. "I'm sure we can use you for something around one of my practices."

Riley smiled. "I'm flattered, but I'm going to have to pass. Thanks though."

As she turned and walked away, he said, "I guess some people are too afraid of success."

Natalie scoffed.

Riley took a deep breath and hummed one of Granny's favorite mantras: *All the gold in the world can't hide the insecurity and ugliness hidden inside.*

These people weren't ugly. They just had a lot. Even the youngest of the bunch was sporty. As Chris waved her over, she couldn't help but stare down at his bright white shoes. Those tennis shoes must've cost a month's rent.

As she approached Chris, she noticed his smile grow wider with each step. He stood alone, watching the party like a typical wallflower. Something was appealing about his hazel eyes and fair skin. He looked a lot like AJ must've looked ten years ago and a few shades lighter. Either way, she felt herself stepping into a comfort zone and away from the horrible people in the parlor.

"What can I get for you?" she asked.

"Mmm. I haven't decided yet."

"Alright, can I help you with something else?" she said.

"I figured you could use a break from those assholes. Are you okay?" he said near a whisper.

"Yes." Riley sighed. *Great. He can tell I'm annoyed. Not good.*

"It's alright to yell back at them. I work in the food industry too. It sucks ass, right?"

She chuckled, feeling her mood lighten for the first time in hours.

"That's a nice tattoo you got there." She eyed the thick, upside-down cross stretching down the right side of his neck.

"Oh, this old thing? I got it to piss my mom off. Worked like a charm."

"I bet it did."

"Does it bother you? I can cover it up if it does. I'm not trying to make enemies like those people."

"Oh God, no. That's your choice. I have no right to judge it."

He looked down. "I like your tattoo too."

She felt her face get warm.

"You don't have to explain it. It's just really nice needlework. You got your message across."

"Oh, you're sweet."

"Nah, just honest. How long have you worked here?"

"Just for tonight."

"Nice. Well, maybe later I can order you a drink. I feel like you'll need it."

She smiled. "No, I don't drink on the job."

"You consider this a normal gig?" He smirked.

"You know what? No. No, I don't."

"Yeah. It's not every day that you get an invitation to a haunted hotel."

"Yeah, but I'm sure it's a gimmick. I mean, I haven't seen anything that states otherwise." *Other than the strange man who sat on the couch.* Riley was convinced she was seeing things.

"I saw something."

She cocked her head in disbelief. "Really?" Her heart raced. "Wh—what did you see?"

"Allen. That guy looks like the Crypt Keeper."

She laughed.

"I mean it," Chris said. "That man could fork over at any moment and come after all of our asses." He shivered once as he peered around Riley. "It's like staring into King Tut's tomb. His ass *is* the haunting."

She laughed harder, placing her free hand on her chest.

"There's that pretty smile," he said.

"Thanks, I needed that."

"No, thank you. I needed to see a beautiful woman smile."

She watched him watch her and fought the need to sneak a few drinks with him. He seemed fun and carefree.

And a little bruised.

"Do you need ice for that?" She pressed her own finger to her cheekbone. The dark blemish on his face looked fresh.

"Oh no. This isn't... It's alright."

"You sure? It looks like it hurts."

"It doesn't. You're so attentive. Can I take you with me when I leave?"

"Oh, stop it."

He snickered. "Nah, I'm just kidding. Well, if you want, I mean, I can sneak you a couple drinks? That way, we can have our own party watching these jackasses go at it. Come on," he lulled. "You know you want to."

She shook her head, failing to curb her wide smile. "Have you decided on your drink yet?"

"Yeah. I'll take a rum and Coke."

"Sorry. I'm only allowed to serve this bourbon or the whiskey or wine on the shelves. There's, uh—"

"*Ugh.* I hope it's not Michigan whiskey. It's the worst shit on the market."

They laughed. Riley didn't drink much of anything, only wine here and there. Whiskey and bourbon were too harsh for her taste. Luckily, she had her hands full this evening. Although Chris was cute and sweet like her AJ, she still had a job to do.

But she was tempted.

"Do you at least agree?" he asked.

Riley shrugged.

"Okay, okay, I get it. You want to, but can't. Never bite the hand that feeds you. A very wise thought from a very beautiful woman. Well, if that's what's going through your mind anyway."

She must've blushed because he went on. "It *was*, huh?"

She nodded wildly, trembling at the lips, trying to hold back a burst of laughter.

"Don't worry. It'll be our little secret." He took a deep inhale, puffing his chest out. He eyed the wall he stood in front of and looked over the shelves stocked with a variety of whiskey. "Alright, can I have a triple shot of Forest Red whiskey on the rocks?"

"You're getting wasted before dinner?" she asked, peeping around to make sure Allen and the others were too preoccupied with one another to notice she'd been talking to Chris for a while.

"Why not? Might as well fill up on fine whiskey while I can."

"I guess." She couldn't argue with that.

"My name's Chris, by the way," he said. He extended an open hand.

Meeting his palm with hers, she clutched and shook. *I guess everyone here isn't a huge asshole after all.*

"I'm Riley. It's nice to meet you."

"Pleasure's all mine, *Riley*."

Grinning, Riley said, "I'll bring your drink over as soon as I can."

Riley made her way back to the waitress station and set her platter down.

"My new house in Florida is…" She tuned Dr. Myles out, happy he was boring Natalie and Randy to death with his stories. Dan still sat on the couch, watching a fireplace with no fire and no man sitting next to him. It was as if the mystery man disappeared into thin air.

Maybe he went to the bathroom, or maybe…

"You need your rest," AJ's voice sounded in her mind. She rolled her eyes. Maybe he was right. But she was so close to her goal, she could feel it. All she had to do was get through the night, no matter how weird and sneaky Allen was or how rudely some guests behaved.

She sighed and looked at Allen and Brenda, who kept their spots behind Dan. They watched and snickered, mumbled and whispered.

Riley knew those kinds of people. Her parents would've fit in perfectly. She grew up in Birmingham, an uppity town just outside of Detroit. Her strict parents set high standards for Riley, forcing her into ballet, tennis, track, and The National Success Society, all in the efforts of stuffing her into a prestigious medical school. She was supposed to take over Mom's OB/GYN practice, the business that made everything happen for their small family. Dad was sure of it. He'd even begun teaching Riley the ins and outs of office management and medical billing. It was all money and no play for Mom and Dad, and they did everything to make Riley as uptight and strict as they were. But that changed when she wasn't worth their time anymore. Or maybe they finally realized that destiny had other plans for her when they learned the name of her real fate: Stephen Wells.

"Appetizers!" Natalie's exclaim pulled Riley from her trance.

"Right away," Riley said. She crossed the hall into the kitchen. "Lord, God, please give me the strength to get through this night," she whispered.

She gathered the plate of hors d'oeuvres and turned to head back to the parlor.

A thick shadow rushed up the hall, passing the kitchen door frame, freezing her in place.

Her hands shook, and her heart slammed against her chest. The thing moved too fast to be human, was too thin to be material, and too big to be an animal.

What the...?

Slowly, she crept toward the door. With a stiff neck, she peered around the corner and up the hall.

No one.

Anxiously, Riley stepped slowly on shaking limbs. As she crossed the hall and entered the parlor, she recited:

"Even though I walk through the darkest valley, I will fear no evil, for you are with me; your rod and your staff, they comfort me."

She checked the room and found the guests and hosts standing around just as they had before.

If everyone is here, then what was that?

She closed her eyes and shook her head. *Dear Lord, please help me get a grip*, she thought. The sleeplessness and creepiness of the place wore on her.

She jerked at the shoulders when she opened her eyes to find Allen staring at her. The tint on his face intensified, and the cracks in his cheeks and forehead deepened with more than just age. She watched his eyes darken, engulfing the whites around his pupils. Chills shot through her as time seemed to stand still. An overwhelming sense of dread cloaked her as she quivered, afraid to speak or move as his evil demeanor sucked the life from her veins.

With shaking lips, she uttered:

"The Lord saw that the wickedness of man was great in the earth and that every intention of the thought of his heart was only evil continually."

Allen's face crumbled as he separated his lips to speak. His lips gave way to white, sharp, jagged teeth.

"Well," Brenda started, pulling Riley back to the party and out of Allen's strange grasp. Allen turned and smiled; his face abruptly switched back to that of the snarky old man who worked for the hotel. "We have…" she held her wrist up to her eye level, "…forty-five minutes before we have to head out to the ballroom for dinner. I hope everyone is hungry for the finest cut porterhouse steak and baked red potatoes."

"My cook makes the *best* steak and potatoes," Dr. Myles said.

Brenda chuckled. "I'm sure he does," she said. "Drink up and enjoy the appetizers, but be sure to leave room. The night has only just begun."

Chapter 6

Allen pushed a cart through the flopping doors against the back of the ballroom, wearing a wide-mouthed grin. He parked it near the bar.

"Dinner is served!" he announced. Plates sat on silver platters as they rattled against one another. Riley followed close behind with a silver platter full of red wine. She set it on the bar and went to his side. They uncovered the plates and set them in front of guests, starting with Randy.

Chris grumbled. *What kind of party dictates what you drink? And who the hell doesn't have rum?* He glanced at the bar sitting behind the people on the opposite side of the table. Randy sat between the empty corner seat and adjacent to Chris. The seat directly across from Chris was also empty. Dr. Myles had his back just in front of the crystal triangle emblem on the bar. For a second, Chris wondered if the thing was removable. The way the red light scattered once it hit the crystal emphasized authenticity. It might've been a diamond. He'd have to do the fog test to make sure it was real and worth his time to chisel off a piece or two.

He glanced around. There was a plethora of pricey shit for the taking, just as he thought there'd be. This night would cost him nothing compared to life on the road, an experience that would start in a little over six hours.

"Mmm. Something smells good," Brenda said. "Have you guys ever had porterhouse steak grilled on a stone? My husband used to love it that way. God rest his soul. I pulled up the recipe and threw it right on the menu to commemorate his exceptional taste." She looked at her steak with happy eyes.

"I'm sure you did," Natalie said before rolling her eyes and laying them on the porcelain plate Riley placed in front of her.

"We're the only place that does it in town," Allen said as he sat in the empty seat at the head of the table, next to Randy and across from Brenda, whose back was to the archway just past the hostess station.

"There's a restaurant up the road that does that," Randy said.

"You live in town?" Brenda asked, cocking her head.

"Oh. No. No, I, uh, visit from time to time. I'm from Muskegon."

Liar. Chris sniffed Randy's bullshit from across the table. Judging by Brenda's faint smirk, she must've thought the same.

"Actually," she said, "I don't know that much about any of you. But we'll get to that shortly. First, though, a toast."

Brenda stood and raised her glass. Everyone at the table did the same.

She parted her lips to say something, but then stopped and looked at the bar.

"Riley, would you care to join us?"

Riley leaned against the bar next to her drink platter. Her brown eyes widened like a deer caught in headlights. "Uh—"

"Please, dear, don't make me have to ask twice. We're wasting precious minutes."

"Oh, okay, it's just—"

"You are a guest. So what if you're working the event? I would love for you to join us for dinner. Allen's sitting. It's only fair if you join too."

Riley shrugged, grabbed the extra plate and glass of wine from the platter, and sat across from Chris.

He smiled at her and studied her confused look. Her dark pulled-back hair and fair, creamy skin screamed *Carla* in his mind. Their mannerisms were strikingly similar, from that sensual strut to the way those big brown eyes glimmering in the candlelight. He felt his heart melt all over again. Although she didn't look it, he sensed she was older based on the dates on her tattoo and how she handled working for the elite dipshits at the dinner table.

Yeah. She's older, meaning more experienced. For a second, he wished he were her apron because he'd get to hug her slender waist. She was gorgeous, and if he weren't working, he'd try to get her back to his room. But his priorities didn't include searching for Carla's replacement.

Riley's face softened when she caught his eye.

He mouthed, "Bottoms up."

She nodded.

"Now, that's better, isn't it?" Brenda turned her attention to the rest of the table. "To new friends and a wonderful dinner. May this be the first of many."

"Cheers," Randy said.

Riley raised her glass to Chris. He met her gaze and raised his glass to her. As he took his drink, he watched her, hoping for a way to fit her into his life, if only for the evening. He'd like her full lips on his and his arms around her, just like he had with Carla for years.

But the thought of Carla came with baggage and a reminder of tonight's goal. He dismissed the thought of him and Riley and moved his attention to the hostess, or *Master of Ceremonies*, at the head of the table. Brenda took her seat. "Now that that's out of the way, let's—"

"Is this place really haunted?" Randy asked.

Brenda cleared her throat. "Mr. Morris, let's save the questions for a little later. I would like for all of us to get to know each other a little better first. I'll start. I'm Brenda Scott, and I've owned this historical treasure for more than forty years. I took it over from my father, who bought it in 1948. I love this place so much that I live here."

Chris let out a soft sigh. This was going to be a long night. He peered at the portrait of a man wearing a top hat hanging against the wall behind Brenda. Chris didn't know much about art, although Uncle Jay had mentioned learning more about it so the Gang could up the ante. He was probably getting bored with break-ins, and after the mishap in Bloomfield, it was time to expand the repertoire. But Chris knew the enormous diamond on Brenda's forefinger was worth more than his car. The diamond was so big that it would be impossible to sleep with it on. He wondered if she was a cougar, because the way she latched onto him earlier hinted as much. The gold dragging from her neck and leaking from her wrists also had to be worth more than the paintings. The way she stared at him with soft eyes when she showed him his room let him know she wanted him. Perhaps by the end of the night he would stop by her room and give her what she wanted so he could take what he needed, time permitting.

"Alright, alright." Brenda stabbed her steak with her fork and sawed at it with her knife. "Mmm. Nice and red. Just like I like it. Dr. Myles, would you mind taking the floor? Who are you? What do you do? Where are you from?"

"Mm," he said through cheeks full of steak. He grabbed his handkerchief and patted at his thick lips. "Well, I'm Dr. Donald Myles, and…"

Chris watched the man spew off accomplishments. Dr. Myles wasn't top shit. He wore a button-up that he grabbed from some department store. His designer woodgrain glasses? Seven-hundred-dollar May-Tans. But who didn't own a pair of those? Chris had about ten pairs. Dr. Myles didn't wear a watch or a ring either.

"…proud owner of the Lamborghini parked out back." Dr. Myles reached in his pocket and pulled his keys free. He waved them over the table.

Good to know. Chris lodged a red potato in his mouth. His heart picked up, and his palms itched. Maybe he would ditch the Charger, scrap the Lambo, and pick up dump cars as he made his way south. He made a note to stop in Chicago and search for Eddie, Uncle Jay's contact in that area. Eddie would do anything for a set of wheels like that, including keeping his mouth shut.

"Oh, very nice," Allen said.

"Yes, thanks for sharing," Brenda said. She looked up from her plate. "Riley?"

"Oh, I'm fine." She looked to her right. "You can go, Randy. I don't have much to share."

"Nonsense. I want to know more about you," Brenda said.

Riley stroked the nape of her neck. "Okay. Uh…" She cleared her throat. "I'm a server from Birmingham. Not the one in Alabama, the one outside of Detroit. I spent some time in college. I—"

"Tell us about the tattoo on your arm," Brenda said.

"Uh... I don't feel comfortable talking about that."

"Were you ever married?"

"That's something else I—"

Brenda sighed. "You know what? You're right. I'm sorry. I just figured since we were getting to know one another that I'd take the chance to know who *Nicholas* was and why he left you so early in his life."

Bitchy move, Chris thought.

"I didn't mean to upset you," Brenda went on. "Perhaps we can talk later?"

Riley showed a fake smirk.

"Randy, would you mind telling us more about you?" Brenda said.

Riley gulped her drink down. "Does anyone want anything else to drink?"

Natalie raised her empty glass, and so did Dan.

Riley stood, grabbed the bottle from the bar top, and refreshed their glasses.

"Randy?" Brenda asked.

Chris looked over at the man to find him staring hard. Chris dropped his brow.

"Randy?" Brenda asked.

"Huh? Oh, it's my turn. Yeah, uh, I own a landscaping company in Muskegon."

"You alright? Why are you so nervous?" Natalie asked before chuckling.

Chris cocked his head. *Do I make you nervous?* He smiled.

"Oh, no, I'm fine, it's just… Is there peanut oil in this, or…" He cleared his throat.

"No, there shouldn't be. We got your note about your allergies," Brenda said.

Randy shook his head. "Oh, okay." A nervous giggle. "Anyway. Yeah, that's all there is to know."

"What's the name of your company?" Allen asked.

"Mar Landscaping. We service the Muskegon and Grand Rapids area, and I just opened another branch in Fort Worth. Now we're working on expanding to the Chicago area."

"Interesting," Allen said.

Randy was clearly lying, Chris was sure. Randy's face moistened, and he struggled to pick his words. And the way he watched Chris was unbearably awkward. Randy was sneaky, and the last thing Chris needed was eyes on him. Chris stabbed his fork into his steak and watched the blood run free and onto his plate.

"Allen, you're up," Brenda said.

Allen rolled up his sleeves. "I'm Allen Hunt. I've lived and worked here at this beautiful hotel for thirty years."

"Times one thousand," Natalie mumbled.

Brenda's fork smacked her plate as a look of astonishment washed her face.

"Oh," Allen said underneath a devious smirk.

"Oh, come on, it's just a joke. You know, because you look so old," Natalie said. "Shit, I'm in my fifties and you don't see me bitching about it."

Everyone laughed, even Chris.

"Oh, I needed that laugh," Allen said. "But remember, everyone gets old and perishes."

An awkward silence swept the room.

"Well, isn't that the truth," Brenda said. "Isn't this fun? Daniel? You're up next."

The big man sat up in his chair. "Yeah. So, I'm Daniel Marsh, but you can call me Dan. I'm a United States Army veteran."

"Ohh," Allen said facetiously.

Dan sneered. "Yeah. I served in Iraq, Iran, and Jordan, just to name a few."

"When?" Brenda asked before stuffing potatoes in her mouth.

"2004 to 2010."

"Nice. What did you do out there?" Randy asked.

Chris glanced over at him. If Randy wasn't a cop, he was something just as nosey. The way he stared at Dan with that quizzical gaze and the way his hands were tucked under the table showed just that.

"I patrolled the major city streets, mostly on the night shift, keeping the peace. Sometimes, we'd go on missions to take out crime lords or people who threatened to incite the locals, making our lives harder."

"Why'd you leave?" Brenda asked.

"Discharged."

"I hope it was honorable," Allen said.

"No, it was the opposite. I was accused of foul play, causing the people to riot. I was sent packing in order to redeem the peace."

"Accused of what kind of foul play?" Brenda asked.

Dan balled his fist and pressed it against his mouth. He cleared his veiny throat. "I—uh—well, a couple of the guys in my platoon had a habit of stealing from the locals."

"Stealing what?"

"I'm not at liberty to discuss that."

"Oh, well, excuse me. I'm sorry I overstepped."

Dan's face reddened as Brenda patted her cherry lips with her napkin. "I'm sorry, Dan, do I make you nervous?"

He shook his head. "No. Absolutely not."

"Hm. Well, maybe it'd be better for Allen to ask you questions. Don't you agree?"

Before Dan could answer, Allen picked up where Brenda left off. "You close with your family, Dan?"

Dan scowled. "What?"

Allen drew his head back. "I'm sorry, I thought the question was clear."

"It was clear to me," Natalie said, taking down the last of her wine.

"I heard it," Randy said, watching the man closely.

"I heard it clearly as well," Dr. Myles said as he used his fork to scrape up what little food he had left on his plate.

"I *for sure* heard you," Brenda said as she placed an elbow on the oak surface and rested her chin on the back of her hand.

Dan chortled. "Why does that matter?"

"Oh, come on. We're amongst friends. We're getting to know each other. Why not share something more personal?" Allen coaxed.

"You didn't ask anyone else—"

"Correction. *Brenda* didn't ask anyone else. But I'm asking now."

"You think that's fair, huh? To have him ask me personal questions like that?" Dan asked Brenda.

"Well, to be honest, I'm interested in understanding that aspect of your life. I want to know if you have a family. I've always wondered how army men stayed away—you said six years—for so long and held down a household. A man of your stature and grace definitely had a woman fall for him before you joined the army, maybe? And I'm not talking about for Iraq or when the war on terror—"

"Or innocent people," Randy interjected.

"It's war every day where I'm from," Natalie said.

"...or ·whatever." Brenda went on. "You said you were a lieutenant, so our government trusted you enough to give you the responsibility to train, watch, and even take care of a platoon of younger soldiers who put their lives on the line every day in a foreign place. Some who were just hot to hold an assault rifle, and others who were just confused about what they wanted to be when they grew up. No. You *have* experience. So, you've been on the fighting career track for quite some time. Now tell me—or better yet, tell *us*—

about the woman who has the other half of the wedding ring budget wrapped around her finger?"

Huh, Chris thought. He'd planned on taking Dan's ring at some point this evening when everyone was drunk and passed out.

Dan sucked down a deep sigh and pushed it through his pointed nose. Without looking Brenda in the face, he said, "We're separated."

"Oh?" Allen raised his brow.

Dan met his eyes. "Yeah. She took our two daughters and moved to Alaska with her sister. We met in Montreal on my very first tour. Her beautiful silky black hair and caramel skin hooked me before she could say hello. Her name is Laura." He picked up his glass and gulped it dry.

"Riley, get the man a drink," Allen said with triumph across his face. "And fill mine up too, while you're at it.

Brenda shook her head. "Oh, Mr. Marsh, you are an enthralling man. Backward as a palindrome, but definitely an interesting addition to our get-together."

"I have to agree," Allen said.

"A trip, ain't he?" Natalie said as she took a drink from her freshly poured glass of wine.

"Christopher, you're up," Brenda said.

"Pass," Chris said as his heart raced.

"Nuh uh, cutie. You have to share," Brenda said.

Chris huffed, hoping to ease the jitters in his gut. "Uh. I'm from Warren—"

"The Detroit area? Nice, and not too far away," she said as she raised a hand to tell Riley to stop pouring.

"I'm a cook at a diner."

"I'm sorry," Randy interrupted. "How are you elite?"

Chris raised his brow. "Dude, what?"

"Honestly, you look like a little punk who took his parents' invitation or something. I mean, I thought this was an elite invite-only event."

Chris tilted his head. He saw himself hopping over the table and crushing Randy's neck with his bare hands. But that would get him arrested and ruin his plans for the night. He had to focus. He took a deep breath and smirked at the nervous man.

"I'm sorry, Randy," Brenda said. "You had your turn to speak. Now it's Chris's turn. And if you must know, not like it's any of your business, he was invited just like you were. Now please, settle down and let the young man talk."

Chris bit the back of his lip and watched Randy stare back at him. *Who the fuck is this guy, and why is he on my ass?* "That's all I have to say."

"Well, that's too bad," Brenda said.

Chris didn't blend well. But Brian would've. He would instigate to keep himself and Chris entertained. Too bad that all fell by the wayside. *Thanks a lot, Carla.* He shook the thought when Natalie bellowed out a hysterical laugh at Randy. He quickly averted his eyes when Chris caught him staring.

"Natalie, you're up," Brenda said.

"I'm from Detroit…"

Chris was done listening to the chattering from these odd strangers. They were all piggy banks in his eyes, and he couldn't wait to rob them blind.

After many years of practice, he was more than a thief; he was a con artist. But he started small with "sticky fingers," nabbing candy and small toys. The typical guardian would explain this behavior away by saying, "Oh, he just picked it up and forgot to make me pay for it." But not Uncle Jay.

One day, Uncle Jay turned at the waist with a scowl, his brown eyes threatening in the splash of orange from the late afternoon sun.

Chris's heartbeat ripped through his chest as the pockets on his coat burned against his body. So did his crown, where he hid the Crispy Rings underneath his knit hat. He shivered as he prepared for the sting from Uncle Jay's palm swiping his cheeks.

"Empty your pockets, Chris," Uncle Jay had said with a throaty husky voice.

"I—"

Uncle Jay turned around and adhered to the emerald stoplight.

"We don't want your ma finding out, huh?" He chuckled as he merged onto the highway.

Chris's eyes bulged as he spit out a heavy breath.

"But empty your pockets," Uncle Jay said nonchalantly.

Chris smiled and reached into his two front pockets and pulled out a yellow clay tube and six miniature cars. He pulled a Choco Bar from underneath his glove, a red pop from between his waistband and thigh, and the small bag of Crispy Rings onion chips from underneath his Ninja Katz hat.

Uncle Jay shifted his glare to the rearview mirror. "Damn, kid." He snickered. "How long?"

Chris pulled the ends of the chip bag open and tossed a fried onion ring between his braced teeth. "I don't know."

"Well, it's yours now," Uncle Jay said with a grin as he reached over and turned the radio up to its loudest.

Chris smiled, warm and thankful. They never talked about it again, and they never told Mom about it.

Chris spent most of his time with Uncle Jay while growing up. He was the only father figure he'd known, especially since the day Mom had enough of Dad's drinking and punching fits. Since that day, Chris was shy on the details about his father's leave. He woke up, and Mom packed him and his little brother, Will, in the car. They would never see or talk to Dad again. After a few years, Dad tried coming to get Will and Chris, but the courts wouldn't allow it. So Dad was reduced to sitting out front, drinking and stalking them at their grandparents' house for hours. Then he'd leave.

The last time Chris saw him was when he lay still in a casket after he was stabbed in the chest during a bar fight. Chris was ten, and Will was six.

Two years after the funeral, Mom saved enough to move them out of their grandparents' house. He'd never forget that big smile she wore when she rushed in excitedly, going on about this cute, small house off I-696.

"It'll be easy to get to work, and you guys will get your own rooms!" she exclaimed. Mom was excitable. She'd giggle and smile at the dumbest things. The glow in her hazel eyes and that big toothy smile used to put him at ease as a kid. He'd miss that about her.

***

Allen's laughter pulled Chris back to the dinner table.

"Oh, so you have women in your family who left your pasty-ass, and now you think you can come and talk to anybody else any kind of way?" Natalie exclaimed. "Mothafucka, I'll chop your ass up and dump you in Bush Lake. Keep talking yo shit. Lying fucker!"

"Bitch, watch what the hell you say to me!" Dan fired back. "I'll put your black ass in the ground!"

"Hey, hey. Stop arguing," Allen said through laughter.

"I guess I'll be clearing up now," Riley said nervously.

"I ain't done with my steak!" Natalie raised the blade of her steak knife and pointed it at Dan. The edge almost touched Chris's nose.

Why the hell did I sit between them?

"Listen here, bitch. My own kid didn't get away with talking to me like that. *No one* talks to me like that. You better sleep with one eye open." Natalie rose from her chair and dusted her silk dress that hugged her thick thighs. "I'm done with this shit," she snapped. "I need to get some rest, otherwise somebody might die tonight."

"Alright. Good—" Riley started.

"Bitch, just—" Natalie raised her hands and choked the air. "Just don't talk to me. Just—" Her loud threat fell to a low grumble as she marched off.

74

"I guess we'll be serving dessert to her room later then," Brenda said. "Are you all tired? Would you like dessert sent to your rooms?"

"Well, just because she's upset doesn't mean it has to ruin the night for everyone else," Allen said.

"You know what? You're right." She peered around the table. "Do you guys have questions for me?"

"Yes," Randy said.

"Well, shoot."

"Is this hotel really haunted? I've read about some paranormal investigators claiming it to be, but I wanted to hear it from you. Have you seen any ghosts roaming around here?"

She snickered. "Of course I have."

"Do you mind telling us about them?"

"But that'll suck the fun right out of it for you, I guarantee it. You'll see them. Everyone does. I mean, trust me; they don't hide their presence." She peered at the threshold just behind Allen and her face dropped, bleeding all color. "There's one standing right there."

Chris's neck froze as he held Riley's petrified gaze.

"Gotcha," Brenda said.

They all let out a nervous laugh except for Allen, who only sat there resting his chin on his knuckles.

"No, no, in all seriousness, the ghosts are real, and they live here. There's a cluster of them too. They've been here since the original building burnt down back in 1921, just a couple years after the place was built. It killed around twenty-five people, and as punishment, the townspeople hung the owner. As a matter of fact, she was prosecuted and hanged right outside the door."

"Hm," Randy said as he took a sip from his glass.

"Then," Brenda went on, "there was a carbon monoxide leak in 1990 during a get-together much like this one. It claimed six lives, but the building didn't take too much damage."

"Did you get hurt?"

"I suffered acute poisoning, but I'm fine. I survived. It was a sad day for Holloway though." She rubbed her wrist and drifted off.

"It sounds like this place is prone to death," Randy said, stuffing a cube of steak in his mouth.

Brenda's gaze went glassy. "Why, yes. It appears so."

"What was it like taking over the hotel with its history and all?" he asked.

"Oh. I was a beautiful young entrepreneur, just turned twenty-five. The first woman in my family to own a thriving business and the first one to get any real respect from everyone in town, including the mayor. I don't do what I do for status, but it feels good to run a tight ship, with or without help from a man." She glared at Dan, who stared at the bar. Chris knew the man wasn't listening to the stuffy old woman go on about her accomplishments. It was boring. But Chris sat attentively, loving the attention that Dan was taking from him, making his moves for the evening much simpler.

A small smile spread across Brenda's face. "God, everyone was so proud of me."

"I bet they were. And you don't look a day over fifty," Randy said.

"Why, thank you, Randy. That's so sweet of you to say. Do you have any more questions?"

"Do you ever think about selling this place? It's gotta be worth millions."

"No. I will not be selling this place. It's a huge token of my success."

"Really? Why not sell it to the town? That way, it'll be well kept and cherished as a landmark. I understand that this place holds a dear place in Holloway's heart."

She chuckled. "Oh, Randy. I know what you're thinking. *She's old. What does she need with this place anymore?* It's not like I have children or a family to pass it on to. And if I did, they wouldn't know how to appreciate it. They'd probably sell it straight away."

Randy winced and jutted his head back a little as if shocked at her remark. "So you don't think Holloway deserves the hotel as an important piece of history?"

"Well, no. It's my building for now, and if I feel like selling it, I will do so to whoever I feel deserves it. But for now, selling it is off the table, and if Allen is still kicking by the time I leave, it'll be left in his care. He knows this place better than anyone besides me."

"Hm. Well, after dinner, is it alright if I look around? Maybe I'll meet one of your ghosts."

"Feel free. The night is yours."

Chris frowned. *Great. Another asshole lurking around, making it harder for me to get shit done.* Maybe Randy was a cop, watching Chris. Perhaps he knew what happened and came to stop Chris from leaving town. Did Uncle Jay spill the beans? No, he would never do that. Snitching was forbidden, and there was more blood on Uncle

Jay's hands than Chris's. *Shit.* Chris had to get on the road fast.

Calm down. You're overthinking. That cop doesn't know shit, he thought. *Just wait it out.* Chris would follow Randy to find out which room he was in; then he'd wait for Randy to finish his solo tour. *That'll work.* It'd keep Chris at Gallagher Hotel a little later in the night than he wanted, but he wasn't risking being found out before he hit the road.

Chris sliced a piece of steak and shoved it in his mouth. He chewed slowly, pleased with his new plan.

That'll work. The sooner this dinner ends, the better.

Chapter 7

Riley took a plate from the top of the stack of dirty dishes and placed it in the sink. Sudsy water splashed and licked her cheek before the plate landed at the bottom, clattering against a cluster of used utensils.

How embarrassing. She had suffered her fair share of humiliation throughout her life, mostly bought on by herself. She owned up to that. But these people were a different breed. If they weren't vain, they were just plain rude. No wonder the pay for the gig was so much. The guests were a handful.

Still, Riley's own mistakes landed her here. She could've been a doctor, working next to Mom, delivering babies and giving professional, sound, lifesaving advice. But instead, she served and catered to the rich. It wasn't like they didn't deserve it; they all seemed to work so hard for what they had. But what gave them the right to treat her so horribly?

She slammed her fists into the wet surface, overflowing the water onto the tan and white marbled counter. This wasn't how things were supposed to go. Her eyes watered as she rested her hands in the dishwater. Where'd she go wrong? She tried so hard to do right by everyone. Mom. Dad. Steve. Nick. Yet she stood alone, facing a world that loved chewing her up and spitting her out.

It's just for one night, she thought. *One night, then you'll never see these assholes again...*

Tears flowed down her cheeks.

Riley never allowed anyone to mistreat her. Not even Steve after Nick was born or when he fell back into one of his famous relapses. But here she was, allowing these horrible people to speak to her like common trash.

Am I garbage? Riley thought. Everyone was *so* successful, even Chris. He *says* he's a cook, but those shoes and jeans say otherwise. Riley's parents used to buy those things for her as a child, so long as she kept her grades high enough. It was easy to get straight A's. It was her thing. She earned awards for Dad to stick on the mantle and track trophies for Dad to show off at the country club.

God, I used to be so smart, she thought. She was destined for greatness and set up to have it all. Now she was a worthless adult, barely making rent most winters when people didn't go out to restaurants or need a contract server for events.

I used to be so...strong. She sucked back sobs, swallowing the mourning for her past self. She deserved to bask in the glory of her accomplishments, not wondering why she was so mediocre.

Why did I... No.

She wiped her face clean with the back of her cuff and picked up the plate from the bottom of the sink. *No point in crying over spilled milk,* she thought. *It's over now.* If only she hadn't given Steve the time of day... *Things would be perfect.* She'd have a nice big house in Birmingham, two new cars, and the finest silks in the world to wrap her body.

Things fell apart when she fell in love.

Stephen Wells approached her on orientation day at the University of Ann Arbor, two days after moving into her dorm. The Student Center teamed with new students swarming kiosks, picking up class schedules, paraphernalia, and financial aid advice. The early afternoon sun lit the common area as they cluttered the bright, wide space in front of the cafeteria.

Steve's dusty blond hair swept across his prominent brow as he swaggered over, thumbs lodged underneath the straps of his backpack. He watched her with a big smile and eyes as blue as Lake Huron out in front of her family's cabin. Riley felt herself blushing. She hoped he didn't notice that she was defeated before he could even say hello.

He stopped in front of her. "Hi. Can you help me out?"

"Uh, yeah. What do you need?" She tried curbing her wide smile, but she couldn't help it. In high school, she crushed on boys like him: pretty eyes, tanned skin, a loose-fitting t-shirt with jeans ripped at the knees, and high-top Chucks. These boys were trouble because they were charming.

But she melted in his hands. His faintly sun-kissed fair skin, the small mole on his lower lip, and his easy, husky voice set her heart on fire.

"I need to find Bradford Hall," he said. "Can you show me where it is?"

"Sure. Uh. Do you have a map?" She looked over her shoulder at the cluster of students standing at the kiosk with a huge *HELP CENTER* sign over it. She pointed at the woman sitting behind it. "She gave me one."

"Oh. Well, they didn't give me one, and I don't have time to stand in line. I don't want to be late for class. I'm sorry, I thought you were like a sophomore or something. Is this your first year too?"

"Yeah," she said. "I also have a class there in a couple hours. Math 250?"

He drew his head back, stunned. "No, Math 098. Wow. You must be really smart."

She giggled like a schoolgirl, then snorted. *Oh God,* she thought. *Get it together, Riley!*

He looked around. "Well, maybe we can go look for it together?"

"Alright." She followed him through the path he made, clearing the crowd.

From that point on, they had always been together. Riding around in his old school Monte Carlo, hitting party after party and date after date. They ate breakfast, lunch, and dinner together, and they even spent nights together in their dorms. Steve quickly became everything.

Back then, she never thought things would change. Now, she wished they had sooner.

She set the plate on the drying rack and went to grab another one from the stack of dirty dishes.

Allen entered the kitchen, pushing a cart. He parked it next to the stove and pulled a cake from the walk-in freezer just behind Riley. She kept her back to him. The less she entertained, the less she'd be noticed. She wished she'd picked up on that since the time she strode through the door at the beginning of her shift. His petrifying glare was enough to put her off. That chilling instance haunted her through dinner. She didn't care to speak or look at him. She felt pure hate in his aura. But he didn't seem to notice or care that she peeped something dark about him; he carried on as if he hadn't scolded her in the parlor with a sinister affliction. Luckily, this was the only night they'd have to deal with one another. How anyone worked with him at all was a mystery to her, one she didn't care to solve.

He slammed the door shut behind him. "You seem to be in a mood," he said.

Riley dropped her chin to her chest. "Is it that obvious?" she asked.

"You can say how you feel out loud. There's no judgment here," he said. He placed the cake on the counter next to the drying rack. Its creamy white surface gleamed with red sprinkles. "You know we have a dishwasher, right? You don't have to make things harder for yourself."

She set the plate she'd been scrubbing in the water and looked over at him. He might've been strange, but maybe he could offer some sense to this whole thing. The fluttering in her belly needed to stop. Maybe he'd say something—anything—that'd make her feel better. "Why'd she have to sit me down?"

"Who, Brenda?" he asked while crossing his thin arms over his chest and leaning his hip against the counter.

"Yeah," she said. "It was embarrassing." She felt her face grow hot.

"Leave then."

"No. I—I need this job. I just thought it was unnecessary, don't you think?"

"Brenda is going to be Brenda no matter where she is or who she's with. But if you insist on being sensitive about it, leave. No one is forcing you to stay. Sure, you'll lose pay, and sure, Bruce will hear about it, but it's your choice. Stop playing the victim and go on with your duties." He pushed himself from the counter. "Now, if you don't mind, I have to deliver this to our guests since everyone decided they wanted to check in early." He opened the cabinet just over his head, took out a stack of white plates, and placed them on the counter. Then he pulled the drawer by his waist open and took out a cake slicer. He cut a slice and placed it on the top saucer. "This is for you." He placed it on the counter. "Brenda was right. Even though you're the help, and you're getting paid to be here, I'm not going to treat you like a dog." He stuck his finger in his mouth, wiping the icing on his fingernail clean. "Mm. White chocolate buttercream frosting. My favorite."

He placed the whole cake on the cart top and put the plates in a neat stack next to it. He pushed the cart, leaving Riley alone. She rolled her eyes and dropped the plate in the water. Leaving would be too hard to explain to Bruce. She needed her job, and she needed the money. Riley sighed. *Stick it out*, she thought. *It's only one night. And besides, everyone is winding down.*

She snatched up the hand towel next to the drying rack and dried her hands before stepping over to her slice of cake. She picked up the plate, took a clean fork from the drying rack, and dove in.

"Mm," she said. "Pretty good." The red velvet cake melted on her tongue.

Stop playing the victim and get on with your duties. Allen's words were so fresh that she peered around. His oddly present words bounced around as if he were repeating himself while standing right next to her. She yawned. *Must be tired, or going insane.* She went with the former. She shook it off, then took another bite.

A peculiar, soft clinking sound pulled Riley's attention over to the pots hanging over the stove across from the sink. *That's strange,* she thought. Slowly, she stepped closer to the disturbance and watched the skillets and small pots shake and pat against one another. Could there have been a wind blowing through? The clatter was soft, but loud enough so that she should've noticed sooner. She looked around and found the closest vent on the floorboard near the door.

Riley set her plate on the counter and listened. No rumble from the air conditioner kicking on, and the air would have to blow pretty hard to get the pots to move at all. She looked over at the drapes just beyond the pot and pan rack. They stood still.

She rubbed the gooseflesh along her arm and went for the vent. Nothing blew at her ankles. She dropped to her knees and peeked. Nothing blew back at her face.

"Huh..." she mumbled.

She got to her feet and headed for the stove. Before she could touch the rattling pots, she peered inside the sink. The water trembled, making small waves that crashed into one another. Suds dispersed, making way for the disruption. She watched as small waves ricocheted, faltering outward from the center as if an invisible faucet leaked small drops inside. *What the heck?*

The clattering came to an abrupt stop as the pots and pans froze, seizing all movement. The bubbles in the sink slowly came back together, closing the gap they'd made in response to the quavering house.

Dazed and wavering, her head spun, making her go light on her feet. She shook her head and widened her eyes. The room seemed to spin, dizzying her to her surroundings.

She pressed her hands against the counter, begging the kitchen to stop turning. Her vision went cloudy, and her mind flipped inside her head, threatening to take her off her feet.

Through sharp breaths, she grunted. She looked down at the cake. It sat half-eaten on the counter where she'd left it next to the sink.

What was in that cake? Or d—did I drink too much? What...what...? Her thoughts tripped over each other.

That strange but euphoric feeling threatened to send her back to a place she hadn't been since...

She looked at her forearm. Nick's birth date and death date drifted into focus.

She huffed through flared nostrils. "No. No. No," she roared. "I promised you I wouldn't. I swear I didn't, baby. I swear." She closed her eyes. Tears seeped out as she clutched her forearm. "I promise, Nick, I didn't."

"Hey!" an unfamiliar, impatient voice.

Riley popped her eyes open and looked at the kitchen door. A pale-faced man stood there, leering at her with a displeased scowl. His glossy black hair was slicked back, and he sported a black serving coat, white apron, bowtie, and creased trousers. "If you're done going through menopause, I need those fucking steaks!"

"Steaks?" Riley asked. Her feet stood on steady ground, and her head stopped spinning. All had calmed except for the man who she hadn't seen all night. She winced at him. "St—steaks?" she asked again.

"Yeah," he quipped. "I need one...*do do do*," he sang as he pulled a notepad from his pocket. He dragged his pointed index finger along the page. "Ah, there it is. One medium rare, three rare, and one well. Do you have them yet?" He stuffed the notepad back into the front of his apron and watched her.

"Steaks? The restaurant is closed for the night. You shouldn't be here," Riley said. She motioned for him. "Here, I'll lead you to the door."

He squinted his dark, beady eyes. "What the *hell* are you talking about?" He snapped his fingers. "Hey! Wake up! It's time to work. Do you have the steaks or not?"

"No," she said. Was this man a drunk that staggered in from the street? Couldn't've been, because she could smell his sweet cologne, not alcohol. And he was well kept, nicely groomed.

He stomped his foot and his face flushed. "Did you forget who was out there? Huh? Governor Fisher and his new wife are terribly upset with these ridiculous wait times. I hope you know that."

"I—I—"

"Fuck this." He turned his pale face up the hall and yelled, "Tell them five more minutes! It's not ready yet." He looked her up and down, then he shook his head. "Why they've got women working in a professional kitchen defies me. You belong in a kitchen, but not this one. Get it together! We've got a long night, and Governor Fisher is already outdone with the service. I'll see to it personally that Trudy cuts your pay for this."

"W—who?"

He turned and rushed off. Riley followed just to stop short past the threshold.

"Watch it!" A man, dressed a lot like the one from before, whisked past while balancing a silver platter full of drinks. She pressed her back against the wall, allowing him to pass. He disappeared through the flapping doors that led to the ballroom.

87

Others went by, rushing into the hall from the kitchen where Riley had been.

What? She turned and looked inside the kitchen. Women wearing long black dresses covered in paper aprons pulled plates from the cabinets and flipped steaks on an iron stovetop.

Perplexed, Riley stared at the new faces as they bustled and hurried, shouting orders at one another and disappearing into the second half of the kitchen where the other ten-burner stove was. Smacking oil burst and popped, barely loud enough to sound off over their voices.

Who are these people?

A soft tap on her shoulder made Riley spin around. A woman with cherry lips and short, curly black hair stood just behind her in the hallway. "Hey, do you have the chicken order up? Sheriff Louis is getting *pretty* impatient out there. God, you should see him getting all red in the face." She chuckled.

"N—no. I'm not a cook," Riley said as she studied the girl. She was young, or at least that's what her clear, pale, plump face suggested.

"Oh, stop toying around, girl. No need to be bashful. Go get the chicken while I spin a tale. Look, how's this..." She cleared her throat. "Gee, sir. I'm sorry, but there's a five-minute wait on the chicken. You see, our chef wants to make it especially *good* for you." She smiled big. "How's that? Huh? Am I good or what?"

She laughed and slapped Riley on the shoulder. Riley watched with worry dragging her heart.

"Can I let you in on a secret?" the girl said. She leaned in and dropped her excited voice to a whisper. "I planned on spitting in his potatoes anyway." A chill shot down Riley's back as the woman's freezing breath pressed against her ear. "He's such a prick. Promise you won't say anything."

The girl backed away and went back to the ballroom, passing through the doors, allowing the sound of clacking glass and chatter to sail through.

Riley cocked her head. It sounded like a full house out there.

But how?

She stepped carefully, keeping a shoulder against the wall. Servers passed by with silver platters on their palms full of food or drinks, focusing hard on the tasks at hand. She watched each of them go through those doors, disappearing into the busy ballroom.

Riley reached a shaking hand out and planted it on the door. "Very good, sir!" The waiter from earlier came pushing through. She shoved her hand to her side and backed away. He stood in front of her. His smile faded as his eyes went blank. He stared at her, holding her gaze with empty, dead eyes. His shoulders dropped, then he stepped slowly, approaching her while raising his big hand. A waitress walked behind Riley, making her stop in her tracks long enough for the man to make contact. He reached for her face, moved his hand over her cheek, and caressed her with an icy touch.

"I used to be like you," he whispered. He frowned, and his lips trembled as his eyes glossed over. "I used to be like you," he whispered again. With every second that passed between them, his cheeks sank, and his eyes receded into his skull.

Riley gasped and stepped back slowly, ignoring the busy servers hustling around her, making their way to the ballroom. "I—I don't know what that means. Who are you? Where'd you come from?"

"I want to be you!" the man yelled. His cheeks charred, blackening between his cries. Burnt skin flaked and fell loose from his face. He took a sluggish step toward her. "How come I can't be you?" He slapped the wall. His hand left a sooty print.

Heart thumping, Riley went into a hurried back step. Her back hit what felt like a frozen corpse. She spun around.

"Watch out," the girl with the red lips said as she looked down at her apron. Half of it was a smoky gray, and the other half was made of fiery embers. "You almost knocked me over, warm body." She chuckled as she looked up at Riley.

Riley yelped and tossed a hand over her mouth. Half the girl's face was gone, burnt down to a browning skull from her crown down past her neck. Patches of pink flesh clung to small spots along her throat as if they were melted between bones.

The girl smiled with the half of her face that was still intact and headed off, holding Riley's eyes as she kept her pace for the ballroom and ignoring the man that had gone silent and only stared. The girl winked with her good eye and headed straight for the man.

The woman walked through him as if he were part of the air.

"Oh my *God*." Riley backed up frantically, using the wall to keep herself on her feet. "No. No. No. This can't be real." She peered at the floor and listened to the excited laughter, which seemed to subside. *This can't be real. This isn't real. God, please don't let this be real.* She pulled her gaze from the floor and peered up the hall once the noise fell silent. The man had gone, the bustle of a busy kitchen died to silence, and the ballroom fell quiet on the other side of the flapping doors.

Riley turned and raced for the kitchen sink. She turned the faucet on and cupped her hands to collect cold water. She threw it in her face and gasped harshly.

"It's okay. It's fine," she said. "It isn't real. You're just seeing things. That's all." She hugged her waist. *But if you're seeing things, then you're going crazy.* She sobbed. "No, I swear I'm not using again." *Or maybe this place is truly...haunted.*

"Bullshit." She rushed from the kitchen and back into the hallway. She stopped and looked up and down the corridor. *What if he comes back? What if... Stop it, Riley,* she thought. *There's no such thing as ghosts.*

Prove it.

Heart thumping, she marched up the hallway and charged through the flapping doors. The ballroom was silent around Allen as he fussed with the curtains next to the front door. Burgundy and thick, they flowed effortlessly to the floor like blood. His cart sat at the base of the stairs with nothing on it but an empty platter. The tables were cleaned off, chairs pushed up. But they were all...slightly different. The cushions were brown, and the bar was all wood with small candles lighting up the shelves full of liquor against the wall behind it. The wooden hostess station was shorter and sandy brown.

"Did you change the furniture?" Riley asked.

He continued fluffing the curtains, unmoved by her question, if he heard her at all.

"Allen," she said in a small voice. He went on messing around with his curtains, dusting and fluffing them like pillows.

She cleared her throat. "Allen?"

"What?" he asked. He peered at her wearing an annoyed look on his face.

"Did you...did you see people in here?"

"Yes, Riley. I do see people in here."

Her heart dropped. "Oh, thank God. Where did they go?"

"Well, there's one person who's working on the curtains, and there's another person asking stupid questions instead of cleaning the kitchen as she should be." He went back to his curtains. "What do you see?"

"I'm not talking about now. I'm talking about the people that were just here. After the..." Her face flushed. She felt silly mentioning this to Allen.

"After what?"

"After the shaking. It was like the house was shaking under my feet. Then it stopped, and there was a man and a whole staff and—and laughter. And...I know I'm not going crazy. Did you feel it?"

He sighed. "Feel *what*, Riley?"

"The shaking. It was like a mini earthquake."

He huffed. "No. I feel annoyed that you're asking such ridiculous questions. I feel frustrated that you're talking to me at all. Please find something to do before I lose my mind. You can finish the kitchen. You can mop the floors. You can check on our guests and see if they want anything with their cake. Please, just…go away from me and make yourself useful for once!"

She looked over her shoulder. The flapping door stood still in the shadowy corner. "But I—"

"Look, I don't have time to deal with you," Allen snarled.

Patience worn, she snapped. "Look, I know you don't like me and that's fine! But there is something seriously wrong here! I can feel it."

"Can you feel it? Hmm. I'm off to bed. Please, don't disturb me. And you better believe that I will be calling Bruce in the morning and letting him know about your rude mouth, constant questioning, and just…" He rubbed his temples. "See if you get a dime for all the help you've been tonight."

Riley huffed and rushed for the kitchen. She paced the floor. *All the help I've been? What the hell is he talking about?* She put up with the abuse all night from those people. She'd done everything he wanted her to do. She…she…

She had to go. Hopefully, AJ was still awake and didn't mind the drive up at such a late time. She went back toward the ballroom and headed for the steps.

A shrill from above stopped Riley midstride. A sharp, electrifying pang shot through her body.

The scream sounded again, but slightly muffled. It was coming from the second floor…where the guests were staying.

"Help!" A screeching cry.

Riley rushed up the steps and found Dan and Randy standing in front of Room 3.

Chapter 8

Chris set the leather backpack on the twin bed and opened it. He pulled a small black case out and set it on the long oak dresser against the wall. He released the Velcro and rolled the kit open. His pocketknife, screwdriver, and lock picks lined the inside, organized in that order, nice and snug in the kit's slots. He pulled at the tightly fitted cuffs of his black cotton shirt and patted down the pockets of his dark cargo pants. He was about ready to head out. He pulled the pocketknife and its leather holster free and fastened it against his waist just behind his pistol holster. He took up the screwdriver and shoved it inside his left calf pocket. The fifteen lock picks went into the opposite pocket. He smirked as his gut flared with anticipation. He'd done this hundreds of times per the Gang's mantra:

Rule #1: Make sure it's worth it.

Rule #2: Survey and survey again.

Rule #3: The exit is more important than the entrance.

Rule #4: Move fast and quiet.

Rule #5: Never leave empty-handed.

Rule #6: Do not get caught.

The Rule of Six was tried, true, and fail-proof, thanks to Uncle Jay.

Chris sat on the bed, then leaned over to pull the thin laces of his army boots tight before tying them. The metal railing creaked under his weight. He'd never seen such a dated design for a hotel room. When he thought of a hotel room, he thought *laid and lavished*. Thoughts of a huge flat-screen TV, a corner jacuzzi, Egyptian cotton bed dressings, glass tables, and a killer view of the Detroit River flooded his mind.

But this wasn't that kind of place. In fact, it looked like it had been pulled straight from the year 1900. The pink and white floral pattern on the wall faded into an ashy gray. Thick, red velvet curtains hid the room from the outside, giving way for the lamp on the oak end table, which was shielded by an ugly floral-patterned shade, to light the room in a dim yellowish glow. A chest sat against the wall next to the private bathroom, and the bed was the size of a toddler's beginner bed.

The only thing modern about the room was the mahogany desk that sat opposite the bed. But the obnoxiously huge portrait of Ulysses Gallagher hanging just over the desk aged the room another century. The picture spanned from the desk up to the ceiling. Ulysses' pale face looked serious as he sat in a chair, leaning over one of its shiny arms that reflected the flash from the camera. His clean face stared off to the side as if he weren't thinking of anything at all.

Chris got to his feet and crossed the carpet to the bathroom. He flipped the switch and met his face in the mirror.

He scoffed. At least the bathroom had a typical design: a sink, toilet, and tub. All he could ask for. He turned the faucet on and ran cold water.

Flutters burst in his gut as he leaned over and cupped his hands under the freezing water.

I've done this hundreds of times.

He put his face in his wet hands, allowing a refreshing chill to wash over him.

This will be like any other time.

He turned the water off and grabbed the white hand towel from the rail over the back of the toilet. He ran through the plan one more time.

Chris had trailed behind the others as they climbed upstairs, so he knew where everyone stayed. He planned on standing behind his door with an ear against it, listening to make sure there was no movement in the hallway, especially from Randy. The man hadn't left Room 5 yet. Chris was sure of it. There was no movement in the hallway since Allen dropped off the cake.

Chris spat out a heavy breath.

Maybe Randy changed his mind.

Chris clenched his teeth. *Or maybe he's waiting on me to go out there.*

He shook his head. *Focus, dude. No one knows who you are.*

Chris would step out, going for Natalie's room first. She was so tanked that it was only a matter of time before she passed out.

Fuck, he thought. His mind scattered, and his plans shuffled over one another. No longer clear. No longer straight.

He hit his head with his palm. *Come on, dude. Come on. This isn't hard.* He glared into the mirror. "What the hell is going on, man?" he asked himself. "Change is good," he reasoned. Especially this change. He'd needed it to happen for weeks now, and he finally took the way out.

Chris huffed and dropped his chin to his chest. A violent chill shot up his spine. He refused to back out now. No. He needed this.

So go over the plan, he thought.

He'd creep across the hall, listening hard and watching like a hawk. Then, he'd kneel and jab the lock with his screwdriver and ease the blade of his pocketknife deep inside. He chuckled. Or *softly fuck it until that sweet click sounds off,* as Brian used to say.

"Yeah," he said. He'd slide inside, closing the door behind him, slipping into Natalie's room like a snake in the grass. His pistol would be ready with the silencer fully engaged.

"Just in case she wakes up," he said.

He'd snatch up the goods and go on to the next room: Dr. Myles.

No one would suspect a thing. If bodies piled up, he wasn't worried because by the time they surfaced, he'd be long gone.

"You can do this," he said. "You don't need Brian. You don't need Uncle Jay or the Gang. You can do this."

He patted the pockets of his cargo pants. He felt the outline of his screwdriver, ready to use. Then he rubbed his waist. The hardness of his pistol welcomed his touch, the silencer pressed against his right thigh.

He smiled. He was ready. But the small shake in his legs and hands begged to differ.

He paced the room, trying to smooth the shakes out of his limbs.

Why was he so nervous? Granted, he hadn't been out in a few weeks because of Uncle Jay's orders, but it wasn't like he'd never been solo before. He grew up solo until the day he met Brian.

Chris cringed. It was a day he slowly grew to regret.

It had been two years since Dad died when Mom moved them into a ranch-style brick house in Warren. The bustling neighborhood was nothing like Granny and Grandpa's. Mom raved about the abundance of neighbor kids and told Chris and William to mingle and make friends. But Chris was a loner and wanted nothing to do with them, so he made an excessive effort to isolate himself from the mass of kids that migrated on their bikes at the corner house. Congregating with the crowd was far from his style because congregations talked, and whenever they chatted, they'd reach conclusions, and when they met those conclusions, they'd gang up on the one who knew exactly where their missing bikes, games, and allowances had gone. He preferred riding alone and refused to have it any other way. Besides, Mom and William deserved to ease into their new lives without the drama.

Chris didn't have a problem with this, as he preferred staying in his room, playing video games, and trolling religious forums. God wasn't real, and he felt that those nut bags should know that.

Chris only left his room to get fresh air every now and again when he rode his bike to school or up to the gas station on 10 Mile to take a few bottles of Red Pop, Well Made hot chips, and a few chocolate bars.

When he made it back home one sunny, humid day, he rode up the driveway and leaned his bike against the brick wall near the metal gate that opened to the back yard. After slamming and locking the steel gate behind him, he pulled his very first house key from his basketball shorts pocket and jabbed the lock, allowing himself inside. A chilly breeze welcomed him, clinging onto his wet t-shirt.

Just as he climbed the three steps that led into the kitchen, his muscles locked. Two women, one being Mom, gossiped about kids and husbands. They laughed aloud and slapped knees, going on and on, chattering like chickens.

Chris took a breath and walked on his toes through the kitchen to the opening of the hallway. He peeked left, glaring at the wooden doors to the rooms and bathroom.

No one there.

He peered right. The sun beat hard on the red couches and the cherrywood china cabinet. Although he could hear them, he couldn't see them from where he stood.

Back against the wall, he slid out into the hallway and made his way to his room. He pressed the shaking pop bottles and crumbling chip bags between his hip and waistband tight, silencing the noise.

His room door was in his sights, straight ahead. He walked on his toes and listened hard to the women.

Almost there.

He grasped the doorknob and turned it. He pushed the door in and cringed when the dry hinges squeaked.

"Chris," Mom called out. "Chris, honey, come say hi to the Bentleys."

Ugh, he thought as he threw his head back and rolled his eyes at the ceiling. He didn't *want* to talk to strangers, and it sounded like there was more than one. *The Bentleys. Plural. No thanks.*

"I can't, I have—"

"Come here, Chris," she hissed.

Defeat. As much as he didn't want to talk to them, he didn't want Mom slapping the side of his head in front of them either.

He turned on his heels and headed up the hall for the living room.

Mom's smile shone as bright as the sun that lit up their new furniture set. Her long, silky, raven hair flowed behind her with some tucked behind her ear, showing off her sterling silver crucifix earrings. Her soft latte skin glowed in the sunlight that beamed from the window behind her.

Next to her on the loveseat sat a tub of goo. Chris figured the peach-skinned woman had to be 400 pounds. She was coated in a thin, sleek layer of sweat that she wiped away with her forearm. Her breath picked up speed when she leaned forward and lifted her stubby hand out to him.

"Hi, honey. I'm Mrs. Bentley." She forced up her overweight gullet. Chris felt his face crumble as he watched the woman, hoping she wouldn't choke and die from a heart attack just then. He thought carefully before saying anything back because he didn't want to spark up a conversation that could risk her life or appetite.

"Chris, where are your manners?" Mom folded her arms and raised a brow, her silent way of asking if he wanted to be embarrassed.

"Hi," he said, dismayed. He hoped she caught a clue and waved the conversation off, freeing him.

"This is my son, Brian."

Brian sat on the suede recliner in the corner. His

chubby face was scarlet, and his ham hock forearms spilled over the chair's arms. His round belly hopped with every breath as he glared with his beady eyes.

They didn't speak.

"Sweetie," Mom said. "Take Brian to your room and show him your games and movies. Sheela, would you like a cocktail?"

"Of course," Mrs. Bentley gobbled.

They didn't move. Instead, they looked over at either Brian or Chris as if their happy hour rested on their shoulders.

"Um—" Before Chris could finish his half-thought, Brian soared from the seat and shuffled past him. Chris followed behind him, squinting. Strange. The kid knew to lead Chris straight up the hallway and into his room.

"So..." Brian flopped down onto Chris's futon. It squealed underneath him. Chris cringed, hoping Brain wouldn't leave a crater in the mattress.

"So?" Chris flipped on the console and handed Brian a controller. Then, he took a spot on the bed next to Brian.

"You don't have a dad, right?" Brian asked.

"Right." Chris winced at him. *What an odd question.*

"So how can you afford all this stuff?" Brian gazed around.

Name-brand jeans and t-shirts lined the open closet, and posters of rappers and rock stars hid the dark walls. A 40-inch TV and stereo with surround sound and every game console known to man lined his mahogany entertainment center. Bundles of games were stored in the shelving units of the entertainment stand; the most popular and rare, to be exact. An aluminum telescope was stationed on a tripod in front of the window, and comic books lined a floor-to-ceiling bookshelf.

"All what stuff?" Chris asked, trying to blow the nosey bastard off.

Brian cast a dull look at Chris and then asked, "How

do you have all *this* stuff?"

"My mom and my uncle."

"I don't think so, dude."

"What do you mean?"

"Your mom works at the diner, right?"

Chris wasn't surprised that Brian knew that. He was sure Brian had his fair share of pizza and pie at all the diners around Warren. "Yeah."

"And she's a bartender at The Unwind, right?"

Chris's cheeks grew hot and his palms began sweating. "Why?" he spat.

"I'm just saying, I have both parents. My mom's a teacher and Dad works at the plant. I don't have this much stuff. Well, not from them anyway."

Chris scrunched his face and wondered how loud Brian's jaw would sound once Chris cracked it with his fist. "What the fuck is that supposed to mean?" he snarled.

"What I'm fucking saying *is*…I do the same shit."

"What?" Chris narrowed his eyes at him.

"I steal from Mr. Giovanni. He's too fucking old to keep up with his comic book inventory. I steal from the lesbians that own the video game store up on Hoover. What I'm saying is…I get it."

Flabbergasted, Chris stared at the side of Brian's face.

"And what I'm also saying is," he went on, "you're good."

"I'm…good?" Confusion flooded Chris's mind. *Who is this kid?*

"Yeah, I've been trying to pick up that game *Late Salvation* for months, but they all follow me around. But since you're new here, they won't bother you."

"Oh?"

A smile crept across Brian's face. "You're not going to deny it?"

Chris shook his head. "I mean, it's the truth, so…" Then he narrowed his eyes at Brian again. "How did you know?"

"Like I said, I do it for a living, so it's easy to spot a fellow thief."

Chris gritted the backs of his teeth and grumbled. "Don't call me that!"

"Hey." Brian raised his hands and calmly said, "That's fine. I won't call you that. Okay? I wanna teach you some things." He chuckled. "I'm on your side. We're the same."

Chris scoffed, growing impatient with every second. "What can you teach me that I don't already know?"

"Dude, I live here. I was born and *raised* here. I know everyone. I know how to get in and out without so much as a bat of an eye. I know the store owners' schedules, bus schedules through town, and everything in between to get us there and back. No suspensions. Pockets full. And our parents won't know a thing. My mom is too fat and lazy to check up on me, and my dad works about sixty hours a week. I bet your mom spends most of her time at work too, right?"

"Y—yeah. Bus schedules?" Everything Chris took up was during trips with Nana to the mall, Pop Pop to the Pal-Mart, and Mom to the grocery store. He'd whine about being bored or dehydrated, then take their car keys after they whisked him away for some much-needed peace when, all the while, he headed a few storefronts down to have his own *personal time*. Chris stowed his stolen goods under the passenger seat and headed back just in time to help them load the car. Once home, he'd wait several hours before sneaking the keys again and removing his gifts. He'd never thought of taking the bus though.

"Yeah," Brian said, "bus schedules. It's the best way to get around. I got sick of waiting for my parents to go anywhere or do anything. So I went at it on my own. I do most of my swiping after school."

Chris didn't say anything. He only wondered, *Why hadn't I thought of that before?* He imagined the things he could've gotten from Greatest Buy and Wireless Shack.

"So, are you in? Can you meet me after school?" Brian asked, brow raised and eyes full of hope.

"I don't know, man," Chris said. "I mean, Mom is real fickle about who I hang out with, especially after she and my uncle had a falling out. He taught me some cool shit, and...well, I figured it best to work alone to keep her off my back."

Brian scoffed. "You really think she doesn't know that you're taking shit? Has she never been in here before?"

"Well, I mean, maybe. But she doesn't think I do it anymore since she stopped Uncle Jay from coming around. It's bullshit if you ask me." He recoiled. He missed going out in Uncle Jay's old-school Impala, listening to him talk about his recent scores and favorite tricks. He'd talk Chris through them, then take him to the mall to try them out. Surgical tubes between the legs, scissors, and fake receipts were Chris's favorite tools. These tricks worked out just fine. No need for overexertion. "And besides, she's been in a good mood since we moved out on our own from my grandparents'. I don't need to give her a reason to worry."

Brian set the controller on the mattress and pressed his hands together. "Look, dude, I get it. You don't want to call attention to yourself in a new place, but let's be honest: you won't stop. Your shorts are stuffed with shit right now. Where'd you go, the gas station?" He shook his head. "I'll give it a month before Hassan catches you. You have to go a few miles down, across 8 Mile, and into Detroit. They'd be so busy watching everyone else that they won't bother us."

Chris dropped his brow.

"Fucked up? I know. But you have to take advantage wherever you can. Fact is, you will never stop. You're incapable. I only know because I'm the same way. Now, I'm not going to beg. I'm not going to worry. I just know that you're new, no one has caught on to you yet, and we can really use each other's help. Now, are you in?" He gazed at

Chris with hopeful eyes.

Brian was right. Chris had no intention of stopping. The itch was intense, and he scratched it however, and whenever, he could. Besides, since Uncle Jay, Chris hadn't run across anyone else who understood his needs enough to help him benefit. Maybe this kid deserved Chris's time. But there was something that needed to be cleared up first.

Chris nodded. "Sounds good."

"Yeah?" Brian said through a big smile.

"Yeah, but first answer this." Chris rolled his shoulders. "How did you know where my room was?" His heart thudded. Chris knew what the answer was, he just wanted to hear Brian say it.

"I looked around on my way to the bathroom earlier," Brian said with ease.

He can lie through his teeth, Chris thought. A red flag went up. "Did you take anything?"

Brian smiled, then stood. He reached into his cargo shorts pocket and presented a disc. Cuffing it on all sides with his chubby fingers, he flipped it over. It was the game that Chris "borrowed" from his cousin: *Late Salvation.*

Chris snatched it from Brian's grip and trudged over to the entertainment stand. He snatched out the case and replaced the disc. Slamming it shut, he let out a hateful grunt. He'd pulverize another kid for taking a piece of candy from him, let alone a video game.

Chris took things. People didn't take from him.

Glowering, Chris said, "I want to make something clear. Don't *ever* take anything from me or my house again. Understood?"

"I understand," Brian said, his voice fixed. "I hope that wasn't a deal-breaker. I swear it won't happen again."

Chris wished he'd whisked Brian away from his room that day. If he'd known the trouble Brian would drag him into, he would've kicked his ass then told Mom he was a thief. A *filthy* thief.

But he didn't.

***

Chris smirked and then sighed. *Crazy how shit happens.* He stopped pacing the hotel room and sat on the bed. He listened. Quiet. He checked the hand clock standing on the side table, next to the lamp.

"Hm," he grunted. 10:46. One more hour, and then he'd head out. Those assholes could still be awake. He headed for the desk and took up the plate of cake Allen dropped off not too long ago. That guy made Chris shudder. He wasn't sure if it was his gray face, wrinkled cheeks and forehead, or his dull black eyes, but there was something that seemed dead about the old man. It was like his skin was a mask, hiding him from the world. Chris knew he couldn't trust him. He still hadn't said much to the man, and he hoped he would never have to.

A chill made Chris's body convulse. *Ugh.* He'd skip out on finding where Allen slept. No need to be too greedy. He didn't want to know the man and could go the rest of his life without seeing him again.

Chris dug his fork into the velvet cake and took a bite.

Although he could promise not to see Allen for the rest of the night, he couldn't promise he wouldn't see him in his dreams when he stopped over in Iowa City.

Or nightmares, he thought.

"Mmm," he hummed. The moist red velvet melted on his tongue, and the sweet white frosting swooned around his mouth.

Just like Mom's Christmas cake.

He ran over the plan one last time.

105

First, Natalie. Then Dr. Myles. He didn't want the Lamborghini anymore. Too risky to drive around in a stolen car. But he had to be sure there was nothing else of value in the doctor's possession. Based on his constant gloating, there had to be something in his room worth taking.

Then Randy, the cop, or whatever he is. A high risk. Randy couldn't be trusted. It might be easy to put him down. He was slightly thinner than Chris, so choking him out wouldn't be so hard. Chris snorted. He hoped Randy was awake, because he would love to shoot him between the eyes instead. He placed the fork on the plate and quickly drew his pistol. He pointed it at the portrait over the desk, aiming at the man's forehead. *Say something now, uptight prick.*

Smiling, he set the pistol on the desk, freeing his hand to take another bite.

Then, Dan, the musclehead. He might be a problem. An ex-soldier with an attitude, Dan might shake himself awake like those vets in the movies. Chris shrugged. *Maybe it'd be better to forget about the ring altogether.*

"Mm hmm," he said, agreeing with himself.

Riley didn't have anything Chris wanted other than a pleasant chat and the chance to watch her do almost anything. There was something humbling about her that he found comforting, much like his conversations with Mom or Carla. He wished there was more time to get to know her, but there wasn't, because once he finished collecting his pay in the parlor, he'd be off to his car, disappearing into the night before anyone noticed he was gone.

Still though, it would've been nice…

He placed the empty plate on the dresser and grabbed the clothes he'd worn earlier from the chair. He stuffed them inside his backpack, all except the shirt that Morgan burned earlier. He looked it over and grimaced. A hole surrounded by ash sat dead center. There was no repairing it.

Fucking Morgan.

He wished he could go back and put a bullet in her head. But there was no going back. An empty, sinking feeling came over him. No more Mom or William. No more Uncle Jay.

Chris went over to the bathroom and—

The pearly white bar of soap trembled and slid down into the sink. The toilet seat rattled softly, clinking against the porcelain backing. Chris winced and stepped closer to the disturbance.

He watched the water inside the toilet bowl rattle slightly in response to the commotion.

What the hell? he thought. Michigan has earthquakes. Most places did. But they were so slight that they'd go unnoticed.

So what the hell was going on?

He shrugged. This place was old, rebuilt in the 30s, almost one hundred years ago. Surely it was standing on its last leg. *Nah,* he thought. *Maybe there's an old sump pump that shakes the house every time it kicks on,* he thought. *Or maybe...* A soft hum from behind made him stiffen. The song intensified, humming the lyrics to Carla's favorite song, "Everlong."

His breath hitched, and the bathroom walls spun, tossing him into an uncertain space. Vomit threatened to force its way up his throat as his gut tucked. A dull haze blinded him to the room he stood in. He let out a helpless gasp. He grunted and groaned, fighting to grab hold of his mind as it twisted. Dizzy, he pressed his hands to his eyes.

"Chris?" the voice hissed.

His chest shook as his heart slammed into it.

"Chris?" she said again. "Come back to bed."

Slobber dribbled from his lips and puddled on the floor as his vision sharpened, refocusing on the walls and mirror.

"Did you hear me?" she asked.

He pulled a shaking hand over his wet lips.

"Come on, crazy. You know I can't sleep unless you're here with me."

"No," he whispered. "No, there's no way."

Slowly, he peered into the mirror over the sink. He found the reflection of the bed behind him. He glimpsed at the end of the bed. Legs moved underneath the white sheets a lot like Carla's did before she finally got comfortable enough to fall asleep.

"Ca—Carla?" he asked in a broken whisper.

Her legs stopped moving.

Air burst through his mouth and nose as his hands tightened on the edge of the sink.

"Carla!" he called out again.

He whipped around and marched into the bedroom.

The bed was as he left it, nicely made with nothing but his leather bag on the mattress and a print from where he sat.

He gasped and put his hand on his forehead. *What the fuck?* He flopped down on the bed and put his elbows on his knees.

"What the hell was Morgan smoking earlier?"

You're seeing shit. You have work to do and a long-ass drive after that. He patted his cheeks hard and forced air through his pursed lips.

Chris stood and hopped on his toes like a boxer ready to jab at his opponent's face. He jabbed at the air with Mayweather's speed and technique, knocking the small shreds of dizziness loose.

Get big. Get ready, he chanted in his head.

"I don't love you anymore," Carla said.

He stopped and spun around.

Nothing.

"Dude, come on!" he said. He closed his eyes tight and put his hands over his face.

"I'm sorry." Carla's crying face hid behind his eyes. He froze in place and dropped his arms to his sides.

"I hate you!" Her screams pierced his ears. "I hope you fucking die!" she wailed.

He searched the room. "Where are you?" he shouted.

Her sobs grew louder, swallowing up the space around him.

"How could you do this?" she shrieked.

"Where are you?" Chris hollered. He dropped to his knees and looked under the bed to find it bare.

"Come out, Carla!" He rushed over to the bathroom and yanked the white shower curtain back only to find an empty tub.

Her painful sobs muffled, but not too low that he couldn't follow it. He rushed to the bed, pulled it out, and stared.

Carla's whimpering sounded like she was just behind the wall.

"Carla!" Chris yelled. He banged a fist against the wall.

"I hate you. I fucking hate you!" she screamed.

He patted the wall and pressed his ear against it. *This can't be—*

A high-pitch shriek forced him to whip around, placing his eyes on the door. This shriek was nothing like Carla's. It was unfamiliar and formidable.

Chris backed away from the wall and stepped slowly for the door.

Footfalls banged against the hallway floor.

"Hey! Is everything alright in there?" Randy yelled.

The answer came in the form of another ear-splitting cry.

Chris pulled the door open and peered up the hallway. Riley came rushing up the steps to meet Dan and Randy, who were huddled outside Natalie's room. Riley banged on the door only for it to be answered with more agonizing shrills.

Chapter 9

"Natalie!" Riley knocked frantically while twisting the knob. "Natalie? Natalie, are you alright?" She glanced over her shoulder to find Randy covering his mouth with a shaking hand, and Dan, who put his hands on the hips of his flannel pajama pants.

An eruptive thud sounded from the other side of the door, and Natalie shrilled. "Oh God, please! What do you want from me? Somebody help!"

Riley turned her attention back to the door. She balled a fist and banged on it. "Natalie!" she called out. "Natalie, please, unlock the door." Riley turned the knob. It stopped short with a dull click. The thing didn't budge.

Face hot and heart thudding against her chest, she turned to the men. "Help me get the door open!" she demanded.

"What's going on out here?" Dr. Myles said as he approached, fastening his evergreen silk robe.

"You don't hear that?" Riley asked, her voice cracking. She looked at Chris, the only guest fully dressed in something other than pajamas aside from Randy. "Help me get the door open, please!"

"What the fuck?" Chris uttered as he dragged his almond eyes down the length of the door, more curious than frantic.

What is wrong with these people? It was like they couldn't be bothered to help, but they *could* be bothered to watch someone else suffer. There was no time to figure it out. Riley turned to her side and threw her shoulder into the door. It stood unscathed. A sharp pain shot down her arm.

She groaned, ready to launch her body into the door again, but with a running start this time. She rushed to the opposite wall and ran, ramming her shoulder into the door.

Nothing.

Natalie's shrills reduced to a gurgling muffle. "Help—me!"

"Natalie!" Riley kicked the door over and over. Exasperated, sweat trickled down her forehead. She turned to the guests and pleaded, "She could be dying in there!"

"Move," Dan said. He shoved a shoulder into the door two, three times. It didn't move.

"There has to be another way inside!" Riley said. She searched around.

"No, I got it." Dan tucked his lips between his teeth and kicked the door with his barefoot. He grunted, then lodged his shoulder into it again.

Riley marched up the hallway and stopped at the end. Nothing but a window covered by a thick curtain.

"Hey!" Dan shouted. "I said I got it. Just—" He rammed his body into the door again.

Riley ran back toward the group but went into the room next to Natalie's: Randy's room.

A professional-grade camera and laptop sat on the desk. She veered for the bathroom and went to tear the shower rod loose. It was plastered to the wall by bolts.

"Shit!" she yelled.

Dan's shouts grew louder, and the thuds against the door fiercer.

Natalie's cries fell into a sickening gag before a thud shook the floor.

Riley rushed back out into the hallway where Dan slammed his shoulder into the door, and the guests stood by and watched with worried eyes.

"I can't find anything," Riley said. "Oh God, we need to help her!"

She went back for the wall opposite the door and waited for Dan to clear the way. She gave herself a running start and slammed her shoulder into the door.

"You're not helping! You're just in the fucking way!" Dan shouted.

"You don't seem to be doing any better yourself!" she yelled, baring teeth.

Dan dropped his shoulders and ran a big hand over his moistening face. Once Riley ran for the opposite wall next to him, he ran for the door and growled when the thing didn't move.

She followed suit once he cleared the way.

"Woman, you're in the way!" he yelled.

Ignoring him, she charged for the door again. Before she could make contact, she felt someone grab her arm and yank her back. Dan hefted her up to eye level, pulling her feet from the floor. "I said I got it!" he barked, suffocating her with the smell of whiskey.

"Get your hands—" she started. Dan tossed her. Her body slammed into the wall just left of the door. Her head jutted back, slamming into the wall. She stumbled forward, landing on her knees and palms.

"Ah!" she shouted.

"Stop!" Chris yelled. Pouting, he marched over toward Dan. Dan stood sternly, his chest rose, and his fists balled.

"Watch out!" Chris said as he slid past Dan for the door. Shaking his head, he reached into his pocket and waistband as he kneeled on one knee in front of the door. He pulled a knife and screwdriver free and lightly jabbed at the lock for all of three seconds. The lock clicked. Chris pushed the door in, and his face went pale.

Riley crawled over to his side, and her eyes widened. "Oh my God!" she shrilled.

The smell of blood and spoiled meat turned her stomach. She peered around the silent room and found Natalie's body lying at the foot of the bed. Her split neck spewed blood as it poured out like a red waterfall. Her eyes were wide and lifeless, aimed at the group.

The room seemed to shrink as Riley watched, deafened by the sounds of her own heartbeat and Randy's shrieking.

It was almost like Natalie had done it to herself, because from where Riley was, there was no one else in the room with her.

But Riley wasn't interested in finding out.

"This can't be happening," she whispered. "This can't be real." She closed her eyes and shook her head. "This can't—" She gagged. "Oh God in heaven, save us from…" she prayed, but stopped when her mouth moistened and stomach flopped. She vomited on the floor.

Chris moved back while letting out harsh gasps. Riley shot up to her feet and grabbed the doorknob. She locked the door from the inside and slammed it closed.

"Fuck this!" Dan yelled.

He and Randy took off up the hallway and down the stairs. Riley followed close behind, stomping down the steps, headed for the door. Dan skipped over every other step, leading the way and leaving them behind.

He slung the door open and ran outside with Randy and Riley just behind him. They ran out to the porch and halted.

Dan stood frozen at the top of the steps.

Icy snakes squeezed Riley's gut as she searched for light beyond the porch. Slowly, she stepped to the railing and looked down. A blackened abyss swallowed them whole, surrounding them with nothingness.

She looked up. The stars and moon hid somewhere out there, wherever *out there* was. The dim yellow porch light offered them enough light to see the porch and the top step, which descended into what seemed like emptiness.

She looked down and found a lone pebble next to her foot. She kicked it and watched as the darkness swallowed it whole.

A tightness grabbed hold of her neck. Heaving, she backed away, pinning her back to the brick wall.

"Oh God. Oh no. Where—wh—where's Holloway?" Randy said, pressing his hand against his chest.

"I—" Riley's mind jumbled, skimming over possibilities. *This isn't real. It can't be.*

"What the fuck is this place?" Dan whispered as he glared about. He grabbed the railing with one hand and leaned forward. He extended his arm and spread his fingers.

He waved, feeling around in the darkness. "Nah. It doesn't—
" He switched hands and grabbed at the air.

"What is this? Where the fuck are we? Huh?!" Randy said.

Dan spun around, tucked his lower lip between his teeth, and approached Riley. His face reddened as he stepped toward her with a slow stride. "I'm going to ask you once," he started. "What is this? Is this some kind of joke?"

Riley furrowed her brow. "What?"

"You heard what I said. What—is—this?"

"H—how am I supposed to know?"

"You work here, don't you?" His menacing calmness made her quiver.

"No!" she yelled. "I'm a contract server—"

"They put a black box around this place or something? Is this some sort of experiment?"

"I don't know!"

"Don't lie to me!"

"I'm not! I swear. I don't know—"

"Shh." He put an index finger up.

"What?" Randy asked, his face growing paler with every heavy breath.

Dan walked over to the railing and shouted, "Hello!"

They listened.

Nothing.

"Fuck," Dan said.

"What?" Randy asked.

"There's no echo." Dan shook his head slowly. "There—there's nothing out there, not even anything to toss my voice back. It doesn't— I've never seen anything like it." He picked up a small stone and threw it. The stone disappeared in the silent void.

"No. No," he said. He grabbed his hair with both hands, then turned his attention back to Riley. He dropped his hands to his sides, then charged at her.

She darted for the door but fell victim to his monstrous grip on the back of her shirt.

"Ack!" she yelled.

He wrapped his arms around her waist and hoisted her up.

"Put me down!" she screamed while kicking at the air and jabbing at his head.

"Fucking gladly." He hung her over the edge of the porch where the stairs would have been.

"No!" she shrilled. "No! Please don't!"

"Start talking then!"

"I don't know what's going on! I don't—don't know!" She felt her heart leap in her chest as she clutched his tank top and watched her tears fall into the blackness below.

"Let go of my shirt," he demanded.

"No!" she wailed.

"S—stop!" Randy shouted.

"Talk, Riley!" Dan ordered.

117

"I—I don't kn—kn—know!"

"I know the fucking way out!" Randy said.

Dan turned his attention to Randy.

"I—I know the way out," he repeated.

"Well... Talk!" Dan said.

"Put her down on the porch, please. My head is throbbing right now, and I can't think with all the screaming."

"How do I know you're telling the truth?"

Randy scoffed. "What do you have to lose?" he snapped. "Now, please, put her down."

Dan huffed, then pressed his mouth to Riley's cheek. "If I find out you're lying, I will break your *fucking* neck. You understand?" he said.

"Yes!"

He threw her onto the porch. She skidded across the cement, rolling to a stop at the door. She curled into a ball and sobbed. She flinched when she felt a hand touch her shaking shoulder.

"It's alright. It's just me," Randy said. "You're alright."

Breathing heavily, Dan said, "Well, talk, sunshine."

"I'd rather us go inside. I don't feel—"

"After you."

"Come on," Randy said. He pulled Riley to her feet and helped her inside. Dan followed close behind.

"Sit here." Randy sat her on the bottom step and pulled a sterling silver flask from his trouser pocket. "Here. It isn't water, but I'm sure it'll help calm your nerves a little."

She snatched it from his hand and unscrewed the silver top. She pressed the small opening against her lips and sucked the piercing alcohol down her throat. She wasn't sure what it was, but she welcomed the warmth as it pushed down her shaking limbs.

"Alright. So, I have a few questions," Dan said after he shut the door and flipped the lock into place.

"Go ahead," Randy said, pulling the flask from Riley's lips and replacing the cap. "Save some for the rest of us, aye?"

She wiped her lips with the back of her hand. "Sorry…" she whispered.

"Where are we?" Dan asked.

"I don't know," Randy replied.

"You—" Dan chuckled. "You don't know? So how the hell do you propose we get out of here?"

"Look, I grew up in Holloway," Randy said. "There are all sorts of urban legends about this place. I can think of a place in this house that could get us out or tell us how to get out."

Dan squinted his eyes at the man. "An urban legend? You mean those fairytales that kids tell each other? You want me to put my life in the hands of a campfire story?"

"It doesn't look like we have a choice."

"We had a choice, and we still do." Dan reached for Riley. She fell back onto her hands and crawled up the steps, wide-eyed at the red-faced man.

Randy stepped in his way before he could reach her. "She doesn't know shit!"

"How the hell do you know?"

"As I said before, I was born and raised in Holloway. I know everyone in town and everyone that works here. She's not one of them. In fact, I've never seen her until today. She's just working the event."

Dan snarled and turned away. He placed his hands on his hips. "Then what?"

"There's an urban legend about the lady that used to run this place. She was obsessive over every detail. She controlled everything down to guest relations, management, and even the events that took place on this block. I'm talking block parties, street fights, fancy balls. She was a real control freak in a time when women weren't—"

"Get to the point!"

"Uh—" Randy babbled. "She—she spent a lot of time in the attic. It was an escape for her. She went up there to plan the layout of the stores she bought, tally her investments, fuck politicians and bootleggers... That attic is the pinnacle of this place. It hides all the secrets. My friend Liza, Brenda's private assistant, told me that no one's allowed to go up there. The maids can't even clean the attic because Brenda's afraid they may ruin its historical integrity. That attic will help us find the way out of here, or at least help us understand what the hell is going on."

"Well, it looks like we don't have a choice, do we?" Dan asked.

"No," Randy said.

"Does your urban legend tell you how to get up there?"

"No. But I've taken the tour many times. I know where the door is. But I need to get to my room first."

"No way. Out of the question! Did you see what happened to Natalie? Who's to say whoever did that to her won't come next door to your room and kill us?"

"I need to go to my room. I have files and photos of this place that I'd hate to lose. And besides, if the attic doesn't pan out, maybe there is something in the documents that could help us."

"I'm not interested. The only thing I need to know is the way out!" Dan roared.

Riley kicked herself for agreeing with the deranged man. All she wanted was a way back home. Possibilities rammed her mind on all sides with one thing gnawing at her conscience, making her feel incomplete. "We should go find the others," Riley interjected.

"What?" Dan said.

"I *said* we should go find Chris and Dr. Myles. Did you notice they didn't come outside with us?"

"That's their problem." He tossed his hands up. "Maybe they found a way out."

"I doubt it," Randy said.

"So you want to go look for them too?"

"Oh no. Keep up with the group; that's what I say," Randy said.

Riley stood up. "I'll go find them myself then," she said. "We'll find the attic and meet you there."

"Nope. Absolutely not. I'm keeping my eye on you," Dan said.

She scoffed. "You're not in Iraq anymore, Dan. I'm not the enemy. I just want to go find the others."

He pointed a sharp finger at her. "Don't ever say *shit* to me about my war. You got that? I don't trust your ass, and I'd rather have you close by."

"Well, I guess you're coming with me."

"I—"

"Look," Randy said. "We have to pass my room to get to the attic. That's the last place we saw them. Maybe they're still up there. We can look for them then. Hell, they may even be in the attic already. Fair?"

Riley gave a stiff nod.

Dan scoffed.

"Alright. I'll lead the way." Randy climbed the steps, getting just in front of Riley.

"I'll take the rear," Dan said, eyeing Riley.

She followed Randy, limping on her cramping knee.

Doubt eroded her mind as they approached the second floor.

What happened to Natalie? Who were those people she saw in and outside the kitchen? They turned into burn victims right before her. Where was Allen? His face pierced her mind. His satanic scowl haunted her, shoving her deeper into a vulnerable space.

Riley prayed to herself:

Dear God, please protect us as we trudge between the walls of Satan's nest. May we find our brethren safe and fall into salvation. Please lead the way.

Riley sobbed, hoping to find Chris and Dr. Myles before the house did.

She imagined Chris trying to go through a window only to find himself falling forever. She also feared for Dr. Myles. What if he was killed by whatever killed Natalie? His room was right next door to hers.

PART II

Chapter 10

"I always liked seeing you in that suit." Trudy stood in front of Ulysses' portrait, marveling at his winning smile. "That gray three-piece brought out the color in your eyes." She chuckled as she basked in her alcohol-induced light-headedness.

She paced the carpet with easy steps and picked up her ball glass from the mahogany end table next to the glass lamp. She sat down on the loveseat. With her free hand, she rubbed the velvet cushion next to her. She peered at the portrait over the fake fireplace against the glossy mahogany wall and sighed. "You always had a way of charming people with that smile. It's the reason I fell in love with you, you know? Every morning when I wake up, I see you in your tuxedo, approaching me at Mayor Tucker's gala. You were so handsome. You swaggered over and swept me off my feet." She rolled her wrist, swirling the whiskey inside her glass.

She bit her lower lip.

"I wish I was with you, you know, all the time. But I got the next best thing. When Allen approached with his offer, I was happy to break free from that damning place and inject myself into this new world. He gave me the opportunity to pick up where I left off with our dream. I jumped at the chance. But I was so naïve, trusting a demon. I didn't know the repercussions that lay ahead. Instead, I found myself caught up in this..." She pressed her eyes closed and cocked her head. She smirked. "No use in crying over spilled milk, right?" She put her arms out shoulder-length, biting back tears. "I am who I am, and you always loved me for it. I always made a way whether it was intended or..." she peered around, "...unfathomable. I always make a way, always sniffing out *possibilities*." She threw her head back and glared at the ceiling. "Ugh, I'm rambling like a drunk old fool."

Trudy sighed. "But after what they did to me, I had to find a way back here to you. To our *things*." Triumph overcame her. "At least I got to keep my soul. But I wish I got to keep my name. *Trudy*. It was more than a name, it was a…it was a personality. It was something that no one could replicate. No one could be. They could only watch me excel and wonder what it was like to be the woman of Holloway. I was doing something that no one could, man or woman. I had a voice. I had grace. I had money that I collected on my own," she said.

Ulysses stared back with his leg crossed over his knee as he sat on an evergreen loveseat a lot like the one Trudy sat on. He leaned against the far-left couch arm with his palm against the side of his face.

She remembered setting up that photo op. Ulysses bashfully sat there, worried about the decision he made that ultimately separated them. But Trudy refused to be upset about it any longer. The least he could do was leave her something that reflected his good side until he came back from France. It took her days to convince him to go along with the photoshoot. "You don't know if you're coming back. The least you can do is leave your dear wife a few tokens with that handsome face," she'd told him. He smiled, although Trudy was convinced he was happier about her letting up on the fact he'd rather go fight in foreign lands than to stay with her and take over Holloway.

"It would make us look better," he'd told her. "People respect veterans."

The next day, they went over business scenarios, prepping her to keep his real estate company, The Estate, going. They planned to save enough to start a new business, deal in hooch, and open a hotel in the town square.

"*Trudy* had so much because of you," she said to the portrait. "But no matter how much I want to go back in time and be her, it'll never happen." She frowned. "If we're talking about wishing and wanting, I can tell you that sometimes…sometimes I…" She gazed into her cup of brown liquor. "When you're in hell, all you think about is how you're stuck there forever. You're deafened by screams and pleas from the others and beaten by Satan's Over Watchers until you're raw with pain. That place is more than a place. It *becomes* you. It makes you see who you were and who you will always be—a sinner lost amid a hateful realm. You don't even get to see Satan because you aren't worthy of anything beyond where you've landed."

She shook her head.

"But the Over Watchers, the souls that accepted their fate and accepted the call of the Devil, get to meet him. Oh yes, those, those scarlet-skinned, jagged-toothed demons get to become an extension of Him. They get to watch and whip, cackle and feast on the parts of your soul. You don't get those chunks of flesh back. Yeah, the fire and molten rock burns off your flesh just so it could grow back and burn again. But the worst part is when an Over Watcher has a taste for a soul. They grab you up with those scaly red palms and lodge you between their spiky teeth.

"Allen didn't leave that part of him in Hell either. That domineering sneer and hunger for hatred came along with him… Satan fed him *so much* power. He's so strong that he provides us both enough energy to stay connected to this place." She peered around and scoffed. "You've seen him around here, barking out orders and…" She sneered, denouncing the cold sweat on her brow. "*Eating.*"

An intense heat pressed against her face, and a splitting migraine struck her head. "Whatever he says…goes, and he said that my name is Brenda Scott and I am a seventy-two-year-old breast cancer survivor with no kids—never married. I was born into a rich family, and my grandfather was one of the most celebrated sheriffs in Holloway's history. Want to know what he did?" She sipped her drink and looked at Ulysses. "When he was a deputy, he caught the culprit responsible for the murder of the town's mayor and the state governor." A tear fell loose from her blurred eyes. "You see, Allen and his boss, Satan, have a sick sense of humor." She dropped Ulysses' gaze and peered down at the couch seat next to her. "I'm not that woman who defied the odds when women couldn't become lucrative on their own, I'm a woman who is related to a man who took it away from us."

On the side table against the arm of the loveseat was a picture of them on their wedding day. She rubbed a tear away from her cheek.

She looked over at Ulysses. "At least you get to stay young forever, wherever you ended up," she whispered. Envy coursed through her veins. She missed her fair, smooth face and deep dimples. Not the mess of burnt skin and scars. She wanted to grow into her own body and take on her aging spots and complications specially tailored to her. Not this. "I see through someone else's eyes every day when I'm over there in the material realm," she said.

She dropped her head shamefully. "I looked for you when we climbed up from the depths of hell. I never told you that." She peered at him. "Whenever I could, I searched the entire way up, although Allen told me not to move my eyes away from the Vessel because it was one of Satan's veins, and it would lead us to the material world where I'd be born again. He told me to focus only on the climb. I agreed. I agreed because I wanted our world back."

She pressed her fist against her lips. "I..." She dropped her fist to her thigh and snatched up the velvet pillow from the couch corner. "I defied Allen's demand. I couldn't help it. As I dug my fingers into the Vessel, climbing back to this world, I glanced around to see if your face stood out from the masses of tortured souls. Each layer was...*so* damned. They were hard to watch. But I never stopped looking for you. Deep down, I hoped I'd never find you. I know deep in here..." she placed her hand on her chest, "...that you were good enough to go northbound." She pointed to the ceiling.

"I guess this is the closest I'll ever get to you, and I'm fine with that."

Trudy reached over the couch arm and picked up the bottle. She refreshed her glass. "Ah... You know what? I never thanked you for the gift." She set her glass down and held up the bottle. "The best whiskey in the world." She gazed at the bottle and caressed it. Its gold label spoke to its exclusivity. "I know how much you love your whiskey, but I couldn't stand that pungent taste of heavy liquor. I was all, 'Wine, please.' But I picked up the habit since I've been back, and now we have a room dedicated to our favorite drink." She smiled. "It's hard to imagine that this room was full of storage and junk when the original Brenda Scott ran this place. Now it's your whiskey parlor." She laughed. "What am I saying? Of course, you know that. You sat up there and watched me toss things out and..." She peered around at the glass shelves that lined the walls. "It's a vivacious display of the world's finest whiskey. Can you believe the variety of whiskey in this world now? Back in our time, it became illegal to cross county lines with it, let alone have a room dedicated to it."

She stood and admired her collection. Over one hundred of the world's most renowned whiskies. She turned, allowing nostalgia to pull her into the past. "Ulysses, remember how we used to dance around the house?" She waltzed and hummed, making her way to the record player in the far corner of the room.

"Remember our wedding day?" She placed the needle on the record. A piano's smooth melody filled the room. She swayed her hips. "God, I was a mess. My makeup ran down my face, and my sisters didn't know how to fix it." She snickered. "I didn't think I could go through with it because you were better than me. I didn't deserve you, and we both knew that. But there was something about me that drew you in tight. You weren't like my other suitors. You didn't just want a quick fuck behind another woman's back. You weren't controlling, forcing me to take your hand and push out your children. You were different in all the right ways. So, as I stood there, ready to step out into the aisle, I froze. I wanted to run as I looked at the faces in the crowd. My sisters were happy that I wasn't the hardware store clerk anymore, or that girl who dropped out of the schoolhouse to help them and their husbands with bills. I was married to an accountant with a degree and his own business. You were my pure, unstoppable *strength*. I watched your smile widen and light up with every step I took down the aisle. My heart melted in your hands, and I knew yours belonged to me too. We were forever bonded; I needed you, and you needed me."

She sipped her drink. "I would kill to feel you again." She teared up. "You had a special way of putting me at ease. That was your power. You were so diplomatic—so charming and relaxed. No wonder you went into real estate."

She took her seat as the song drew to an end. The next track started.

"We were the power couple around here. *Ulysses and Trudy Gallagher.* We built Holloway up from a poor, out of the way town into a sanctuary for people who wanted a reason to spend money. You and I did that." She raised her glass to him. "No one can take that from us. Cheers to us; you can't have one without the other." She cleared her glass, and her face tightened as the bitter whiskey tunneled down her throat. "There's no telling what we could've accomplished if you hadn't..." She shook her head. "Never mind that. I promised last time I wouldn't get all emotional about the past. You don't need to keep seeing me like this. Just...a pleasant conversation is all I want. That's it. That's all." She ran a thumb underneath her eyelid, catching tears and black eyeliner.

She smiled and nodded to rhythmic riffs. "Oh. This right here...this is my favorite..." She tapped the air with her fingers, playing along to the piano's trill. "Mozart was a genius, but Heff was the best damn piano player I've ever heard. Remember how we used to sit in the parlor back at our house and listen to this very song? Then you'd get up and say, 'Stop this talk of business. Dance with me.' I'd object, but you'd shut me up with a kiss. I can still feel your soft lips against mine." She ran a finger down her lips.

"I'd give anything to see you again. To feel you. Talk to you. I'd give all this up just to be with you. But that's not an option because Allen wouldn't allow it. My future in this place is laid out already by him and Satan, and I'd take it just to watch your frozen smile and admire your many faces. It's the way it has to be thanks to..."

She narrowed her eyes at the portrait, failing to curb her impending fit. "Why...?" Her voice cracked. "Why'd you leave me? I—I did so much since you've been gone, and you weren't around to see it. I made so many mistakes and did things I wouldn't've done had you been around." She sobbed. "I... It almost *killed* me to sell The Estate to that snake, Rather. You worked so hard to get it off the ground and you taught me everything I knew about business and... But I couldn't handle it. That office reeked of you. Your essence was so...strong. I didn't have a choice...I— Why'd you go? Why weren't you here to stop me from planting those bombs? Huh? Why didn't you intervene? You would've come up with another way of doing things. I know you would've. But when the sirens of war rang, you ran to the military. You just got on that plane like I meant *nothing*. The last thing you said was, 'I'll come back.' But you didn't, did you? You came back in the form of some medal and bad news. All I heard was, 'He died serving his country.' Bull fucking shit!" she yelled.

She stared at the portrait, hoping he'd answer back.

When he didn't, she went on. "So yeah. Yeah. I did it. I took the money from selling The Estate and your life insurance and opened my own shit! I started my own businesses using everything you taught me. I was just like you! Whenever I was in a bind or needed a clever way out, I thought, 'What would Ulysses do?' Then I'd think, 'He'd make that deal with that shady-ass bootlegger. He'd invest in the railroad. He'd build that hotel on the town square.' You easily would've made those things happen. Not only did you have that boyish face, that glowing smile, and confidence, you had a *dick*. I don't have a *dick*. Back then, I had the next best thing. So I did what I could to keep our dreams alive after you gallivanted around Europe, dying in *pits*!

"Yeah, I blew this building up because I built it! Not them! I built this place because I loved you, and I loved our dreams, and they wanted to take that away from us. So nobody gets shit!" She sniffed and headed for the bottle. She refreshed her glass. "I'm living in my own hell, Ulysses. It wouldn't've happened had you stayed here and not marched off to war."

She turned to the painting. "I love you and the freedom you gave me. You treated me like a human, not an object." Her face grew hot as she took a sip from her glass. "You never should've left me," she snarled. "But you, the *patriot*, the loyal citizen, the caregiver, just had to go trek in mud and get your fingers dirty with gun powder. You think I like the idea of my beloved husband dying in a hole somewhere?"

A chilly slither shot up her spine. She swayed her head to shake the dizzy spell. Blood ran down her throat, and a horrifying shriek shot through her ears.

She looked at Ulysses' frozen smile. "Don't say it. Don't *you dare* say it. I always do what I have to do, and you know that."

She gulped her glass dry and then refilled it to the brim, hoping to wash the fresh blood down her throat.

"Don't you *dare* judge me. Natalie was as dead inside as the bodies she ripped apart and tossed in that *disgusting* river. You should've seen her at dinner, talking like she owned the place. If anything, she deserves to be devoured by the Vessel." She cleared her throat, failing to stop Natalie's fresh blood from flowing down. The disgusting taste made Trudy cringe. "But you know what? She has bigger balls than anyone I know. To make an example out of your kid takes some real…um…" She sipped her glass.

"We could've died old together, proud of our accomplishments as we moved on to heaven. But that didn't happen because of *you*. Do you think I like being stuck here with that pretentious piece of shit from the bowels of hell? None of this would've happened had you been around to stop them from passing that law that shut me down!"

133

She launched her glass at him; it shattered across the portrait, leaving a wet splotch on Ulysses' face.

She put a hand on her aching forehead.

"You know, no matter how long you carry on with this pointless banter, that photo won't talk back," Allen said.

She turned to find him sauntering over.

"Shouldn't you be feasting?" Trudy asked as she wiped tears from her face.

"You know I like to take my time between bites," he hissed.

She sighed. "How was it?"

Allen sat in the leather chair across from the loveseat "Delectable. Although I have to say the marinade broke down her pride a little. I hate when they regret what they've done right before I take that first bit. They taste best when there is a struggle of wills."

She almost vomited in her mouth. She could go without sharing his dinner plate. But with the linkage, it was inevitable. "I thought the ones ripened in guilt tasted better? Is that not true anymore?"

He smiled. "You should be able to tell me. You can taste it too, right? I can tell there's something *special* about this bunch."

"Well, narcissism comes in all shapes and forms, but according to the list from the Vessel, Natalie isn't quite the worst of the bunch."

"Really? A woman with the will to chop up her son and toss him into a watery grave with the rest of her victims isn't the worst?"

"No, but the thought of killing your own child to make a point is just...baffling." She looked over at Ulysses. *We were supposed to start a family.*

"Oh, give it a rest." Allen snorted. "You wouldn't've been any different. It's best that nothing grew in your wretched womb," he hissed. She hated hearing her name from the demon's mouth. The way he spat through his rows of shredding teeth made her cringe. "You burned down your own *hotel* just to prove a point that landed you at my doorstep."

"I know."

"You shouldn't pout. You were such a beautiful young woman." He stood and approached her. Her body stiffened as he drew close. A hot sensation suffocated her, making her cringe all over as the underside of her skin crawled. Allen caressed her face. Her skin tightened under his scaly touch. She winced and pulled away, hating the way she looked when she wasn't Brenda. Sure, in this realm, she was Trudy again, but the soul bears scars. Hell engraved many on her once beautiful body.

"Too bad you can't look like this on the material plane," he said, breath reeking of hot iron. "I probably would've gone with a different persona: a young married man." He smiled, showing off his bloodied teeth. "Twenty-nine-year-old me was quite a sight. When I wasn't soaked in the blood of peasants or kings of foreign lands, I was the most handsome man in the Arabian Peninsula."

"You get to choose, and you chose to be...old?"

"Yes. So?"

"It isn't fair."

"Oh, but it is. I've been dead for so long that no one would recognize me in this realm. But you? You left a scar on this world, going down in history as a cold-blooded killer. Do I need to remind you that your punishment still stands whether we are at the feet of the Master or connected to him by one of his veins?"

Weary of the constant reminder, Trudy rubbed her temples. "Is there anything else you need, Allen?"

He sighed. "No. No." He turned on his heels to head for the door. Then he stopped and raised a gray, bony finger. "Uh, there is one question that's been bothering me all night. The girl... Riley. What's she doing here?"

"Well, she's not who I asked for. I asked for what the Vessel wanted: Bruce, the undercover serial killer. Not Riley."

"You think I believe you, Trudy? She said she was *requested*. I go to the Vessel, collect the names from the Book, and give those names to you. You get those souls here. Easy enough, right? So, I'll ask again. Why—is—she—here?"

Her legs went numb. "I wanted to surprise you. I did some research on necromancy and the human soul. Satanists sacrifice pure, God-fearing souls to the Master as a gift or token of appreciation. Satan takes these gifts and enjoys them because not only do they taste good, it's a slap in the face to God. I thought I'd change things up and show my appreciation for allowing me to come back here. I wanted it to be a surprise because I was wondering if a God-fearing soul would taste any different from the evil ones." She watched him closely as he scowled, hoping he'd take the explanation as the truth.

He smiled. "I'd have to sort some things out, but I guess you're right. I wouldn't mind a little dessert with my meal, and I'm sure the Master would love it." His smile fell back into a scowl. "Trudy, don't make me regret trusting you on this. We don't want to repeat what happened last time you tried to pull one over on me, do we?"

Her heart raced as she shook her head. "N—no. I wouldn't do anything to risk you or the Vessel," she said.

"You need me," Allen said. "I don't need you, and neither does the Vessel. Don't forget that."

"You need me because you need this place. Without this place, you have no doorway to anchor the Vessel," she said carefully.

"You really think that?" Allen spread his toothy grin. Gore riddled his crimson smile as fleshy chunks dangled from sharp edges. His oversized maw leaked onto the beige carpet. "Cross me again, and you'll find out."

Chapter 11

Chris pulled himself across the carpet, putting an urgent distance between him and Natalie's bleeding body. He twisted at the waist, put his hands against the plushy carpet, and clawed at the floor until he got to his feet. Although he heard the door to Room 3 slam closed behind him, he didn't look back. He only rushed into his room and shut the door behind him as the others rushed up the hallway and down the stairs. He pinned his back to the door and gripped the pocketknife in his hands, holding it tight against his chest.

W—what the fuck? Did Allen…? Did Brenda…?

Spending the night with a couple murderers wasn't ideal. *What if they're assassins sent to pick Natalie off?* He thought about how she threatened Dan at dinner. Natalie was a killer. Her words and menacing demeanor said as much.

What if I'm next? He knew the Gang would strike, but not like this. It wasn't Uncle Jay's style.

Chris stood on shaking limbs; freezing sweat poured down his face.

Fuck!

Chilly tears rushed down his cheeks as he trudged for the chair. He snatched up his leather bag, then scooped up his tennis shoes from the foot of the bed and crammed them inside, crushing them. He reached under the pillow, took his wallet, and shoved it into his back pocket.

He threw the bag's strap over his shoulder and searched the room. He spotted his keys on the desk, rushed for them, then froze mid-stride.

The portrait moved.

He stepped closer, wincing. Ulysses' chest flared as if he were breathing. Chris listened. The wall had a pulse that thumped like a heartbeat. Chris held his breath and leaned over the desk. An imprint as thick as a tree trunk spanned the length of the portrait with every thump.

The portrait was alive, breathing and watching him.

Slowly, Chris reached down for his keys. Then he froze as the thumping sped up. He yanked his hand back as if he'd just touched fire.

Chris stared at the picture. Ulysses' stern face stood frozen in time while the canvas pulsed hard. Something was stuck in there, and it wanted out.

Is that what killed Natalie?

His mind ventured back to the sobs and laughter he'd heard earlier, just before Natalie's cries for help. Carla was alive in his hotel room. He heard her. *Saw* her.

But there was no way that could be true.

There was something wrong with the house, and there was something off about *that* painting. Before he could stop himself, he marched over to the door and scooped his knife from the floor. He headed back for the desk, dropped his bag, and pulled the rolling chair out. He stepped on the chair and then onto the desktop, standing face to face with the portrait. He stabbed the left side of the picture, carving it out as Uncle Jay showed him. Chris carefully sawed, keeping the blade close to the frame, careful not to rip or destroy the photo. As he went across the top, his blade shook when it hit whatever had been moving back there. He pulled his hand back as his heart thundered in his chest. The knife fell from his fingers, landing underneath the desk.

He glared at the bloodied blade that lay on the carpet. Then he peered back at the painting. A thick stream of blood poured over Ulysses' face, hiding it under a wet, crimson coat.

Chris cocked his head. "What the hell—" Then he smirked. Whatever was back there, it was about to die at his hand. With the other guests out of the way, he could eliminate the threat and take what he wanted. After what he'd seen lying around, he wasn't leaving empty-handed. He didn't have a choice. His new life was a few hours away, and his very survival rested on it.

Chris stepped down from the chair and picked up the knife. Holding it up and pointing it at the painting, he carefully leaned over the desk and tucked his fingers underneath the left side of the canvas.

Dammit, he thought. He'd have to tear the painting free, destroying it. But it didn't matter. Whatever was in the wall couldn't move much. It was totally at his mercy. If he put whatever was lurking around behind that photo out of its misery, everything after that would make up for the trouble.

He took a deep breath and yanked it loose, ripping the paper across the middle.

Chris's jaw dropped. He backpedaled with his eyes plastered on the mess of bloody plant entrails pinned against the wall. A thick red vine swarmed behind the desk, up the center of the wall, and penetrated the ceiling. The stems overlapped and slithered like a colony of live snakes. Thick drops of blood leaked from its withering branches and the fresh cut. He backed up slowly, snatching his leather bag from the floor. Chris ran, pulled the door open, and hit the hallway with an urgent stride.

Oh shit, he thought. *Oh shit. Oh shit.*

Rushing up the hall, he passed Room 3. The door was still closed.

Chris passed an open room just across the hall from the staircase, then abruptly stopped before he hit the first step.

"Shit! Shit!" Dr. Myles said. Chris took a few steps back and peered into the open room, putting the struggling man into view.

Dr. Myles tussled with a green duffel bag just in front of the open door. Hundred-dollar bills fell from his frantic grasp, landing on the carpet in clusters as they spilled from the bag. Chris eyed the bag. Based on the size and the amount of money pouring from it, there had to be close to one million dollars up for grabs.

It's been a while since he'd seen that much money, and when he had, he had to split it with Brian, Uncle Jay, and the Gang.

He looked up the hallway. Not a peep. All clear...or clear enough.

"Uh," Chris said. He cleared his throat.

Dr. Myles shot him a disapproving glare. "Well, don't just stand there, help me!" he said.

Chris looked over his shoulder at the staircase, then back up the hallway. This could be the hit of all hits. That bag held his salvation.

It looks like I won't be leaving empty-handed after all.

He stepped inside the doctor's room with eyes still plastered on the money flowing from the bag and falling from Dr. Myles' hands.

"Look, kid, are you going to help me or not? Standing there will not get us out of here any faster!" he said. The man's thick butterfingers couldn't keep the money inside the bag. It was almost comical to watch him struggle with something so menial. *How'd the bag break open in the first place?*

Dr. Myles sighed, finally cramming some money inside the bag. He reached a hand underneath the bed and picked up bills that had spilled and scattered. "If you help me get out of here, I'll pay you."

"What makes you think I want to help you?" Chris asked. He could've shot Dr. Myles right then and took the bag. It would make things much simpler than standing there trying to figure out why the humble doctor had that much money outside the bank. At least that's what Chris thought people like him did with their money, anyway. Not like the Gang. Banks were for daytime job money.

"What makes you think I don't know what your true intentions are," Dr. Myles snarled. "You're clearly a thief."

"You don't have any proof of that," Chris quipped.

Dr. Myles stood straight and gave Chris a quick look up and down. He put a flat hand out, pointing at Chris with all five fingers pressed together. "You said you're a line cook?" He slapped his thick thigh with his flattened hand. "You can't afford the stuff you're wearing with a line cook's salary. *Tsk.* You must be stupid to think anyone is naïve enough to believe that. And who walks around with a screwdriver and pops open locked doors so easily?" He went back to hustling, scooping up money, and mumbling underneath his breath.

Chris dropped his brow. "You don't know shit about me, so don't start with that high and mighty bullshit because I'll punch your teeth in."

Dr. Myles raised his hands but kept his eyes on the scattered bills beneath him. "Don't get shitty with me. I don't care about what you have going on with all..." he looked Chris up and down with wide eyes, "...that. That's your business, and I have my own shit to worry about. With that being said, do we have a deal or not? If not, kindly fuck off!"

Chris stepped inside, pulled the other strap of his bag over his other shoulder, and crouched, picking up a wad of cash just behind Dr. Myles. Chris pulled the green bag by the strap, bringing it closer to him. He stuffed the money inside. "We need to move if you want to catch up with the others."

"Are you stupid?" Dr. Myles snapped. "I'm not going anywhere near that damn cop."

Chris snatched up single one-hundred-dollar bills from the area near the bathroom door. "You really think that guy's a cop?"

"You don't think so?"

Chris scoffed. "Nope. You saw how he acted in front of Natalie's room? He took right off after Dan. If he's a cop, he's a coward. He didn't investigate or nothin."

"Did you hear all those questions he asked earlier? And based on the way he was looking at you, he probably already knows that you're a thief."

"Stop fucking calling me that," Chris warned as he scooped up the bills that had fluttered onto the chilly bathroom tiles.

"He could be here watching me. Oh my God, I thought I was *careful*." Dr. Myles clenched his fists, grabbing the taut sheet on the bed. He got on one knee, and his breathing quickened. "I can't go to jail. I'm *not* going to jail. That's not a place for me. I'm Dr. *Myles,* dammit! People like me don't go to jail!"

"Calm down," Chris said as he walked around the room, picking up stray bills that made it to the far walls.

"I wanted a nice weekend away!" Dr. Myles nagged. "But then this motherfucker wants to show up asking questions, and these people decided they wanted to pull childish pranks! I don't have time for this shit!"

"You think they're pulling a prank?" Chris asked as he dropped the bills off into the bag. He stood over Dr. Myles. *I could put one right in the back of his head,* Chris thought. He grasped the pistol in his waistband.

Dr. Myles met Chris's eye. He pulled himself up and sat on the edge of the bed. "Well, yeah, boy. Do you believe this shit? I think Brenda is pulling a stunt just to have a massive grand opening for the hotel part of this place. She's got the whole haunted angle working just fine for her."

"But Natal—"

"The bitch is an actress. She's alive in her room, probably preparing for her big reveal. Did you see how dramatic she was at dinner?" Dr. Myles bent at the waist and pulled the duffel bag onto the bed next to him. "And who confesses to a murder in a room full of strangers, huh? I'll tell you who: an actor. And that's exactly what she is. Open your eyes, kid. It's all a game, and we are the randomly selected guinea pigs in for the shitty ride." He got to his feet and fastened the duffel bag. "They ain't using me for this game. No, sir." Chris watched as Dr. Myles walked across the room to the desk and dropped to his knees. He reached underneath and picked up a stray hundred-dollar bill that Chris had missed on his walk around the room.

The doctor's logic was plausible, but it didn't explain the voices, Carla's sobbing, or her lying in Chris's bed. It didn't explain the breathing vein in Room 6 either. But Chris would keep that to himself. Even though the doctor seemed sound and grounded in his explanations for what was going on, he was sweating and trembling, struggling to put money in a bag. *Who drops this much money on the floor? A hack. That's who.*

But it didn't matter. Chris had a new plan. Dr. Myles had his back to him as he eyed the corners where the carpet and the walls met. Chris reached for his pistol and dragged it up his thigh. He released the grip when thuds from heavy footfalls sounded off at the base of the staircase across the hallway. Chris pushed the gun back into its holster, and both men glared at the open door. Chris's heart raced as he glared at Dr. Myles.

"Close the door," Dr. Myles whispered.

Chris rushed over and closed the door softly. He pressed his ear against it.

"Chris? Dr. Myles?" Riley's voice. "Are you guys up here?"

"They're gone," Dan said.

"We would've seen them go by," she said.

Pffst. "You really think that? After what the hell we just saw?"

Someone had crushed Natalie's throat, and they didn't know who or why.

Chris's palms went clammy. They *all* saw it. Her corpse looked so real. *Yeah, an actual prank. A gimmick to get the most haunted building in Michigan some press. I ought to burn this fucking place to the ground.* But adding arson to his list of convictions wouldn't help. No. He needed out, and Dr. Myles was coming too.

A new plan came into view. Chris would wait until he and Dr. Myles got outside and around the back of the building. Chris would put a bullet in the back of his head and toss him into the trunk of his Lambo. By the time people found him in the morning, Chris would be long gone.

He peered over at the back of Dr. Myles' head. Or he could do it now. Take the man out, clean up the money mess, and proceed to his car out back. He pouted. But to avoid having the body found before he left, it would be better if they made it out of the building first.

Chris sighed. The new plan would have to stick. It wasn't the original plan, but it was a plan.

"If you don't have a plan, make sure you at least have an escape plan," Uncle Jay always said.

Uncle Jay said a lot of things. He also told Chris there was nothing he could do that'd put him in the hot seat because he was blood. But that turned out not to be so true.

Chris shook his head as he stood quietly, listening to Riley and Dan go back and forth.

The truth was, Chris was no different from the Gang, and if this plan fell through, he'd go the way of ol' TJ. His gut turned at the thought of that night. He and Brian had met up at Uncle Jay's for a party where he pumped them full of rum and coke, and they watched girls strip and give lap dances.

Uncle Jay approached Chris as he sat poolside, leering at the redhead who tripped and toppled over into the pool. She had already removed her bikini top, and he and

Brian had a bet going on how long it'd take for her to remove her bottoms.

"Hey, nephew," Uncle Jay said. He reached for Chris's beer and put the bottle to his lips, gulping it down.

"Hey, I wasn't done with that, Unc."

He pulled the bottle from his lips and burped. "I know. But I gotta talk to you about some real shit."

"Yeah?"

"What are your plans now?"

Chris chuckled. "What do you mean?"

"Hey, Brian," Uncle Jay called over to the pool. "Come over here. I gotta talk to you too."

Brian pulled himself up from the pool. "I'll be back," he yelled over his shoulder to the redhead and her blonde friend in the pool. He ran a hand down his face as he approached them. "This can't wait until... I mean, I'm kinda in the middle of something."

"Nah, it can't. Get over here," Uncle Jay said as he set the bottle on the ground.

Brian took a seat next to Chris, who sat in the middle. "Yeah, what's up?"

"What are your plans now? I mean, you guys are done with school, and you work where?"

"The diner," Chris said reluctantly.

"I'm going to work for my uncle as an electrician," Brian said.

"Yeah, that's all fine and good, but how would you feel about working for me?"

"Doing what?" Chris asked. He hoped it wasn't bullshit like cleaning up after Uncle Jay's parties or clearing the gutters of his new house.

"Joining up," Uncle Jay said.

"Yes!" Brian said. Chris threw him a look. He'd told Brian about the Gang before, but only in confidence. He hoped his friend's overenthusiasm didn't reflect poorly on him.

"It's alright, Chris," Uncle Jay assured. "You're not kids no more. I'm sure you know about what goes on out here with me. Your ma didn't stop talking to me for no reason. You know that."

"Yeah. I mean..." Chris cleared his throat. "Yeah, it's just that..."

"You don't know? Look, I know you've been pocketin' shit. That diner didn't put that watch on your wrist or those nice-ass shoes on your girl. What's her name?"

"Carla."

"Yeah. Carla. You buy her a lot of nice shit on amateur pay. Imagine if you could buy a house like this? A car like that?" He pointed to his Mercedes parked on the opposite side of the pool in front of the garage. "And if shit doesn't work out with Carla, you could get girls like that." He pointed to the two girls making out in the pool. Both had gone fully nude, allowing their bikinis to float around. "Join up, and I can make that happen for you."

Brian scoffed. "What is there to think about? You said Carla was a pain in the ass anyway! Let's do this shit!"

Skipping college and the military altogether was a done deal. If he could make more money off doing what he loved, he couldn't imagine a happier life. "Yeah." Chris shook his head.

"Yeah?" Uncle Jay asked.

"Yeah. Yeah. Let's do it."

Brian clapped his hands together and smiled big. "Fuck yeah!" he shouted.

"There's one thing you gotta do first," Uncle Jay said.

"Shit, what's that? Take something? I can do that shit in my sleep," Brian said.

"Nah. Nah. You gotta attend an arbitration."

Chris dragged his brow, confused.

"What's that?" Brian asked.

"Aye," Uncle Jay yelled at the pool. "You gotta leave."

"What? The party's over?" the redhead asked.

"Yeah. Leave. Now."

The girls grunted as they fished for their bikini tops and bottoms. They exited the pool and snatched up their beach towels from the chair next to Chris, and headed up the driveway, grumbling and sulking the whole way.

"So, what do we have to do?" Brain asked.

"Hold on. Be quiet for a second," Uncle Jay said, lifting a finger.

The sound of a lone engine starting up and a car pulling off answered back.

"Alright," he said. "Follow me."

149

They followed him through the side door and down the steps leading to the basement.

The walls were plastered in posters of porn stars and rock legends. A single lamp lit up the space in a deep red light, shielded by a black lampshade with a white skull on it. Chris leaned against the ping pong table that had been moved up against the wall next to the arcade games. The Gang, including Morgan, Mikey, Slater, and Zed, stood over a chair in the center of the basement. Tied to the chair was TJ. His once bronze face was bloodied and purple.

"Gang," Uncle Jay started. "We have our replacements."

"Two for the price of one," Morgan said. "How fun."

"What's going on?" Brian asked as he stepped closer to the sobbing man.

"What's going on is the conclusion to an arbitration. You see, boys, we work together, eat together, and decide together. This is a true democracy, not the bullshit the government tries to feed you. This is a real community. A real *family*. We have a set of codes we live by. These codes keep us together. Keep us thinkin' straight. But when one of us breaks one of those fragile rules, they are no longer fit. Whether it be an ass whooping, a temporary suspension under close surveillance, or death, the punishment is harsh. But we vote as a group. We agree as a family and carry out and execute punishments to a fuckin' T. Whatever we vote on goes, and in the case of ol' TJ here, he broke two rules. Morgan, what are the first set of rules?"

"Do not steal from the pot. The communication pipeline is king. Do not harm anyone in the Gang without consent from the arbitration ruling. Do not share information about the Gang to anyone on the outside."

Chris's heart dropped, and his face flushed. *You're not even in the Gang yet, and you've already broken a fucking rule.*

"Chris, I know you told Brian about us. But that'll be a freebie because you haven't been initiated yet. Relax. Besides, that's only one set of rules. You'll learn the tried-and-true Rule of Six shortly."

Chris let out a silent sigh of relief.

Uncle Jay looked over at Morgan. "Morgan, which rules did TJ break?"

"Do not steal from the pot. The communication pipeline is king."

"Thank you, baby." He peered at Chris. "Yes. This twat waffle went on a job, killed the target, failed to resend such important information to the Gang, and he planned on splitting town with his kid and wife. That's a no-no, TJ. Lucky for you, your kid and wife will be left alive. But you? Well, we'll see about that." Uncle Jay searched the faces of his congregation. "What's the verdict?"

Morgan pointed her thumb down.

Slater shook his head.

"It's gotta be done. He put us at risk," Zed forced out his thick gullet.

Mikey pointed his thumb down. He swaggered over to TJ while undoing his navy button-down. He set it on the couch and pulled brass knuckles from his trouser pocket. "I want to go first. I have to be home in time to tuck the kids in."

"No! Please! I swear I'll never do it again. I swear, please. I have a *son*!" TJ begged.

"You shoulda thought about that before you went off and did your own thing," Morgan said. She picked up the Louisville Slugger bat standing against the arcade game.

"Wait," Uncle Jay said. He put his hand out, gesturing for the bat.

She handed it to him with a faint smile.

"Mikey, I know you got shit to do, but I think our new members should go first." He pointed the bat toward Chris and then moved it toward Brian. "Well, it's already too late to turn back. You saw what you saw, and you know what you know. Who's on first?"

The group chuckled.

"Shit, I'll go first." Brian snatched the bat and slammed TJ over the head. The metallic clang bounced off the walls, piercing Chris's ears. TJ's eyes rolled into his skull as he shook violently and drooled blood from his mouth and left temple.

"Your turn, nephew."

Chris pushed himself from the table and grabbed the bat from Brian.

"Make it count," Brian said.

Chris peered down at the man. His eyes flickered as blood poured from the gash in his head. *I'd be putting him out of his misery anyway*, he thought. Besides, Chris didn't know him. At that moment, he realized what he'd do for money and respect; take another life just to better his own. Chris swung the bat, clocking TJ over the head. The hit snapped TJ's neck, making him go motionless.

***

A soft knock on the door.

"Dr. Myles? Are you in there? It's me, Riley."

Chris looked over at Dr. Myles.

The doctor shook his head frantically and mouthed, "No. Don't open it."

Chris gave a stiff nod. He wished she were alone. If she were, he'd let her in and split the money with her. With all the shit she'd dealt with all night, she deserved as much. But he reminded himself that she wasn't the goal. *Escaping* was the goal.

Another knock at the door. This one louder than the first.

They waited in silence. Riley let out a harsh sigh, and footfalls trailed off up the hallway where she began knocking on another door.

"Chris? Chris, are you in there?" she asked.

"Hey," Dr. Myles whispered, waving Chris away from the door.

"What?"

"Once they leave the hallway, I say we make a run for the front door."

Chris listened as their voices faded with distance. A door closed somewhere down the hall.

"Alright," Dr. Myles said as he zipped up the duffel bag and patted his silk pajama pants down.

Chris pulled the door open and rushed for the steps on his toes. Dr. Myles did the same thing, following close behind. The sensation of being watched and chased made Chris's body tremble as he skipped down and past the vase and another portrait.

Damn, he thought. He'd miss out on the things he wanted from that place. But priorities shifted, forcing him to find the exit earlier than he'd planned. Everything happened for a reason, and that bag over the doctor's stubby shoulder would make up for everything.

Once they made it to the end of the staircase, the men froze. Tables and chairs blocked the door, stacked high, and the words engraved into the door read, *NO EXIT.*

Chris's chest shriveled. They were trapped. Locked inside like prisoners.

"What the hell does that mean?" Dr. Myles whispered sharply. "Is there another way out? There has to be another way out of here!"

He was right. There had to be a way out of the house other than the front door. Then Chris remembered his walk around the outside. "Relax," Chris said. "I saw storm doors in the parking lot earlier. We just need to find the basement."

"Do you know how to get down there? Oh shit, why didn't I take that corny tour earlier? How the hell will we find the—"

"Dude, I don't fucking know."

"God, I don't remember Brenda mentioning anything earlier about—"

A soft piano riff sounded from the ballroom behind them. Chris turned to find flickering candlelight on tables full of patrons.

Servers in paper aprons and long, thick black dresses pushed through the flapping door on the wall opposite from where he and Dr. Myles stood. Meat sizzled, and glasses clinked as happy patrons dressed in three-piece suits and big dresses clapped at the smiling waitstaff who served them up.

154

"What the hell...?" Dr. Myles said as he took a step closer to the hostess station.

Crystals from the massive chandelier reflected pale and olive-toned faces. The center table was the biggest, where women wearing diamonds and gold around their necks chattered and laughed as they leaned over the empty seats next to them. Chris watched the people move about, nearly gliding with grace, with big smiles and easy laughter.

"Who are these people?" Dr. Myles asked.

"I—I don't know..." Chris said. "But..." He looked over his shoulder at the barred door. "I have a feeling the basement door is through that door over there." He glared at the double doors against the back wall. "It's our only way out."

"Al—alright," Dr. Myles said.

Chris took a step forward and watched the faces. A woman from the table in the center of the room caught Chris's eye midway through her laughter. Her ivory face dropped as she glared at him. Her emotionless eyes sent a skitter through his body, threatening his legs to stop and run back. But there was no going back.

He needed out.

He snatched his eyes away from the woman and kept moving forward on his toes. The way to the basement was through those doors. He just knew it.

A cluster of men rushed through the double doors and made their way toward the center table. They laughed and slapped each other on the back while sipping brandy from crystal glasses. They wiped hysterical tears from their eyes and eased down from their high when they glimpsed Chris and Dr. Myles passing by the bar.

"Hey!" one of them said.

"M—me?" Dr. Myles said.

"Keep moving," Chris demanded.

"Hey, you!" The man with a pencil mustache pointed and marched through the ballroom headed right for them. "What are you doing here? You shouldn't be here! It's a private party!" His words made the floor tremble under Chris's feet. His heart slammed urgently into his chest.

Chris picked up speed, pushing past a waitress balancing a platter on her palm. The platter toppled over, spilling brandy all over a bigger woman and her massive floral hat.

"Hey, you little prick! Sheriff! Sheriff, arrest those men!" the man said. "They're not allowed to be here! They—"

A fiery orange blast from the bar sent everyone aghast. The man turned his attention to the flames that engulfed the shrieking bartender. Another blow from behind the bar sent the place into a wild frenzy. Flames hopped up and coated the bar, and glass shards splintered out, slashing Chris across the cheek.

"Holy shit!" Dr. Myles said.

"Come on!" Chris shouted.

They kept heading for the flapping doors as the patrons rushed past them for the exit. They pushed past one another, stomping on others, fighting to get to the blocked front door.

"Shit, shit!" Chris said as he pushed past the doors.

Smoke filled the corridor, forcing Chris and Dr. Myles to choke on the thick air.

Chris's eyes burned as he passed by the kitchen. A third blast pulled his attention to the cooks and waitresses, screaming as flames engulfed them from the wood stove in the corner.

Another blast engulfed three of them, tearing them down with flame and bringing the ceiling over the kitchen down.

"I don't see any stairs!" Dr. Myles said.

"Come on!"

They rushed through the doors and back into the ballroom.

Dresses burned, and people dropped from smoke inhalation. The foundation shook as another blast from a table tore a hole in the wall.

Sweat trickled down Chris's brow. He pulled his shirt collar over his nose and hopped over smoldering bodies.

The wooden roof crashed down onto the bar, taking out the top floor.

They rounded the wall just before the foyer and entered the area where Ulysses' obnoxious golden statue stood. An area Chris hadn't noticed earlier. Next to it, a door.

Chris touched the doorknob, winced, and pulled back from it.

"Fuck," he yelped. His hand reddened from the burning metal.

"Move!" Dr. Myles said as he pulled his hand inside his silk shirt and turned the knob, welcoming them to a dark staircase.

Chapter 12

Where'd they go?

Riley was sure she would've seen them pass by at some point. She looked over her shoulder and met Dan's eye. He watched her closely.

She rolled her eyes and peered at the stairs up toward the end of the hall, just past Randy. *Maybe they went up. But why would they? Why didn't they follow us downstairs?* Surely there couldn't've been anything *that* important to pull them back into their rooms.

"Hang on," she said. Dan stopped in his tracks, but Randy kept his urgent stride for Room 5.

She backtracked, passed Dan, and stood in front of Room 1, Dr. Myles' room. She knocked softly. "Dr. Myles? Are you in there? It's me, Riley." She waited and listened. Nothing.

She dropped her shoulders and peered across the hallway. *Maybe they went into Chris's room.* Before stepping away, she knocked louder.

Nothing.

She huffed and marched up the hallway toward the steps that led up. It was as quiet as the space outside. She quivered. Dr. Myles and Chris needed to know. Luckily, they barricaded the door so the guys wouldn't fall into nothingness.

She passed Randy's room and saw him shuffle around while rustling papers and zipping up bags. She stopped in front of the adjacent room, Room 6, and knocked.

"Chris? Chris, are you in there?"

No answer.

"Huh," she said. A daunting heaviness laid on her shoulders. *What if they're already... No. No, they couldn't be.*

A sharp pang hit her in the form of a migraine when she met Dan's eyes. He stood next to her, watching her as if she were a criminal and he was the cop escorting her to the electric chair. "I don't know where they are. I'm really worried," she said.

He lifted his big hand and pointed at Randy's room.

She shook her head and stomped ahead of the stubborn man. She wished she could shake him because he wasn't helping, he was *hindering*. If they ended up stuck in this place, it would be because of Dan's big-headed control issues, something she'd had her fair share of dealing with in the past. She refused to deal with it tonight.

She stepped inside Randy's room, and a bloom of spicy cologne welcomed her. The dim light from the lamp on the side table lit the space, outing his neatness. His toiletries were placed on the oak dresser top. His cotton sweatpants laid out nicely on the made-up bed. A silver laptop sat on the desk against the wall near the bathroom, just as she'd seen earlier. She moved toward the desk as Dan locked the door behind him and leaned against it. He crossed his thick arms over his chest and laid eyes on Riley.

"I'm not the enemy here," she reminded him. But he grunted, keeping his eyes fixed on her every move.

As Randy swiped up his toiletries from the oak dresser top, Riley studied the things on the desk. Leather-bound notebooks sat next to the open laptop, and two stacks of pictures sat on the opposite side. On the top of one stack was a black-and-white picture. On top of the other was a copper-toned, hazy image.

Riley frowned as she picked up the black-and-white picture. She stared at the smiling couple. The man's familiar face seemed to smile the hardest. Scraps of paper faltered around, catching the brim of his top hat and the shoulders of his tuxedo jacket. The woman's bright dress looked lavished, laced, and embroidered over her bust. The design was undoubtedly of its time, meaning the couple was wealthy. Their young faces beamed with joy as the woman cozied up to the man's side as he wrapped an arm around her waist.

Riley lifted the picture toward Randy, who made his way for the desk with his brown leather laptop bag. He froze.

"This is the man from the portraits in the parlor and on the staircases. Why do you have this, Randy? How did you get it?" she asked.

He snapped from his trance and avoided her eyes, getting back to the task at hand. "My name's not Randy. It's Neil. Neil Logan."

"What? What do you mean?" Riley said.

Dan huffed.

"I'm undercover." He closed his laptop and pulled the charger from the wall. Then he peered up at her. "Put that down, please."

"Why do you have this?" she asked again. "Is there something you need to tell us, Ra— Neil?" She frowned. "If there is, you should start talking." She looked down at the copper-toned picture. An array of people stood clustered together out in front of a wooden building. At the bottom, it read, *Gallagher Hotel: Holloway's place of comfort. Come stay with us*. Mostly women, they wore paper aprons with

160

long black dresses underneath. Three men stood amongst them wearing three-piece suits and bow ties. Their faces were blank and unmoved, except one woman. Riley pulled the photo closer, and her mouth dropped. The woman with the baby doll face smiled hard. Her dimples sank deep into her cheeks. Her head was cocked playfully, nearly touching the shoulder of the pointed-nosed man who fell apart before Riley's eyes earlier that night.

Her hand trembled as she glared at the picture.

Neil reached for it. "Hand them over." He bent his fingers quickly, beckoning her to pass them along.

"Who are these people?" she asked in a shaken, low voice.

Neil sighed. "Well…" He cleared his throat. "In that picture," he started, pointing at Riley's left hand, "it's Ulysses and his wife, Trudy. She's the woman who built this place and then burned it down in 1921."

Those people who she'd seen in the kitchen were real, living, breathing husks. But not anymore. And based on the sickening burnt flesh hanging from their faces…

A shiver skittered up her back. "T—Trudy?" She peered at the staff photo.

"Yes, the woman who owned and opened this place destroyed it." He nodded at the staff picture. "In that other picture are the people who worked here. They, uh, perished with the first building in that fire."

"Oh God." Riley side-stepped, sitting on the edge of the bed. "I—"

"Are you going to give me those pictures?" Neil asked, irritation drowning his tone.

161

"I've seen these people," she said.

"What?" Neil said. "Where? How?"

"Downstairs. Right after... Did you feel a rumble or something? The kitchen shook, and I thought it was an earthquake. It didn't make sense."

"Yeah. I thought maybe it was the wind or something. I didn't pay it any attention," Neil said as he crouched in front of her.

"When?" she asked. "When did you feel it?"

"While I was sitting at the desk eating that disgusting cake."

Her memory rushed back to her, hitting her hard. When she ate her cake, she felt that uncomfortable wavering in her head that threatened to knock her over. She suppressed the uneasy feeling by staring into Neil's dark eyes as he knelt in front of her.

"Why does it matter?" Dan said. "I felt it too, and I thought an old furnace kicked on or something. It doesn't mean shit. Now give him his pictures so we can get outta here."

"Did you feel something else?" Riley asked, ignoring Dan's request and focusing on the concern in Neil's eyes. She winced. "A lightheadedness? Like you were...high?"

Neil's cheeks went red. "Did you?"

"Yes. I did. I—I felt sick in the head and then..." She lifted the photo of the waitstaff. "This man started shouting at me about steaks and the governor and...and Trudy. Neil, tell me about Trudy. Why'd she burn this building down? Why'd she kill these people?"

"Well, she didn't burn *this* building down. This was the brick and mortar rebuild that was reopened in 1935. Yeah, they learned quickly that wood burns to the ground. *Shocker.*" He rolled his eyes and turned away from Riley as he got to his feet and continued stuffing his laptop and its charger inside his leather case.

"Those people felt so real. Neil, they *were* real. They talked to me." She rubbed her cheek. "One of them touched me, and it was almost like he cursed my existence by suffocating me in his own nonexistence. He couldn't understand why he couldn't be me… '*I want to be like you,*' he said. He kept saying it, even after…" A tear slid down her cheek.

Neil stopped stuffing his bag abruptly and dropped his shoulders. Dan dropped his hands to his sides.

"I—I remember Brenda mentioning something about the building coming down in 1921…but it doesn't make sense. I know what I saw. I know what I felt." She raised the photo of the waitstaff. "These people are still here, along with the governor and the mayor. Everyone is still in this house." She sobbed. "You should've seen them. Their faces melting off. And—and that waiter. That poor, poor man. He stared at me with blackened eyes. It was like he was lost in thought before he touched me, like I was an anomaly. Like I was…" She shuddered as she watched his face in the photo. His stern lips and serious eyes didn't know what damnation awaited him in that building he stood in front of. "He was so *disappointed.*"

Neil set his laptop bag on the bed next to Riley and pulled up another bag, this one stuffed to the brim with file folders. He grinned as he pulled the strap over his shoulder. "This…this is excellent."

"Why?" Dan asked, moving from his post at the door and closer to Neil, who looked at the man and took a step back.

"If what Brenda said is true and we all haven't been eating roofied food all night, then this place is really haunted. The legend is real!" He picked up his camera and messed around with the winder.

"Who the hell would listen to anything Brenda had to say? The woman is a hack, just doing this to get the word out about her hotel. People do that shit all the time," Dan said. "And I'm not drugged."

"*You'd* think that. It doesn't seem like you pay any mind to women at all, if you ask me."

"What the fuck does that have to do with anything?"

"I'm just saying if you cut that macho shit for two minutes, you might learn something. How do you explain what happened to Natalie? Huh? She died in an empty room. And how do you explain the traveling, gaping openness outside? Huh? Face it, Captain Ass, you don't know the answer to this puzzle," Neil said.

"I—"

"Neil, what happened here that night?" Riley asked. "Why'd Trudy do this, and why are we here now?"

"Right," he said, keeping his eyes on Dan, who stood firm with his fists balled at his sides. "Trudy got angry, set bombs up in the kitchen and throughout the ballroom. She even set those janky, homemade explosives behind the bar. She locked those people and some authoritative figures inside while they burned the collapsing building. They say she listened to them scream and laughed as they did." He pulled the strap of his camera bag over his shoulder. "I think she did it out of spite. Prohibition was setting in, messing with her bootlegging business, and the politics in town turned against her." He pulled a news article loose from his bag of files. "She didn't get an actual trial because she killed the judge, sheriff, and district attorney. She was hanged here by the deputy, in what used to be the town square.

"The story about her killing those people is true, but I'd love to have clearer references on that. I've tried for years to get the court documents deciphered once they finally made them a couple months after she died." He handed her an article. "But the *haunting* was nothing more than an urban legend until now."

Riley squinched her eyes, struggling to read the withering article. The paper was thinner than a strand of thread and threatened to tear under her touch. She held it lightly. The title read: *Wo n Ha ed in To n Squ r after Ma s Murder, Gov r Fisher.*

a ong the D d.

Words in the article faded in some spots, forcing Riley to strain her eyes to read them.

"June 19, 1921. Trudy Gallagher was hanged in the t wn's sq r after pl ti explos that cla med t e l ves of Governor Brighton J mes F sh r, Ma or icha d Tuc r, Mrs. Lou e er..."

"I can't read this," Riley said.

"So you feel my frustration," Neil said. "But that part is squared away, passed down by word of mouth. Everyone in Holloway knows about the history of this place. But the real mystery is what goes on behind these walls now. I tried to figure it out by piecing together strange instances that were reported by the townspeople, bizarre disappearances, and all the peculiarity in between. But none of it makes sense, and I always find myself starting back at the beginning, before the bombing."

She handed it back and watched him file it away.

"Trudy Mona Lisa Gallagher is known by the people of Holloway for the crimes she committed," Neil said. "Once Ulysses died in France during the Great War, she reacted in interesting ways. She slept with powerful men and used them to keep her and Ulysses' dreams alive. She was the queen of backdoor dealings, taking meetings with bootleggers and opening the floodgates for crime to lurk in this town at such a vulnerable time. She paid for the railroad to cut through here, which brought all types of crooks and madness to this place. That woman accomplished so much by the age of twenty-nine. She was rich and beautiful and wasn't afraid to use what she had to get what she wanted."

"Alright, we're done with the history lesson," Dan said. "It's time to go."

"It's rumored that her wrath is very much alive in these walls," Neil continued, glaring around at the floral printed wallpaper. "Legend has it that she claims the souls of those who bear the same crimes. Well, at least that's what paranormal investigators claim. In my opinion, you should never mess with a woman who is betrayed or scorned. Especially not a woman as powerful as Trudy was."

"Arguably," Dan said.

"Look, this isn't a dick-swinging contest. According to these researched documents I have, she was powerful for her time."

"Like I said…"

"Call Webster if you have a fucking problem with it! Anyway, the mayor was taken by her. She was—she was very alluring, sexy, and smart. Ulysses bragged about the woman until he went off to France. Before that, he didn't go anywhere without her. They were *the* power couple, making all their decisions and lots of money together. So, when she was widowed, the mayor took her for a ride and treated her like a high-priced whore." He scoffed. "And you better bet your ass that she took advantage. Trudy had the mayor on her side, meaning she had Holloway on her side. She turned this fucking place into a war zone for drunks, convicts, bandits, and rich folks who wanted to act an ass for a week or two. Things got out of control, turning this place into the *real* Saloon Alley. It brought a lot of money into town, but crime shot through the roof." He snickered. "I can promise you that."

"You some kind of Ghostbuster or something? Christ." Dan threw his hands up and motioned for the door.

"Not really."

"Then what the hell are you? Why do you have all this shit? And why do you know so much about this place? Why do you *want to* know so much about this place?"

"It's complicated. Trust me. You should focus more on getting out of here."

"Look, faggot, don't tell me what the hell I'm supposed to focus on—"

"Hey, hey, man, calm down. I'm just saying that there isn't enough time to discuss this. Alright? It's just too long of an explanation, and it's *classified.* You understand, right?"

"Ugh." Frustration tugged at Riley's nerves, pulling her from her seat. This was too much to handle. As the men argued, she rushed off to the bathroom and pulled the door closed behind her.

She watched her red eyes as tears fell loose into the sink.

"We have to get out of here," she whispered.

"I love you," a soft baritone from the other side of the wall.

She froze and stared at the wall just behind the toilet.

"I love you, Riley, and I'll be there for you."

She recognized that voice. The low tremble and comforting warmth cleared her of the frightful night she found herself lost in.

But it couldn't be him. She pressed her hands against her ears and glared at the wall. The house played tricks with her mind, taking her back to that day in college when she stood in the bathroom, staring down at the test.

Her phone vibrated on the counter and she read the text from Steve: *Alright, I'll bring over some tacos, and we can watch that movie. WYD now?*

She picked up the phone and hesitated. No need to stress him out this time. The first two times she thought they made a mistake bought her the silent treatment for a week. She was sure this was another one of those times.

She replied: *Nothing. Missing you.*

She placed the phone on the counter next to the sink and brushed her tongue against the roof of her mouth. Her mouth felt like cotton, and a mild cramp shot through her belly. But that was normal, even though she was three weeks late.

It's fine, she thought. She and Steve had been unprotected since freshman year. She was convinced he had slow swimmers thanks to the Oxy.

She chuckled. He sure knew how to keep it rolling, entangling them both into a floatable high, pushing everything and anything stress-related out of her mind. And her grades were better than ever. If she wasn't at a party with Steve and Marcy, she was studying or running around campus prepping for another track meet.

College was easier than high school in many respects because of him.

Her face reddened in the mirror. Too bad Mom and Dad didn't feel the same about Steve. The first thing they asked when she brought him home for Christmas was, "Is that kid a pill head?"

"No!" she objected. And that was that.

Steve wasn't an addict. He was peaceful. Stress-free. Confident. Sexy. It wasn't like he was sticking himself with needles or anything. Those pills were good for him, keeping his anxiety at ease and helping him love her. They made him happy, and they made her better.

She flicked at her bangs.

So why are you taking this stupid test then? she thought. *It's only going to come back negative anyway.*

"To be careful," she said aloud. She sighed. It wasn't like she hadn't been abnormal and bloated like that before. It happened almost every time they binged for weeks.

She peered down at the test. A sign came into view.

Her heart thudded against her ears.

"No," she whispered.

She shook the thing. The plus sign grew intense, plastered across the test window.

169

"No. No. No. Shit. Shit. Shit!"

Going weak in the knees, Riley raced from the bathroom and down the hall. She pushed the door open, went to her bed, and snatched up the Ridge Pharmacy bag. The extra pregnancy test fell loose, landing on her plushy gray blanket. She snatched it up and raced for the bathroom.

Questions rammed the edges of her mind: *What will Mom and Dad say? Will I have to drop out? Could this be a false positive? What will Steve say?*

She slammed the stall closed, pulled her track shorts down, and sat on the toilet.

"Come on. Come on." She shoved the welted end of the stick between her thighs.

"Come on." She sobbed as she watched the back of the stall door.

***

"Riley, let's go. We're leaving," Dan said.

She wiped her face dry with her sleeve and pulled the door open to find Neil covered in bags with two straps around each arm. Dan watched her over his shoulder with his palm wrapped around the doorknob.

Chapter 13

Riley followed behind Neil as they climbed the steps to the next floor. Dan followed close behind her. She hefted Neil's laptop bag strap over her shoulder and rolled her eyes. She and Dan hadn't bothered going back to their rooms to grab a thing. Neil? He had to have all his stuff. But instead of acknowledging the nagging thought, she kept her pace, following him to the exit. Whether Neil was a cop or an investigator of some kind, he was the only one she sort of trusted. He seemed kind, but on an urgent mission. She wondered about the work he was doing in the hotel and how it became such an obsession.

They climbed the staircase, stopping midway in front of another portrait of Ulysses. Riley looked around. Two out of the three paintings that lined the staircase were of Ulysses doing various poses for what seemed like a sports magazine. In one black-and-white photo, he struck a running pose with his tennis racket held high. In the other, he leaned on a golf club, with a gentle breeze slightly picking up his plaid kilt.

Still no photos of Trudy.

"Why the hell have we stopped?" Dan asked.

"Oh, calm down, Muscle Head," Neil said. "I need to capture this. I've never been up this way before; it isn't a part of the tour." Neil stopped and aimed his camera at the ceiling. "Beautiful," he whispered to himself. The camera clicked and clacked, tossing bright flashes, and made a small whirring sound once he was done. He allowed the camera to dangle off to his side as it hung from one of the two straps around his shoulder. He continued up the steps for the oak door at the top.

"What are the pictures for?" Riley asked.

"My work," he said.

"Your work?"

"Yes." He stopped and turned to face her. "My exposé will reveal the truth about this place. It's anything but normal." He turned and continued his pace, only to stop and snap a few shots of Ulysses in a black-and-white photo, posing in an old school army uniform. The guy used his famous glare, staring off and away from whoever took the picture as he stood in front of a dark backdrop. His balled fists pressed against his hips with his elbows bent. He looked like a knock-off superhero, not so much a man going to war.

She scrunched her face, curious about Neil's exposé. He hadn't mentioned it before, and it made every bit of sense. Her heart sank, and for a second, she felt like she and the men were chasing a wild goose all for a quirky reporter, or a random crazy, to fill in the blanks from his faded news article and urban legends. She wanted to peer over her shoulder at Dan, but she avoided the motion. Dan was impatient, and if he was thinking the same thing...

Please, Neil, don't set this man off. She figured it was best to keep Neil talking instead. "I'm sure everything you need to know is in your urban legends, right? I mean, I told you the people were still lurking around here. That was true. So, the rest of it must be true. If I knew about the myths, I wouldn't have bothered showing up."

Neil held his camera with both hands and glared at the photo. "Wonderful," he mumbled under his breath. Then he met her eyes, a glimmer of irritation in his own. "Well, sad to say, I'm drawn to this place, and I have been since I was a kid. Everyone in Holloway knows it's haunted. People have...seen things. But no one has gone on record with proof of murder since the original building blew up... Well, not until now."

"Hm." Natalie's lifeless body on her room floor was more than enough proof of foul play outside of the apparitions Riley had seen lurking around the kitchen area. There was more than enough evidence that the house was dangerous. What more could he need?

"The people of this town cherish this place," he said as he looked around the staircase as if searching for another distraction. "Yeah, Governor Fisher's murder left a big, nasty skid mark on our history, but this hotel holds a place near Holloway's heart. It's the biggest mystery full of holes that need to be filled with information, and I'm hungry enough to find out everything there is to know. The town deserves it."

"What's there to know other than the ghosts and the nothingness outside? It's like we're stuck here." She felt air depleting from her chest. Hanging over nothing struck her, making her knees shake. Neil hadn't mentioned a legend about that, and if his myth about the attic wasn't true... "How can you be so sure that this is the way out, Neil?"

"Look, I know everyone in town. From the Kimballs by the tracks to the Yodels across the street, everyone has had an experience with this place."

"And?"

Dan grunted. They ignored him as Neil went to snap more pictures of the dark carpet and the door at the top of the steps.

"Alright." He dropped his camera to his side. "Let's take the Yodels, for instance. Mary Yodel, the wife, jogs past here every morning around four am. At least once every few months, she catches a red glare beaming from the attic window. She comes here for dinner at least once every other week, so she's very acquainted with Brenda. She asked her about the light, and Brenda claimed it was a red lightbulb they put up sometimes because it's easier on their old eyes.

But she doesn't believe that for a second. It's not the blaring light that threw her, it's the things it made her hear and feel. She heard voices, dead voices. Voices of her parents reading her bedtime stories at night. She heard her grandfather talk about the dangers of cardiac arrest and how she should take care to keep a proper diet so she didn't end up with his fatal disease. She reported feeling entranced and lightheaded, guilty, and fearful for her own spirit. The light pulled at her, trying to drag her toward it, but she'd keep running, too afraid to tell her husband about it for fear of sounding insane."

Dan *tsk*ed and stopped. "That doesn't mean this is the way out."

"Or, alright, let's take the Kimballs then. They came here for dinner one night. Their youngest child glimpsed a pale-faced man wearing a thin mustache staring at him from behind the kitchen doors. When he went to use the restroom next to the whiskey room, the man was waiting outside the door for him. He beckoned the boy, leading him up to the second floor. Then he brought him to these steps. The boy described it as if the man wanted him to come up here. Brenda stopped him from climbing the steps." He huffed. "When anything happens here, or anyone sees anything strange, they call me. I get their eyewitness account and attempt to investigate it."

"I saw him too," Riley said. "He was sitting next to Dan in the parlor earlier."

"Well, you're not the only person who claimed to see him. I did some research and found a few men that attended that party that had pencil mustaches. He could've been Mayor Tucker, but I can't know for sure. Either way, people all over town claimed to have seen him lurking around the hotel, but the Kimball boy is the only one who reported having him lead him to this set of stairs."

"Why are you so bent on exposing anything? Why not just leave well enough alone?" Riley asked. "If you had, you wouldn't be stuck here now."

He sighed. "Because I need a straightforward story, and I'm so close to getting it all figured out. I know Brenda's assistant, Liza. She's a girl I've been friends with since daycare. She is literally my best friend, and we've always shared a curiosity for this place. Whenever we got an allowance or paycheck, we'd flock here to take the hotel tour and eat the award-winning food. This place was always so interesting to me, and to have a friend on the inside was a blessing. It took almost a decade to get Liza to open up about certain things. The attic was one of those things, and so was her boss. The attic had always been the core of our suspicions, but not as suspicious as Brenda and Allen.

"It's like... Okay—Brenda is a part of this town. Her father bought this place after Trudy's sister sold it. When he passed, he left it to Brenda. Before her fight with breast cancer in the 1980s, she was lively and involved. This place looked different—it was modern. But after she fell into a coma because of complications with cancer, things changed. She woke up as a new person. She became a loner, never spending time at town events like holiday parades or attending mass. She even turned her family away. It's almost like she denounced them, or never knew them to begin with. Regardless of her giving a cold shoulder, never leaving this mansion, and the fresh stock of furniture and portraits..." he pointed to Ulysses' army pose, "...she's still a part of this town, and people know who she is. But Allen? No one knows where he came from or how long he and Brenda have known each other. Liza says their dynamic is complicated. Yes, Brenda is his boss when guests are around, but they barely talk during the off hours. In fact, she went as far as to say that Brenda is afraid of sitting in the same room with him once they close in the evenings."

He peered over Riley's shoulder at Dan.

"Anyway, Liza got me on the list for this party as Randy." He turned and faced the door. "She directed me to the attic. She said, 'No matter what happens, go to the attic.' Her face turned paper-white when she told me that. 'You'll find what you're looking for.' I wanted more information— begged her for it. But she wouldn't say. She left my office, and I haven't seen or heard from her since. It's been three weeks."

"I'm sure she's fine," Riley said.

"Don't be naïve. I've been in this business for ten years. I know a threatened witness when I see one. My friend was petrified."

"You're..." Riley winced at the frowning man. "You're a reporter."

"Oh, great," Dan said. "I should've known."

Neil scowled at Dan. "During the day? Yeah. But when I'm in here, I'm a curious citizen looking to fill holes. It's such a fickle concept. The only things passed down are the things people find worthy, and even that information doesn't have to be true. But I know there is a hidden truth here. Somewhere, deep in this place, a secret is waiting to be revealed."

"Or it could all be a set up to get more dumb saps to come and spend money here," Dan said.

"Ah, and the nonbeliever speaks loudly, as he loves the sound his ass makes," Neil said. "I can see why you may say that. The exclusive private party. The ghosts they advertise on their website. The bloody history of this place. Yeah. I get it, and I can see that. But that doesn't explain what Riley and the others saw, and it for damn sure doesn't explain what happened to Natalie."

The sound of her name pushed a violent chill down Riley's back.

"We all saw blood spilling from the gash in her neck. She's dead. And she died *here*. We need to know what that means," Neil said.

"We *do not* know if she's dead. She could be some actress, helping them out with freaking their guests out," Dan griped.

"If that were true, why'd you run for the door? You've seen death and blood before when you were at war, correct? You can't tell me that was fake."

Dan's face reddened, and his brow dropped.

Neil smirked. "See, I know what's going on here. The captain doesn't know when he's defeated. It looks like—"

"Fuck off!"

"Me? Fuck off? Tell me, Captain, is there something you're hiding from? Is there a reason you don't want to believe any of this? If there is a pattern, then your minutes might be numbered."

"What?" Riley asked, heart speeding up, eyes searching Neil's face.

"Remember what I said earlier about the urban legend: Trudy snatches the souls of those who were just as greedy and prideful as she was. Remember what Natalie said in the parlor when Lieutenant Straight Neck over here set her off? I have a feeling it was all true. She is what I like to call a *Lady Boss*. She got off on telling me about her accomplishments and how happy she was with her business."

177

He gave a sideways nod. "If you get people drunk and rub their ego the right way, you'll find out a boatload of dirt. Natalie killed her son and over two hundred hit men, drug dealers, and crackheads. She was the Godmother of Detroit."

Riley gave him a sideways glare.

"That doesn't mean a damn—" Dan started.

"Among the people on tonight's repertoire that Liza shared with me is a host of nightmarish humans. Granted, I had to put the pieces together myself, but with one important clue from Liza: she harped on the idea that everyone was invited for a reason. Natalie was a Lady Boss, Dr. Myles is a narcissistic pig, that Chris boy is obviously a thug of some kind, and you...you are a disgraced army veteran."

Dan rushed up the steps, pushing past Riley, and grabbed Neil's neck. He slammed Neil's body into the wall, next to Ulysses' army portrait. Neil dropped his file bag, and it slid down the steps. At the bottom, the latch loosened, sending papers and photos scattering across the second-floor hallway.

"No," Neil croaked. He wrestled Dan, throwing his hands every which way, pounding against Dan's chest and cheeks. But Dan squeezed his fingers hard against Neil's throat, sending him into a choking fit.

"You better pick your next words wisely, reporter," Dan snarled.

Neil responded with a round of harsh coughs.

"Stop it!" Riley yelled. She rushed up the steps and pulled at Dan's muscly arms. She watched Neil's eyes go bloodshot. "You're hurting him!"

"Good!" Dan barked. "Now listen here. This might be a fucking goose chase for you, but the only thing I need to hear out of your mouth is a way out. I don't give a fuck about your shit history, your hunches, or your Podunk town." He moved closer, his trembling lips nearly touching Neil's darkening face. "I've seen death enough to know that ghosts aren't real, and if they are, you will join them here shortly if that attic isn't the way out."

"Hey!" Riley yelled. "Hey!" She clawed at the man's arms and grip, but he only seemed to tighten his fingers around Neil's neck. Neil wheezed, and his eyes drifted up as they fluttered.

"I oughta break your neck clean off your shoulders."

"Stop it! That's enough!" Riley demanded, but Dan remained unfazed.

"Have you ever felt someone's life bleed out into your hands, reporter? It's a powerful feeling that I'd been missin'," Dan hissed.

Gooseflesh tore through Riley's skin as she dug her nails into his arm. They slipped with her failed attempts to pull him loose.

Neil's gasps slowed, and his face turned violet.

"Stop it! He can't *breathe*!"

"We're going to go to the attic," Dan drawled. "You're going to show us the way out. You're going to do this now!" he snapped. "Understand?"

Neil's eyelids fluttered to a close.

"Let him—"

Dan dropped Neil. Neil buckled at the knees with his back still against the wall. Holding his neck, he gasped and coughed as he held onto the railing.

"Now that that's out of the way, shall we?" Dan asked through a grin.

Riley shot Dan a look, hoping he felt every welt on his arms and hands. "You're a monster," she croaked. "You could've killed him!"

"He's alright." He looked at Neil. "Walk it off."

"*Gah—fuck—you—*" Neil hacked.

Chapter 14

Neil pushed the attic door open and stepped inside. Riley followed him.

Dan stood near the door after he closed it. He crossed his arms. "This doesn't look like a way out, Neil," he said.

Riley frowned. The room only had a long oak desk to the right, stationed in front of a double door closet, and matching file cabinets on either side.

Neil cased the room, making his way to one of the two filing cabinets. He pawed around inside the hutch of the first one, moving books across the shelves. He yanked at the drawer. It stopped short, locked.

"Dammit," Neil said. He pressed a hand against his chest and extended his neck, clearing his throat.

Riley went over to the opposite file cabinet near the cloaked window. She grasped the handle and pulled. Locked.

"Well, this isn't ideal," Neil said as he went to the desk. "Liza wouldn't have sent me up here if…" He rounded the desk and peered at the oak double door closet behind the office chair. He shoved the chair, sending it rolling away.

"Uh…Riley."

She approached the closet and gasped. A dim red glow seeped into the office through the cracks surrounding the closet door.

"It's…" Neil cleared his throat. "Th—there's something in there."

Dan moved from the door and toward the desk. "The way out, I hope."

"I…" Neil put a hand on the knob, then drew back with a wince.

"What's the problem?!" Dan said.

"It…it, uh…" Neil stepped back, tripping over his foot and stumbling into the desk. He pressed his hands against the surface and gasped. "It—it—hurts." He coddled his hand. "It burns."

"Move!" Dan went and grabbed the golden knob. He stood frozen. He grunted and howled before twisting it. It clicked under his efforts. He withdrew his hand. "Fuck!" he yelled. "There has to be a damn key in here somewhere!"

"What if—if Brenda has it?" Neil asked.

"Look around!" Dan trudged around to the cabinet near the window. He yanked at the handle two, three times before destroying the latch, sending metal and wooden particles flying across the room. He pulled file folders and threw them over his shoulder. Papers spilled out, crossing the carpet.

Riley went to Neil, who was wide-eyed and pale in the face. His gaping eyes stared at the closet.

"Neil?" Riley said. "Neil? Are—are you alright?"

"It—it— Whoa. I—"

She touched his shoulder, and he jerked. "Shh. Shh. It's okay. Talk to me."

His lips tremored. "I, uh—I don't want to…" He trailed off as tears slipped down his face.

Riley frowned and peered at the closet. Light bled through crevices, welcoming them to find it. Her insides shuddered as she lifted her hand, playing with the light. It caressed her skin, rubbing her in a familiar warmth. She moaned, hugging her body and rolling her lightening head over her shoulders.

"When I was thirteen," Neil whispered, "my brother and I got into a fight over a baseball mitt because I didn't want to play with it. I wanted to watch the nightly news with Mom. I didn't care about the childish things Charlie did. I wanted to dig into cold case files and look into the murderer of the month. I wanted to watch trials and investigate the fraud allegations down at the railroad company..." He chuckled.

"As an act of revenge, Charlie grabbed my journal and ripped it to shreds. He tossed the torn paper in my face as I sat there, watching that show, *Prime Time Murder* with Gayla Michaels. I hopped up from the couch and slapped him across the face, leaving three parallel red scratches. You should've seen him. I called him Tiger Boy for a week." He chuckled. "I even got the kids at school all riled up, and they jumped on the bandwagon. Anyway, he grabbed a bat and went to swing it, hoping to clock me over the head. But Mom stepped in and told me to go cool off. She always took my side, and Charlie hated me for that. So did Father. He told her she was making me soft. I didn't care though. I did what I was told. Pissed, I left the house that night and went to the ice cream parlor because they had peanut butter chocolate soft serve. It was around nine pm."

Riley looked over to find Neil's eyes trained on the closet door, then she moved her gaze back to the mesmerizing light. Her feet felt numb, and her head floated on mixed thoughts.

"I loved that place. I mean...*loved* that ice cream..." he said. "By the time my heated stroll led me there, they were closed. So I decided the park was the next best place. I passed this hotel, heading there. Then I stopped. A red light shone so brightly that it broke through the curtains, painting a small spot on the street. It was so…*strange*. I—I never noticed or saw it before. All the years I lived here I—"

He sniffed.

"I crossed the street to make sure it wasn't a glare of a taillight or something. It was a stupid thought because I was the only person out that night. I crossed the street and stopped just shy of the yard. Then I felt my chest go…empty. My body felt like it floated off the ground. I was entangled in every thought I ever had. Every idea I ever dreamt up and the faces I'd seen since birth flashed by. Every well-done pat on the back and every moment I lived to forget came rushing back. Then I heard her…" He gulped. "I just about wet my pants at that moment. My grandmother had been gone for twelve years at the time, but I remembered her voice. It was clear as the night sky. She beckoned me. 'Come to Granny, Sugar Baby.' The memory of her face was clear as day. Her cracking old voice sang deep in my ears. But as I walked up the walkway for Gallagher Hotel, her voice faded back to the depths of my memory, and my subconscious jumbled, bringing on a splitting headache. It felt like my thoughts were tossed, revealing a new hatred for Charlie and Father. I felt vulnerable. *Confused.* Upset and trapped in my mind." He scoffed. "I remembered thinking, 'How come I'm not like them?'

"As I climbed the first step, I stopped mid-stride. Froze in place. Brenda slung the door in, asking me what I was doing out so late. Just as her words entered my mind, those feelings of confused emptiness went away. Faltered right out of sight and out of mind. I was more embarrassed than afraid. Since that day, I vowed to—"

"I felt it too," Riley said.

Neil whipped around and met her eyes. She watched his eyes tremble under the red light. "What do you mean?"

"I felt it when I first got here. Some magnetic pull on my thoughts, emotions... A past I wanted to forget rushed to the surface. I felt it."

"Did you see the glare?" he asked urgently.

She shook her head. "No. No. The sun was still out. But I felt the same intensity when I was in the kitchen before Natalie's screams."

He smiled. "This is good, Riley. It proves there is some kind of force in here, hidden deep, possibly strong enough to keep us tied to it and strong enough to keep the waitstaff and party guests here." He peered at the closet. "And I think we found it."

"Move!" Dan said. He shoved Neil aside and pulled at the desk drawer. "I'm not dying here!" He pulled at the locked drawer wildly.

Riley backed away from the distraught man and gasped at the state of the place. Cabinet doors barely clung by a hinge to either file cabinet. Drawers dangled free; two lay smashed in the middle of the room. Papers, files, and bits of wood chips and metal shards were scattered across the floor.

A loud clang rang out, and Dan slammed the dismantled drawer on top of the desk. He pawed around inside it and pulled a ring of keys loose and held them up. "I knew it!"

He looked over at Neil. "Here, figure out which one of these opens the closet."

"N—no. You do it!" Neil protested.

Dan bared his teeth and stomped over to Neil.

"This was your idea! I'm not touching the fucking thing again!"

"Why not? Are you hiding from something?"

Dan grunted and went to grab Neil.

"Stop it!" Riley shouted. "Don't touch him!"

"Riley...you've—"

"Don't you dare!" Riley shrieked. "Who are you pissed at, Dan? Because it's not me. It's like you forget that you're not the only one trapped in here. We all are! Now, I don't know what you're hiding from, and I don't give a shit! I—"

"You got kids, Riley?" Dan asked.

She frowned. His question knocked her off balance. "What? No," she said.

"Hm. So whose birth and death date are those on your arm then?"

She clenched the backs of her teeth, then sighed. "Why does that matter?"

"Answer the question. It's your own fault that I noticed. Saw it when you tried pulling me from the reporter's neck."

She shook her head. "It's not up for discussion."

"I think it ought to be. If we're trying to figure out why we're here, we should get to know more about each other. Try to *trust* one another. You want me to trust you, right?"

She shook her head.

He chuckled. "Cute. But seriously. A story for a story. What happened?"

"Tell him, Riley. You might be able to open that door, because there is a reason he won't. And I sure don't want to touch it again. Your memories might not be as bad."

She looked down at the weeping angel. "I had a son. Nick."

"What happened to him?" Dan asked.

She looked up at his curious gaze. "Life got in the way."

"Hm." Dan smacked his teeth.

"What?" she contorted.

"Well, you're young. Maybe about thirty-two? The death date on your arm implies you had him young, which is why you dropped out of college."

Riley narrowed her eyes at him.

He snorted. "Yeah. Old Brenda made that known when she had her righteous rant about women earlier. But you would've protected the kid with your own skin if you could. Something happened that stopped you from being Super Mom. Or maybe that was your own doing."

"You bastard. I—"

"Then tell me what happened."

Her heart lurched up to her throat. She gulped, fighting to push that day to the far edges of her mind. But the hotel wanted different. Nick's painful shrills jolted her mind, searing her memory with an agonizing sight.

Dan cocked his head and grinned. "There's a reason why we're here. So what's your reason, huh? Why do you believe you're here? I deserve to know, don't I? I mean, if we're all here for a *reason* and—"

"Why are you here, Dan?" She blinked the tears back. "I mean, w—why has death surrounded you?"

"What?" he spat through clenched teeth.

"Remember on the stairs how *you* said you've been surrounded by death more than enough to know that ghosts don't exist? When and why? Yeah, I know you've been to war, but how many people have you killed? How many innocent people suffered from the wrath we've been seeing from you all night?"

There was an eerie silence as he laid a hateful glare on her. But she kept a steady eye, waiting for him to drill her.

Instead, he scoffed. "I did a tour in Iraq. Saw my men blown to seared pulp. I've seen kids without arms and legs. I've seen fathers torn from their homes and gunned down in cold blood in the hot, sandy streets. I've seen it all." He shrugged. "It was another day at the office. I was just taking orders." He chuckled. "That's one thing the enemy and I have in common. But it takes being outside of it to know that no one wins. There's only the ever-crawling body count and the faces of your victims to greet you every night when you fall asleep alone. No one wants to be around a cold-blooded killer. But I was fashioned this way. Chiseled to take orders and doomed to relive a job well-executed with every breath I take."

He peered at the door, and Riley's eyes widened. "You're...you're afraid. Aren't you?" She looked past him. "It's the door. It showed you something, didn't it?"

"It did." The tremble in his throat decayed the hard exterior he'd thrown around since they'd met. No matter how tough he was, or pretended to be, Dan was broken.

"How many?"

Dan turned his cheek to her and dropped his head. "That's not up for discussion."

Riley sighed, curious about a pattern. By the sounds of it, Dan was a warlord working for the US, and if Neil was right about Natalie, then there had to be some pattern. She kept digging. "I was hired to work at this event. Neil got a special invitation from his friend. How'd you get invited?"

"I got an invitation in the mail. It's funny, because I told myself to get out more and meet a new woman. But with the next woman, I wouldn't make the mistake of telling the truth about the night terrors. As soon as I told my wife, she packed the girls up and hot-tailed it to Alaska." His voice cracked. "She promised not to tell the police what I said as long as I promised never to contact them again." He chuckled. "Can't run away from these memories fast enough."

His words made her raise a brow. For once, they agreed. Dan was afraid. His memories scrambled his brain much like hers had since she stepped foot inside the hotel.

"But you know what, Riley? I still can't quite place *you*. You say that you had a kid, and now you don't. Since you refuse to share what happened, I have to assume it's your fault. *Heh*. My hunch isn't clear about you, and that makes you dangerous."

"I'm not a threat," she assured him.

"Oh?" he asked. His cynicism made her quiver. "Then, here." He tossed her the key ring. "Open the door."

"What?"

"Open the door. If you have nothing to hide, then you shouldn't have a problem getting that door open and helping us find a way out."

She looked at Neil. He avoided her eyes and dropped his glare to the floor. "Coward," she whispered. "Fine."

She turned to the door and stepped forward. Voices and whispers loaded her thoughts. Sunny picnics with Mom and Dad. Her Valedictorian address at her high school graduation. All the faces. All the unsuspecting, cheerful faces.

She jammed the first key into the keyhole and cringed.

Mom and Dad sat on a wicker patio sofa with the rose garden in the background and a small crackling bonfire burned in the center of the firepit coffee table. Riley stood on shaking legs, hands across her belly. "I'm two months pregnant," crept past her lips, sending Dad to tears. Mom's face sat still as stone as she glared at Riley. Her father's red eyes peered up at her.

"You're on your own," he said before storming past her and slamming the glass sliding door behind him. It shattered, littering the cement patio, leaving Mom to stare, disappointment taking over her face.

When the key refused to disable the lock, Riley quickly pulled it from the keyhole. It felt like she came up for air from a memory that tainted the back of her mind for over a decade.

"Hurry!" Dan shouted.

Riley took up the next key and shoved it in the keyhole.

Nick's nightly screams for food or attention rang out in her ears. She turned on her side to find Steve sitting on the edge of the bed, throwing his head back after moving his cupped hand from his mouth. "Your kid's crying," he said. Riley pulled herself from the bed, fury boiling deep in her gut.

"Our kid!" she said.

"I didn't want that crying bastard!"

"How could you say that?" Tears brewed underneath her anguish. She rounded the bed and snatched up the baggie of pills from the nightstand.

"Hey!" Steve yelled as he reached for it.

"Steve, stop using this shit! You're not a kid anymore. I need your help with Nick! I need you in your right mind! This stuff is killing you!"

He rolled his eyes. "You don't have anything more interesting to say?"

Face burning, she stomped off, headed for the bathroom.

"Riley!" He chased after her. She quickened her stride and dumped the Oxy in the toilet.

"No!" He shoved her as she flushed it. Her body flew, and her legs hit the tub. She shrieked at the sharp pain as she fell inside, taking the shower curtain down with her.

He reached inside the toilet, throwing water onto the floor. He screamed, "No! No! You bitch! You fucking bitch!"

He fell back and balled up on the floor, sobbing.

Riley pulled herself from the tub and limped over to him.

She held him. "Shhh." She sobbed. "I'll help you get through this. I need you, Steve. Nick needs you. But you have to get clean."

He pushed her away. "Get off me!" He leaped to his feet and rushed out of the apartment.

Riley pulled the key from the knob, and the keyring fell to the floor.

"Riley! Hurry!" Dan said.

"I—I'm trying!" she snapped.

She scooped the keys up and stuffed another one in the keyhole.

The day Steve came home, she didn't hear or see him come in. She went to use the bathroom after putting Nick down for a nap. She pushed the door open and shrilled. Steve lay naked on the bathroom floor, face pale and lips blue. His glassy eyes gazed at the ceiling, and a note on a torn envelope laid in his open hand.

"I'm sorry," it read.

Riley pulled the closet door open and took a step back. She panted and put a hand on her chest. "Oh my God…"

Neil and Dan rushed over to her side.

The white pedestal stood in the center of the empty closet. Dan pulled the other door open, giving them a view of the pulsating thing inside. Red vines as thin as veins wrapped the column and swarmed the platform where a copper book lay open. Judging by the pages lying on the left side, it was near the beginning of the book.

Riley stepped slowly, trying desperately to push the invading thoughts away, striving to focus on the book's tanned pages.

The back of the page on the left was full of crimson words, a passage that continued from the page before. But the page on the right had light gray words.

"I don't recognize the language," she reported.

No one responded. She only heard snaps and shutters from Neil's camera.

"Did you hear what I—" She stopped. It felt like icy fingers clenched her gut. There was a phrase across the middle of the page that she recognized. She read it aloud:

"Daniel Martin Marsh. Ludington, Michigan. February 26, 1974."

"W—what?" Dan said in a small voice. He rushed to her side. "Th—that's me."

Three symbols marked the page next to his name.

"What does it say? What does this mean?" he said.

"I told you, I don't know. I can't read this."

"Let me see," Neil said.

He glanced it over and scoffed. "Oh no," he said.

"What?" Dan yelled.

"This is a dead language. Aramaic."

"How do you know?"

"I took a few philosophy classes in college, and we explored the—"

"If you can't read it, how the hell are we going to get out of here!" Dan grabbed his hair and stormed off. He crouched next to the desk and mumbled to himself.

"Oh, what's this now?" Neil pointed to the symbols following Dan's name.

"Do you know what those mean?" Riley asked.

"Yeah." Neil smiled. "I do. They, uh…" He snapped his fingers, capturing a memory. She imagined he wrestled with the many others that cloaked her mind as well. "Dante's *Inferno… The—The Divine Comedy*." He snapped his fingers. "You read it, right?"

"I think so. Maybe in an English Lit class. Why?"

"I picked it for a book report in that philosophy class. These symbols are shorthand because the original ones are animals, but I know what they mean!"

"Well?"

"Ah. Right. Uh. Let me see." Carefully, he looked over the symbols after Dan's name. "The eyes with the triangle underneath it means pride. The sigmoidal line across the circle means lust, and the star means wrath."

"Are these spiritual crimes?"

Neil shrugged. "There's only one way to find out."

She looked to find Dan still crouched with his hair tight between his fingers.

"Not that way." Neil raised his chin to the book. "Turn it back a page. I wonder if the last passage belonged to Natalie."

Or Dr. Myles or Chris.

She touched the page with a steady hand, then stiffened at the wrist, holding her hand in place. Natalie's shrills erupted in her ears, sounding as fresh as they had earlier. Fingers trembling, Riley searched the passage, each word soaked in red ink, each letter dripping down the page as if they bled a story into the old paper. The metallic smell made Riley's belly turn, but she kept her hand in place as Natalie's essence returned to her.

Riley felt the hacksaw in her hands. She heard the taunts spewed toward the black man hanging naked and upside down by his ankles in the dank basement. His shoulder missed an arm, his face missed a nose, and blood soaked him down, adding to the puddle underneath his matted hair.

The man screamed for mercy. "Ma! I'm sorry!" Blood mixed with drool as it leaked down his face. "Please stop," he wailed. Riley's lungs tightened as she laughed Natalie's sick cackle. The man's warm blood ran free from her hands as she put the saw to his neck and ground it until his head dangled by a shred of skin.

The passage stopped, leaving the page blank for a few lines, and then the words picked up again. Riley wanted to pull her hand away, but fear and intrigue kept her fingers glued to Natalie's story.

Riley saw through Natalie's eyes as she sat on the bed, rubbing lotion on her hands. She felt the silk gown against her skin and watched Room 3 through her eyes.

She heard the bathroom door creak open. She whipped around to find the disturbance that brought the smell of rotting meat along with it.

But it was too late.

Riley's throat burned with Natalie's screams as an atrocious being grabbed hold of her neck. Natalie's legs dangled about a foot away from the carpet as it lifted her from the bed. Her red nightgown fluttered as she kicked and clawed at its grip. Thick maggots tunneled from the small openings in the thing's brown face and burrowed their way through an orifice in its deteriorating cheek. The monster's beige wrist held onto its pale forearm by wired threads. Green sludge seeped from the openings where the twine missed connections between the joints. A tattoo of a rose head etched its papery neck, and the stem was interrupted with a tattoo of a spade symbol where its moss-splotched chest began. The naked thing's body was as bloated as a water-damaged ceiling. It was impossible to tell how many people made that cacophony of death and sea of bile whole.

Aside from the monster holding her by the neck, Riley heard thuds against the door and her own voice calling out for Natalie to open it.

Natalie gagged for air as the monster pulled her in slowly until her cheek met the hole in its face where a nose might've been.

"I love you, Ma," it grumbled past copper teeth.

Its hands squeezed, and Riley tasted Natalie's blood surge up her throat.

Riley pulled her shaking hand back and panted hard, trying to slow her heart and ease the tightness in her chest. The closet blurred underneath her tears.

"Natalie Ann Hope. Detroit, Michigan. October 2, 1968. Pride. Envy. Greed. Hm," Neil said before snapping a photo of the page. "Turn it back a page," he said.

"I can't." Riley sobbed. "Oh God in heaven, please help us."

196

"What?" He finally looked up at her and his eyes sagged in worry. "Riley, did you see something?"

The images burned her mind. That poor man begged his mother for mercy as blood drenched him down. But Natalie didn't care. She got off on torturing her son. Her *child*. "I can't! I can't touch that damned book. I— Oh God, it was horrible!" She sniffed and pointed to the book. "It showed me everything! I know how she died— Oh *God*. How could she do that to her own son?" she yelled.

He shushed her. "What did you see?"

"Her son... She killed him and—and he—he came back as a mess of body—" She sucked in a harsh breath, struggling to breathe. "He was stitched together like a puppet made of leftover parts! She killed him, and he came back! He was here, in this hotel! He *killed* her," Riley shrilled.

"Are you sure?" Neil asked. He glared down to the floor. Then he smiled. "Trudy snatches the souls of those who were just as greedy and prideful as she was. Don't you see?" He peered at her. "It's real, Riley! The myth is real! The urban legend isn't just a story. It's all true!"

"N—n—no. This is a nightmare." She closed her eyes. "Oh God in heaven, protect us from this evil as you guide us to your arms. Deliver us to your sanctuary, as Satan is alive and taking us one by one." She wept as she wrapped her arms around her belly. "Please help us."

"Look, Riley, I'm sorry for whatever you saw, I really am. But I need you to turn the page back again. I mean, this is what I've been looking for. The people of Holloway need to know."

She opened her eyes and frowned. She felt rage build up as her face went hot. "You do it!" she shrieked.

"Who's going to take the pictures?"

She pressed her hands against his chest and shoved him, lodging him into the door. It smacked the wall as he took on an astounded expression. "What the hell?" he shouted.

She raced from the closet and put a hand against the desktop.

Dan stood. "I'll do it."

Neil peered at him. "Really?"

"Yeah. If it helps us figure out why we're here, I'd like to know. Besides, whatever she saw got her shook. I—"

"How could Natalie do that to *anyone*?" Riley asked. She bent at the waist, fighting the urge to vomit. She watched her tears fall to the floor.

"I don't want my dirty laundry aired out unless it's by me," Dan said.

Dan stepped over and entered the closet. Riley heard the flapping of the page as he turned it.

He grunted.

"What do you see?" Neil asked.

"A lot of shit. People dying."

"Hm. Move your hand. It looks like a ledger from June 9, 1990. The letters look like copper or old blood. Not unlike Natalie's page. Hm. It's like a summary, maybe because these names are listed." He snapped another picture.

"Let me try something," Dan said. It sounded like his finger ran across the page.

"Wendell Connally. Newburg, Michigan. March 9, 1958. Pride. Greed," Neil read. "Do you see anything?"

"Hang on, I... Yeah."

"So, when you touch the words, you see their crimes and death, right? Tell me about Wendell. What do you see?"

"He was a murdering loan shark," Dan said.

"Alright. Let's go to the next one. Shanna Taut. Madison Heights, Michigan. December 16, 1964. Pride. Lust. Greed."

"Man-eater and thief."

"Gerald High. Bear Lake, Michigan. May 25, 1945. Pride and envy."

"Serial killer."

"Mitchell McLeod. Hell, Michigan. August 7, 1968. Pride."

"Serial killer."

"Huh. *Carbon monoxide poisoning* my ass. These people served another purpose here," Neil said. "Flip the page forward. FYI, you might want to rush past Natalie, because whatever Riley saw..."

Dan didn't respond. The pages flipped quickly, then stopped.

"I—I don't see anything," Dan said.

"Well, maybe it's because it's your page. Flip it again."

Dan did.

"Demetrious Howell Myles. April 8, 1975. Grand Rapids, Michigan. Pride. Greed," Neil read.

"Nothing," Dan said.

Neil snapped a photo and Dan flipped the page.

"Christopher Anthony Styles. July 1, 1997. Warren, Michigan. Pride. Envy."

"Still nothing."

"What's strange is that your pages don't have blood on them. At least that's what I'm assuming that awful red ink is. Since Natalie is dead, her page is complete. There's a story to tell there. Maybe…maybe that means you guys still have a chance to get out of here."

"I hope you're right," Dan said before turning the page.

"Oh, wow," Neil said.

"Oh, wow is right," Dan said.

"Riley," Neil called out. "Riley, we're not in here. There's an entry for Bruce Paul Price, but that's it. There is a ledger summarizing everyone else's names, but we aren't on that either."

She stood straight and watched Neil as he pulled himself from the book and drew closer to the desk.

"We're not?" Her chest tightened. "You mean we…we're not supposed to be in here?"

He shook his head with a giddy smile. "And I'm thinking maybe we can find a way out of here." He peered into the closet. "I think that thing may be writing in the book. It's powerful enough to make your thoughts collide and tug on your deepest fears. It even brings out the past—parts we don't want to see. It's—it's life. It's death." He looked at her. "It might help us get out of here. We just need to find out where it starts."

"I was thinking the same thing," Dan said before he launched his bare foot into the pedestal. It rattled and chipped where his foot landed.

"Wait, wait!" Neil said. He grabbed his laptop bag and opened it. "Put the book inside."

Dan cuffed the book's hardcovers and yanked at it violently. He grunted and yelled as small vines snapped and squirted thick red liquid like ripped arteries. Before long, the vines gave, letting the book loose. Huffing, Dan closed it, dropped it into the bag, then went back to kicking the pedestal. It toppled over after the third kick. He and Neil peered down the hole it covered.

Dan smiled. "Looks like a way out to me. The damned thing goes all the way to the—"

"Basement. Of course. Why didn't I think of that? Liza told me that Brenda and Allen sleep in the basement units. How else would they get out of this…limbo or—or—"

"Purgatory," Riley said as she approached them.

She peered down the hole. The vines crossed over each other against the floor, oozing blood onto the carpet. Thick drops leaked, falling down the hole and entering the darkness.

"I'm headed to the basement," Dan said. "Come or don't. I don't give a shit. But I want out now."

"We're coming with you," Riley said. "Maybe us being with you is keeping you alive." She looked at Neil. "And if that's true, then Chris and Dr. Myles are still alive around here. If we find them, we can keep them alive too."

"They better hope we run into them on the way down to the basement," Dan said. "I don't want to be here any longer than I need to be."

Dan rushed for the door and Neil scooped up his bag. Riley didn't bother with grabbing his other bag. Everything he needed was already hanging from his shoulder. Book and all.

Chapter 15

After they stepped out of the office, Riley winced as she inhaled specks of sand, flying free, riding a thick, humid breeze. Small holes riddled the yellow clay walls, and the sounds of war erupted underneath desperate cries just outside the sunlit room. Riley stepped slowly, careful to step over the yellow drape splayed out on the hard, gravelly floor.

Dan stood in the middle of the room, staring at the bed on a thin metal frame against the opposite wall.

Riley gasped when she caught sight of what he leered at.

A girl, no more than ten years old, lay on the thin mattress. Her long dark hair hung over the edge of the bed. Her eyes sunk into her shriveled face, and her body hid under a white sheet from the neck down. Blood soaked the sheet where a knife handle protruded, its blade buried in her chest.

"Oh no," Riley uttered. "Dan," she said. "Dan, what—"

"I was out all night surveying the villagers and scoping out threats," he said. He stepped forward and turned to face them. He frowned as tears rolled down his face.

"I stopped at a house—this one, to be exact." He bit his upper lip and nodded. "A local tipped us off that this girl's father had been making pipe bombs in the basement. He sold them to the radicals, causing the deaths of over forty US soldiers within a month. He planned on wiping my platoon out when we passed by in the Humvee on our nightly rounds..."

Riley backed away until she felt her back against the hot clay wall. She frowned as Dan sat on the bed next to the lifeless girl.

"What did you do, Dan?" Neil asked as he moved just beside Riley.

"My platoon and I burst inside the morning before the proposed strike, gunned down his wife, young son, and, hell, even the damn dog."

He looked over his shoulder at the corpse. "We saved her for us as a treat."

Riley gasped. "You—You—"

"Monster? Bastard?" His voice cracked. "You don't know what it's like."

Riley dropped her jaw, wanting to find the words and questions. She shook her head. But Dan's heaving chest, wet eyes, and shaking hands said it all: He was a dangerous predator, and unfortunately, the young girl fell prey to men ten times her size and girth.

Dan was supposed to be the hero that promoted peace in a savage land, or at least that's how the news put it. Instead, the girl watched her family get massacred and then got brutalized by strange men in her own home.

"How could you do this? You have daughters, for Christ's sake!" Riley shouted.

"You don't know what it's like over there, Riley. No one does," Dan said. He found her eyes and sobbed.

"What?" she said through tears.

"It's lonely. It's sad. Death's everywhere. It's enough to make you lose your mind and forget that there's a line between right and wrong," he said.

"You—you hurt a *child*, Dan. What's there to question?" Tears trickled down her face.

"Death was everywhere. I—I thought I was saving her... Her family was dead, her home, ransacked. And we were so lonely. I—I missed my wife. I—I was depressed and—and—" He looked at the floor. "I needed her. And then I had to kill her because no one could know."

"Bullshit!" Riley shrieked. "You didn't have to do that. Going over there was your choice! You did this! God, you didn't have to *hurt* her."

"I had to kill her because no one could know what happened here. No one could know what we did to her and—and the others."

"Oh my God," Riley said, covering her mouth with a shaking hand.

"God's not here, Riley," Dan said. "He's not there either."

Riley's chest caved as her thoughts were assured. She watched Dan, stunned. He was so sure the hotel was nothing more than a marketing ploy not too long ago. But as she watched Dan crumble, she realized he had been hiding from his own truth: Dan was no hero. He was a rapist and murderer. Riley clenched her teeth. As she scolded Dan, she contemplated attacking him. "You were found out, weren't you?"

He let out a trembling sigh. "The murder sent the people into an uproar. They demanded my platoon be removed or the explosions and firefights would increase."

"You should be in prison," Neil spat.

"I have friends in high places that are into some of the sickest shit you could imagine. Instead of prison, I was dishonorably discharged, lost my family, and I never sleep without seeing those girls I killed. They never stop crying and bleeding." He sobbed into his hands. "Oh *God*. They broke me." He looked up at them. "This is hell, and I'm sorry, but we're all going to die here."

The floor shook underneath a rash of loud thuds. A small hand crept out from underneath the bed, pulling its own corpse. Her long, silky mane covered her face. Clumps of mud clung to her hair and pink cloak. She had to be no older than thirteen. She hissed and clawed at Dan's ankles, using them to pull herself forward.

Dan tried jumping up from the bed, but his efforts failed as the girl yanked at his ankles, bringing him down on his belly. He yelped when his body flopped to the floor. As the girl in pink clawed up his body, he kicked and pawed, screaming, "Have mercy on my soul!"

A thin, cinnamon hand jutted up through the blemished earthen floor. It grabbed Dan's face, tearing at his skin with its boney fingertips.

He screamed and struggled to pull it away to no avail.

Riley cupped her mouth as she watched the man beg for forgiveness as the girl in pink pulled him toward her and away from the corpse pulling itself from the floor. The tall girl wore a light blue cloak with brown splotches of what could've been old blood riddling her clothes with copper stains. Riley went cold when it fully emerged from the floor. The hole in the back of the girl's head opened straight through to the front. Her hair matted around the wretched opening that was littered with bits of ripped skull hanging loose from her split scalp.

The girl in pink dug into his stomach and ripped it open.

He spat blood and gurgling cries. The girl in blue dragged her feet to the crying man and dropped to her knees. She joined in on digging into his flesh.

Riley's skin crawled as defeat and realization washed over her. Dan's cries and screams confirmed it: they had to be in hell.

The girl on the bed rose. She sat up and yanked the knife from her chest, letting out a gushing *splat* as she groaned. She stood from the bed, allowing the sheet to fall from her body. A ripped orange cloak wrapped her from her chest to her scraped knees.

The girl watched him weep as he barely clung to life as his breaths went short and sporadic while he bled from the mouth.

"Pl—please," he whispered.

She lifted the knife and jabbed it deep in his chest.

He let out a gurgled cry as blood poured from his open gashes.

Riley cried.

The one in pink rose to her knees, lifted her hand, and dug her nails into his face, tearing off a cheek. The one in blue continued pulling guts from his stomach. The one in orange tore at his lap.

Riley's head spun. So much carnage. So much blood. Fighting to catch her footing before she fell over, she grasped the wall. Hissing and smacking teeth made her regurgitate. The room had grown hotter, and she felt her skin singe as the walls took on a new color: spritzed, splattered, and coated crimson.

Dan was everywhere.

"Riley!" Neil's desperate cry.

Why am I here? she thought.

"Riley!"

Am I next?

"*Riley*? You have to move," Neil yelled.

Her limbs seized as hopelessness swept her off her feet.

We can't be saved.

As her mind raced, the sick sounds drifted farther away. Dan was reduced to a pile of bloody pulp.

She could see Neil shouting in her face and pulling her by the arm. But his lips didn't match the voice in her head:

Lust. Pride. Lust and pride. Bleeding words. Bloody vines. Hell. This is hell, and Satan is coming for us.

Chapter 16

The door slammed behind them, taking the light away from Chris and Dr. Myles' new path. The screams on the other side subsided as they descended the narrow staircase. The burning air dissipated, making it easy to breathe again.

Chris led the way, stepping into the shadows, blind to what hid in the darkness.

Dr. Myles' heavy breaths deafened Chris as he listened hard to the silence in the space at the foot of the steps.

A shiver crossed Chris's body. He hadn't taken the time to check this part of the mansion. He didn't plan on checking it until it was time to leave. He arranged for a different turnout all around. Those people in the ballroom weren't part of the plan.

What were they? Apparitions? Ghosts? They seemed so real. They breathed, laughed, talked, and even called him and Dr. Myles out. Chris's soul felt bare, stripped of all being as he walked amongst them. Images of the man who came out of the parlor haunted his mind, a distraction that made his gut flip with anxiety. The man knew Chris and Dr. Myles didn't belong. The way his dark eyes watched and his accusing tone deepened with each step he took shook Chris down to his core. His heart almost leaped from his chest when the man's shouting made the room shake underneath his feet.

And even that woman sitting at the table glanced them over. Her eyes were just as dark and curious, hungry for an explanation.

Those things knew Chris and Dr. Myles didn't belong at their private party. It was like he and Myles had stepped out of a time machine and right into the hotel's history. Raw and uncut. There they were, watching the ghosts of a violent past. Then they decayed underneath fiery blasts, carrying them back to the death that claimed them before.

Was—was it because of us?

Chris remembered watching TV shows where the cartoon characters traveled back in time and accidentally changed an important course of events just by stepping on an ant. The accident caused massive ripples in time, killing everyone in the past and altering the future. The burning bodies and chaos broke out almost instantly when the people noticed that Chris and Dr. Myles didn't belong.

Chris swallowed the lump in his throat and shook the thought.

It didn't matter. All that mattered was finding the way out. That's all he needed, along with the bag of what he assumed was stuffed with about a million dollars. What the doctor was doing with it went over Chris's head by a long shot.

What if someone's looking for it?

Couldn't be, he reasoned. Dr. Myles didn't seem like the type of guy that would do something shady, such as taking it from someone else. That was Chris's job. *He* was the expert in that area.

But he also thought Gallagher Hotel was just an old hotel. It turned out to be much more than that. Based on what he'd seen, the place sucked up blood like a sponge. From the people in the parlor to Natalie's mysterious death, Gallagher Hotel was much more than just an old mansion; it was a graveyard.

A sickening jitter made him shake hard and brought his efforts at climbing down the steps to a quick pause.

"What?" Dr. Myles asked, lightly bumping Chris's backpack.

"N—nothing. I thought I heard something."

Chris continued making his way down the steps, toes leading the way.

Elaborate scheme or not, something was wrong with the hotel, and the sooner he got out and snatched that bag, the better. He'd be long gone before anyone noticed that some guy from Detroit made off like a bandit, hot-tailing it across the country while Dr. Myles lay dead in his awfully expensive trunk.

Chris cringed at the sound of the man's heavy breathing as his eyes adjusted, finding small comfort in the darkness. But his body still tensed, hating every second.

"Can you keep it down?" Chris said. If something were waiting at the foot of the steps, it could sneak up and snatch him, leaving nothing but the sounds of the doctor's heavy breath in Chris's ears.

"I'm not saying anything."

"Yeah, I know that, but your breathing is loud as shit!" Chris whispered.

"Don't worry about what I'm doing! Get us out of here, now."

"What the hell do you think I'm doing? You think I like walking around in the dark?"

"I don't care about what you like. I'm not paying you to talk about your feelings! I'm paying you to get me to my car! Now feel around for a light or something, will you?"

Chris rolled his eyes. If it weren't for that bag around his shoulder, Dr. Myles would be left alone, not having the pleasure of holding Chris back to begin with.

But there was no way he was leaving the place empty-handed. He didn't have a choice.

Chris patted the darkness. Drywall welcomed his touch, offering no guidance to a light source.

"You sure there's a way out down here?" Dr. Myles whispered.

Chris's knee almost buckled when his foot hit solid ground. He looked over his shoulder. His eyes adjusted, barely making out the doctor's round silhouette against the dim light that outlined the door at the top of the steps.

"This is the last step," Chris said. He continued straight with open hands, feeling his way around. His muscles jerked when hands rubbed against his shoulder.

He whipped around, fists balled, ready to swing.

"It's just me, kid. Where the hell are the walls?"

Chris grabbed the doctor's hand and yanked his wrist, pulling it toward where he had been pressing against the wall. He placed the hand there.

"Thanks," the doctor said ungraciously.

Their hands brushed against the wall as they continued forward, walking straight. Chris imagined touching something warm and clothed with a belly that expanded with deep breaths. Before he could figure out what it was, it'd snatch him up and drag him to its hole. Or maybe his hand would waver over something fleshy and wet with blood.

A chill skittered up his back.

Come on, dude. Focus. Gallagher was getting under his skin.

A strong sense of vulnerability coursed through him, and a familiar uncontrolled openness pushed at his mind, shoving him deep into an anxious whirlwind.

For years, he had felt his way through the dark, something he'd promised he'd never do again. But back then, he wasn't in *literal* darkness. He was awake with tons of light to see Carla drifting away from his grasp. From the way she got jealous of him spending so much time with Brian to the way she snarled at any of Brian's girlfriends when they came around, she put more effort into lodging a wedge between them than she did with saving their deteriorating relationship.

With the way she nagged and accused, Chris was sure Carla *hated* Brian.

Carla had just crawled into bed after dealing with her morning sickness for the fifth time that night. Her skin felt cold against his, prompting him to turn on his side and search her brown eyes.

"You alright?" he asked, rubbing her bare shoulder.

"No," she said.

"You're freezing," he said. He pulled his blue flannel comforter over her shoulder. "Is this a part of your morning sick—"

"He's doing it again," she said, frowning.

Chris huffed and turned on his back. "So..."

"You don't hear that?" she said, maneuvering to her back.

"You always hear something," Chris grumbled.

"*Shhhhh.*"

Chris smacked his teeth. "You woke me up, now I have to shut up?"

"Shush! Listen!"

Grunts and moans lurked from beyond the door and through the wall.

"They're fucking," Chris said, curving his smile. Brian had a way of choosing them at the bar every night. It was a wonder how the guy's dick hadn't fallen off from slut rot.

"That girl was screaming," Carla said. "They woke me up! I'm going to say something." She threw the cover off her.

"No!" Chris sat up. "Don't get involved."

She scoffed and sat up slowly, crumbling at the face as she held her round belly. "Why?"

Chris leaned over and grabbed the controller off the nightstand. "I don't know or care. You shouldn't either." He powered the TV on and turned up the volume.

"Doesn't he know that I have to work in the morning and that you worked a long shift? Does he even *care* about anyone other than himself?" she griped.

"Come on, Carla. Not tonight," he said, raising his voice over the laughter from the TV.

"Then when, Chris? He's only going to keep—"

Thuds against the wall made her rush from the bed and glare at it. "How am I supposed to sleep with him constantly bringing his whores here? Doesn't he know that I need my rest?" She rubbed her protruding belly.

"Yes, Carla, and so do I and the whores. You make it known all the time. Can you just ignore it and go to sleep?"

"No! I'm so sick of you letting him do whatever he wants! You let him run over you and treat this house like a fucking playground! How are we supposed to raise our kid with him around, bringing all types of trash in here? I—I just can't do this!"

She rushed over to the dresser. She yanked the top drawer open and pulled her clothes loose, tossing them onto the bed.

"Man, come on, Carla." Chris pulled himself from the bed and opened his arms as he went over to her.

"No, Chris!" She sobbed. "You need to choose right now! It's him or me! I can't keep dealing with his shit. He's disrespectful, he doesn't acknowledge me, he..."

Chris drew his head back. "Why do you care if he acknowledges you or not?"

"What the hell are you talking about?" She turned her back to him and went back to taking her clothes from the drawer.

"It almost sounds like you're jealous of his hoes."

"Do you know how stupid that sounds?!" she growled. She slammed her hands against the top of the dresser. "I want him to go away so we can raise our family without him being around doing that disgusting shit that he does. I can't...I can't...*ugh*."

"Is there something you want to tell me?" Chris asked.

Carla turned and faced him. She peered up from his chest and then into his eyes. She drove her tongue over her top lip before biting it. "Yeah. Yeah. Actually, there is."

She moved closer, expression growing dimmer with the shrinking distance. Her protruding stomach pressed against his groin.

Chris gulped, curbing the need to wring her neck. It all made sense. Carla's constant complaining about Brian and her perpetual nagging over what he did hinted at jealousy. The awkwardness between the three of them had to be the worst when they sat in a room together.

He balled his fists and watched her with intent, ready for a slap to the face, whether it be from her fists or her words.

"If you don't kick him out of here, you will not be in CJ's life. If you don't leave the Gang, you will not be in our *family's* life. You will pay child support and will not be in

215

my life. Is that what you want, Chris? Huh? To be pushed out because you don't want to get your playmate under control?"

Chris shook his head. "You want me to leave the Gang? How the hell am I supposed to pay for the baby's shit?"

"Figure it out!"

"Whatever." Chris waved her off and flopped down on the bed. "You think the diner will pay for rent here? Huh? Or how about that Jeep you whip around? Or the house you want? Do you think I can afford this shit from what I make at the diner? You're stupid as hell!"

"Don't call me stupid, fucker." She snatched the closet door open and pulled a black duffel bag free from the clutter. She shoved her clothes inside.

"Where are you going?" Chris got to his feet and rushed for the door, blocking it.

"I'm going to Mom's because you're not man enough to tell Brian to knock his shit off, and you clearly don't plan on being in our lives!"

"I never said that!"

She huffed as she sauntered over to leave. "Move, Chris."

"No! You're not going anywhere with my kid."

"Move, Chris," she said again.

"You're—"

"Move the fuck out of the way, you piece of shit!"

"You know what? Fine." He stepped aside. She turned the knob and pulled the door open.

"So you're just going to leave after everything? Huh? I don't mean shit to you now?" Chris asked.

Tears fell down her face. "I need a break from this. I want our kid to be healthy. Safe. I don't think I can trust you with making sure that happens. I—I'll come back to get the rest of my stuff in a few days."

He frowned. He wasn't sure if it was her hormones or what, but she seemed serious this time. "Come on, Carla. You don't have to leave. We ca—"

"This will never change! So, if you love me or care about me, you'd just let us go."

***

Chris's finger brushed against what felt like a metal switch. He flipped it.

Dim white lights flickered on, stinging his eyes, forcing him to wince and put a hand up to shield him from the harsh brightness.

"Thank God," Dr. Myles said.

They stood in a long, narrow hallway with one door on either side. A blackened room sat at the end of the hallway where Chris had placed the cellar doors that opened to the parking lot. Dead silent, no one had ventured down there, and nothing strange hopped out at them.

Chris smiled as his plans had changed. Dr. Myles wasn't leaving the basement.

Dr. Myles grunted. "You don't know where you're going, do you?"

"Come on, man. I'm trying to figure something out," Chris said as he stepped forward, surveying the hallway on both sides. He carefully laid out the rooms beyond the wall, configuring it with what he knew about the floor above. Those rooms had to be massive and probably full of storage.

A cold sweat broke out across his forehead.

Or bodies. With what he'd seen, he couldn't back the doctor on what he said about the place because it didn't explain what they'd seen in the ballroom.

"Still, uh, think this is a hoax?" Chris asked as he trudged along slowly.

Dr. Myles twisted the doorknob to the room on the right. It stopped short with a click. "Yeah. I do. It's easy to set up smoke and mirrors just to scare people. I'm not falling for that shit."

"You seemed pretty scared to me." Chris kept his eyes open, half-ready for someone to round the corner at the end of the hall.

"I was startled because I wasn't prepared for that." Dr. Myles checked the door across the hallway. Locked.

"Hm. Naw. You were scared."

"What the hell do you want me to say, kid? That we're stuck in a haunted house? Is that what you're thinking right now? That the spooky house is going to get us? Do you want to know what I think? I think this is the work of some bitch who'd do anything for attention at a time like this. Do you watch the market? Do you even know what the stock market is? No offense, but you're not the smartest guy here, so whatever you're thinking, it's probably best for you to think the opposite. It'll keep you alive until we get to the damn exit."

A dense heat dawned on Chris's nerves. "You think you're better than me?"

"No, kid, I *know* I'm better than you, and if you want to get paid, I suggest you treat me with more respect and stop this childish talk about haunted houses and shit. It's annoying me."

"Is that what's annoying you? Or is it the idea that this place is really haunted? You can't deny that you saw them, because I did too."

"Smoke and mirrors!"

"Keep your fucking voice down, asshole."

"Then focus up, or I'll make you focus up!"

Tsk. "Is that a threat?" Chris stopped and faced the man. His dark brown skin was drenched in sweat. He clutched his bag tight over his shoulder.

"Do you want it to be a threat?" Dr. Myles asked.

Chris grinned as he felt the pistol burning against his hip. He fought the urge to grab it and shove it down the doctor's throat. If he did that, he would be stuck with a body

218

on his hands, leaving the chance for potential witnesses to find them.

Chris huffed and grinned. "Just keep up, will you? We're almost out of here."

"Good."

Chapter 17

Chris's face crumbled at the thick dusty air in the opening at the end of the hallway. He put his hand over his itchy nose. The light from the hallway behind them shone just enough to give the furniture silhouettes, outlining couch backings and thick chair arms, offering the path to the cellar doors. Chris peered ahead at the far wall against what should've been the back of the house. He looked up at the dark ceiling which seemed to give to a curvature filled with a thick blackness.

There, he thought. *The doors should be over there.* He smirked. *Freedom is only a few feet away.* He grasped the grip of his pistol. *That money is mine.* He looked over his shoulder at the man following behind him. Dr. Myles was looking down at his feet while he walked on his toes, careful not to get his corduroy house shoes destroyed in that dusty room.

Chris chuckled to himself. *You'll be worry-free real soon.*

He looked ahead and kept his careful pace, heart thumping hard against his chest as he imagined the feel of that money in his hands. He'd be in Mexico soon enough. He'd put some money down on an oceanside condo and maybe take up a job bartending. An ease came down on him. He'd be far and out of touch. No Uncle Jay. No Gang. No past.

Then a familiar emptiness set heavily on his mind. Too bad he hadn't run into Riley. He'd much rather lead her to safety than lead Dr. Myles to his death. It'd almost be like bringing Carla back to life. He wouldn't mind the good deed before disconnecting from that life altogether.

220

But there wasn't time, and no matter how much he wanted it to be, it wasn't a priority.

He looked around. The dark cancelled the patterns on the old furniture, so Chris imagined faded, dingy, floral-patterned cloth just barely covering withering wood. The furniture was a lot like the people upstairs—aged, irrelevant, lost, and forgotten.

It was a wonder the damned place hadn't gone up in flames again since 19-something. The dryness could've made his nose bleed.

"Look, if you don't know where you're going, you need to tell me now!" Dr. Myles said. He stopped, pulling his feet across the floor.

Chris turned to find the man standing still in the dark. "What do I gain from lying about something like that?"

"This bag. Admit it. You brought me down here to shoot me, take my money, and run."

Invisible lightning surged through Chris's body. His palms went clammy as he flexed his fists. "What the hell are you talking about?"

"I didn't think you were that much of a coward. Why didn't you just take me out upstairs, huh? Is it because of the witnesses? That's what it was? Was it because of that cop?"

"Look, I don't know what you're talking about." Chris turned and pointed to the ceiling. "The door is right over there. Why would I bring you to the exit when I could've come alone? Do you hear yourself right now? I don't even have a gun!"

Dr. Myles motioned to the curvature in the ceiling. "You're lying. There's no door over there. I didn't see one when I came in this place earlier."

Chris frowned. "Dude, I have no reason to lie about something like that. I know there's a door over there. I saw it when I came in. I remember because I passed it to come through the back door."

"There's a back door? Why didn't we—"

"Because the thing was chained closed."

Dr. Myles shook his head wildly. "That doesn't make sense, kid!"

"If I wanted to take you out, why would I walk ahead of you? Listen to yourself, man."

"I know an assassination when I see one! How did you know where to find me?"

Chris narrowed his eyes at the frantic man. "What?"

"I know he gets creative. But this? This is elaborate. To make this place up like this and hire actors to scare us into the basement... He owns this building, doesn't he? This is his party, isn't it?" His voice shook. "He owns everything. I should've known that invitation was a phony. God. How could I be so damn stupid?" He slammed his palm into his broad forehead.

Perplexed, Chris asked, "Are—are you talking about Allen?"

"I *know* he sent you. Oh God. He knows where I am! He *knows*. He—" He stopped and dropped his hand to his side. In a calm voice, he said, "I'll pay you double whatever he's giving you. What's he paying you? Come on. You can tell me."

"Who the fuck is *he*?" Chris's face scorched. This conversation was pulling him from salvation. *What the hell is wrong with this guy, and why did he have to break down right here of all times?* Chris would have understood if the man broke down upstairs in the sea of dead partiers. He'd even understand if Dr. Myles had broke down during the explosions that tore the place apart. But here? When they were almost out? It didn't click.

"You don't have to keep playing dumb! I'm striking a deal with you," Dr. Myles spoke slowly. "Do you know what that is? Take the bag. Take all of it. I'm not dying over this."

Chris stared at the man.

"Don't look at me like that!"

"As I said before, I don't know what you're talking about," Chris growled.

"You know damn well what I'm talking about! He sent you to kill me and to take the money back. But I swear, I didn't say shit to the cops. It was my damned PA. I needed his help during the surgery and—and I know we agreed that we'd use Nurse Maggie during the surgery, but she was out. So, I had to go with my PA. I told him he was in for a half-million, and he—he agreed and..." Dr. Myles drifted, dropping his chin to his chest. "He didn't ask questions. The kid was ironclad. He—he told me he was up for it, so we did the deed, just like Francisco wanted. Beelo died right there on the table, just as planned. But my PA... He—he *lied*. The bastard lied. Lied to me. Lied to... Well, you might as well say he lied to Francisco because he went on and—and—and hey, look." He opened his hands out to his sides. "Look." He clapped them together and rubbed them against one another. He held them up. "Our hands are clean. He's gone. I took care of him. He won't say anything else to the police because he's gone." He chuckled. "He's no longer a threat and our hands are *clean*."

"I—"

"Tell Francisco he can trust me! I didn't say a thing to the police when they called me in. I told them it was a risky procedure and that we all knew it was risky, but we had to act or he wasn't coming out of the coma. There was no way we could've saved him. And—and they believed me because they didn't have a choice. I'm the best heart surgeon in Grand Rapids, and they're just the stupid-ass cops. They don't know a damn thing! Alright? So—so please take the money and leave me alone. I'll disappear. I'll change my name. Just take it and go."

Chris dropped his shoulders and huffed. A migraine pressed at the front of his skull. Things needed to get back on track. Calmly, he said, "Dude, I don't know what the *fuck* you're talking about." He pointed a sharp finger at the ceiling. "The door is right over there, and we are about to get out of here. You can pay me like we agreed and go on your way. You go your way, and I'll go mine. See? We're not even going the same way. You're out of Grand Rapids?"

Dr. Myles gave a stiff nod.

"Well, I'm from Detroit. I'm headed east, you're headed west. You will never see me again. I promise you that. So let's keep going, alright? No one is out to get you here."

"I'm not going anywhere until you take the money." Dr. Myles tossed the bag midway between their feet. "You say you don't have a gun, but I know you're lying. Please. Just take it, give it to him, and, hell... Tell him you killed me. I'll do anything for the threats to stop."

Chris looked down at the bag. It looked like a dark lump on the cement floor.

"Take it. I'm tired of running."

Chris shrugged. Since Dr. Myles was giving it up, he didn't have to waste a bullet on him. And with the bag in his possession, he couldn't give three shits about the man making it out at all. Chris stepped for the bag, bent at the waist, and reached for the strap.

Dr. Myles slammed into Chris's shoulder, sending him back flopping onto the floor.

"*Ack!*" Chris yelped.

Before he could turn, Dr. Myles rushed over and grabbed Chris by the neck from behind. Dr. Myles put Chris in a headlock, pressing his neck hard. Chris swung up and over his head wildly, hoping to land a punch. He missed, but forced Dr. Myles to lose his footing. He stumbled back, taking Chris back with him. Chris landed in the man's lap, his backpack lodged between them. Dr. Myles' thick arm tightened, sending Chris into a choking fit. The soles of Chris's boots scuffed the floor as he kicked and stomped, trying to shake himself free.

Chris reached for the pistol, but Dr. Myles slapped his hands away.

Chris's head lightened as the room darkened. A hot flash convulsed through his body as he went numb.

Dr. Myles reached down to Chris's waist and pulled the gun free. He shoved Chris forward, forcing him onto his hands and knees before climbing to his feet.

Chris's throat burned as he coughed and hacked to the floor, his sight sharpening.

"Get up!" Dr. Myles yelled.

Slowly, Chris climbed to his feet, using an end table to pull himself up. He raised his head, then raised his hands.

Shit.

"You *are* stupider than I thought, kid! There's a silencer on this? Why didn't you just kill me earlier?"

Because I didn't want anyone to find you until I was gone... Regretting the decision, Chris didn't say anything. He gazed, watching the chamber, ready for it to blow.

Dr. Myles fixed his pajama pants, twisting the waistband straight. Then he clutched the strap over his shoulder. "You thought I'd let you put a bullet between my eyes? Do you think I don't *know* who you are? I've seen you carrying that pistol around, putting your hand on the grip, ready to pull it out and shoot me in the face!" he spat. "Tell me, did Francisco know you were a hack when he hired you? You his kid or something?"

Chris said nothing.

"Don't play stupid with me, boy! I know he sent you to take me out. It was only a matter of time before they found me. My wife told me about them trashing my cabin up north and threatening my kid at school." He bared his teeth. "They even went as far as threatening to kill her. Francisco will never find my family or me." He shook his head. "And he's not getting this money back. I told him I didn't say a damn thing to anyone, and I took care of the problem. I deserve this money!"

"Dude, I don't—"

Dr. Myles gripped the pistol and moved a finger for the trigger. "Lie again if you want to," he said through grinding teeth. "Now you're going to let me pass through that door first, wait twenty minutes, then you do whatever the hell you're going to do. You go back to him, and you tell him you failed. He can take his anger out on you. If you move before I leave, I will kill you, and I don't care who knows."

"Alright," Chris said.

"Good."

Dr. Myles stepped slowly toward Chris, keeping the barrel and his eyes on him.

Chris stepped aside, allowing the man to pass. Dr. Myles took a quick glance at the path ahead, allowing Chris time to duck and drive his hands underneath Dr. Myles' wrist. He jutted the man's arm upward, and a muted shot went off into the ceiling. Thick dust rained down on them as Chris gripped the man's wrist and pushed back with all his weight. Dr. Myles stumbled back, falling between two couches and into the wall. Chris banged Dr. Myles' wrists into the wall, grunting frantically as Dr. Myles let out a painful groan.

Dr. Myles pulled his head back and sent his forehead into Chris's nose. A blinding flash knocked Chris back. He faltered on his feet but didn't go down.

As the flash and small colorful spots cleared his vision, the butt of his pistol cracked his forehead, sending his feet up and his body over an end table. He landed on his back, face wet with blood. His eyes fluttered as the darkness engulfed him. The rules swarmed his mind as he fought the need to sleep:

Rule #1: Make sure it's worth it.

Rule #2: Survey and survey again.

Rule #3: The exit is more important than the entrance.

Rule #4: Move fast and quiet.

Rule #5: Never leave empty-handed.

Rule# 6: Don't get caught.

The chant was almost a mantra, lulling him into his unconscious mind.

Chapter 18

The moon sat at the highest point in the sky on that still, quiet night. The trivial mansion stood tall in the middle of the block. The bright spotlights shone hard on the six pillars that lined the porch. Hidden underneath the fog was the deep evergreen yard with thick brush, all surrounded by a tall wrought-iron fence.

Frost nipped at the tip of Chris's nose, prompting him to pull his face mask down, covering his face. The leaves rustled next to him before he felt Brian nudge his side. Chris flashed him a scowl.

"The fucking white house of Bloomfield, aye?" Brian chuckled. In the night, Chris could barely make out Brain's face as he pulled his thin lips back into a mischievous grin. His chiseled chin scrunched, and his dark eyes gleamed with excitement.

Chris couldn't afford to play into Brian's enthusiasm, especially with the shit from Carla a few nights before. Brian still hadn't acknowledged the breakup or the fact that it was his fault.

Chris opted for a level head instead, preparing for the hit of all hits if the place were laid out the way Brian and Uncle Jay described earlier. Chris had scoffed at the poorly drawn layout on the crumpled-up Lion's Diner napkin. He hated feeling insecure at work.

He sighed. But that was the job for the night: a mansion in Bloomfield.

Chris focused up. "Which window?" he whispered.

Brian pointed at the tall, double-paned window off to the far right. "You see that one to the far right? There's one just around that corner. That's the one I unlocked earlier when I did her electrical work. I doubt she locked it back. The woman is old as dirt. She told me she was pushing ninety."

Chris nodded. Brian was a perfect surveyor. He got in, did his job, and charmed the people enough to know everything about them.

"Alright," Brian said as he patted his black hoodie and the sides of his cargo pants. Chris did the same thing. His palm rode around his belt, moving over his steel LED flashlight, screwdriver, and empty holster. There was no need for heat. The woman lived there alone, and she could barely walk. Chris snorted to himself. Mr. Late and Great left the hag a fortune, some of which would be his soon enough.

He looked over at Brian, nodded, and moved fast while he crouched. They followed the shrubbery, staying deep inside it as they walked along the front of the yard. They stopped just in front of the window.

"Alright, stay close to the gate." Brian pulled his mask down, darted out into the yard, and followed the gate up to the side of the house, careful to avoid casting a shadow from the bright spotlights. Chris followed. Frosted grass crushed underneath his weight as he pounded the lawn to the point of entry. He grimaced with every step. They could always do without noise. It could call for attention from a neighbor—or worse, wake the lonely occupant.

His eyes widened at the side of the house, fighting for sight. But the sound of the window sliding up with ease under Brian's hands calmed him. This would be like any other night. Planned out. Careful. In and out.

Brian hoisted himself inside. Chris did the same with hot heels and the thought of a hungry Rottweiler hitting the corner at any moment. Although Brian claimed the woman didn't have pets, the fear popped up every time Chris crept into a sliding door or climbed through a window.

Chris spun on his ass and planted his feet on the white carpet.

"Fuck." He gasped and smiled hard at the bounty.

The living room gleamed with glass coffee tables, a white plushy carpet, and fine furnishings. The white leather couches shone under a layer of plastic, and small white elephant statues stood on the glass end tables. The china cabinet against the far wall near the double door that led out to a hallway was stacked shelf to shelf with figurines and porcelain dishes. A silver picture frame glistened against the wall as the bright spotlights in the yard crept through the sheer curtains. Blue and red abstract paintings also lined the walls between portraits of what Chris assumed to be family members, both short and tall, young and old.

Brian walked over to the china cabinet and gently pulled the top drawer out. He reached inside and pulled out silverware. Holding it up before his face, he snickered.

Expensive, Chris thought.

Chris's heart fluttered and his palms itched. If he weren't a man of the dollar sign, he'd declare that room priceless. Unobtainable. But everything had a price, and he was sure his net worth would skyrocket if he filled up on the things in that room alone.

Chris was more interested in something else. A box Brian gloated about at lunch.

Chris glared around. No box in sight.

Brian must've read Chris's mind, because without looking away from the drawer, he said, "The glass box is upstairs in the office. First door to the left."

Chris nodded and let himself into the hallway. More paintings and portraits lined the walls. He darted up the spiral staircase, skipping two steps at a time like a kid on a toy shopping spree. It was all his for the taking. No restraints. No struggle. In and out. And he'd be a couple thousand dollars richer than he was an hour before.

He grinned when he reached the top floor. The first door to the left was ajar. Chris went inside, pulled his flashlight, and flipped it on.

In the center of the room, on an oak desk, sat a silver crystal box. Its icy blue shimmer bounced his LED light off it, almost blinding him. The diamond drawer handles glistened, and roses embroidered the mirrored surface. He couldn't look away from the rare beauty.

Carla'd love it so much, she'd give him a second chance. They'd forget the fight and raise CJ together. He'd even get a ring to go along with it. They'd been through worse; they'd get through this. He wasn't leaving the Gang, but she didn't have to know that. He'd bury the lie if that meant keeping her and his kid around.

Possibilities pumped him with optimism.

He quickly pulled his drawstring backpack free and opened it. With careful hands and a wide grin, he picked up the box and slid it inside.

"*Ah!*" A shriek from behind.

The hairs on the back of his neck rose as his limbs stiffened. He held his breath in his throat.

"Robber! Get outta my house!" a shaken voice shrilled.

Chris whipped around. A thin, old woman stood in the doorway. Her pasty face shivered as much as the mess of plastic rollers in her hair. Her white nightgown stopped at her knees, showing off the blue and purple veins pressing against her thin, papery skin.

She breathed hard and lifted a quaking hand. "I—I'm calling the—"

She choked on the last few words. Brian's face peered over her shoulder from behind. He hooked an arm around her waist and pulled a blade across her throat. She pawed at the gash as blood spritzed the walls and painted her nightgown scarlet. She fell to her knees, choking and gagging with shocked eyes and a bloody face. She reached for Chris, the word *HELP* screaming in her eyes.

Chris gripped the end of the desk as his heart slammed at his chest.

Brian lifted his foot and stomped the back of her head, forcing her face down onto the carpet. He bent over and hammered the hunting knife into her back. After the

231

twelfth gut-wrenching slash, Chris nearly lost his footing from shock.

So much blood. And Brian wouldn't stop.

There wasn't a rule for murder, but the Gang never resorted to it unless they needed to put down a member. Not a target.

Chris finally got his mouth to move. "Stop! We gotta get out of here!"

Brian stopped and glanced at Chris with heavy eyes as he stood straight. He huffed like he'd just done a round of hurdles. Blood drops scattered across his face from his chin to his forehead. "Okay. Let's go," he said dryly.

With a running start, Chris jumped over the dead woman. His boots smacked the crimson puddle with a loud, sloppy *splat*. But he kept his hustle, and so did Brian.

Once they reached the steps, Brian stopped and bent down.

Chris turned. "What the hell, man?"

"I'm taking my shoes off. I'll carry them the rest of the way."

Not a bad idea. Chris did the same before bolting down the steps and through the living room. They darted for the open window, nearly diving through it.

Rule #1: Make sure it's worth it.

Rule #2: Survey and survey again.

Rule #3: The exit is more important than the entrance.

Rule #4: Move fast and quiet.

Rule #5: Never leave empty-handed.

Rule #6: Don't get caught.

There wasn't a rule for murdering a target, but there was one for leaving empty-handed and not making sure the woman was sound asleep. Chris replayed that night over in his head while he and Brian sat at home on probation per Uncle Jay's orders. The woman had to have heard them at some point to shake herself awake.

For the first time, someone had the balls to break multiple rules, namely rules 4 through 6.

Unfortunately, it wasn't the last time Chris broke any of the Gang's rules.

He couldn't say that much for Brian.

Chapter 19

Chris awoke cheek-down in a puddle of his own blood. He groaned and pressed his hand against his leaking face.

"Fuck," he said.

He tremored.

What the hell happened?

A breeze wafted through, prompting him to turn on his back.

Worry consumed him.

How long was I out? He grimaced. There was no way of knowing.

His mouth was cotton dry, and when he coughed, it burned his throat.

Groaning, he lifted his head from the floor. The cold sweats mixed in with the blood on his brow as he commanded his arms to reach up and pull him from the floor. But he stayed still.

I need to wake up from the nightmare.

But he remembered Uncle Jay, and his heart slammed.

Get up, man, he told himself.

The doctor had gotten away with the money and…

Chris looked over to where he'd been lying. He frowned as worry flooded his chest.

Where'd my bag go?

Panic ensued, forcing the blood to pour from the cracks in his face faster.

He wasn't going anywhere without his keys, and there were no windows down there.

What if it's morning? What if Uncle Jay is outside waiting for me? He envisioned Uncle Jay and Morgan sitting out front, ready to carry out the verdict. With all the trees and dead lands around Holloway, there was no way Chris was going back to the city alive.

The Gang was *still* ruling on what he and Brian had done in Bloomfield. But the second thing? There was no coming back from that.

Chris had to go, and he had to go fast.

His heart raced as he clawed at the end table, gripped the end, and pulled his body from the floor. Every bone in his body ached, fighting his efforts. He breathed harder, filling his cramped chest.

When he got to his feet, he peered around. The basement was as it had been before Dr. Myles flipped out. Dark and full of old furniture organized in a way that offered a path through to the...

He looked over at the curvature in the ceiling. There was still a blackness that hid it.

He walked on wobbling legs, not giving whatever blood he had left in his body a chance to congregate downward.

There had to be storm doors there in that curvature. He knew what he'd seen earlier. *The exit is more important than the entrance. The exit is more important than the entrance... The exit...*

He stopped at the foot of the steps and peered up at the shadowy curvature. But it wasn't a curvature at all.

He smirked and closed his eyes, welcoming the calm night just beyond the open storm doors. He'd never seen the sky so dark before.

A high-pitched rhythmic beep made him frown. Maybe it was a tow truck in reverse, or maybe it was the police looking for him. His heart thudded, making him feel sluggish. They probably pulled his car apart, looking for anything to attach him to what happened. Maybe that was Uncle Jay's plan: turning Chris in and letting the cops sort it out.

Chris stepped back a few steps.

The beeping was too high-pitched to be from a police tow truck. It was familiar. Almost like a hospital monitor he'd heard before when he spent a week there for pneumonia.

He climbed the steps and emerged into the parking lot.

Blackness immersed him, pushing him into an uncomfortable headspace. The parking lot wasn't there. Instead, he was in a big room that seemed to expand forever beyond the figure and machinery stationed a few feet away. A glass box enclosed a brown, burly man who stood over his patient.

The surgeon was surrounded by state-of-the-art equipment which he used on his patient, who was stretched across an operating table.

The surgeon wore a face shield and a white surgeon's gown. A light blue mask covered his mouth.

Chris squinted at the dark man lying on the table. A violent chill shot through him.

"M—Myles?" Chris asked weakly.

A low but urgent hum came from the patient.

Chris's eyes almost popped from his face as he drew closer.

The surgeon didn't acknowledge Chris's presence. He might as well not have been standing there to begin with. But he stood there, eyes glued to the travesty before him.

Light blue drapes hung from silver railings, hanging down to the floor. Crystalline fixtures blasted bright lights. Wires and tubes went in, out, over, and under the table from a machine that sat just to the right of the patient.

The surgeon reached for the surface of one of the two carts to his right, setting down bloody scissors and swapping them for a thin blade which sat next to a pair of oversized tweezers, knives of various sizes, and a cluster of gauzes. The tools lay on an open blue cloth. The surgeon peered up at one of the three monitors that recorded vitals, two of which were riddled in crimped lines and numbers. But one, the biggest of the three which sat in the center of the setup, was stationed the highest against the drapes.

Chris's insides jerked as he cupped his hanging jaw, eyes fixed on the center monitor.

Brown skin lay split open. Clamps held each flap down against Dr. Myles' trembling chest. In the opening, blood-soaked flesh housed a pumping heart. Dark branches expanded across the plump chambers, and yellow gristle coated pieces of either side of the muscle. The surgeon picked and prodded at it with the tweezers and blade, freeing bloodstreams that added to the dry coat around the incision.

Chris dropped to his knees and landed on his hands. He vomited.

"Myles!" Chris sobbed. "No, dammit! Myles!" he screamed.

A frantic outcry responded, but nothing that made words.

Eyes coated in tears, Chris looked on. There was no parking lot. There was no way out. His body froze, plastering him in place, forcing him to watch.

"Bypassing," the hushed voice of the surgeon boomed over the PA.

The beeping sped up as Dr. Myles' heart pulsated, nearly leaping from his chest. But the surgeon remained unmoved, continuing with his poking. He showed no hustle to slow it down or panic to save his patient.

"Doctor," the surgeon began. "You always told me I would be a good *you.*"

He reached for a napkin and pressed it against Dr. Myles' open chest, who growled underneath his pressed lips as an array of squelching sounds blared through the PA, making Chris's own chest cramp.

"You said, and I quote, 'You can be almost as good as me one day.' Then you laughed and waved it off."

Dr. Myles could've let off an overpowering shrill, but his plastered lips didn't allow it.

"You said, 'Pruitt, you have ambition, but no patience.' You said, 'I'll teach you everything you need to know about this medical business,' and you'd fix me up with the people I needed to know to make me rich. You even agreed to pay for me to get my MD."

The surgeon cocked his head, staring down at Dr. Myles' teary face. "It isn't fun being on this table under someone's hand who is so much like you, is it?"

Veins popped from Dr. Myles' head as he lay still, unable to plead. His eyes were wide open, his body paralyzed.

Dr. Pruitt let out a muffled chuckle. "I was going to quit working at your office because I couldn't deal with your arrogant words, your cocky prose, or your shitty attitude toward anyone who you considered your subordinate. But who was I kidding? The *world* is your subordinate."

Pruitt set the tweezers on the table but kept the blade. Carefully, he pressed it against the pumping heart.

Dr. Myles let out an agonized groan.

"I was going to leave, but you begged me to stay. You took it a step further and took me out on you and your wife's boat. You fucked me at your cabin and bought me gifts and wrote me love letters."

Pruitt positioned the blade underneath the yellow fatty sac just over the top of Dr. Myles' heart.

"I promised to keep that secret, so long as you kept loving me the way you did. And I kept it for six years."

He drove the blade up, peeling the sac from the muscle. Dr. Myles' scream stopped shy of his closed lips.

Pruitt sighed. "I kept so many secrets for you. The lies I told the authorities about your need to harass your nurses. The lies I told your wife about our out-of-town conferences. The lies I told your daughter about how I was her Godfather. Lies. You made me tell so many *lies.*"

He put the blade on the table and picked up the tweezers. He stopped and gazed at Dr. Myles.

"But I'd do anything to keep you happy and keep you in my life. You were good for me, the patients, and the Cardiology Association of America. You were a true Corrigan of our time because of your ingenuity and intelligence. You were greatness, and when you let me work for you, I—I knew my career was made. But that was until I got to know the monster that lived behind all that intelligence."

He used the tweezers to pick up the detached fat and set it on the second table inside a small plastic container.

"All the lies and deceit weren't enough to make me turn my back on you because I knew—I just knew—there was a man with a big heart underneath it all. You've shown him to me frequently. Remember the United States Doctors of America Ball? You took me on that ship, and we sailed away to Barbados. It was the best week of my life because I got to rub shoulders with genuine success, and watching you claim that achievement award was a blessing. We were on our way to becoming a strong, powerful couple, and at that moment, I vowed to never leave your side."

He set the tweezers down and picked up the blade.

"I knew I would never have you the way your wife did. I would never have you the way the spotlight did or your admiring colleagues did. But dammit, I had you in *some* way, and that was enough for me."

He scraped at the fat that sat front and center on the heart. His head swayed.

"But when I found you sobbing in your office that day after your meeting with those men, my heart broke. I've never seen you so defeated. So vulnerable. For once, you didn't have an answer, and I knew I could save you as you cried like a child and shivered like a leaf. You were afraid, and you needed me, just like I always needed you. So I sat there, opposite your desk, and begged you to speak up and tell me what was on your mind. It took hours to get you to speak.

"But when you finally did, I hated your voice. You planned on harming a patient, and your mind was made up. I could tell from the way you spoke under fake tears. I was too in love and too dumb to realize it was a setup. For once, you needed me to pull this off. No one else. Not the nurses I protected you against and not Dr. Wells, who was on her way out the door. They would've reported you and made you pay for what you had planned. But not me, because of the promises you made. You promised to leave Nancy and that we'd go away together. There was a million dollars in it for us, and you knew I'd jump at the chance to move away with you. We'd live our lives in Mexico, in love. Together.

"I didn't object. I only got ready for surgery. I watched you walk around the office, smiling like we hadn't sentenced a man to death, like we didn't give up on a patient for profit. I watched you. But even so, I didn't say a word. We went through with it, and I watched you botch it. I watched you let him bleed out on that table. I watched you wait until his heart stopped before taking action. I watched, and it gave me nightmare after nightmare.

"I tried talking to you about it, but you only yelled at me. I threatened to turn you in when I went a week without sleep, and you said, 'You think the board would believe you over me? Ridiculous. It was too late for him. He would've died in a day or so when the surgery was over.' But I knew that was a lie. And if I knew it was a lie, so did you. I broke down in your arms and listened to you try to make sense of what we'd done.

"'It's better this way. Trust me. Keep your mouth shut. Understand? You keep your mouth shut, and we'll be home free shortly. They'll deliver the money tonight.' Remember that conversation?

"I found solace in those words and agreed that it would be alright fairly soon. Then I found myself at the police station, emptying my broken heart on the table."

There was silence.

Chris's throat constricted and his mind reeled. Dr. Myles wasn't a healer or a lover. He was a killer. Chris crawled to his feet and stepped back as his gut swarmed with icy butterflies. "I'm going to die in here," he whispered. "We're—"

Damned.

Pruitt pulled his face shield and mask free and tossed them on the floor. Then he pulled his operation gown from his scrubs. A thick slash opened his neck. Dry blood painted his brown skin burgundy. His nostrils flared, and tears ran free. "When you called me to talk at the cabin, I didn't know it would end with me buried deep in a shallow grave by our rose garden. I didn't know you never loved me. You only basked in the attention and love and praise I gave you every waking moment of six years.

"You killed the person who truly loved you. And I will never stop loving you. Your heart belongs to me just like mine belonged to you until the day you stopped it."

Pruitt raised his hand and drove it into Dr. Myles' chest. He wrapped his long fingers around the racing heart and squeezed it. Dr. Myles convulsed, and blood ran through his nose. His stiffened limbs trembled and shook, barely lifting from the table.

Pruitt snatched the heart from the cavity and clenched it, causing blood to spew, licking the inside of the glass box in spots. It leaked down his forearm and onto the black floor. Some had splashed onto his cheeks, nose, and neck.

Dr. Myles went still, and his vital signs flatlined. Crimson splatters coated Pruitt's eyes and splashed his face. A gory splatter hit the glass walls as he pulled the heart away from his clenched teeth and smacked on it as if it were tough meat.

"Holy shit! Holy fuck!" Chris screamed. His heart fluttered, threatening to burst. He blinked hard and beckoned his legs to run, begged his mind to erase what he was seeing. He struggled to make sense of it all.

Run. Wake up. Oh God, went on in his mind as thoughts jumbled and tripped over one another. But his stiff neck and locked knees thought otherwise.

Pruitt peered up at him, still chewing.

"Oh fuck," Chris said as his feet came to. He shot up and tottered over a few steps, hoping to run into the doors. His calf caught hold of something protruding from the floor, and his body went toppling down cement steps.

"Ack! Ah!" His bones hit each step as he went tumbling down.

He rolled off the bottom step, slamming into the front of a couch. He turned on his back, bruises aching and new blood spilling onto his clothes.

He spat out harsh, painful breaths as the room maneuvered and spun. His gut buckled and his body weakened. His vision shook as he grunted.

He screamed, emptying the air out of his chest. "Fuck! Just fucking— *Ahhhhhhhhhhhh* fuck!"

Chest pumping, he growled and roared.

He was alone in a place that made no sense.

There was no exit.

There was nothing fixed to survey.

He was leaving empty-handed.

Nothing was worth it, and Gallagher Hotel caught him in its web of torture and uncertainty.

He pulled himself up to his feet and sat on the couch, grimacing at his pained body.

He shook his head, decided he was better off sitting still and letting whatever happened next happen.

He surrendered, allowing his tensed muscles to relax, and he sobbed.

Chapter 20

Trudy placed her silver brush down on the vanity and flicked at her brown bangs as she sat, fixing her running makeup and crooked wig. She hated when she and Ulysses fought. It allowed her emotions to run free, entangling her in a web of uncertainty, a place she dreaded whenever Allen brought them over the line.

Aside from the minor outbursts and drunken tears, she couldn't help but feel relieved.

She smiled.

The dreadful lieutenant was dead. He and that pompous doctor.

Men: demanding, controlling, and illogical. They'd let many down in their pathetic lives. She knew it personally because Allen tasted their deceit and sins. He feasted on their thoughts and sentiments. As Allen and the Vessel devoured their souls, she felt their blood run down her throat. She felt their sins burn her tongue as both men writhed in guilt and spiraled deep into the realization that they'd exited purgatory. Their crimes against humanity doomed their souls to the walls of the Vessel, as Satan found them wretched enough to strengthen his vein's hold on the hotel and the material world beyond it.

She cleared her throat and removed the lid from her ivory foundation. She placed it on the vanity tabletop.

Allen always passed the scraps onto her as if she needed them as much as he did. She fought the urge before telling and showing him she liked material food. It didn't make her nauseous like it did Allen. It didn't make her bloat or crave anything different either.

Watching Dan and Dr. Myles suffer was enough for her. She saw their souls stick between Allen's teeth as he chewed. She heard their groans as their essence was digested. It made her smile. But the taste made her sick. It always did.

She ran a pinky under her eyelid, straightening out a stray line of mascara. She admired the mirror for giving her razor-sharp vision of her skin. It took decades for her to look at her pure soul without crying or cringing. She didn't get to be Trudy in the material realm, but she got to see her true self in purgatory.

Hell had done a number on her soul. Charcoal stains blemished her sunken cheeks. Her burnt skull held onto a few strands of hair that turned white from terror. Deep-welted crevices riddled her legs and arms, left from chunks that the Over Watchers took with their teeth. Her boney fingers were stained black from the times she shoveled lava. She scooped it from one pit and dumped it into another. She wouldn't be done until all the pits were empty. They never were. And last, the most prominent scar, was the triangle pointing to a lazily drawn eye. It reminded her of her sin whenever they crossed the line: pride. It stung underneath the makeup, forcing her to sweat and rub her forehead more than she wanted.

Her insecurities subsided when she found the silver vanity a little over a decade ago. After she died, the keepsake went to her sisters, and she couldn't help but yearn to add it to her collection from her lifetime. It wasn't easy to get ahold of it either, as Belle moved to Kansas and Mary died from pancreatic cancer shortly after she remarried and gave birth to her son.

To take Trudy's mind off her entrapment with Allen, she sent Liza traveling, searching for the mirror. Luckily, Mary's son had it in his garage, picking up dust. Now, the vanity sat in Trudy's basement, only for her reflection to see.

She ran a hand over the side of the mirror, admiring the carvings of small elephants with their trunks up and tails down as they stood in line, heading somewhere. She was convinced the vanity, just like everything else she owned, was the best in all Holloway. Back then, Trudy was the most interesting woman in Holloway with the best things, the most money, and an abundance of respect before those people put her on trial for...

She tsked. Sometimes, she couldn't decide which offense came first.

She shrugged and dabbed the blush with a pad. Then she covered the spots just around her eyes, burying the coal blemishes. She frowned. There was nothing she could do about her soul's condition, but Brenda's deteriorating body wasn't much better, and Allen was enjoying it. He loved watching her get old and worn with brittle bones and saggy skin. She'd been stuck in that body for thirty years, entering it when Brenda was forty-two.

Trudy snatched up the glass bottle next to the foundation. She put the spout to her lips and took a few gulps before setting it down. She wiped the alcohol dry with the back of her hand.

Brenda would be turning seventy-three shortly.

Her eyes watered. Trudy didn't live past twenty-nine. She never got to live the life she planned out for her and Ulysses. She was robbed.

However, Allen got to live his human life on earth until the ripe old age of 90. In his casket rested an empty skull full of secrets. Dead bodies floated in every sea and hid in every desert around the Arabian Peninsula. His reign as a ruthless dictator left millions dead, starving, and homeless.

She scoffed.

All because someone had to prove they could care for the land better than the other.

A dick swinging contest: the cause of Ulysses' death.

But she hadn't started any literal wars or caused hunger and homelessness. She tried running a business on the underbelly of light and was hanged for it. She technically didn't get a trial either. A twenty-nine-year-old widow was killed for doing what men have been doing for centuries: gaining and maintaining power.

Hell was full of those types, and Dan or Dr. Myles wouldn't get the chance to join them. If they had, their foreheads would be ingrained with a short sigmoidal curve or the dreaded pyramid sign. Then they'd be shoved into the lava pit where they'd wrestle with others like them, fighting to escape without vision or separating lips.

Luckily for them, their souls served a different purpose. They were a better fit for Allen's diet. They were fit for the walls of the Vessel.

She was happy the Vessel chose Dan.

Trudy rolled her eyes.

She hated the sight of the man. Dan walked around with his chest out, spouting off about how he'd been to war and how he'd been around death and caused hell. When, in fact, Trudy had *been* to hell. Dan didn't know a thing about pain or power, and he never would. Not in this life or the next.

She dipped a finger in her aging cream and rubbed it on the front of her chin.

The way Dan stomped around with his flared nostrils and stern pout under that hooded brow made her ill. She hadn't felt that sick since the last conversation she had with Richard Tucker.

Mayor Tucker looked into her eyes on that starry night after they rode around Holloway, just as they had for years. She remembered looking back at him with the mismatched feeling of disgust deep in her gut. She was repulsed by those nights, sitting with that dog in his car, talking about what he wanted to put in her mouth, and all the things he wanted to do to her. He'd pull her clothes off and enter her, and she'd let him, all just to get to the true nature of the ride. He wasn't the best at making love, but he was always willing to cave in to her requests.

As she tightened her tunic around her waist and he pulled his trousers up, she said, "I hear you're going to have the governor staying with you at the mayor's mansion during his visit."

Still panting, he pulled sweat from his brow by driving a handkerchief across it. "Yeah. I figured it'd give me a chance at chatting him up and getting his support for my campaign once I run as his successor." He shrugged. "I have to win the second term as mayor first, right? Speaking of which, we need to—"

"Why not have him stay at the hotel?" she interrupted. "It's new, the people love it, and I honestly can't think of a better place for him to stay. Don't you agree? We spent so much time and money getting that place built, we should show it off to the world. And besides, if people know the governor stayed there, they'd travel just to visit. That means more money."

He ran his fingers along his pencil mustache. "Yeah, but—"

"Richard, come on. You know it's the best place for him." She rubbed his thigh.

"I don't know, Trudy. I already have it all planned—"

She moved her hand to his lap. "Come on. You know it's a good idea." She winked.

He grumbled.

"Richard." She smiled. "Don't make me beg."

He let out a heavy sigh. "Alright. Alright. Maybe you're right. It is new. It is *nice*."

"Yes?"

"Yes…"

She shrilled happily. "I have so much I want to do for this! We're going to take down the curtains and put up sheer white ones. Then we're going to get these gorgeous crystal candlestick holders and—"

"…under one condition."

His foreign, authoritative tone made her uneasy. "What's that?"

"I heard a couple people in Saloon Alley saying that you should run for mayor."

"What? Really?" Her smile grew wider. "Stop while you're ahead. You're really making my day." She considered tearing his trousers off and going for another round. What better way to celebrate good and shocking news? Besides, if she got the mayor, she could help him prepare to be governor. His added support to her campaign and her reign as Holloway's mayor during his run for governor would add to her power. Her mind reeled with ideas of how she'd run the town.

"Yeah. But you know that can't happen, right?" he said.

"Of course not," she lied. She collected her wits, quickly remembering who she was speaking with. Although her running for mayor against him would've benefited them both, she was still a woman stuck in a man's world. She trod lightly. "I'm still leading your reelection campaign as promised."

"No, you're not."

She frowned. "What?"

"I talked with Clyde. He thinks I should separate my political interests from you and your underground activities. It could reflect negatively on me."

"That doesn't make sense, Richard. If the people love me enough to be mayor, they would definitely back you up if I were on your team. You need me."

"Hm. You know, I thought the same thing, but Clyde begged to differ. With the alcohol law rolling in and Michigan agreeing to be a clean state, the people would have no use for you if they realize you're a criminal."

Her heart sank. That damn DA had a way of sticking his nose in places it shouldn't've been. Since he'd been elected, he preached about alcohol and how it poisoned Holloway's streets, turning the town into a war zone. He had it out for Trudy, and so did Sheriff Louis. "So, you're going to take his advice?"

"It's not advice, it's what's going to happen."

She narrowed her eyes at him. "Did you just fire me?"

"Trudy, I plan on running for governor in four years, and the Eighteenth Amendment is in full swing. If I want my career to continue soaring, I can't be involved with you."

"So why can't I run for mayor then? You don't want my help, so I'd just help myself. You said it, the people want me."

"A couple people said that, but they don't know *what* they want. They don't know about the trafficking, and some people don't realize that it's not good for this town. Trust me, they'll comply once the law hits and goes into full swing. Holloway will be fine, just as it was before you and your bootleggers started ripping and running around."

"Ripping and running?" She scoffed. "What nerve? Our *ripping and running* put money into this place." She pointed to the colorful lights off in the distance. "We grew Holloway from a dead farm town, struggling to build a town square, to a metropolis full of businesses and entertainment. Our town is a sanctuary for the working class. And you were alright with it, if I remember correctly. You accepted city taxes every year, and you've sat in those saloons every day. You're a hypocrite, and Holloway deserves better than that! They deserve me! Someone who knows how to make things happen. I'm making this place flourish, and you and those other assholes will not stop me."

He leaned in, eyes fixed on hers. "Listen, because I don't want to have this conversation, or any other, with you ever again. If you run for mayor, I will see that you do not win. You'd be humiliating yourself if you tried. Don't do it, Trudy."

"You're intimidated by me, aren't you?" she hissed.

"No, I'm—"

"You're scared of being beaten by a woman. The same woman who kept you in her pocket for years. I'm the reason this town has money and railroad tracks. What have you done but sit back and get your pecker sucked? You collected the same money I did. You, Louis, and even Judge

Rowls. All of you share in on the pile that is now Saloon Alley, but I'm the one getting booted? You want my railroad, *and* you want my bootleggers gone. Hell, next you're going to want my saloons and hotel."

"If you can't convert them into restaurants only, they'll have to close. They're outlawed under the new amendment. I have a buyer lined up for you. Rather Hunt is ready to buy your saloons and the hotel."

"What?" she shouted. She'd already given Richard what he wanted: her time and "love." Their time together followed a pattern: she'd deliver, then he'd fulfill her wishes, no questions asked. So what was happening? She pressed the backs of her teeth together and waited.

He sighed. "Trudy, don't make this harder than it needs to be."

"If the saloons and hotel are closed, then...what about business with Reggie?"

"If it doesn't stop, and he's seen anywhere around town, he will be arrested and charged for manufacturing and distributing alcohol. They're putting bootleggers away, Trudy. Don't risk his freedom."

"You're serious about this?" she asked.

"Yes. Look, I want to save this town! Some people are afraid because of all the violence on Saloon Alley. The drunken bar fights and shoot-outs. Prostitution. It's turned that side of Holloway into the Wild West. Yes, the money is good, but it's changed this town too much, and with this law going into effect, I can't risk letting Holloway become a beat town where everything illegal and unjust happens. I'm sorry. You need to end your contract with Reggie and prepare to sell your saloons and the hotel if you refuse to convert them. There's too much alcohol money tied into those things. You can serve alcohol on the night the governor comes by because he requested it be available wherever he stays. We'll call it a private party. But the saloons need to change now."

She drew her head back, weary of his unfair request. "We opened so many lucrative businesses here because of Reggie. We got a railroad and tourists… You want to stop this now?"

"Trudy, my hands are tied. You're going to have to end the contract, or the sheriff will be at the train, waiting to handcuff Reggie and take him in."

"Hm. So I walk away with nothing? That's shit!"

"Keep your voice down!" he growled.

"Why? So people can't hear how you're ripping me off? I can't believe this. After everything I've done…"

"Don't you dare go down that repetitive list of shit you've done. It's old, and you're a woman, sweetheart. All your accomplishments are actually mine or someone else's. The only things people associate with you are the stores, saloons, and that hotel. They think, wow, her husband's death paid out."

She dropped her jaw. "How dare you speak to me like that!"

"Calling it as it is."

"It's a good thing you kicked me off your campaign. I would hate to be on a sinking ship."

He chuckled. "Oh, really? You're upset now?"

Face scorching, Trudy snapped. "I hope your wife and kids wake up and realize that you, the great Mayor Richard Tucker, are a walking pile of human garbage. You took part in the alcohol trafficking—don't *act* like you didn't. You're a serial cheater and a coward, and I hate when you shove that puny thing you call a cock inside me. You aren't a man; you are a leech and a user that can't fuck good!"

His palm struck her cheek, shoving a blinding flash before her eyes. Aches seared her face as she shouted and grabbed the door handle. He grabbed her hair and pinned his big hand against her mouth. He hissed in her ear, "This isn't a game, Trudy. I will not allow you to fuck this up for me. Sell the saloons and hotel and end your contract with Reggie. That's all I need you to do. If I hear that you're not doing any of those things, I will kill you. Now nod if you agree."

She nodded.

"Make this the last time we talk."

He shoved her head forward, leaving her weeping in the passenger seat as he drove her home.

He pulled onto the curb, right out front of the two-story red brick house.

"Get out," he barked.

She shoved the door open and ran up the pebble walkway for the front door with a face full of tears. No one, including Ulysses, had ever treated her that way. She'd never been so embarrassed or betrayed.

That evening, Trudy cried in her room to her sisters. Mary stood next to the lilac Victorian bench at the foot of the double king-size bed. Belle sat next to Trudy, who soaked her lavender silk sheets with tears. She picked her face up and rubbed her burning cheek.

"There was so much hate in his eyes," Trudy said. "He was so upset with me." She shook her head. "I just don't understand it. I've only done good for the town. How could he dismiss me that way?" She sniffed. "I shouldn't have sold The Estate because I never would have used the money to invest in the bootlegger Ulysses met in Detroit. I—wanted our legacy to move on with the times. But now, I have nothing." She sobbed, thinking about Gallagher's Saloon. She'd bought a storefront on the dead side of town for a low price and transformed it into three saloons: Gallagher's Saloon, Lady Night's, and The Piano Club. Then, she ventured into town and bought an ice cream parlor, a boutique, and a café along the town square. All three places sold bottled alcohol.

When the Wilson twins bought the land next to her saloon front, they built four more saloons: Bottom, Blue's, The Brothel, and Doggy's Saloon. That was Saloon Alley: a gateway into Holloway's nightlife and an excellent source of income.

Although Trudy owned many businesses, she looked for different projects. She had her eye on a patch of land downtown off the town square. It was a perfect place for a hotel, somewhere tourists could stay while they ventured in and throughout Saloon Alley.

She bought the land on that corner and had a wooden mansion built, calling it Gallagher Hotel. It was wildly successful, grossing thousands of dollars a month, prompting Trudy to invest in a women's organization called She Lives. She spent her days teaching women and girls about entrepreneurship and how to gain independence and her nights paying Reggie and stocking her saloons and business with hooch.

As she sat there in her thoughts, her sisters watched. Belle had a look of concern as she frowned and rubbed Trudy's hand. Mary, however, stood with her arms crossed over her chest. She stared blankly at the floor, probably not listening at all.

"At least you still get to plan the gala," Belle said. "And then after that, who knows what we could get into? We could travel or maybe start over somewhere else." She smiled. "I always thought California would fit us."

Trudy pouted. "Thomas wouldn't want you to leave. This was his *home*."

"*Was* his home, Trudy." Belle sighed. "I hated the days when we all found out, one by one, that the guys weren't coming back from Europe. Thomas is dead. I hate it, but it's true. We've made many strides toward independence, and we achieved it without the men. It helped me realize that we can do anything together. I think it's time to move on. Let's leave Holloway together and go see the world."

Trudy shook her head. "Why would I want to leave our home? It's wonderful here."

"Yeah, you're right, but sometimes taking a break from the madness is good for the soul. Besides, you shouldn't let this town consume you. You've done well. You have many other businesses. It's time to let it all go. It isn't worth fighting for."

"Belle, I can't let them take what I worked for because of a *political agenda*. I can stop this. Do you understand the pull I have in Holloway? I made things happen simply because I whispered in the right person's ear. I am Holloway, and there's no way in hell I'm going to let them take over what I worked so hard for. If you don't understand that, then you can leave," she said.

"Trudy, I'm just trying to help. You don't have to fight anymore. We have more than enough money to move away from here. Sell the businesses."

Trudy scowled. "How dare you give up on the shit I worked so hard for? How dare you be so willing to turn your back on the shit I did for us?" she hissed.

"I'm not trying to upset you. I know you worked hard for everything we have, and I appreciate it. I just think it's time to cash in and move on."

"You don't get to make those decisions! You're just as bad as Richard, telling me what I should do with my shit! Get out! Get out now! Both of you!" Trudy picked up a pillow and launched it into Belle's face. Belle swatted it away before it could make contact. It hit the wall and landed on the floor.

Mary turned and calmly walked out into the hallway.

Belle stood and looked at Trudy. "Think about it," Belle said, before turning and leaving.

Trudy hated when Belle made her reservations known. She was always the voice of reason for Trudy, and in most cases, she'd take the advice. But not that time.

Although Belle's advice didn't link up with what Trudy wanted, she was right about one thing: Trudy was still running the gala that year in the hotel, and her threats would be there alongside the governor.

Trudy met with Reggie a week later and told him about the threat over her morning tea. The sun spilled through the blinds, painting the kitchen in a bright yellow haze. Reggie sat across from her with an emotionless expression.

"I want to buy a gun," she said with both hands clutching her hot porcelain mug.

Reggie nodded and stood from his seat. He swaggered over to his suitcase next to her cast iron wood stove and hefted it onto the oak kitchen table. He didn't open it. He just gave her a deceptive glare with his dark eyes. "You know you have to do something about the threat, right?"

"Yes," she said. She rubbed her silk skirt with shaking fingers. Reggie always did that to her. It wasn't because he was black; Trudy thought racism was a waste of time and impeded financial growth. It was because Reggie wasn't afraid to use his guns on anyone. She imagined that in his line of business, there wasn't room for reluctance or ad hoc decisions, only well thought out executions.

He rested his elbows on the table and crossed his arms over one another. He grinned. "I would hate to lose Holloway as a pit-stop drop-off, but if the law's sniffing around, it's bad for business. You understand, right?"

"Yes, I know."

"Of course you know, Trudy. You know everything. So, uh, you plan on shooting them all in cold blood? You know that's a good way to get caught, right? And if you get caught committing a crime with something from my arsenal, I'll find you and kill you before you get canned."

She nodded stiffly and swallowed the ball in her throat. "Yes, I understand."

He sighed. "I like you, Trudy. I really do. You've brought me so much money over the years. It's a shame when the team turns on each other for personal gain. You know the real reason they booted you is because you're a dame."

She scoffed. "The idea came up. I was told all my ideas weren't my own. They belonged to someone else. A man."

"Yeah, I can tell. I can see the heat in your eyes."

She turned away, averting her glance.

"It's alright," he said. "Tell you what, I'm not going to sell you a gun. It's too sloppy and easy to draw back to you, the woman scorned with a good friend who traffics illegals. Nuh uh." He leaned in, forcing the wooden table legs to creak under his weight. "You're going to make it look like an assassination."

"How?"

He pinched his scruffy chin. "Do you know anything about bombs?"

"No. Not much. I know they blow up, but that's it."

"You should plant them around your gala and let it tear them all down."

She gasped. "W—what? That'll destroy the hotel. I can't—"

"Whoa, whoa. Whoa. Hear me out. You will get rid of the problems, and no one would suspect you. The people around here know how much you love that place. They know how much time and effort you put into building it up from the ground. You're a superwoman around here. It'll look like some radical crazy set out to kill the governor. Case closed."

"I—"

"You know I'm right, Trudy."

He was, and she was out of options. She didn't want to die in prison, but she didn't want Richard to take everything she had. Once the building went down, she'd get it rebuilt and start over. She smiled as the plan sat in plain view.

"Alright," she said.

"Hm. Are you trying to bring the building down or a single room? I suggest bringing the whole thing down."

"Yes, the whole building," she said. If she brought the building down during the gala, they'd all perish. It was the perfect plan, satisfying revenge.

"I'll drop the artillery off at the hotel in the morning. How does ten small ones sound? They have a silent timer and a mighty blast impact."

"Good. How much?"

"For you? One thousand."

Once the bombs arrived, she stored them in the hotel's basement until the day of the gala. She sent the staff home that afternoon, telling them to return at the start of the party and to get some much-needed rest for the night ahead. Happily, they obliged.

Trudy circled the mansion, deciding where to plant the bombs. She set the timer just as Reggie showed her. She shoved two underneath the wood stove and the bar, one underneath the table closest to the exit, and another underneath the table closest to the kitchen. She taped two against the underside of the long table in the middle of the room, one inside the piano, and one beneath the hostess station.

As guests poured in that night, Trudy kept an eye out for Richard, Sheriff Louis, and D.A. Clyde Albright. She'd figured she'd clear the air with them and share a whiskey, toasting to Richard's success to shake any suspicions should anyone live.

She was sure none of them would.

Once she spotted them being chauffeured to their table by the hostess, she beckoned them to the whiskey parlor.

Richard leaned over to his wife, who sat next to him wearing a pearl dress she'd gotten from Mary and Belle's boutique.

"I'll be back," he said.

Mrs. Tucker smiled and nodded before passing a fake smile onto Mrs. Louis, who sat two seats to her right.

Trudy's gut twisted with envy. *How dare he kiss her in front of me?* He'd never done that before. She smirked as she turned and headed for the parlor.

And he'll never do it again.

"It looks nice in here," Richard said, a look of amazement on his face as he entered the parlor. "I mean, you have the honey-glazed walls and glass shelves with different brands of whiskey. Is that Sherman's scotch blend?" He swaggered over to the glass shelf nearest the wood stove fireplace.

"Grab it, and I'll pour us a glass," she said, fighting to maintain her smile.

He grabbed it and passed it to her.

As she poured their drinks, she eavesdropped on the men as they huddled around the fireplace.

"...yeah, there was a portrait of Ulysses Gallag—" Richard started. "Trudy, where is the portrait of the American hero?"

"I moved them back home. I felt more comfortable with them being there. They are a priceless possession for me, and I wouldn't be able to live with myself if they were damaged by one of the guests or anything," she said. *I don't want them to perish with you,* she thought. "Drinks are ready!"

The men chuckled amongst themselves as they walked over to Trudy and picked up their drinks from the end table next to the evergreen suede loveseat. Clyde eyed her with a disgusted glare. She averted her eyes, afraid he'd find her plans in her hidden scowl.

"Gentlemen," she started. "I just want to say that I support the direction you're taking this town. Having an alcohol-free county is for the safety of the people, and I would never do anything to stand in the way of that. From tomorrow on, may this be a good start to a new future."

"I'm happy you see it our way, Trudy," Clyde said as he sat on the loveseat.

She pictured herself shoving her glass into his freckled face. "Yes." She smiled. "And I also want to share some big news."

"Oh, what's that?" Richard asked as he stood next to the fireplace, sipping his whiskey.

"I sold the saloons and the hotel. As of Monday, they will all be under new management," she lied.

"Oh, well, that's good news," Louis said as he raised his glass.

"Thank you," she said as she raised her glass. "To new things."

The men raised their glasses and drank.

"Well, you gentlemen are free to stay in here as long as you'd like, but I must excuse myself. The gala isn't going to run itself."

"Oh, that's fine. We'll see you in a second," Richard said.

She nodded and went for the door.

"Oh, and Trudy?"

She turned. "Yes, Clyde?"

"You made the right decision." He winked.

Trudy smiled and turned for the door. She cringed as she walked out into the hallway, rushing past her busy waitstaff who swarmed the hallway, and her pianist, who tickled the ivories, playing a calming waltz. She watched happy people dine on good food and enjoyed the moment as it was.

Trudy picked up speed before she could change her mind about destroying such a beautiful place. It was a part of her and Ulysses' dream to build and own a hotel in the town square, and she made it happen.

But Tucker, Albright, and Louis had to go before they stepped too far in her way.

You'll build another hotel in this spot, she thought. *You'll have it all back.*

She charged past the doors and shut them behind her. She ran down the steps and reached underneath the wooden porch, pulling a long, thick, heavy plank out. The scraping from dragging it against the pavement was so loud that she looked over her shoulder.

No one was in the town square, as they shouldn't be. Sheriff Louis put a curfew in place for seven that evening to keep Holloway looking like an obedient town. She cringed as she dragged the plank up the steps and lodged it into the door handles. This new town wasn't her town, and she'd do anything to have the old one back.

Once she heaved and grunted, pushing the plank in place, she ran down the steps and up the street, disappearing into the night.

Those men didn't deserve to live, just like Dan and Dr. Myles didn't deserve a heartbeat or merit either. But because of their status, they thought they'd get away with treating people like shit.

They got their suffering, and it felt good to witness.

PART III

Chapter 21

Chris trekked his way back to the stairs. If he didn't get out soon, he'd have to face Uncle Jay.

He'd seen death and felt nothing about it. He'd even caused it, but there was something different about what happened in Gallagher Hotel. The murders seemed purposeful, like the world was better off without people like him or Dr. Myles. Or Natalie. For a second, Chris wondered what the cop's ordeal was, or if Dan was invited to the hotel for the same reason.

Chris teared up.

He was going to die, he just didn't know when. But he had a few ideas on how. Stuck, he pondered.

"I'm not scared," he whispered. "I'm not scared!" he yelled up the staircase at the closed door.

"Come get me! Just come do it!" he shouted.

Nothing answered back. The house was silent.

He climbed the steps and walked into the hallway off the kitchen. The smoke cleared, leaving the place as spotless as it was when he arrived. But the tables and chairs were still different from the ones at dinner. They were dated and set up without people, or ghosts, sitting at them.

He dropped his head, wide eyes pinned to the floor.

This place was *going* to kill him.

His heart dropped.

Outside wasn't there anymore. Everything was a vast blackness around that glass box. He'd be crazy to explore the world outside of there.

Am I in hell?

Too afraid of the answer, he decided he was better off sitting and waiting. He pulled a chair out from the table closest to the door and glared at the clean mahogany tabletop. The candle on the table flickered for him, the lonely patron.

He was finally alone, clear of the Gang, and left to think about how he'd gotten on their bad side.

Where'd I go wrong?

Chris's life was set up for success. He had money, cars, and a caring family, things a lot of people died without.

But that night at his house changed everything; he crossed a line, and there was no going back. Uncle Jay fought for Chris every time he'd blown up on a member at a party or threatened a cop here and there. Uncle Jay was even fair with Brian and Chris's punishment for what happened in Bloomfield. They were laid off for a month or until the heat was low.

Chris wished he'd fled right after Bloomfield.

He laid his forehead on the table. Then he smiled. *It's a game*, he thought. If he were the last man standing, he should get out alive. It was only fair.

He scoffed. *Fairness.* He harped on that word more than he wanted. The Gang's planned retaliation wasn't fair. Gallagher Hotel wasn't fair.

It wasn't fair that he didn't know how to get out. The irony was baffling: a thief who broke into places for a living couldn't figure out how to escape a public building.

Someone cleared their throat, prompting Chris to shoot his head up from the table.

A girl with short black hair and thick smiling cherry lips looked down at him as she cupped a notepad and pencil in her hands. A long black dress covered by a paper apron draped her short frame. "What'll it be?"

Chris stared at her, envious of her kind smile and calm demeanor. He racked his mind, searching for her face. He was sure he'd never seen her before.

"It's alright, toots. I'm not like the others. You just look *really hungry,* and I think you should eat something. I'll pay for it."

"I—I'm not hungry," he said in a low voice.

"Well, what's the matter? You're all bruised up and beaten down. Do you need someone to talk to?"

"I—" he whispered. "I'm lost."

"Lost like you need directions, or lost as in depression lost?"

He sobbed. "I—I tried to curb it. I tried to make things right. But then—but then I still lost."

She put a freezing hand on his shoulder and frowned. "It's life. We all end up losing. But think about it like this: You're only as defeated as you want to be."

"I don't—understand."

She set her notepad on the table and pulled the chair out across from him. She sat down and held his eyes in her comfortable gaze. "It's like this… You did whatever you did to end up here. You were chosen, there is no doubting that. But you are as guilty of your convictions as you choose to be. It's never too late to forgive yourself and vow to be better."

He moved his gaze to the now wooden bar, staring at the stools that lined the front of it.

"You can claim your sins and extinguish them. But first, you need to acknowledge them and then let them go back to the past where they belong. You don't have to be down. You don't have to run. You don't have to wish or cry. You can choose to move on and be happy. You can apologize. You can pray. You can do so much."

Her light voice and kind words made him wonder. "Are you stuck here too?"

She cleared her throat. "I don't like to think I'm stuck anywhere. I think of this as my resting place until I'm set free." Her smile grew wide. "I know that'll happen. I pray for it all the time. I mean, I miss inhaling the summer breeze or sniffing my flower garden. I'd love to live those moments again. I just have to accept my fate for now. You can too."

"But—"

Hurried footsteps pounded the stairs. He looked at the archway. *This is it,* he thought. He was getting what he deserved. He'd take it all, just as long as it meant he'd be free.

Riley rounded the corner with Randy following behind. Her hair had fallen to her lean shoulders, and dark rings rounded her eyes as she raced into the ballroom. She froze, then threw her hands over her mouth. "Oh my God! Chris?"

He turned to the waitress to find her gone. He frowned and turned to watch Riley approach.

She crouched and pulled him into a tight hug. He rubbed his mouth against her shoulder, balling.

"I thought you were dead," he said.

"No. No, we're here." She pulled away. "And we know the way out." She smiled.

"Where?" he asked. He'd seen most of the house, and other than the storm doors, there wasn't a way out. He was sure of it.

"We went into the attic and found some things."

"Things?" he asked.

"Yes, Chris. Neil and I believe that most of the people here were singled out and brought here on purpose."

"Who's Neil?"

She cleared her throat and peered at Randy.

"My name's not Randy. It's Neil. I'm working undercover to—"

"You're a cop?" Chris asked.

"No. I'm a reporter putting together an expose on this place."

"*Tsk*. Get comfortable," Chris said.

Riley looked over her shoulder at Neil.

"There was a book in the attic," she began. "It has people's names, and it stores their essence, giving it off to anyone who touches the pages." Tears filled her eyes. "It makes you relive horrible things that those people did and how they died." She wiped a tear away. "I saw Natalie. I *was* her."

He winced at her. "I don't get what you're saying."

"In the book, there are entries. The ones closer to the beginning are written in deep red, almost like old blood. When I flipped to Natalie's page, it dripped by the letter. I pulled my finger across the page and re-lived what she had done to her son. She—she hung him upside down and hacked him apart." Pain crossed Riley's face. Then she wept. "And then I saw what happened to her. A man, made of many bloated, damaged body parts, squeezed her neck so tight that it broke open." She dropped Chris's gaze and looked at his knees. "It was her son. How could anyone treat their child that way?"

Chris set his hand on her shoulder. "A person who deserves to be here would do something like that."

She went to speak by separating her lips, but she stopped and wiped her tears away instead.

"Who else was in the book?" he asked. He knew he was in there. The crime fit, and so did the chilling coincidences. He and Dr. Myles ran away from their homes and issues only to end up at Gallagher Hotel. Based on what happened on that operating table, Dr. Myles was toxic, killing the people around him. He was an arrogant, selfish killer, and based on what Riley said, so was Natalie.

Chris was no different.

"Dan," Riley said.

Chris raised a brow.

"When we found the book in the attic, we didn't know what to do with it. Thick red vines held it in place on a pedestal. Dan took the book and kicked the pedestal over. The ripped vines bled onto the floor." Her face crumbled in disgust. "When Dan moved the column, we saw that it went down a long way. We figured it went down and through the basement, and as soon as we left the room, we ended up in a clay house out in the desert somewhere." She drifted, and Chris watched her frown. "He was a rapist and murderer."

"Well, Dr. Myles wasn't a standup guy either," Chris said. "He was, uh, fucking around with someone he worked with. His PA, Pruitt. Dr. Myles killed him over money, so Pruitt came back and performed open-heart surgery on Dr. Myles before ripping out his heart and... It was the worst thing I've ever seen. The guy took a bite out of..." Chris's voice cracked, "...Dr. Myles' *heart.*"

She put a hand over her mouth. "I'm so sorry, Chris."

"Nah, it's alright." He pointed to the gash in his forehead. "Dr. Dickhead got me good before he decided to step outside."

"You—you've been outside too?"

Chris sensed the worry etched deep in her voice. "Yeah. We went through the storm doors."

"You didn't fall?"

"No. He got surgery in a glass box sitting where the parking lot is. Why would I fall?"

"Because there's nothing out there. It's all nothing. Blackness. Emptiness. I'm so happy you didn't sink..."

His heart raced, making his body tremble. There was something about the thought of falling forever. *You never land.*

"How is that possible?"

"I think I can answer that," Neil said as he picked his camera up and started taking photos of the ballroom. He stopped and looked over at them. "The original hotel didn't have a parking lot. In fact, there were a few more rooms that extended out into where the parking lot is now. During the rebuild, they decided that cars had become prevalent, justifying the construction of a parking lot."

271

"So you're saying I would've fallen if I—"

"Yup," Neil said as he went back to snapping photos of the now oak bar.

Chris felt his lungs deplete of air as a heavy heat dawned on him.

"Chris, when you were in the basement, did you see the vines?" Riley asked.

His mind went back to his room earlier. Those things looked more like veins wrapped around a wall, carrying blood from the basement and up to the attic. But she didn't need to know about what he'd seen because there was no point. Gallagher Hotel had them. "No," he said.

"I say we go look anyway." She gave him a faint smile. "I'm so happy you're alive." She pulled him in for another hug. He welcomed it but refused to feel her pain or concerns. He'd reached the end of the line, and that book was going to prove it.

"Am I in there?" he asked.

She pulled away and dropped her head. She nodded slowly.

"Can I see?"

Neil stepped over and handed Chris a laptop bag. "Be careful touching it. It will make you see things. Horrible things."

Chris opened the bag and reached inside. He pulled the old book out and opened it on his lap.

"Y—you don't feel anything?" Neil asked.

"No," Chris said. The thing reeked of metal, and the old pages were crusty with blood. He stopped on the page with his name across the top. The letters on his page were gray just as Dan's and Dr. Myles' were. He turned the page quickly and saw a list of names. He furrowed his brow. "Your names aren't on here," he said.

"I know," Riley said.

"So, what does that mean?"

"I don't know."

Chris stared at her. If they weren't in the book, then why were they in Gallagher Hotel? Why did they share the same hell as he did? Judging from what Riley said, Dan and Dr. Myles' pages should be complete and covered in blood. Chris didn't see what happened to Dan, but he knew Dr. Myles was dead. So why wasn't his page covered in wet blood like Natalie's? He declared it meaningless. Just another ploy in that house of death. It didn't mean they were safe, and it didn't bring him any closer to thinking it'd release them from the house. It was another dead end. "It's just a book," he said. "It doesn't mean shit."

Chris launched the book across the room. It slid once it hit the floor, stopping near the window next to the barricaded front door. Once the book hit the wall, the pages fell loose, shooting every which way and spreading across the foyer floor.

"Hey!" Neil yelled as he rushed after the book, picking up loose pages and shoving them between the covers. "What the hell is your problem?"

"A *book* doesn't tell me when or how I'm going to die. Fuck that! It's just a book."

"It'll help us get out of here!" Neil yelled.

"How do you know? It can't even explain why you're here! You're not in it! So why the fuck are you here?" Chris shouted.

"What does it matter?" Riley asked.

Chris glared in her eyes and found Carla's face the last time he saw her. Regret coursed through him. He was in that book that took people's stories and wrote them in blood. He was in there alongside a rapist and murderers. And with good reason. It was hard to say he was jealous that Neil and Riley had a chance of breaking free, but Chris's intuition told him to get comfortable. "It matters because I hate being the worst guy in the room."

"What are you talking about? You're still alive, so you have a chance," Riley said.

"No, I don't," Chris said, eyes full of tears. He dropped his wet gaze to his lap. He nodded. "I belong here. I'm just as bad as those guys in that book."

"No you're not," she said. "Don't say that, Chris."

"Yes, I am. I—I hurt someone—a couple people—that I loved, and I did it out of anger and jealousy." He looked into Riley's eyes. "I see her face every time I look at you."

"Allen?" Neil said. Chris looked at the foyer to find Neil clutching the book against his chest as he peered up the staircase. Neil's eyes widened as his mouth dropped open. "Oh my God!" he exclaimed before he rushed over into the ballroom. He stood next to Riley, hands shaking violently around the book. She stood up and watched the foyer, fists balled against her sides.

274

"What's—" she began before gawking at Allen as he silently stepped into the foyer. He sauntered, holding his head back as if he were nursing a nosebleed.

"What the fuck?" Chris whispered as he shot up from his seat.

Riley gasped when Allen stepped into the flickering lights and dropped his face enough for the blood to flow from his twisted nose.

Allen's black eyes bulged underneath peeled back eyelids. His dingy skin sagged down his face, splitting at the cheeks, giving way to bloodied gashes. His dislocated jaw hung loose, barely holding onto his face by his elastic skin. And instead of his uniform from dinner, he wore a black and white three-piece suit as if he just rose from the coffin at his funeral. He breathed heavily through his mouth full of long, jagged teeth soaked in blood. He glared at them, then he slowly turned his distorted face to Neil.

"You need to give that back to me," he shouted. His thundering, deep voice shook the floor.

Neil held the book to his chest. He shook his head. "N—n—no."

"Give me the book!"

"No! This book is going to the police and—and everyone is going to know what's really going on in here."

Allen flexed his neck and grunted. "You've been a thorn up my ass since the day we met. Your intrusive stalking and questioning have run their course, and whether you give that book to me or not, you're going to die."

"I don't care about what you do. You're not getting this book. The people of Holloway are get—"

Allen charged Neil with an open hand and grabbed him by his jaw. He lifted him high, taking Neil's feet off the floor. He kicked and let out muffled cries behind Allen's red, scaly hand. Allen used his other hand to tear the book from Neil's grip.

"Stop it!" Riley yelled. She rushed for them, but Chris reached out and grabbed her arm. There was no way she could save him. Allen had what he wanted. No sense in her and Neil both getting hurt by what looked like a storybook demon. A shiver broke through him.

Allen could've been Satan himself.

"Stop it!" she shrieked.

"You want me to stop this?" Allen asked.

"Yes!"

He grunted. "I'll let him go if you let me have you."

She dropped her brow. "What?"

"Riley," Allen growled. "You're pure at heart and enough energy to"—he twitched and jerked at the shoulders—"restore me until the book is back in place. I'll leave him if you give me you." Allen glared at her hard. The stillness between the two was intense, bolstering.

She nodded. "Set them both free, and you can have me. Set them free and give them the book."

"What?" he hissed.

"Riley, no," Chris objected, never moving his eyes from Allen.

But she ignored him, carrying on with her proposed deal. "Set them and the book free, and then you can have me."

"But the book belongs to the Master. The book belongs *here*."

"I know, but without that book, no one else will end up trapped here. No one else will fall victim to you, demon."

He snickered. "A bold statement by such a small woman. Hm." He glared at Neil and sighed. "No deal," Allen said. He peered at Neil. "Say hi to Liza for me." He pulled Neil's face forward and opened his mouth full of rugged knives.

Neil shrilled as Allen brought his teeth down on the sides of his face. The sound of crushing and crumbling bones smacked the walls as Allen took a mouthy gouge from Neil's skull.

"Neil!" Riley shrilled.

Chris watched as Allen tore the front half of Neil's face loose, chewing on his skin, bones, and flesh, leaving a bloodied mess of ripped bones and yellow brain matter. He threw Neil's body off to the side. It slammed into the wall before falling to the floor.

Chris turned to find Riley stomping legs free from a chair. She pulled it loose, making a sharp edge.

She went to toss it to Chris, but he waved her off with a shaking hand and pulled his pocketknife instead. Allen would have to fight for his next meal. Heart slamming, Chris moved his eyes back to Allen, who was still chewing on the bite he took out of Neil.

Riley rushed Allen, shoving her shoulder into him and sending him toppling onto his side. He hit the floor and groaned after the sound of snapping bone erupted.

She ran over to him and slammed the sharp edge of the chair leg into his neck. He hacked up blood as he grabbed the wound. Blood from the wound pooled around his hand and spilled onto the floor.

"Help me!" she cried.

Chris rushed over and kicked him in the face, sending blood splatter across the room. They stomped and kicked Allen until he stopped coughing. His hand let up on the wound, allowing it to pour out onto the floor. He went still, and his black eyes closed.

They stopped and stepped back, breathing hard and clutching their weapons.

Chris froze when Allen coughed. Then he laughed.

"Impossible," Riley whispered as she watched him with wide eyes.

Allen clutched the book with one hand and pulled the chair stump from his neck with the other. He threw it against the wall; it landed next to Neil. Allen rolled onto his stomach and picked himself up.

He grinned a bloody, toothy smirk.

Chris approached with an urgent stride, knife up, ready to pierce Allen's chest. But Allen grabbed Chris by the neck and hoisted him up, pulling his feet from the floor. Chris kicked and choked as Allen's grip tightened. Chris lodged the knife into Allen's eye.

Allen roared as his jammed eye socket squirted blood. But his grip only tightened, making Chris go numb in his arms and legs. His face grew hot, and his crown sizzled as his vision blurred.

Allen moved his hand with the book still in it. He used his long finger to snatch the knife from his eye. He tossed it aside. "You're mine, boy," Allen hissed as he pulled Chris close to his opening maw.

Chris kicked and yelped.

Riley ran up and stomped Allen's leg at the knee. It caved, sending a sickening crack through the room.

The beast shrilled, loosening his grip, sending Chris down to the floor.

Chris sucked up air and beckoned his limbs to work.

Allen batted at Riley and missed as she ducked and fell to her hands and knees. She crawled toward the foyer with Allen following close behind, dragging his useless limb and holding the book against his chest.

Limping and struggling to get air back into his lungs, Chris raced for the table nearest the hostess station and picked it up. He slammed it across Allen's back, sending him belly flopping to the floor.

Chris then grabbed Allen up by his collar and flipped him on his back. He slammed his fist into Allen's sagging face, grunting and screaming as he drew more blood and added to the gashes on the old man's face.

"Chris!" Riley called out. She pulled a chair from the clutter blocking the door and pulled the curtain back from the window to the right of the door. She slammed the chair into the window.

Allen let out a gurgled cackle, dragging Chris's attention back to him.

"You will die here, *Chris*. Nothing you do will stop that from happening. You belong to the Vessel! It wants your sins, and we will suck down your soul with one gulp because you are damned! You will die, and I will savor your insignificant spirit! You are dead, and it's all because of *her*!" Allen cackled hysterically as Chris raised his fist and crushed the man's twisted, pointy nose.

"Dead!" Allen shrieked.

"Shut up!" Chris demanded.

"You're dead!"

"Shut up!" Chris said as he wept.

"Chris!" Riley called. "The window!" She'd cleared the window enough for a body to go through it.

"You're dead!" Allen yelled as Chris dragged him across the foyer and up to the window. "Boy, your soul is marked! You're dead because of what you did to *them*!"

Chris hefted Allen up and pressed his body against the empty windowpane. "Fuck you!" he said.

"Push him out!" she said as she lifted Allen's legs, ready to help.

"You're dead, boy! Dead! You hear me?" Allen said. "The Book says so!" Chris glared at the book. Allen hadn't let it go since he'd taken it from Neil. Chris tried tugging at it.

"Forget about the book! Push him out now!"

"Carla would have never loved you because she always loved him more!" Allen said.

"Fuck you!" Chris pushed Allen back, and Riley shoved his legs forward. They watched him fall... and fall...and...

Chris's breath shook as his chest imploded. The darkness swallowed Allen whole, taking him into nothingness. "Oh God!" Chris said. "Oh my…"

There was nothing out there, and the book was gone, sinking into the blackness. He shuddered. Sure, Riley had mentioned it. But to see it…

There was nowhere to escape in the massive void.

Chapter 22

"We're all made of energy," Allen said. As he spoke, his lips didn't move; Over Watchers communicated telepathically. He gawked at Trudy with his wide black orbs. Black patches riddled his scarlet bald head, and his red scaly skin reeked of sulfur. He moved closer to her on thin legs, nearly pressing his bare swollen belly against her.

Trudy dug up molten rock and moved it to a pile that slid loose and buried her feet. She could feel her hands and legs blister and burn under crackling skin. But she kept digging, listening to the cries of a man not too far from where she stood. He whined about being alive and how he wasn't meant to be in hell.

"This is a mistake!" he screamed.

Trudy knew better. His misery boosted morale for the Over Watchers. Allen especially got a good laugh from the man's cries and joined in, torturing him from time to time.

Trudy felt the burning aches from the work, and it made her want to scream. But with her mouth sewn shut, she couldn't complain if she tried.

"People don't realize that energy has to go somewhere. It doesn't dissipate when the body dies and decays, it is recycled, never fading. It's one of the many sparks that light up this universe." He sighed. His deep, monotone voice shook Trudy, making the ground move underneath her feet. Whenever he spoke, he impeded progress, making her lava hill fall over.

He went on. "There is something about your spark, Trudy."

She froze. She hadn't heard her name in what seemed like centuries.

"It sounds good, doesn't it? *Trudy Mona Lisa Gallagher*. Has a nice ring to it."

His voice swooned her mind, wrapping her in a forbidden nostalgia. "Your name feels good to say. *Trudy*," he hissed. "That name carried a lot of weight in your town. What was it called? Holloway?"

She groaned as the demon watched her. She cringed. His thin red lips curved into a smile with long, sharp, bloody teeth.

"The Master and I have been watching you. We know where you're from, and we think you can help us with a little project."

She dropped her head as memories of Holloway circled her mind, beckoning her to immerse in the past.

She saw Ulysses, and the last time she kissed him before he stepped into war. After she received his remains and laid him to rest, she locked herself up in his office at The Estate, where she broke down and gorged on his whiskey collection. That pain was helpless. It felt like the floor had been pulled from underneath her feet, pushing her into a pit of nothingness. She had no reason to live anymore. After weeks of binge drinking, she made a rash decision. Ulysses was gone, and she had to bear that in mind whenever she showed up at their home and his office. She sold The Estate and pursued their proposed endeavor for when he returned: saloons and alcohol.

"They took everything from you," Allen said. "Even your *lover*. That wasn't your war. That wasn't *his* war. But he answered the call to duty, all to die for another *man*. Men have always been a problem in your life. They're the reason you're dead now."

Her thoughts ventured to the day the noose choked her, ending her reign. She remembered what she said and how it felt to be betrayed by her family and town.

"You want that place back, don't you?"

She nodded.

"I know. It's attached to your soul, and so are the souls trapped there. You killed so many people in such a surprising way that their spirits stumbled over one another, clogging the Gate to the other side. They are stuck there now. You made a doorway to the spiritual world, ready for use. Are you listening to me, Trudy?"

She shook her head.

"You're going to get me into that hotel, and it will become a door to hell to which I have the honor of guarding."

Over Watchers aren't Gate Keepers, she thought.

"I am now, my dear Trudy. And that's all thanks to you."

He walked circles around her. "My intuition is spot on. Your soul is like a magnet, drawing us to you." A sinister chuckle. "Your pride is so overbearing, and your anger is searing, almost too hot for me to touch. It makes you the perfect morsel."

She didn't understand what he wanted, but she stayed still, waiting for him to find a point and reach it fast. Although they had an eternity to do so, she wasn't interested in spending it listening to Allen.

"How would you like to go back with me?"

284

She felt her brow drop. No one left hell unless they were commissioned, and even that was rare.

"I have it all set up, and once we get back, you can pick up where you left off. And don't worry, the people of Holloway wouldn't even recognize you."

Dreams of her lavish wardrobe and beautiful house rushed back. She basked in the sweet admiration she had gotten from men and women alike. Even without Ulysses, she accomplished more than any other woman she knew. The chance to start over pumped her full of optimism. She nodded hungrily.

"Wonderful. I'll take you back to your building, and you'll run your hotel like you always had. I think you'll be surprised to know that things aren't like they were when you died."

She nodded again.

"But there is a proposition and a few things I should cover."

She listened.

"You can run the hotel as you like, but when I speak, you are to follow my every command. I know best."

She nodded, hesitantly.

"You must be wondering about the project. Since you spilled blood on that ground out of pure hate and then died in retaliation on that very spot, it belongs to you. You are spiritually linked to that place. You died there last and made it over to this realm. The others are stuck, meaning they belong to that place, giving it loads of spiritual energy, all thanks to you. The energy there is enough to keep me and the Vessel linked, giving us an expanded outreach."

The Vessel?

"One of the Master's veins connecting straight to his heart, better known as hell. It's a complex system made of his flesh and blood. It starts in the deepest depths, or the core, and rises through the ranks of hell. It pierces through the different tiers of this place and through purgatory, a black void of uncertainty. It will end at the base of the Gate, or in this case, your hotel chock-full of spirits, lost in purgatory.

She nodded.

He grabbed her hand and pulled her along, lifting her feet from the ground with his hustle. They crossed through lava craters and walls of fire. They raced by clusters of burning souls, screaming for mercy as they tried to claw their way out of lava pools. A few climbed out, using the others as a stepping stool. Over Watchers shoved feet in their faces, kicking them back inside.

They quickly approached a fleshy red stalk protruding from the red clay ground. It rose high over them, entering a hole in the crimson ceiling.

"Grab it," Allen demanded. "You're going up first."

Trudy glared at the mess of veins that wiggled along the surface of the stalk. She grabbed it and fought the urge to draw back. Slimy and wet, the thin wormlike vine swarmed around her hand and wrist. She grimaced. It felt like tentacles trying to pull her in.

"Relax," Allen said. "It will not allow you to fall. But you need to climb, and don't stop until I tell you to. Now put your other hand up there."

She obeyed, allowing it to fasten her onto the stalk.

"Now, climb a few paces without letting go."

She did.

She faced the stalk and watched the vines cover her hands and climb up her arms. It smothered her in blood, or at least that's what it smelled like: burning iron.

"Now, find the trunk. It's in there somewhere. Once you do, use that to pull yourself up."

Reluctantly, she dug through the vines, snagging at pieces that snatched away from her grip. She found a vine that was as wide as a person and hugged it, pressing her body close to it.

"Now pull yourself up. All the other mess will clear the path once we move."

She pulled herself up and wrapped her legs around it. As Allen said, the thin vines cleared her path. Once her foot was off the red, molten clay, Allen latched onto the stalk just underneath her.

Before they hit the rocky ceiling, Allen yelled out, "Once we pass this plane, you are not allowed to acknowledge anything. Do not move your eyes from the stalk, or *they* will pull you down and keep you."

She nodded and passed the small opening in the ceiling.

They came up through a muddy forest floor. Trees covered every square inch around them. The thickness of the strange canopies made of thin twisted branches and yellow leaves her hand's size cast a thick shadow on the forest floor, making it impossible to see past the small opening made for the stalk.

"Keep climbing and don't look," Allen said.

She shuddered at the sounds of growling beasts mauling a helpless person who let out a blood-curdling scream. She didn't know where the person was or where the attack was happening, but it set fear in her gut, making her stir. Her throat trembled at the squelching sounds from nearby.

"If it makes you feel better, they'll wake up to outrun the beasts another day…for eternity."

That didn't make her feel better. In fact, she felt suffocated.

The next plane wasn't any easier. They came through a snowy floor and climbed through a plane made of ice blocks. The brisk winds attacked her bare body with frostbite, making it difficult to climb. The metallic sky covered the realm in a stormy gray gloom, and the icy air made it hard to breathe.

She peered at a group of souls chipping away at the ice block a mile or so past the stalk. They stood in an S-formation and swung pickaxes at the frozen block they stood on.

They'll never get through those… she thought. The blocks were as tall as skyscrapers and thick as a whale.

"You'd be surprised to hear when they started. Hm. I think it was about ten centuries ago? I'm not sure. I just know that it's breakable, and when it breaks, they'll fall into water that's so cold that it might as well be acid. Keep looking around, and you'll join them," Allen said.

In the last realm, wild winds kicked up red sand from the flat land and whipped it around. Dunes ate up the horizon and succumbed to violent tornadoes ripping them apart. Bolts of lightning crashed onto the land, shooting holes in the ground, burning it.

There weren't any souls. There was only a wasteland made of storms and ruby sand.

The stalk tilted as a dull red tornado full of planks and trees drew close.

"Hang on," Allen's voice. "But keep climbing."

She groaned as sand and debris snagged her torso, face, and arms. But she kept climbing on the tilting stalk until they reached the next plane.

Nothingness.

"Yes," Allen said. "This is the void, and it looks like we're almost home."

She peered up. The stalk burrowed through the bottom of a wooden base. She cringed. A house could've been falling on them.

"What a silly thought," Allen said.

They climbed for what seemed like a year. Her arms grew weary, ready to buckle as they approached the base.

"Oh, relax. We're almost there." He paused. "Although we are close to the material realm, this isn't exactly like it. Unlike the wasteland we just passed, this is much worse. It's nothingness, and it preys on everything that's *not* that."

Trudy dropped her brow and shook her head.

He snickered. "Oh, right. Separate your lips."

She pulled her lips apart, groaning as the sewn wires tore the piercings along her top and bottom lips. She shrieked and cried as pain tore through her face. She pushed heavy breaths through her opened mouth. "I—" she began, then fell into a coughing fit. Her dry mouth burned.

"You don't understand?" Allen asked. "The void is free of consciousness and spirituality and hunts down anything that *is*. It feeds on negative thoughts and guilt—it's a vulnerable place for the mind to wander. There aren't any distractions but fear. This is where the doors to hell are. Spirits that go to heaven get the light and the hand of God to usher them northbound. Souls who go to hell get to fall through the void or slide down the inside the Vessel. Lost souls get to stay here, lost in their own consciousness, or, in the case of the souls stuck in Gallagher Hotel, relive the shock that clogged the doorway to begin with." He looked up at her. "Since you've been to hell, it shouldn't be difficult for you to adjust to this place."

She wasn't adjusting. At that moment, she thought about the day she strapped bombs to the furniture, willing to destroy her own hotel just to destroy a group of men.

"And if you don't...you will, because this will not be the last time you cross over. I will do most of my work on this side, using souls of the damned to strengthen the Master's hold on this location. We will feed sinful spirits to the Vessel, strengthening it, getting it ready to move spirits from this realm to the next. Those souls will also serve as energy for me, as I died in the year 1282. It'll be a while before I'm strong enough to do my duties as the chauffeur or Gate Keeper."

"How do I fit into all this?" Trudy asked.

"This is your hotel, those spirits died by your hand, and your soul is still fresh. You can easily cross over and blend with the material world, providing a cover for our operations. On this side, you will be Trudy, the soul who emerged from hell. But, in the material realm, your name will be Brenda Scott, the current owner of Gallagher Hotel."

"How are we going to do that?"

"Keep quiet until she dies, and then come and let me in."

"How would I—"

"You'll know what to do. Now, close your eyes."

She closed her eyes.

"Don't forget, because even though you'll be in the material realm, your soul will fade if I'm not there with you." He said a few words in an unfamiliar language.

Trudy's body felt warm and contorted as she woke up in a small space. She moved her legs and twisted her torso. She rammed her elbows against the sac that encompassed her. But it held on tight, drowning her in a thick liquid. She tried opening her eyes, but it stung. She tried inhaling, but it ran down her nose and mouth like molasses, scratching flesh as it moved.

She heard voices on the other side, but they were muffled.

Trudy fought to break the sac open for what felt like forever, desperate to break free from the syrupy liquid.

***

The long, high-pitched droning noise changed into isolated short beeps.

"Oh my, God! Brenda? Are you there?" a woman's voice said.

Trudy opened her eyes. A woman with short dark hair sat on the end of the hospital bed, a huge smile on her wet face. Trudy slowly turned her head. Two little boys sat in chairs against the wall. The older boy, maybe around eleven, smiled big and rushed to her side. The little boy, about five, looked frightened as he balled up in his chair, pressing his back against the wall. Tears fell down his face as he watched her.

"What's the matter, Mike?" the woman asked. "Aunt Brenda is alright."

"But she *was* dead," Mike said.

"Ugh," the older boy said.

"Shut up, Frankie!" Mike quipped.

"Then stop being such a chump. She's not dead *anymore*."

"W—what happened to me?"

"You don't remember?" Debbie asked. "You lost your hair during chemo."

"What?" Trudy asked.

"Yeah, but that's alright," Debbie assured. "It's nothing that a wig can't handle. I'm just happy that you're alive!"

Dr. Yodel looked her over with astounded eyes. He listened to her heartbeat and checked her ears and mouth. She sat in the hospital for a couple days, allowing the doctor to pick and prod at her skin and mouth. He sent her down to radiology and made her, Debbie, and the kids wait around for her results on the second day.

He came back to her hospital room, a hand plastered on his head and a huge smile on his face.

"I—I pronounce you cancer-free," he said.

Debbie smiled big and hugged Trudy tight.

"Oh God! I prayed for this." She sobbed in Trudy's neck. "I prayed and prayed and... You're alive!"

Trudy glared at her feet. They were bigger than her size fives. She looked at her legs. A little peach fuzz, something she didn't condone back then. Trudy cleared her throat and looked down at her ivory hands. Her flat chest and small gut were unfamiliar. Her arms were wider than her original form. She felt her head and pulled back when she felt nothing but scalp.

"I've seen nothing like it," Dr. Yodel said. "The cancer metastasized and entered your immune system. It spread through your body like wildfire and shut down organs." He teared up. "Brenda, we lost you to a coma for three days. Based on your charts, you died for three seconds. But now…" He looked at his clipboard. "Now, there is no mass in either breast. Your blood work came back clean. You're the first person to be cured of metastatic breast cancer. Your case is research worthy!

"Brenda, I would like to send you down to see my friend down at the Detroit Medical Center, Dr. Maleena Lynn High. She's an excellent hematology oncologist who holds a MD/Ph.D. She's doing research on eradicating malignant tumors and slowing down metastasis of cancer cells. I think your case would help her research. Who knows how much funding she'll receive and how many lives a vaccine could save."

Trudy glared at the man. How could he ask her something like that? She couldn't care less about what he wanted. No. She was more interested in leaving that room and getting to what mattered most: Gallagher Hotel.

"No," she said.

"Brenda?! Why not?" Debbie asked.

"I want to go back to the hotel. I don't want to be here anymore," she said near a whisper.

Dr. Yodel's cheeks reddened. "Ms. Scott, I understand that you want to get back to your normal life, but I strongly suggest that you see Dr. High. She may want to monitor you for a while to make sure the disease doesn't come back."

"I *want* to go to the hotel now," she said.

Dr. Yodel nodded. "I'll get your discharge paperwork together and send you on your way." He headed for the door, then stopped. "I hope you change your mind. I'll leave her number with your paperwork."

Trudy scratched her arms as the itchy orange sweater scratched her skin as they rode the elevator to the first floor. She cursed Dr. Yodel under her breath as she sat in the mandatory wheelchair. The family stayed quiet in the elevator, just as Trudy wished.

As Debbie drove Trudy around in her minivan, she couldn't help but marvel at her town. The cars of 1990 looked so much better than the vehicles they pushed around in 1921. The buildings stood tall, made of bricks or siding. Street signs plastered every corner and street. People of different cultures mixed in groups as they laughed and talked, sporting jeans and t-shirts with pictures on them. Restaurants, laundromats, and grocery stores made up what used to be Saloon Alley, erasing the work she and her business partners put into that slab of land.

Women drove cars and wore pants and sweaters, tennis shoes, and strangely huge hairstyles. They wore wild colors on their faces for makeup, exaggerating their looks, almost fitting the image of a circus clown.

Debbie pulled up to the hotel. It didn't look the same as Trudy's original building. It was brick with an evergreen awning that bore the same name: Gallagher Hotel. It looked better than the wooden building she designed initially. It was smaller, and it didn't sit in the town square.

"Where is the town square?" Trudy asked.

"Town square?" Debbie asked. "You mean Times Square? It's in New York, silly."

The boys chuckled in the back seat.

Trudy rolled her eyes. "Who ran the hotel while I was in the hospital?"

"Well, you left it to me. I was still looking for a buyer, but I was too busy—"

"There's no need for that anymore."

"Are you sure? You don't at least want to rest for a while? You run a tight ship—your staff is on autopilot, taking care of everything until I—"

"I'm sure."

Trudy peered at the mansion. It sat on the corner of Holly Road and Bend Street. Businesses lined either side of the road, all brick and all with people running in and out, pulling up or driving away.

"Aunt Brenda, are you coming over for Pizza Friday?" Frankie asked.

Trudy looked over her shoulder at the boy. "Pizza night?"

He laughed. "Yeah. You love pizza night still, don't you? Your favorite is Italian sausage and green peppers. You don't remember?"

Trudy sighed. "I'm not interested."

He frowned.

She peered at Mike, who stared at her like she was the monster who lived underneath his bed. Then she turned to Debbie. "I'll be in touch," Trudy said before letting herself out.

She pushed through the honey-glazed wooden door and was welcomed by a house full of guests, sitting at every table.

"Brenda! Oh my God! Brenda, you—" The dark-haired woman wearing a frame-fitting all-black outfit rounded the hostess station and approached her. The name *Ellen* was stitched on her right breast. She looked a lot like Trudy had in her day. "Debbie called and told me about what happened. I'm so happy you're alright!"

"I would like to go to my office. Where is it?"

Ellen cocked her head and then smiled. "Uh, follow me."

The yellow attic was set up with hot pink chairs and a stark white desk. A wood-grained box sat on a glass cube across from the desk. Lava lamps sat atop the smaller glass cubes, and pictures of smiling Brenda plastered the walls. She had curly blonde hair before chemo and wore loud colors like royal blue jumpsuits and hot pink leggings. There were also pictures of Debbie and the boys.

"Are you sure you don't want to take some time off?" Ellen asked with worried eyes.

"No. I'm fine."

"Alright, well, it's almost noon," Ellen said. "Would you like your lunch and your stories? I'd do anything to keep you comfortable."

"Stories?"

Ellen smiled and went over to the wooden box. She pressed a button, and the dark glass front lit up. Moving pictures came into view.

Ellen rounded the desk and pulled out a furry white office chair. She smiled. "Relax, Brenda."

She went over to the chair and sat down, not moving her eyes from the box, or TV as she later found out it was called. "And you are the hostess?"

"Yeah. I'll bring you some water and your favorite from the menu: honey-glazed chicken breast with—"

"Find someone else to be hostess. I want you as my assistant."

"For real?" The girl cocked her head with a peculiar glare.

"Yes. Now go get the menu, financial records, employee ledger, and anything else I'll need. Oh, and if Debbie comes around, tell her I'm busy."

"Are you guys in a fight?"

"What?"

"I mean, Debbie's always up here with you. She's like your sister and your best friend. I'm sure whatever—"

"I'm not looking for suggestions for my personal relationships. I want you to do what I asked you to do. Understand?"

Ellen frowned and nodded. "Alright," she said. "And hey, I'm happy you're alright. We missed you around here."

Trudy waved the girl off and fixated on the screen. Actresses played many parts on the color TV. Commercials showed women playing sports and leading groundbreaking research. Women argued amongst politicians in DC and policed the streets of Holloway. They advertised their dental offices and owned fashion outlets. They were something in this new world, and that very fact fueled Trudy's enthusiasm.

The first step was getting her belongings back, especially those photos of Ulysses and the original furniture and clothes she preferred from her time. For weeks, she sent Ellen out to hunt those things down after Trudy sold Brenda's cottage.

They painted the walls white and replaced those loud colors with gold, beige, and oak.

Getting Allen over had fallen by the wayside until months later when she sat in front of a mirror she had bought for her attic office. She peered at it, proud of the silver.

Allen peered back, his red face with deep slits and eyelids peeled back over his black eyes. She jumped and moved back.

"Do it," he said.

"Do what?"

"Invite me in," he said.

"I don't know how… Do I just… Allen, come in?"

The house rumbled under her feet. The moon went dull behind the curtains, and a blaring red light grew intense behind the closet doors.

The doors opened, and Allen stepped out into the office. His small body looked frail and starved. His maw hung open as he spit out exasperated breaths. He stumbled to the floor.

"I need energy, and I need it now," he grumbled.

As demanded, Trudy picked up another project: finding food.

Allen reported the list of names, telling her they came from the Vessel. Trudy took that information and found those people living close by. She lured them to the hotel for an exclusive party with Ellen's help.

A carbon monoxide leak convinced everyone that their accidental deaths were just an unfortunate event, clearing the hotel of suspicion. But their souls served a different purpose: to strengthen the Vessel and to feed Allen.

Allen didn't disclose how long they'd have to carry out his orders before she could break free. Trudy didn't plan on waiting around to find out. She had another idea.

One of the people the Vessel wanted at the 1990 party, Shanna Taut, was perfect. She was from Madison Heights, a suburb outside Detroit, and she was much younger than Brenda. If she could help Shanna get out, Trudy could exorcise her.

Trudy searched for opportunities that night, waiting to get Shanna alone. But she never got the chance.

As Allen feasted on the damned, consuming their energy and transferring it over to the Vessel, Trudy steered clear, treading lightly until she found the opportunity to strike.

She closed her eyes, envisioning the woman from dinner. Fair skin. Green eyes. A small mole over her left eyebrow. And Shanna had to be alive; Trudy hadn't tasted her essence. With Shanna being the last woman standing, Trudy jumped at the chance. She needed to find her before Allen took her.

She climbed up to the attic and went into the closet. She approached the pedestal and flipped through *The Book of Death*. The words were gibberish, a language only demons would understand. Allen could read the whole thing front and back, whereas Trudy never cared to learn. But she didn't need to decipher the words or the accusations of the meals. She only cared about the images and the gory details that landed them there in the beginning. And just like self-important people, they showed up without so much as a question.

She scoffed. The word "exclusive" bore too much weight on people's decisions. But it wasn't her job to care.

It wasn't until she ran over Shanna's name when the plan came full circle.

Shanna was a woman of the night with a stash made up of stolen goods from her male victims and their dead bodies. Trudy's stomach turned as she reasoned quickly: they got what they deserved.

She had to move quickly, as the words on Shanna's page were filling with blood. Trudy pulled out a book of spells: A Wiccan bible. She flipped through to page seventeen and recited the passage:

Come through and let me in.

Come out and let me consume.

Let me take over, let me live in skin.

Roll in blood, wearing flesh.

Then, she ran her hand over Shanna's page, capturing her essence, filling up on her life, learning her history, and watching her death as it happened. She saw men tear Shanna's flesh on the ballroom floor, which transformed into a skeevy motel room.

A crippling shock pierced Trudy's body. She pulled her hand from *The Book of Death* and dropped the spells. She staggered over to the desk and planted a hand on the surface. She clutched her chest as her heart rammed into her rib cage, shooting cramps through her body. Her skin crawled and ached. It felt like sharp teeth tore into her, grazing her flesh. Blood ran up her throat and spewed from her mouth. She screamed as her insides burned, boiling underneath her skin, shooting sick impulses up her spine and down her extremities.

She fell belly down, screaming and begging the pain to stop.

Minutes dragged on before the pain subsided. She lay there on the floor, heaving, trying to catch her breath and some feeling in her body.

Footfalls made her close her eyes.

"Did you enjoy the show?" Allen asked.

She didn't respond. Instead, she breathed deeply, slowing her heart.

Allen swaggered over and crouched next to her. He ran his fingers through her wig.

"It didn't feel good, did it?"

She gave a stiff nod.

"Next time you try that, you'll be fully digested and become a part of the Vessel." He licked his lips with his serpent tongue. "Consider that a promise."

Chapter 23

Chris and Riley sat at the bar behind ball glasses full of whiskey. Chris gulped his down fast and watched Riley sip hers here and there. Sweat clung to her brow, sticking to hair that fell over her worried eyes. Her wrists shook as she watched her reflection in the mirror behind the shelves across from the bar's well selection.

She sobbed. "I don't understand why we didn't get to go home."

He didn't respond. He poured another glass and wondered if she wanted to finish hers.

"It doesn't seem to bother you. Aren't you afraid?" she asked.

He shrugged and reached over the bar. "Oh shit." He pulled the rum up. "They *do* have rum."

She shook her head at him. "Chris—"

"I belong here."

Her eyes widened. "Don't say that."

"It's the truth, Riley, and once you figure out what's happening around you, it'll go down easier." He gulped down his glass and opened the rum.

"Chris, I don't know why you think that. No one deserves to—"

He filled his glass. "You can stop lying now."

"Uh," she said. She slouched.

He drank his glass dry. "I—I saw what happened to Dr. Myles. And Dan and Natalie were…" He nodded wildly.

"They were shitty people." He filled his glass again, spilling over this time. "They all deserved what they got, and you know it. You couldn't stomach what you saw when you touched the book. You said it. You wondered *how* anyone could kill their own kid. Someone they *loved*." He teared up. "I belong here because I'm no different."

"I—I'm—"

His face grew hot as he rocked back and forth on his stool. He bit his balled fist, then slammed it on the bar surface. "I belong here! I—I got..." He grunted and buried his face in his hands. He hadn't faced that night since it happened. Now, the events resurfaced in his mind.

"I went home after work one night, and Carla, my ex, was waiting for me in my room. I was happy she came back after we'd broken up not too long before. Obviously, she came back around to the idea of us being a family, and that's all I wanted. I was going to be a good dad too. Nothing like mine. He—he liked fighting and got himself stabbed to death at the club when I was ten. I didn't want to be like that. I wanted to teach my son to fish and cook." He snickered. "Play video games and drive. I wanted everything for CJ.

"Anyway, she looked at me, and I got scared. Her face was covered in tears as she's crying and shit. I don't...I don't do well with crying women. I asked her what the problem was and she...she couldn't talk. It was like her jaw was locked and all she could do was cry.

"I was like, 'Carla, what's wrong? I can't help unless you tell me what the problem is.'

"Then she looked at her hands in her lap and started playing with her fingers. She always did that when she was nervous about stuff. She goes, 'I have to tell you something. *Swear* you won't get mad.'" He sighed. "I should've let her choke on the shit she was about to say. Shit. She'd still be there, and I probably wouldn't be here.

"'CJ's not yours.' She said that, and it felt like my world was taken away. Instead of walking out, I told her she was dead to me. Then I asked whose it was." A ball stuffed his throat. "Brian. It was Brian's. My roommate, my work partner. My *best friend*. He shoved his nasty dick inside my girlfriend and got her pregnant. Then she said, 'I don't love you anymore.' Now that is a good way to kick a man while he's down. Those famous words set something off inside me. I—" He swiped tears from his face and cleared his throat. The memory was so fresh. So new. He re-lived every heartbeat and clung to every word as he'd done before. But this time, he knocked denial away, seeing clearly into the past, and accepted each blow.

"I saw...I saw red. I grabbed her by her hair and pulled her to her feet. 'Get out my house then, nasty ass bitch!' I said that to her. She screamed and begged me to let her go, but I clutched tighter, almost dragging her toward the door. She shrilled at the top of her lungs about how much she hated me and how I should die. But at that moment, I wanted her to suffer. I wanted her to lose like I lost. I wanted her pain to be worse than mine.

"I dragged her into the kitchen and threw her down the stairs that led into the basement." He whistled. "Down the stairs she went. Watching her body chuck and slam into the steps and her head crack against the wall still wasn't satisfying enough. As I watched her rock on her side and bleed from the head, I still felt as if her loss didn't match mine. So I waited for Brian to show up."

He sipped his drink. "When he walked in the front door, he was shocked to see me sitting on the recliner with my pistol aimed at his face. I kept it simple—got straight to the point. I asked if he knocked her up. He said, yeah. I asked if he ever planned on telling me. He said, yeah. Then I told him she was lying at the bottom of the steps bleeding out of her head." Chris chuckled. "You should've seen his face. I have never seen the color drain from someone so fast. His face was so pale, it almost spooked me. He tried to explain as calmly as he could, which, I mean..." He shrugged. "That's just how Brian is, or *was*. He's dead as fuck now. I told him I was serious about people not taking shit from me right before I put three in his head.

"I dragged him to the basement and pulled him down the steps. Carla whimpered and yelped from her fall. She was still on the floor, holding her stomach. She screamed when I laid Brian next to her. 'How could you do this?' she asked. I didn't answer because I didn't feel like she needed an explanation. I pointed my gun at her and put one in her forehead.

"I called Uncle Jay, and he came by with the clean-up man. Since then, Brian and Carla have been reported missing. It's weird seeing their faces on the news. They've been on the top of everyone's minds. They're all wondering where Brian and Carla are. I don't know what the clean-up man did with them after we wrapped them in blankets and rugs, but I do know they're dead.

"It all happened so fast. One minute I was happy, then the next, my best friend and girlfriend ended up dead, pooling blood all over the living room floor, the kitchen, and the basement.

"Uncle Jay ordered me to move out that night and lie low in the apartment in his basement. I wasn't allowed to leave, so I sat there for three weeks. Somehow, the hotel sent the invitation to Uncle Jay's house for me, which pissed Uncle Jay off even more. He opened my mail, paranoid asshole. I told him it was a good working spot. He was worried about surveying but let it slide because, at that point, his mind was made up. Either I'd get caught out here, or he was putting me down when I left here." He scoffed. "He was already dealing with my mom lurking around his house looking for me, which was natural because she knew I always hung out with the two who were missing."

He frowned. "Uncle Jay and my gang plan on killing me in the morning. I overheard Uncle Jay talking to one of the guys in the Gang about it. He's been avoiding me, pretended to forget to give me food and water some days. I felt like a dog. It didn't take much to get him to drop me off up here because he knew it'd be the last thing I'd get to do.

"I regret what I did now, and I know I'm going to face it tonight right before this place ends me." He nodded. "I know. I know it's going to happen. Alright!" he shouted. "Alright, I deserve it. I did what I fucking did. I—I killed people I loved!"

His heart sank as he paused. He'd never see anyone anymore. "Mom had been calling me non-stop for weeks. She was excited about CJ, and Carla took that away from her, and I took Carla... I took Carla away from *him*." He crumbled and fell into tears.

Riley shot up from her seat and wrapped him in her arms. She held him with intense care, shushing him softly. "It's okay," she whispered. He clutched the sides of her shirt and wailed, begging the pain to subside. But it didn't. Images of Carla's body lying on the floor with blood pooling from her head and her arm wrapped around her belly haunted his mind.

"I deserve to be here," he said.

"It's okay," Riley cried.

He held onto her, finding a familiar warmth in her embrace. Her smooth voice calmed him. He broke away from the embrace. "Riley, I'm sorry you got sucked into this. You don't belong here."

Riley shook her head. "You don't know that, Chris."

Her frown caught him by surprise. "No. You're not like us. You're not…"

"Neil wasn't either. He was just a reporter digging up information about this hotel." She dropped her gaze to the bar. "I guess Allen was sick of him looking around."

"Yeah, but…you're better than Neil," he said.

"No, I'm not." She glared at him. "I've done my fair share of things." She looked down at her arm. She smiled at the tattoo of the weeping angel. "I know how it feels to lose someone. It hurts the worst when it's your own fault. It feels like your days will never be the same, and your life changes for the worst."

The light in the ballroom brightened behind him. He turned to see a dingy brown couch against a bruised white wall which sat across from a TV, and a bar separated the kitchen from the living room. The restaurant transformed into an apartment.

"I lost Steve a few years earlier," she said as she got up from her stool and eased her way over to the couch. A little boy, five or so, sat on the floor with a butterfly model. He picked up a stick and stuck white glue on it. He placed it carefully against the model.

"I was a single parent, so all I did was work, save, spend, and take care of my Nick. I didn't mind working two jobs because I was going to get Nick whatever he wanted and everything he needed. I was even saving up for our very first house. Things were going great until…"

She sat on the couch and watched Nick with a big smile. "I promised him we'd go chase moths before I went off to work that night. But first I needed a nap. I'd just gotten back from a ten-hour shift at the store. My mom typically watched him on those kinds of afternoons. She'd been a big help, visiting us every day. We spent a lot of time together when I wasn't at work. She almost seemed proud that Steve, my husband and Nick's father, died. But it's wicked to accuse your mother of something like that.

"I went into the bathroom and took two Norcos that I'd stashed. See, it took a year for me to recover from Steve's suicide, and those Norcos helped me sleep." She shook her head. "I didn't want to take them. With my marked-up history, I couldn't drag my parents through that again. I didn't want Nick to grow up knowing his mother chose drugs over him as his father had. I didn't want to seem like Steve, not even a little. But the fact was, my tolerance was way too high for sleeping pills, and I really needed to get to bed so I'd get up early enough to hang out with Nick.

"I laid down on the couch as they played, building his model. I remember how hard he smiled and how my mother, the successful doctor, asked him questions and took his lead. I dozed with a grin on my face. Then I heard Mom's phone ring. She shook me awake and told me she had to go. They were having complications down at the practice, and she had to leave; they needed her help with a delivery. I wanted to beg her to stay and watch Nick, but that would be against her virtues. She loved children and saving lives was a priority. But if she had known I couldn't stay awake, she would've taken Nick with her. I couldn't bring myself to tell her I took a couple Norcos. I was afraid of what she might do or what she might say, so I let her go and fought off sleep the best I could, concentrating on the zany cartoon characters or droning on to Nick about how much fun the park was going to be. He smiled and laughed, looking forward to it. I never fought so hard to keep my eyes open. I dozed and caught myself. Nick watched me; his sad face almost moved me to tears."

The boy stood and walked over to the couch. "Are you tired?" he asked her.

She nodded with tears in her eyes.

"Oh. Um. If you don't want to go out later, we don't have to. I don't really need to go to the park."

"We're still going, Nick," she said. "I just need to take a little nap, then I'll get up refreshed, and we can go add to your collection. We'll fill up the scrapbook and then go buy another one to fill."

The little boy smiled. "That'd be fun. But I want you to get some sleep, Momma. Your eyes are so *red*."

She sighed. "Alright," she said. "Just stay in here until I wake up. I don't want you getting lost."

They both laughed.

He pulled a white throw blanket from her feet and covered her. "Alright. Sleep tight," he said.

"Nick was mature for six. Mom always watched him during the day; I knew she taught him how to be safe and listen when someone told him something."

As Riley lay there on the couch, glaring at the boy through teary eyes, Nick rose from his spot on the floor and motioned for her. He pushed at her shoulder. "Momma," he said.

Riley sobbed and didn't answer.

"Momma, wake up. I'm hungry."

She wept.

Chris frowned. Gallagher struck with a low blow this time. He knew Riley wanted to move and respond to the boy. He could see it in her pained face as she lay on the couch, watching the boy beg her to wake up.

"She's stuck," Chris whispered to himself. "This has already…happened." Much like Dr. Myles, they obeyed their past, succumbing to whatever the apparitions wanted. But the apparitions weren't ghosts like the people that wandered the kitchen and ballroom; these were skeletons hidden deep in their closets.

"Momma, get up! I'm hungry," he said.

Riley parted her lips and asked, "What time is it, baby?"

He looked at the analog clock over the TV instead of the digital cable box sitting on the entertainment center's bottom shelf.

He counted aloud, "Five, ten, fifteen…" He counted on fingers, then reported, "Five seventeen."

"Just five more minutes," Riley said. "I dozed back off. All I asked for was five more minutes. Five more minutes to rest my eyes and dream up the next excuse I'd give him to let me lay down a little longer. I didn't think Nick was hungry. Mom fed him just before I showed up. I told myself I'd take him for ice cream once I pulled myself from the couch. I fell back to sleep."

She watched the boy huff and whine to himself. "I can make it myself," he said.

Riley shook her head. "Nick," she whispered. She only lay on the couch, mesmerized, caught in reliving a nightmare.

The boy trudged over to the kitchen and turned the knob on the stovetop. It hissed, mixing natural gas into the air.

He turned to the pantry and pulled it open. He grabbed a packet of noodles and set them on the counter. Then he went and grabbed a pot from the cabinet underneath the sink before heading back to the stovetop. He frowned. "Where's the fire?" he asked himself.

He glared at the pilot, then said, "Oh, I know what to do."

Nick sauntered over to the drawer next to the stove and pulled it out. He picked up a red lighter and flicked it until the fire came alive.

"No, Nick," Riley wailed as she shook, trying to break away from the couch. But she was stuck. Chris went to move his muscles but sat stiff, plastered to his stool, forced to relive another tragedy.

Nick put the flame against the pilot, and it erupted, shooting a small fireball upward. It disappeared.

"Ah," Nick yelped. A flame caught hold of his pajama sleeve. He waved it frantically. "Oh no, oh no," he yelled.

Smoke alarms went off.

Riley still couldn't move, she only watched.

The flame crawled down his shirt and latched onto his pants. He screamed, "Momma! Momma, get up! Help me!"

Chris watched Riley try to break free. She moved as if her limbs were heavy, paralyzed lumps.

"Get up, Riley!" Chris shouted. "You have to get up!" If she could move and regain control, she'd probably be able to live. "Get up! Don't let it control you. Save him!"

She moved and then shouted, "Oh my God! Nick!" She shot up from the couch as the boy fell to his knees and back against the counter. The fire engulfed the counter and spread to the stove.

She grabbed the throw blanket from the couch and ran for the boy. "Nick!" she shrilled.

Coughing and fighting to break through the fire, she threw the blanket over the boy.

Thuds at the door. "No!" she screamed. "No! I have to save him! I have to— Please don't take me away from him!" The flames took over the blanket, and a bloated fireball erupted, shooting from the room. Riley stumbled back and watched as her son broiled in an inferno.

Chris threw his arm over his face, shielding his nose from the fiery air. He looked down at his legs. He could move. And so could she.

As he made his way for Riley, the fire died out quickly.

He froze. He hoped he hadn't screwed up by walking into her event.

Riley hadn't turned to notice Chris either. She stared at the blackened rubble that used to be her kitchen.

"Riley," Chris said. He reached out for her, then stopped when he heard gravelly footsteps.

Nick stood at the kitchen doorway, watching his mom. His body was restored, unscathed by the fire.

"Do you miss me, Momma?" he said.

She nodded. "Every day."

"Then why don't you come with me? We can still go to the park and get ice cream. I've been waiting like you asked."

"I'm sorry. I'm so sorry about what happened to you. I should've saved you. *No.* It never should've happened."

The boy stepped toward her. "I'm not mad," he said. He raised his arms out. "I missed you, and I'm happy you're here with me."

"Riley, don't listen to him," Chris said. If he'd learned anything about Gallagher Hotel, it was that things weren't what they seemed.

"I was sad about what happened. I think about it every day. But I know you didn't mean to. You were only tired," Nick said.

"Riley, that's not Nick!"

"I'm so happy to see you," she cried, and she reached out to pull the boy in.

"Riley, no!" Chris shoved her, knocking her out the way. Before he could steady himself, arms wrapped around his waist, and flames ate through his torso.

Chris shrilled as pain ate him inside and out. He fell back as his skin scalded and melted from his bones. His body went up in flames, and smoke tightened his chest. A wall of fire engulfed his vision, making breathing impossible. He sucked down the blaze as it took him fully, choking on his screams.

Riley lay on the floor, weeping and screaming, probably sitting with the idea that she was alone.

Gallagher was killing him, taking him down with flames that weren't meant for him. As darkness ensued, Chris wondered if Mom was still looking for him, and if Carla and Brian would ever be found.

As he stopped trying to scream and let death take his soul, a white light broke through the jarring flames, pulling him loose, making him fly.

Chapter 24

Riley's thoughts came in the form of screams as she watched Chris go down. His burning corpse crackled and stiffened as his cries fell silent under the belligerent flames that ate him and Nick whole.

The inferno ate the room again, this time tearing through the carpet and taking Chris and Nick with it. She picked herself up when she realized she couldn't breathe. She ran for the window and peered past the rugged glass shards. The darkness outside stood still.

Sobbing, she ran to the staircase and looked up at the platform. Going upstairs was useless. It was all useless.

The fire tore through the bar, popping glass bottles and cups in its wake. She rushed through the ballroom, skin burning under its intense heat.

She burst through the double doors and rushed into the whiskey parlor.

This is it.

She slammed the door behind her and pressed her back against it.

It's over.

Panicked, she buried her face in her trembling hands.

There is no way out.

Thick gray smoke crept underneath the door. She coughed as the burning cloud made its way up her nostrils and down her throat. She stepped away from the door and watched the smoke invade her space. She backed away until the backs of her legs met the loveseat. She slid down and pressed her face against the plush rug, the only place where the air wasn't tainted.

Gallagher had won. It pulled her son inside and used him as a tool. If Nick had been alive, she wouldn't be there to begin with. Riddled in guilt, she only wept as she watched her oncoming demise: suffocation. Riley wailed and screamed before falling into a coughing fit. She pulled her collar over her mouth and nose, hoping the choking would stop.

She closed her eyes and saw Nick's smiling, playful face. Gallagher Hotel may have her trapped, but it didn't have dominion over her fondest memories of her son. She envisioned Nick as she'd known him on his best days. Not the way the hotel knew him, but in the way she experienced him.

Their last butterfly hunt ended fruitlessly at Tate Park, and Nick walked by her side, dragging his head and butterfly net. He pulled his Detroit Tigers hat from his head and slapped it against his thigh as he walked, frowning.

"Aw, cheer up, Button. We'll catch something next time," Riley said.

"I know. I just *really* wanted to add something to the scrapbook this time." He shrugged. "We don't know the next time we'll be able to come out here."

Riley sighed. "Nick, I bring you as much as I can. You know I work a lot, honey."

"Well, how come Grammy can't bring me?"

She stopped her pace up the thin dirt trail and put her hand on his shoulder. "Well, it's something we do together. You know I look forward to hanging out with you, right? This is *our* thing."

"Yeah, alright," he said, gazing at her with those famous puppy dog eyes.

She stepped in front of him and crouched. "How about this? I'll make it to where we come out looking for butterflies twice a week, and on some days we can get ice cream. How does that sound?"

He smiled. "Okay, Momma. You're on." He fell into her arms and embraced her. She returned his hug and planted a kiss on his forehead.

Once she pulled away and continued walking next to him, he looked up at her and said, "Why do you work so much?"

It broke her heart to hear him ask that. But, as usual, she approached him with clarity and told the truth. "I have to work to take care of us."

"I know, but you *live* at work. I see Grammy more than I see you. You're always sleeping or going to work. I really miss you, Momma."

"I'm not going anywhere, Nick. And I promise that after this summer, I'll quit one of my jobs and replace it with a part-time one. How does that sound?" Riley was close to getting her down payment all saved up for the house. The winter would be a good time to lie low and spend more time with her son. The exciting idea put a smile on her face.

"Alright!" he said as he hugged her legs, nearly taking her down.

"Nick!" she laughed, catching her footing.

"Thank you," he said. As she watched his big gap-toothed smile, her heart filled with joy and pride. He turned out to be such a sweet and courteous little boy. Even without his father, Nick was more than decent; he was perfect.

"Keep that up, and we might stop for ice cream on the way home. I'm getting double chocolate with peanut butter cups."

"Me too. But I'm adding chocolate syrup! I love you, Momma. Now race me!"

Nick took off up the path and she ran behind him, headed for the car.

They hadn't planned on going to the park much after that. Life had gotten in the way, and Riley needed to keep her job at the PJ Saxx. Nick understood that, so he never complained. He settled for the models she brought home for him. The day he died was the first day they'd planned on going to the park in two months.

The smoke grew thin and eventually stopped pouring in underneath the door. Riley stayed there on the floor.

A lot of people showed up to the funeral, even Dad, who'd aged considerably since the last time she'd seen him. Her parents sat in the back pew, watching as everyone cried over the closed casket.

After they buried him, Riley approached Mom at the graveyard. They hadn't spoken since the night Nick died.

"Thank—" Riley began before Mom struck her across the cheek with an open hand. Riley held her stinging cheek as others gasped at the violent gesture.

"How could you let this happen?" Mom asked under her hushed sobs.

"I—"

She put a stiff hand up to Riley. Riley flinched, ready for it to come down hard on the other cheek this time. "I'll see that they put you in jail for this. You killed my grandson because of *drugs*." Mom narrowed her eyes. "You just couldn't stay straight, could you? After all I've done for you? All the time I've spent with you? All the things we've— I can't even look at you!"

"Mom, it was—"

"No more, Riley! No more! They're investigating, and they plan on getting you for neglect. And you know what? I support it. I *advocate* it."

Her heart dropped to the ground, and tears of sorrow and fear mixed in on her face.

"I tried to help you, Riley, but you're a disappointment. From your drug problem to marrying a man who killed himself because he wasn't man enough to begin with. And then *this*? You let your drug addiction kill your only child. You are a real piece of work, and I wish that was you lying in there." She pointed to Nick's tombstone.

Mom's words stabbed like a knife. Riley hadn't felt so much like a failure until that moment.

"I tried to help you, Riley! After Steve died, I told you to move back with me and Frank. You would've had an entire section of the house for you and Nick! Rent-free! You wouldn't have had to work so hard. But *no*. You had to prove your point; you made things hard on yourself!"

"I—I—"

"You are a failure as a woman, and I hope they bury you underneath the jail for what you did to my grandson. You should've died in that apartment."

At that moment, Riley wished her neighbor hadn't bothered bursting in and dragging her from Nick as she tried to save him. Mr. Bent held onto her, stopping her from running back into the burning building.

She wasn't charged for Nick's death; it was ruled as an accident. But the fallout felt like she was sentenced to life in prison. Her parents became estranged, leaving Riley alone. Depression ate her up, making it impossible to leave the bed in her studio apartment. She'd dream of suicide and then reasoned that Nick wouldn't want that for her. Lost, she couldn't break herself from blame. Alone, she couldn't think straight.

She needed help.

It wasn't until she received something in the mail about a new church they built a few blocks up when she decided on her steps toward recovery.

We offer free counseling to the community. Come one and all and praise God with us, it read. The light blue flyer had the address written over fluffy white clouds.

Her parents raised her with their atheist beliefs, pushing the thought of connecting with God from her mind. But the idea of Nick frolicking in heaven gave her the strength to move on and get closer with God.

She left her studio for the first time in weeks and headed for the newly constructed church. The building was as small as a schoolhouse. The white-bricked building had mosaic windows with Jesus' face and arms outstretched, welcoming all to pray with them. The lawn reached up to the road with a dirt patch on either side. The signs on the white picket gates around the plots read, *Community Garden, coming soon.*

Riley pushed through the glass door, letting herself in. She glanced around the empty foyer, and proceeded through a second set of wooden doors, which led into an open area.

Rows of pews lined the open area with a stage set up just before them. Three people stood in front of the first row, laughing and talking.

"I know! I think the bake sale will raise more than enough money for the sound system. That way, we can record and post our sessions on the internet," the young, tanned man said.

"You know what, AJ? I like how you think," a thin black woman with short hair replied.

"AJ is the best maintenance man all around. I can't thank you enough for all your help," a pale older man said. Based on his attire, Riley could tell he was the pastor.

"Well, I have to thank you for giving me a job. It's been difficult since I've been out of prison. I never thought a possession charge would ruin my entire life. God can forgive you, and you can forgive yourself, but it doesn't mean your brothers and sisters will."

"I think it's a blessing in disguise because it brought you to us. You don't have to worry about any of that anymore. We got you covered."

"Thanks, Pastor Miller," AJ said.

"I also have a list of other churches and temples in the area in need of your help. They already agreed to meet with you," the black woman said.

AJ laughed. "Really? I can't thank you guys enough. I always wanted to start my own business. I—" He turned his head and saw Riley approaching them.

Embarrassed, she felt her face turn red. She wore a dingy pair of jogging pants and a holey jean jacket over a white t-shirt. She hadn't bothered washing her hair or taking a shower. As soon as she pulled herself from the bed, she threw her clothes on and rushed out the door before she could change her mind about visiting the church.

"Hi," the pastor said. "Thanks for stopping in." He slowly approached her. "I'm Pastor Henry Miller, and that's Dr. Wanda Phillips—"

"Call me Wanda, honey," the black woman said.

"Yes, and that's Albert Willis, or AJ for short."

AJ waved and smiled at her.

"Mass isn't until tomorrow morning at eight, but feel free to hang out as long as you want. The doors are always open."

Riley teared up as she tried to find the words to explain her visit. "Counseling. Do you still offer counseling?"

"Yes," Wanda said. "Follow me."

She led Riley back to one of the offices by the stage. She felt eyes on her as she followed close behind Wanda.

They entered a wood-paneled office with boxes stacked high and two file cabinets open and empty. A wooden desk sat in the center of the room with two chairs on one side.

"Sorry about the mess. I just moved in here today."

"Counselling is free, right?" Riley asked.

"Of course."

They sat in the chairs. "So, Riley, what brings you in today?"

"I—I—" She wept.

"It's alright, sweetheart. There's nothing that God can't do, including wiping away your sorrows."

"I—I lost my son about a month ago," Riley said.

"I'm so very sorry to hear that," Wanda said. She grabbed Riley's hand and squeezed with a worry deep in her brown eyes. "My deepest condolences."

Riley pushed out exasperated breaths as the weight lifted from her spirit. "It—it was my fault. I slept while he burned to death. I—I killed my Nick!"

Wanda watched her, her look of concern never fading. "Do you want to tell me what happened?"

Riley nodded and told Wanda what happened.

"Riley, that's not your fault. It was an accident. A devastating, horrible accident. I know you're not proud of what happened, but you should be happy that you decided not to allow it to define you as a woman. You're doing something about the situation by seeking help during this hard time. And you know what? I'm here for you. We all are. I understand your family turned on you, but we will never do that. You can find solace here in this beautiful place of worship. You don't even need to attend service. You can come and talk to me or Pastor Miller whenever you need to. We will always be here for you. As a matter of fact..." Wanda stood up and circled her desk. She pulled the drawer open and handed Riley a card. "There is the number for this office, the office at my private practice, and my cell. You can call me anytime."

From that day on, Riley became a devoted member at New Bethel, attending Bible study and mass three times a week. She made new friends and started hanging out with AJ, who she fell for. But no matter how much she liked him, she kept to her new set of virtues: a relationship with the Almighty God and adopting a child to raise on her own.

Through her time at church and with AJ, she got right with God, but she never found the courage to speak to Nick like she had that day she sat with Wanda. She struggled to replace what happened to him with her new life and still cried for him some nights.

She pictured Nick as he was before that treacherous day. Seeing his round face and exchanging his excited banter always made her smile. His kind words and inquisitive mind impressed her with every conversation. His understanding and compassionate thoughts on moths and butterflies radiated through his big gap-toothed smile. He was her kind, sweet child, and she couldn't keep him alive long enough for him to grow up and go through puberty, get into his first fight, or fall in love for the first time. Nick was perfect, extraordinary, and nothing like Steve or Riley. He was better in every way.

Her body relaxed, letting go of the tense feelings of uncertainty and fear as she lay there in the parlor. Nick was a wonderful kid, and she was happy to know him and lucky he was in her life for that short time.

Gallagher Hotel tried and almost won her over, but as she thought of her son, some things came to mind that fed into her growing hatred for the place.

That thing that killed Chris *wasn't* her son. She felt it in her bones as she watched the back of the door. It was a demon sent to replicate a perfect being. She'd watched the serpent try to trick her into a fiery embrace taken up by poor Chris, who tried to warn her.

It had tricked her and cost another life.

Nick wouldn't have done that.

It tried dragging her into this house of sin and death, trying to trap her forever.

Nick would never do that.

It tried to make her feel more guilt and crumble in the hands of an imposter that was a dead-on replica but lacked a fulfilling life and love Nick passed on to anyone he'd met.

Nick was gone, not stuck in Holloway. Not trapped in Gallagher Hotel.

Riley sat up and leaned against the back of the loveseat. For a second, Gallagher had her. It had won, putting Nick in her face, wearing the same thing he wore that day and carrying the same conversations they'd had. Her apartment was spot on, a replica of a place that bore the worst memory of all.

But no more. Nick would not want that. He would want his mommy to survive. She shook her head. Part of her wanted to get up and keep looking around for a way out. But where could she go? She was trapped inside and out.

She dropped her head.

The hotel had won, keeping her there as the last woman standing. *Am I already dead?*

She glared around the room. That was it. The last thing she'd see until…

It didn't matter. She deserved it for allowing the light of a beautiful person to blow out too early.

She froze when she saw something flutter about, around the door. She squinted, trying to get a clear view of the thing. The shadow of a butterfly flapped its wings hard as it flew around like a fly desperate to get on the other side of a window.

She went wide-eyed and covered her mouth with her hand. The butterfly's shadow stopped and rested on the doorknob.

Her heart dropped. She'd gotten good with God, and her spirit was cleansed and new, giving her the strength to carry on with new plans. But she avoided the person who deserved her apologies and newness.

She watched the butterfly and felt her chest cave as she started in on an overdue conversation.

"I'm sorry, Nick," she said. "I feel horrible about how it ended, and I take—I—"

She sucked in a deep breath and expelled the air through pursed lips. "You can do this, Riley. You can do it," she whispered.

"Sometimes, I think of you, and I remember how cursed I might be, and how AJ would be better off without me. Everyone is better off without me because I failed at something that women are born to succeed at."

She wept. "I—I tried so hard to take care of you. I was always so tired. But I thought if I worked hard for it, then it'd all be okay. But it's not okay when I lose the one person I worked so hard for. I'm not good for anyone. Your grandfather says it all the time. He said that I make stupid decisions and allow wishful thinking to be my guide. I messed up. I got so caught up in proving I could take care of you without Steve that I lost sight of the other possibilities that would've made our lives easier."

She drove her hands down her face, making room for more tears to soak her cheeks.

"I'll never be able to make things right, and if I'm dead, I hate the fact that I can't find you now. But know this... I—I fucked up! You're gone because of me, and there's nothing I can do to bring you back.

"When I saw you fall in the flames, I wanted to die. I wanted to die *right* there next to you, but Mr. Bent from next door burst in and dragged me out. He pulled me from you and...and I hated him. I hated him for so long for that, and I spent a lot of nights cursing his name and crying for you. I hoped you would come back, or at least I could see you in my dreams, but you never came. I guess I was too scared to see you again because I was still living, and I had to get better. I had to... Oh *God*. No one should outlive their child.

"I'll never forget what you looked like and what your voice sounded like, or that thing you used to do when you scrunched up your face when you didn't get your way. You did that that day when I asked for five more minutes." She snickered. "That thing in the ballroom didn't do that. That thing...that snake that killed Chris...that...that wasn't you. You would never harm anyone. You would never make me feel guilty."

She peered at her tattoo, then back at the doorknob. The shadow hadn't moved.

"Nick, I love you, and I wish you were here. I wish every morning and night that I could pull you outta bed and tuck you in. But you're in a better place now, and all I can ask for is your forgiveness for what happened."

The butterfly took off from the doorknob and made its way across the room. It lingered around the photo of Ulysses and landed on top of the golden frame.

She picked herself up from the floor and went over to the portrait. Ulysses glared off into the distance as he did in most of his photos. He looked like a man who entertained the idea of a massive photoshoot, not one who wanted to be in one. That was something a woman might love though. She often pictured herself and Steve becoming successful and plastering portraits and pictures of themselves all over their huge house.

Riley peered around. There weren't any photos of Trudy anywhere. She built the place for her husband, Neil had mentioned. Looking around, she remembered thinking the hotel was a sick memory of someone truly obsessed rather than just paying homage. But why would Brenda want so many pictures of this man in her hotel? He died almost a century ago. Two or possibly three portraits were enough for a memorial of the ill-fated owner's husband.

"I guess I should've asked Brenda about that."

She cocked her head.

Brenda. The owner. The woman who prided herself on the hotel and loved its history.

Riley hadn't seen her since dinner.

Is she here?

If she was, Riley hoped she was still taking questions.

Chapter 25

Riley pulled the door open and glanced back at the butterfly that rested on Ulysses' portrait.

"I love you, Nick," she whispered as she made her way into the hallway.

"Brenda!" she yelled as she trudged through the double doors leading into the ballroom. The ballroom was as it was before the fire broke out and tore through the replica of her old apartment. Everything was neat except for the broken window.

"Brenda!" she cried.

Riley rushed through the foyer and up to the staircase, then stopped. She's been up as far as the attic, and Brenda was nowhere to be found. Guests took all the rooms, so she didn't have a room either.

Riley turned and went back through the ballroom, headed for the basement. Chris said he hadn't seen the vines down there.

But he also didn't know about them, so why would he look? she thought.

As she made her way for the double doors, she kicked something and sent it skittering across the floor. She looked down and saw it was Chris's pocketknife. She picked it up and glared at the bloody blade.

"Thank you," she whispered. She folded the keepsake and shoved it in her pocket before going for the basement door.

She pulled the door open and sighed a bit of relief. A dim light lit up the hallway. She took one step down, then stopped.

"Brenda?" she said. Nothing answered back.

Slowly, she stepped down the staircase, carrying herself down into the unknown.

"Brenda, you down here?" she asked as she walked up the narrow hallway toward the dark opening at the end. A door stood on either side of the hallway. There weren't any portraits or statues. No fancy furniture or rugs. Just the cement floor and light gray walls.

"Brenda!" she shouted as her hopes faded. Maybe the woman wasn't there.

The door to the left opened slowly.

"I'm in here, dear," someone answered back.

Riley's heart pounded as she trudged for the opening and stepped inside a museum of Ulysses. Portraits and liquor lined the mahogany walls. Suede couches and lavish rugs made up the fancy room floor.

A woman wearing a long lilac silk dress sat on the loveseat. Her long brown hair flowed over her shoulders as she raised her glass full of brown liquor.

"Riley, you made it," she said. "I hope you know that I've been rooting for you all night. I never left your side."

Riley narrowed her eyes at the familiar face. She struggled, trying to place her. "Who—are you?" she asked gruffly. "Where's Brenda?"

"Brenda?" she laughed. "Oh, where are my manners? You may want to take a seat for this." She rose from the couch and headed for a silver vanity. She picked up the bottle of whiskey. "Would you like a drink?"

"Answer me," Riley demanded as she stayed by the door.

The woman sighed and crossed her thin arms over her flat belly. She leaned against the vanity. "I'm the one that everyone forgets about," she said through a chuckle. She sauntered over to the loveseat.

Riley looked her up and down again. Then she saw the portrait of Ulysses over the fireplace, sitting on a couch—the replica of the one across from the fireplace. "Trudy?"

"Yes."

"What are you doing here?"

She put her hands out. "This is my home. It's *always* been my home."

Riley narrowed her eyes at the woman, not to look dismayed, but to be sure her eyes weren't playing with her head. "Why would you want to be here?"

"Why would I want to leave something that is of my own creation?"

"Because the people you killed are still here."

Trudy shrugged. "It's their own fault they're still stuck here. Hell, it's some of their faults that they died here to begin with."

Riley shook her head. "This— I don't—"

"Don't overthink it, Riley. It isn't becoming of you." She sipped her glass and smirked after bringing it down to her thigh. "Worry ages the skin."

"So, you've been trapped here all this time?"

"No. Only over the last thirty years, but who's keeping tally?" She looked Riley up and down. "Gosh, even with those pregnant bags under your eyes, you are still a beautiful girl. You should be proud of that."

Riley drew her head back, unsure of how to entertain Trudy's strange comment. "Where's Brenda?"

"Dead since 1990."

"So, you...you exorcised her somehow?"

Trudy raised a brow. "Did you enjoy your stay at the hotel? I sure enjoyed having you here."

Riley moved closer to Trudy, stopping just on the other side of the loveseat. "I watched people die here. I saw their sins. I— What is this place?"

"A construction site."

Riley pressed the backs of her teeth together. "Elaborate...please."

"The hotel is trapped in nothingness, a realm called the Void. Some people might refer to it as purgatory. When a devastating incident wipes out a group of people, they clog the door to the spiritual worlds, sticking them in purgatory. Their devastation stops them from moving on. It'll take all of them to realize that they are dead before they can move on. This place is full of spirits, making it the perfect place to make another gate to hell. Attached to this place is one of Satan's veins, or the Vessel. It'll be used to shuttle spirits down to hell. But it isn't ready yet; it's still new. It requires souls of the damned to strengthen its hold on this place. Think of those spirits as a fresh coat of paint for the inside of the Vessel, and believe it or not, since this place is so close to the material realm, it weakens Satan and his soul-sucking servant, Allen."

"W—what?"

"Yes. Allen feeds off the energy from the Vessel. Without it, he's nothing but a brittle bag of bones."

Riley's eyes widened. "So, it's using the souls that died those horrible deaths here?"

"Yeah— Well...not all of them. Me being the owner and the cause of this mess, Allen linked himself to me. I taste the blood of the spirits in the Vessel. I didn't taste Neil or Chris. I have a feeling they went the other way." She pointed to the ceiling.

Riley stared at the senseless woman. She felt like she'd had the place figured out. Unfortunately, talking to Trudy made Riley unlearn everything she thought she knew. A cold sweat broke out across her brow.

"Oh, but, Riley, you don't have to worry about any of this. I'm going to get us out of here."

Riley wanted to be elated about the news. But she couldn't break the feeling that Trudy was untrustworthy. "Us?"

"Yes. You don't think I want to be here, do you? I hate being stuck here under Allen. You've met him. Imagine *living* with him."

"How are you going to get us out of here?"

"You sure you don't want a drink? You look like you could use one."

"Trudy, how?"

"What does it matter? All that should matter is that we're getting out of here. You don't have to be afraid anymore. You don't have to keep running from those thoughts anymore either. You're free. *We're* free."

"But you're dead. You hung a long time ago. You don't belong over there."

"Silly little girl." Trudy scoffed. "I'm more alive than you've been in a long time."

Trudy walked over to the vanity and filled her glass. "Have you ever thought about hell, Riley? Not the way the pastor describes or how those TV shows or movies depict it, but the realness... Have you ever thought about it?"

"Everyone has," she said.

Trudy went back to the couch and sat. Riley inched closer.

"After my neck broke, flashes of my life's events passed by my eyes. I saw the day Mary taught me to walk and the day I tasted my first roast beef *froid* and spat it up. I re-lived the day I lost both parents in a train accident and saw the day I hit puberty and became a woman. I remembered when Joey Patterson asked me out on my first date to the lake. I felt his lips press against mine, and it felt warm all over again." She ran her fingers over her lip. "I saw my Ulysses as he got on one knee and proposed. I saw the hotel built, and the money flowing across my imported white tiger rug. I saw it all and *felt* it all, everything that made me Trudy Mona Lisa Gallagher. Then I fell through the dark, screaming as the wind pushed my skin back and the blackness pulled me down like a magnet to metal."

Trudy gulped, and her wrists trembled. "After what seemed like a lifetime, I saw a small orange pool glowing and growing as I fell. I belly-flopped into the frothing sea of molten rock and shrieked as I tried to swim out. The thick air stabbed at my throat like flying, burning glass shards. I tried to scream as if it would ease the pain. Instead, I was yanked up by the arms and thrown down onto the blistering hot cobblestone. Someone drooled acid on my skin as a pair of scaly hands stuck a needle through my lips and pulled a wire through my skin, sewing my mouth shut.

"Then I was shoved, free-falling deeper than I was before. I landed on a bed of jagged rocks and felt my blood run dry. I remember smiling inside, hoping this was over, and I'd stay in that darkness forever. But I woke up to a skin-splitting strike on my back. Allen yelled at me to get to work. But I wondered if he'd noticed the bubbling blisters bursting all over my body. I wondered if he heard my crackling and breaking joints that never seemed to crumble as I stood on my two feet. I wondered if he cared about my pain. The searing aches. The endless strikes of anguish. Then I realized where I was... I realized Allen didn't care about how I felt. I realized I landed somewhere...somewhere I never thought I'd end up. And honestly, I didn't think it existed. But it turns out that it's the *most* energized place in the universe. Forever awake. Forever feeling. Forever dreadful. It's grief and treachery. Sorrow and hopelessness." She dropped her head. "I lived in the most damned place in the universe for decades, digging and listening. Burning and weeping."

She smiled. "That sweet blackness of death doesn't exist. Your spirit keeps going. It keeps living and wandering, looking for somewhere to exist. But after some time, and thanks to the things I did when I was alive, I made the right friends and ended up here, and now, we can get out of here together."

"Why did I and the others end up here? How'd Allen know who to feed to himself and the Vessel?" Riley asked.

335

Trudy chuckled. "Well, the Vessel wants what it wants. It tells Allen whose souls are best suited for the construction and for him. They need them to keep a tight hold onto this realm until the Gate is ready to usher souls through—I mean, that'll generate enough energy for ages. But until then, Allen needs to feed the Vessel, and whenever a soul is devoured, their essence is recorded in *The Book of Death*. The book is the answer... It ties the two realms together."

"That doesn't—"

"Explain why you and Neil weren't in there? Good observation, Riley. That's because the Vessel didn't want you or Neil. Allen was so tired of Neil's curiosity. He was afraid that one day Neil and Liza would find what they were looking for and spill the beans, bringing too much attention to Allen's operation. Liza stumbled into the attic after she was forbidden to go up there. The Vessel is so powerful that it radiates energy across the realms sometimes, especially when it's feeding time, or it's recording an entry into the book. Needless to say, she is enjoying the view at the bottom of a shallow grave. And Neil, well, I can say it's not something you care to relive."

Riley turned her head. Images of his face being bitten off made her stomach turn. It was truly something she wished to un-see.

"And you, Riley? Well, I invited you. You're perfect. You're beautiful. Lively. I would love to be someone like you."

"You—you did this to me? You brought me here because you want to..." Riley's eyes widened. "You were a disgrace of a woman. You killed people because they didn't get you what you wanted, and now you think you're going to take me like you took Brenda?"

336

"You want to see your son again, don't you?"

"W—what?"

"You heard me. You do want to be with Nick again, right? I know everything about you. When I pulled up information about Bruce, I saw a picture of you and him working an event together on your company's website. You looked beautiful and young, and that short-sleeved uniform looked nice on your slim frame. But what really drew me to you was that tattoo on your arm: the weeping angel with a child's birth and death date. I did more research on you and found out about what happened at your apartment that day. You don't have any social media accounts, but your picture and name are plastered all over New Bethel Baptist Church's website. You're all over the events page. I knew Allen would have a hard time with someone as strong and spiritual as you. You are his kryptonite, Riley. You're a perfect candidate."

"I—I—" Thoughts collided, clouding her judgment. She wanted out of Gallagher Hotel more than Trudy knew. The added chance of leaving and going home to Nick was the best deal anyone had made for her. She'd get to see him again, and AJ would get to move on and find someone who wanted a family with him. It was the best decision. But the idea of Trudy taking her body to do damage in this world nagged at Riley.

"No," Riley said, shaking her head. "I won't let you do it.

Trudy scoffed. "Oh, come on, Riley. Don't you want to see your little boy again?"

"Don't say that. Don't even think about him or say his name!" Riley shouted. "I'd rather be stuck here than release you out into the world."

Trudy shook her head. "Don't say things like that."

"No, Trudy! My mind is made up. I will not let you ruin anyone else," Riley said.

"Ruin anyone else? I'm trying to help you. I know you've been through a lot. You dropped out of school, married an addict, and then lost him *and* your son. Your parents hate you."

Riley's nostrils flared. "And? Your point?"

"You never got the chance to live, Riley. You were always worried about someone else's thoughts or feelings. You've navigated your life around what they needed and expected of you. I can help you change that. I can release you and send you to the only person who ever cared about you. All you have to do is let me in, and it'll be all over."

Riley shook her head and backed away, headed for the door.

"I can tell you don't trust me, and that's fine. I can start by saying that I'm not a murderer, alright? I just wanted something harmless, and people got in my way. Yes, I was mad. But I'm past it."

"The people in the ballroom might think differently."

"Honey, that's old news. They linger around the Gate because they can't forgive themselves for dying. I made this place. Those fires. Deaths. But I didn't know that I created the ball and chain that clings me so tightly to this place. This spot. This land is soaked and nurtured in the blood of the greedy. I created the breeding ground. The door to hell slung inward, pulling me inside and using me to help create a bigger opening, welcoming whoever inside, pride and greed leading the way! I accept that, but it's all over now. I want out. You want out. Let's help each other."

"Trudy, you are evil. Do you understand that? You belong where you've ended up. Me? I got another chance at living, and if that's all used up, that's fine. I'm okay with that. But there is no way I'll let you take me like you took Brenda."

"Oh, is that so?"

"You'll have to *kill* me first."

Trudy rose from the couch. "It doesn't work that way, Riley."

"It won't work at all because you're not welcome."

"Don't say that." Trudy approached, taking a sip from her ball glass.

"I know you aren't good with bad news, but you're going to hear this. You are not taking me, demon. You belong in hell, and you need to make your way back there because no one wants you here."

"Don't call me that," Trudy grunted through clenched teeth.

"But that's what you are. You were a demon when you were alive, and you're a demon now."

"That's enough! You know, I didn't think you, of all people, would give me a hard time. Chris, maybe, but you? We women need to stick together. You can help me get out of here and live the life that was stolen from me, and I…I'll give to God. You'll have your son back."

Riley straightened her back as they stood toe to toe. "No. I'm not interested in what you have to give. In fact, I want you as far away from me as possible."

Trudy snickered. "It doesn't work that way either. You don't have a choice."

Trudy slammed the glass into Riley's cheek, sending her over and down to the floor. The deep cuts stung, and blood spilled from the torn skin. Riley screamed and spun around on her back. Trudy charged her and went to grab Riley's neck with her bloodied hand, but Riley caught it. She pushed it up as Trudy pushed down. She kicked Trudy in the knee, snapping it in half.

Trudy screamed and fell onto the floor. Her wig slid off, unearthing a burnt, cracked skull.

Riley clawed at the rug, trying to grab her footing. Trudy grabbed her ankle and pulled it back, sending Riley belly-flopping onto the floor. She yelped as Trudy pulled and wrapped an arm around Riley's throat and pressed hard.

Riley reached back and clawed at Trudy's face. Her fingers slid down sleek skin and picked up a powdery foundation. Riley swung, catching Trudy in the eye and cheek.

Trudy squeezed tighter, pushing Riley to gag.

"No one tells me what I can't have!" Trudy yelled in Riley's ear. "Now lie still!"

"No!" Riley croaked.

"Come through and let me in. Come out and let me consume," Trudy said.

Riley's arms went weak, slowing her swinging. She gasped for air as flashes crossed her sight. Heat blasted her face as her heart slammed against her chest. A low whir sounded in her ears.

"Let me take over, let me live in skin," Trudy said.

This is it, Riley thought as her hands clutched the rug.

"Roll in blood, wearing flesh."

Riley's limbs went numb as memories rolled over her mind. Her first words to Dad. Her first time on the honor roll. The day she went off to college.

"Let me in, Riley."

She saw Nick's face as she held him in her arms the day he was born. He opened his eyes for the first time and smiled at her. Her heart melted as she truly fell in love for the first time.

"Let me in, Riley!"

She missed his smile. She needed him again. And more than not, she wanted to be out of Gallagher Hotel.

Her eyes fluttered and slowly went to close until movement along the wall took her dwindling attention. The shadow of a butterfly fluttered along. But it wasn't alone. A small boy waving his butterfly net ran behind it. Once he caught it, he jumped for joy and laughed Nick's laugh.

As her heart slowed and tears fell down her face, she thought, *I'm coming, baby. Momma's coming.*

She closed her eyes and let the blackness pull her in.

"Let me in!" Trudy shouted.

"No," Nick said. "It's not your time, Momma. Get up. It's time to go."

But I need to be with you, she thought.

"I'm always with you, Momma. I love you."

I can't do it, she thought.

"Yes, you can. You always did. You work so hard. No point in stopping now. Get up. Get up. *Get up.*"

Riley opened her eyes and threw her heavy head back, striking Trudy in the nose.

"Ack!" Trudy loosened her grip, still holding on.

As Riley panted for air, she reached down to her waistband and pulled out the pocketknife. She opened it and jammed it into Trudy's eye. Trudy abandoned her grip and grabbed her face as she shrilled and kicked at the floor, bunching up the rug.

Riley got up and rushed over to Trudy. Holding her neck, Riley lifted her foot and stomped on the knife, lodging it deep into Trudy's face.

Trudy's blood was drenching Riley's clothes as she kicked and screamed, but Riley kept stomping until Trudy stopped moving. She lay there with a face full of blood, coating bits of charcoal-stained skin and third-degree burns.

Chapter 26

Riley winced as she pressed a piece of cloth she'd ripped from her undershirt against her gushing cheek. She stood in front of the fireplace, staring at the man of the house. She wondered if Ulysses was anything like Trudy: domineering and deadly. Or was he the opposite? Maybe his death changed Trudy for the worse, because no one was born bad; they ended up that way.

She peered over at Trudy's lifeless body. Her eyes were slightly ajar, and half her face clung to the bottom of Riley's nonslip shoe. Riley felt her heart drop for the troubled woman. Trudy came back just to fall forever.

Riley flinched when footsteps sauntered up the hall. Heart slamming into her chest, she dropped the cloth and peered around for a weapon. No matter what happened or how long she'd be in Gallagher Hotel, she wasn't going down without a fight. Her soul wasn't for sale, and if they wanted it, they'd have to bypass her blade. She reached for the handle of the pocketknife lodged deep in Trudy's face. It squelched at the disturbance as Riley pulled the blade free with ease.

As the footsteps grew closer, Riley clutched the handle tight and held it up like she'd seen boxers hold up their fists to protect their chest and chin, but low enough to see what was coming.

The figure's shadow was distorted as it passed by the threshold, forcing Riley's anxiety to explode.

"Come on," Riley mumbled, ready to fight for whatever she had left of her soul as something or someone grew closer.

Allen stopped at the threshold and met her gaze. Smoke lingered from his body as he stepped slowly for Trudy. His white hair was now a dark gray, and fleshy pink patches riddled his skin. His teeth were coated in dry blood. The boils on his face burst with each step. His clothes hung by threads to his deteriorating mess of limbs and saggy skin.

He stopped and stared down at Trudy's body. "She should have listened better, and we would not be in this mess," he said carefully under a thick husk. "The Master is *not* happy."

"What's going to happen to her?" Riley asked with a shaken voice.

Allen peered at her. "She's gone back to hell."

"Is that where everyone else went?" she asked, bracing herself for the answer.

He grunted. "Yes… Well, everyone but Chris and Neil." He scowled. "As you know, I accepted Neil's fake name for my own personal reasons. I needed him dead and out of the way. I really wanted to taste Chris's soul, but when he accepted his fate and tried to save you, his destiny shifted. Let's just say he has to have a long conversation with his God before the final decision can be made."

She frowned. Although the guests were abysmal, everyone deserved a second chance. "What's going to happen to you?"

"Well, I'm not sure. I may be demoted, or I may be back soon. It depends."

His words made her heart tremble. "Am I stuck here?" she asked, still holding the knife up, ready for him to attack.

He snickered. "In my lifetime, I've seen kings reduced to peasants and watched men kill their own families for freedom. I could go as far as to say that I bathed in the blood of a new enemy on a weekly basis. I've seen powerful people turn into weaklings, virtually reduced to nothing. But you? You defy odds, Riley. You are spiritually strong. So much so that the Master doesn't want to touch you. You think you're broken, but you're stronger than ever. I'm big enough to admit when I've been bested. I planned that apparition for you because I fantasized about what a pure, glorious, God-fearing soul tasted like. I hate that you didn't step into a room or open a door first because I would've had you. But you never did. Neither did Chris. You let Dan lead the way into that hut, and Chris let Dr. Myles lead the way out of the storm doors. Both men had their sins on the top of their minds and were convinced that they'd escape scot-free. That's the most vulnerable time for a damned soul.

"When you and Chris sat in the ballroom afterward, I had to choose who to waste my last amount of energy on as I clung to the Vessel after you pushed me out into the Void. Chris had accepted his fate by then and allowed guilt to take him to another level of thinking. He just knew he was going to hell for what he'd done. His newfound regrets acted as a shield for his soul. But you were at your weakest and came around to the idea that you were here for a reason, so I had to strike." He huffed. "But Chris interrupted, knocking me off balance, and sent me back to the depths from which I came. With Trudy dead, no one has to stay here. So, the better question is, do you want to stay stuck?"

She felt the hairs on her arms rise. "No," she said.

"Well, then go back."

She frowned. "How?"

As he approached her, she felt her face twist at the smell of rotten meat. He lifted a scaly hand and watched her eyes. "You didn't belong here." His thin bloody lips trembled as he hissed through clenched teeth. "Your presence was misplaced. I wanted..." He sighed. "Well, that does not matter anymore, now does it?" He peered at Trudy again. "If only she had listened. But when you are dealing with someone so high-strung, head full of pride and greedy to the brim, you get what you get."

He shoved Riley in the chest, knocking her breath loose and sending her backward, free falling to the floor. Her head lightened, and her heart threatened to stop as she struggled to catch air in her throat.

"It's harder going back then it is coming forward. Enjoy your last days on this earth, and hopefully, I never see you again," Allen's dreary voice said as her back slammed into the floor.

***

She sucked in hard as she woke on the chilly kitchen floor. Straining for air, she felt tears run down her face, and a pool of drool encasing her stiff cheek. Bits of shattered plate littered the tile floor around her with the velvet cake not too far off, leaving an array of crumbs sprinkled across the floor.

She curled into a ball on the floor and wept as she begged her sporadic breaths to level out and the pain in her limbs and face to subside.

As the pain mellowed enough for her to straighten out and her vision came to, she glared past the broken plate and found the vent against the floorboard, just a few feet away.

"What—?" She coughed over the last few words of that thought and grunted at the pain in her neck. It felt like it was physically bruising as her body tried collecting air from the house.

Slowly, she turned on her stomach and pushed herself up. On her wobbling knees, she went to take a step only to collide with the counter next to the sink where the dishes were stacked. The suds had depleted, only leaving a pool of water with bits of steak floating around.

She lifted her head to the ceiling and listened.

Silence met her engagement.

She went over to the window and pulled the curtains back. The side of the brick ice cream parlor sat silently in the night, and the full moon glared down, casting a white glow on the sleepy town.

Riley limped off to the hallway and froze, waiting to find people rushing around with platters and drinks. The hallway sat still, just as it had after dinner. Riley trudged into the ballroom. The dinner tables sat with unlit candles, just as they looked when she arrived earlier. The foyer was undisturbed, and the front door was clear of the barricade she, Dan, and Neil put up earlier. Riley went up to the front window and pulled the curtain back. The tall, double-paned window was still intact, and lights lit up the street outside.

She smiled and went to grab the doorknob but stopped.

Freedom was a step away. She knew that.

But then what?

She looked over at the staircase and decided she wasn't done with Gallagher Hotel.

Riley climbed the steps and veered for Room 1. Locked. She peered up the hall and saw all the doors were closed.

"Everything is the way it was before..." Before the dizziness. Before the screams. Before the bloodshed. The hotel was exactly as it was before they'd crossed over, which meant all the doors were locked. She wondered if their lifeless bodies were inside or if they came back over with her at all.

She banged on Dr. Myles' door with the side of her balled fist.

"Dr. Myles!" she called out. She pressed her face against the door and listened.

Nothing.

The more she banged and listened, the more hope faded away. She rushed up the hall to Room 3 and banged on the door, hoping Natalie would snatch it open and scold her for waking her. Riley would happily deal with Natalie's attitude if that meant she was alive.

Nothing.

Riley stood in the middle of the hallway and yelled, "Is anyone still alive?"

She listened. Nothing answered back.

This has to be a nightmare. It has to— Wake up, Riley.

The pain on her face begged to differ, and so did her aching body. She went to her room and pushed the door in. Her tote bag sat on the desk where she'd left it, too busy to unpack and unload her pajamas and toiletries.

She walked into the bathroom and glared in the mirror. The stinging from the glass Trudy thrashed into Riley's face erupted with every step. But once she got to the mirror, she gasped.

There were no marks.

My soul...bears the bruises, just like Trudy's skin was still stained from her time in hell. No one should suffer like this. She scowled.

She thought of Allen's mention of possibly returning. Her heart thudded at the thought of him carrying out another massacre.

Riley shook her head.

"Not if I can help it."

She rushed from the room and raced down the steps. She ran through the foyer and passed by the ballroom, shoving the double doors in where she ended up in the kitchen. She snatched drawers open and pawed around for a cleaver and searched the wall for a fire ax, anything to get the guest room doors open. She stumbled across a junk drawer and pulled up a screwdriver.

"That'll have to work," she whispered.

As Riley raced through the ballroom, she couldn't shake the feeling that someone was watching her.

She stopped before she reached the foyer and turned.

The souls of the guests were already gone. Of that, she was certain. Trudy assured her. But the original party guests, the souls trapped from Trudy's fire, were still on the other side, and needed a guide to get them out of that monstrous house.

Riley sucked in a deep breath and closed her eyes. She envisioned the party she trespassed: the sorrow in the server's face and the burn marks that ingrained their souls and damned them to the hotel. Then she thought of the bubbly girl with cherry lips. They deserved freedom, and they needed help getting there.

"You can go home," she said. "She's gone, and pretty soon this building will be gone. You're free to cross over."

Unsure if her words were enough, she decided to use words from a powerful source. One that helped her when she herself suffered from personal turmoil.

She took in a breath and recited:

And if you faithfully obey the voice of the LORD your God,

being careful to do all his commandments that I command you today,

the LORD, your God, will set you high above all the nations of the earth.

And all these blessings shall come upon you and overtake you,

if you obey the voice of the LORD, your God.

Blessed shall you be in the city, and blessed shall you be in the field.

Blessed shall be the fruit of your womb and the fruit of your ground and the fruit of your cattle,

the increase of your herds and the young of your flock.

Blessed shall be your basket and your kneading bowl...

Tears fell down her face. "Deuteronomy 28. Verses one through sixty-eight." She opened her eyes and searched the room. The dim lights behind the bar flickered.

"You're free to go home now."

A huffed breeze blew through the room, pushing softly against her face. The dim light behind the bar flickered until it went out. Her body went cold, and then warmth hugged her tight.

She smiled. "Safe travels," she whispered.

Riley turned, raced up the steps, and crouched in front of Room 1. She unscrewed the two bolts stationed over and under the doorknob. Once the top plate fell loose, the doorknob fell off. She stuck her finger in the hole and pushed the remaining bit of the knob in. It hit the floor with a dull thud. Then she lodged the screwdriver into the hole and pushed it over until a click sounded.

The latch let up, allowing her inside.

She repeatedly removed the doorknobs from the guestrooms, finding bodies lying on the carpet with plates of red velvet cake either overturned on the floor or sitting on the desk or bed.

She started with Dr. Myles. She hefted his shoulders up and pulled him from the foot of his bed where he'd gone down. She lugged him into the hallway and struggled to pull him down the steps. Once in the foyer, she laid him on the floor and opened the door. The humid night air welcomed her back to the world as she pulled him down the steps and into the plushy yard.

Sweating, she went back and did the same for Natalie, who passed out in bed, and Neil, who fell face-first onto his keyboard. His laptop sat open with a dead battery.

Then she went to Chris's room. Dread stopped her in her tracks. She peered down at the young man, who lay on his back on the bathroom floor. His face had gone pale, and his dead eyes stared at the ceiling.

Nostalgia. It was a horrifying nostalgia. Steve had looked like that the last time she'd seen him.

She crouched and lifted his body. She pulled him in close, embracing him for the last time.

"I'm sorry, Chris," she said.

She laid him down and positioned herself over his head. She picked up his shoulders and pulled him up the hall, down the steps, and into the yard.

As she pulled Dan down the steps, she couldn't help but think of the horrible things she and Neil had seen. Dan was a monster; this was a fact. He *admitted* it. But Riley couldn't bear the responsibility of judging him. It wasn't her job. Sweat soaked her face as she tripped over her own feet, struggling to pull the bulky man.

With all the guests in the yard, she contemplated going to the basement to find Trudy.

As she pulled the cabinets open and snatched up the vegetable oil and long neck lighter, she argued with herself.

Trudy caused so much pain.

Trudy isn't Brenda.

Her mind reeled as she gathered up the guest's belongings and set them next to their bodies on the lawn.

Trudy is a demon.

Trudy isn't Brenda.

As she reentered the house, she stopped in the foyer. One way to the basement. One way to the attic.

Trudy is back in hell.

Brenda needs to be buried by her family.

She ran down to the basement and found the door on the left unlocked. She pushed it open and found the shrine to Ulysses untouched. Then she found Brenda. She sat at the silver vanity with her face laying on its surface.

As she pulled Brenda from the room, she recited:

Come now, let us reason together, says the LORD:

Though your sins are like scarlet,

they shall be as white as snow;

though they are red like crimson,

they shall become like wool.

She laid Brenda's body next to Dan's and watched the faces of the host and guests.

"I hope you all find your peace," she whispered. She frowned. *Although it may be too late for some of you.*

She went back inside for one last thing.

Up in the attic, she pulled the closet door open. The bloodstained pedestal was on its side as it had been when Dan kicked it over. But there were no vines or books. Thoughts or damning memories. There was nothing but remnants of what the thing left behind. She doused it in the vegetable oil.

She outlined the hole with oil, soaking the tight space in the accelerant.

After bringing the lighter to life, she placed the flame against the pedestal and watched it eat the oil, spreading fast across the closet.

A high-pitched shrill filled the room, forcing her to press her hands against her ears and backpedal for the door.

Her heart crashed into her chest as she bolted down the steps, and the high-pitched shrill descended into a low groan that shook the house under her feet. Riley ran down the hallway as flames erupted and swallowed up the staircase. The fire moved rapidly, taking up the carpet in the hallway, hot on her heels.

She nearly slid down the staircase and into the front door. She ran onto the porch and fell over the steps as a blast blew out the windows and shoved her forward.

The house wailed and shrieked as the flames took it back to where it came from.

She grunted at the new aches in her legs and torso as she lay face down in the yard, eating grass as she clasped her teeth.

She turned and watched the fire release a bloom of dark smoke into the sky.

"Hey!"

Riley turned to find someone jogging over from the gas station on the corner. A petite cinnamon-skinned woman ran over to her and crouched.

"Are you alright? Oh my God." She peered at the house and grabbed her own short dark hair. "What—what happened?" She looked at the bodies. "Are they alright?" she asked. "Is—Brenda alright?" Hysteria riddled her voice. "Oh my God. Is—is that Neil? Wh—what happened here?"

Riley's face crumbled at the frightened woman.

"Are—are they…dead?"

Riley gave a stiff nod.

The woman cupped her mouth, and tears fell over her shaking hand. She sniffed. "All right. Okay. Uh…" She pulled her phone from her jean shorts pocket, poked at the screen, and put the phone against her face.

"Yeah, Daddy. D—Daddy. No, I'm not okay. Brenda Scott and Neil from the paper are dead… Yes. Send some units, some firefighters, and an ambulance to Gallagher… Yes. It was like an explosion. The hotel is destroyed, and there are—" She sobbed. "…dead people out here… I know. I am. Fucking hurry, alright? There's someone here who needs help." She nodded frantically. "I know, but she needs help! Hurry okay… Yeah, I'll be here. I'm not leaving until you and the boys get down here." She hung up and watched the building burn hot.

Riley wondered if the woman could hear the otherworldly shrieking that pierced her own ears. She also wondered how Holloway would move forward after being struck with another tragedy.

"Is there anyone you can call?" the woman asked.

"Huh?" Riley asked, vision blurred with tears.

"Honey, is there anyone you can have meet you at the hospital?"

Sirens erupted in the distance, amplifying their urgent approach.

"AJ," Riley whispered.

"Here." The girl handed her the phone.

"I—I don't know his number by heart…"

"Well, does he know where you are?"

"He'll be here at seven."

The girl nodded. "Well, I'll let them know to tell him where you are."

Riley looked around and saw her bag sitting in the yard next to Neil. She had a story to tell, and no matter how crazy it sounded, she needed to tell the right people.

She picked herself up and limped over to her bag. She picked it up and fished her phone out. She pressed the home key, allowing the screen to light up. Nick's face smiled up at her. She smiled back and unlocked the phone.

She pulled up AJ's number and hit the phone icon. Before it could ring, she hung up and watched her tears hit the screen. Talking about what she'd seen was ungodly and unreal. Part of her hoped she was roaming around in a nightmare. There was only one way to know for sure. She took in a deep breath, and texted:

Please come get me from the hospital in Holloway and bring Pastor Miller and Wanda with you. It's important.

Less than a few seconds after she hit send, AJ called.

Excerpt- Netted: A Serial Killer Thriller and Fast-Paced Suspense

Book 1

The Beginning

PROLOGUE

Sully lifted his heavy eyelids. The blue luminescent light stung, making him squint. He grunted, bringing life to his sore throat. His mouth felt like he'd sucked down a jar of cotton balls. He went to move his arms to wipe the crust from his eyes, much like he'd done every morning throughout his forty-seven years of life.

The belligerent clinging of metal sounded as chains smacked the chair's steel arms while they held his wrists down.

He shifted his shoulders and met a sheer resistance. An extended grip spanned the length of his chest, crinkling his dingy black T-shirt underneath it. Chains wrapped him so tight; he felt the chill from the links deep in his lungs and heart. He went to move his legs and found his ankles in a similar condition: pressed hard against the chair's steel legs.

A migraine split his brain, causing him to utter a harsh grunt. This was worse than a tequila hangover from that time he dropped off supplies in El Centro. It was even worse than the time he flew into the grassy knoll off I-64 outside of Louisville, lodging his sleeping face into the thick steering wheel of his rig. This discomfort was a new pain that left his head, from his temples up to his forehead, feeling like aching, useless mush.

Breathing hard, he peered forward with wide eyes. A camera stared back into his face as it sat on a tripod. The dark lens gleamed in the harsh light.

357

Sweat trickled down his forehead as he tried moving his fingers, but they sat stiff, purple and bulged at the tips as if blood stopped flowing past his bound wrists hours ago.

"Help!" he wailed. He cleared his throat to loosen the thick grogginess in his tone.

His heart dropped when a door to his right swung in, allowing a figure to enter.

The figure approached and stood between Sully and the camera before crouching. The only thing Sully could make of the man kneeling before him was the sweater taut against his wide chest and broad shoulders. The cursive letters on his right peck read: Father Paul. A black ski mask hid his face.

"Please...buddy..." Sully cleared his throat again. The stale taste of sleeper's breath coated his mouth. "You gotta help me. I don't know where I am...where my rig is..."

The man only stared, his dark eyes scolded Sully from behind a pair of thick goggles.

Sully passed the stranger a peculiar glare as he tried recollecting thoughts from the past few hours. How'd he get here? The last thing he remembered was the motel room off I 94, a big slab of a road. He and his rig were on the way to The Windy City to drop off some car parts from Albany. He'd made perfect timing, nearly setting a record. There was more than enough time to stop two hours west of the Motor City at a dive, Pete's Grill.

While sitting at the bar, a beaver, Pam, approached him at the bar. Her thick lips and cherry-red hair left him stiffened below the belt. The way that red dress hugged her curvy body made him want to explore what lay underneath it. She was a queen, the type to be his significant other and deep down, he'd hoped to ask her to take on the road with him. She'd be a beautiful passenger seat cover for the old dog. A worthy companion for a man who only knew the road and planned to live out his days riding it. But it wasn't only because of her youthful face and gentle smile. It was the

358

noteworthy conversation; she knew a lot about rigs and trailers. Trucks and tires. More than your typical lot lizard.

After they had a few draft beers, he remembered taking her for a ride up the road about fifty miles and stopping at the Go Go Inn, her idea. Soon after they'd entered the room, Sully complained about how the ugly floral décor looked like baby-sized cockroaches resting on the mattress and curtains before something heavy pummeled the back of his skull. He recalled falling face-first into the scratchy, dingy carpet. The smell of mildew stuffed his senses before the room blurred and his eyes shut.

Now, there was a blinking red light from a camera, bugging his retinas and intensifying his headache. With every shallow breath, the throbbing in his chest hitched, stuffing a sickening ball in his gut.

"Where am I?" he cried.

Father Paul continued to stare up at him.

The black window across from them, just behind the camera, took on a rectangular gleam. There was a TV mounted to the wall behind him. A red skull spun in its center.

Sully tried shifting his weight by rocking side to side. Or at least he thought he was. The chair underneath him stood still. Dizzy with exhaustion, panic riddled his nerves. "Answer me!" Tears fell down his face.

Father Paul's eyes lit up as if pleased to hear another man beg.

The screen behind Sully went black. Then a short phrase popped up in bold letters. They appeared blurry as tears clouded his sight.

He wished he'd read it. But as he batted his eyelids and squinted hard, the words disappeared.

Father Paul stood straight, towering about six feet over Sully, and swaggered over to an oak bookcase.

Sully watched in horror as Father Paul swiped up a rip saw from the top shelf and walked back over with an urgent stride in his step.

Sully fidgeted and shook. Through exasperated breaths, he said, "Wait, wait, *wait*! Please don't. Uh... I'm sorry for whatever I did! Please, just don't—"

Father Paul pressed the saw's teeth onto the bridge of Sully's nose.

Sully sobbed and stammered. "P—p-please!" he said.

Father Paul took a handful of Sully's thick hair and yanked his head back. Sully's scalp screamed as his hairline burned. He tried turning his neck and shaking his head, but Father's Paul's grip only tightened.

The grinding of the blades as they chewed through Sully's face made him wail so loud that his throat strained, and his ungodly squeal filled the room. A hot, sickening impulse shot through his body as his limbs struggled to break free of the bondage.

The sound of cartilage snapping with every movement made his ears pop.

Flashes erupted before his eyes as if he'd been staring into a strobe light. Blood spurted from the fresh cut, coating his deteriorating vision, and turning the room crimson. He choked and hacked as blood ran down his throat.

At the end of his cry, Sully let out a weak *"why?"* as his face sweltered in a blinding pain. His breath seized as his mind tried to comprehend the damage being done to his nose.

The sawing stopped. Sully yelped as Father Paul tore the dangling nose free from the shred of skin keeping it attached to his face. The ripping of Sully's skin sounded like masking tape being torn from a wall.

Sully wept as Father Paul held the nose before the camera.

Sully dropped his chin to his chest. His shoulders jerked with his sobs. Blood ran free from his face to his jeans.

This isn't how he thought he'd die. Mangled and mutilated. Confused and petrified.

All he could do was squeeze his eyes shut and ramble off a quick prayer between his truncated blubbering:

"Dear God, f—forgive me for all that I—I—I've done in this l—life. I succumb to your glory and come to you with an open m—mind and heart. *Please* God. Make this end. Make this torment g—go away and take me in your arms for eternity."

Sully popped his eyes open at the sound of a whirring power drill.

Before Sully could look, Father Paul took another handful of hair and aimed the pointy tip into Sully's eye. As the spinning tip progressed forward, every bruise and scar burned his skin from the many scaffolds and accidents he'd lived through. Passing the CDL exam and buying his first rig, Ricky Red, sat fresh on his mind. Sully heard his first words and felt his first steps in his parent's living room out in his desert hometown of El Paso.

He saw the dank motel room and red-haired Pam.

He belted a horrified shriek when the drill's tip met his right eye.

Continue reading the Netted Box Set (Books 1-3):
https://mybook.to/1D0ntJP

Sign up for updates, advanced review copies, and book recommendations from K.T. Rose:
https://www.kyrobooks.com/subscribe

Made in the USA
Middletown, DE
30 January 2025

70520112R00220